Meg Hutchinson

Meg Hutchinson left school at fifteen and didn't return to education until she was thirty-three, when she entered Teacher Training College and studied for her degree in the evenings. Ever since she was a child, she has loved telling stories and writing 'compositions'. She lived for sixty years in Wednesbury, where her parents and grandparents spent all their lives, but now has a quiet little cottage in Shropshire where she can indulge her passion for storytelling.

Meg Hutchinson's second novel, *For the Sake of Her Child*, is now available as a Hodder and Stoughton hardback.

D0755436

Also by Meg Hutchinson

For the Sake of Her Child

Abel's Daughter

Meg Hutchinson

CORONET BOOKS
Hodder and Stoughton

First published in 1996 by Hodder and Stoughton
First published in paperback in 1996 by Hodder and Stoughton
A division of Hodder Headline PLC

A Coronet Paperback

British Library C.I.P.

Hutchinson, Meg
    Abels's daughter
    1. English fiction – 20th century
    I. Title
    823.9'14[F]

Printed and bound in Great Britain by
Cox & Wyman Ltd, Reading, Berkshire

Hodder and Stoughton
A division of Hodder Headline PLC
338 Euston Road
London NW1 3BH

For my husband, whose patient encouragement and faith in this work remained when my own had failed. Thank you, sweetheart.

Chapter One

'Phoebe Pardoe, I find you guilty of wilful theft. I order you to be taken to a place of imprisonment where you will serve a term of fifteen years' hard labour.'

Phoebe pushed the soiled rags into the hot tub, wincing as the soda bit into the raw flesh of her hands.

'. . . you be taken to a place of detention . . .'

She scrubbed the rags against the ribbed wooden board, the menstrual blood of her fellow inmates turning the water red.

'. . . fifteen years' hard labour . . .'

The words circled endlessly in her brain as they had for the past eight months.

'. . . guilty of wilful theft . . .'

'Put yer back into it, Pardoe!'

Phoebe gasped as the slim wooden cane sliced across her shoulders.

'. . . them bleedin' jam rags won't wash themselves – or p'raps you ain't used to washin'? Yeah, I forgot you once 'ad a laundry woman to do yer washin' for you. Well, you ain't got one now, you bloody thief, so get stuck in or you'll be sorry.'

Phoebe's teeth tightened on her lip; she knew better than to answer back to Sally Moreton, superintendent of the laundry. Built like a man, her mouth was twisted up at the side due to some childhood illness, and her insides were twisted to match. Beating other women seemed the only source of pleasure she had, the cane she carried cutting into their

1

flesh on the merest excuse, and often without any at all.

Squeezing the strips of cloth and dropping them into a cane basket, Phoebe pushed against her hair with a hand as bloody as the rags she had just scrubbed, then picking up the basket she carried it to one of the steaming boilers, dropping her load inside. Now she could take a recently removed batch to the yard and peg them on the lines stretched between the buildings. These were the only moments in her long days that she looked forward to. To see the sky, to feel the clean air on her face, to hear a bird sing . . .

'Leave them!' Sally Moreton's cane came down across Phoebe's raw hands, her cruel piggy eyes gleaming at the scream of pain it brought forth. 'Martha can peg them out. We don't want to risk yer delicate constitution by sending you out into the cold air, now do we?'

'But I always do the pegging out!' The thought of not going outside, even for the few minutes it took to peg the strips of torn sheeting to the lines, made Phoebe forget what so many blows of that cane had taught her. 'Martha does . . .'

The stinging cut of the cane across her mouth stilled the rest of the protest, sending Phoebe crashing backward against the cauldron of bubbling soapy water.

'Martha does what I tell 'er.' The cane rose again, swishing downward across Phoebe's legs, cutting through the worn grey calico. 'Same as all the rest of the thievin', murderin' scum in this place – same as you will, Miss High and Mighty Phoebe Pardoe! An' if you answer me back one more time you might find yerself missin' a tongue to answer back with. Now get that lot in.' Lashing out with her foot, she tipped over another basket of soiled cloths, stained crimson against the stone floor. 'An' get 'em clean. I don't want to see no mark on 'em when I come to inspect.'

'You better be ready to play tonight, you stuck up bitch!' Liza Spittle dropped a fresh basket of laundry at Phoebe's feet as the superintendent moved away. 'Or Steel Arsed

Sal might find a bundle of these pushed up a chimney somewhere.'

'She wouldn't . . .'

'Believe me,' Liza cut in, the beetroot birthmark staining the left side of her face seeming to swell suddenly as though about to burst, 'that wouldn't stop 'er usin' that cane if we was to give her a good excuse. Loves to use the cane does Steel Arse. It's 'er only pleasure. Does for 'er what no bloke would – not wi' a face like that.'

'You're disgusting!'

'Am I?' Liza's large hand grabbed the basket Phoebe had lifted and, bundling several stained cloths together, she shoved them beneath the hessian sack tied about her middle. 'So tonight will mek two of us, won't it?'

The rest of the long day stretched out between jibes and advice as to how to please Liza, but there was no sympathy, that was something these women had had removed from them as cleanly as amputation severed a limb. Please God, Phoebe prayed when at nine p.m. the one gaslamp was turned off, leaving the dormitory in darkness, please God don't let her come near me. But instinct told her that God was not listening.

'So, you've decided to be nice to Liza, 'ave you?'

Liza Spittle sat on the side of Phoebe's narrow mattress, her approach from the far end of the line of ten tight-spaced beds lost among the snuffles and coughs of the women who filled them.

The dim light from outside had faded almost to extinction by the time it touched the beds but Phoebe did not need light to tell her who sat beside her; the rancid stale fish smell that always accompanied Liza, despite the compulsory baths with carbolic soap, told her her prayers had gone unheeded.

'I thought as 'ow you'd see sense . . .'

Liza bent forward, one broad hand pulling away the rough woollen blanket, the miasmic stench of her closing Phoebe's throat.

'Leave me alone,' she choked, swallowing the smell of the other woman. 'Please, leave me alone.'

Liza snatched the blanket further down, revealing white calico a pale shadow in the darkness. 'Is that what you said to the bobbies when they come fer you, or did you let 'em do this?' One hand undid the row of flat calico-covered buttons while the other pressed heavily on Phoebe's shoulder, the snores and moans from the other beds indicating that none of the other women cared what was happening. 'In fer thievin', ain't you?' The nightgown opened to the waist, the older woman pulled it wide. 'A necklace so I 'ear, a very valible necklace . . . Look good over these pretty tits I've no doubt. Did the bobbies tell you you've got pretty tits? Did they feel 'em like Liza's doin'?' A scaly-skinned hand closed over Phoebe's breast.

'Stop . . . please!' Tears poured down Phoebe's cheeks, salting her lips. 'Please stop.'

Liza bent forward, the stale fish smell of her gagging the girl beneath her. 'You'll be a-sayin' please again soon enough but you won't be a-sayin' stop. You'll be begging Liza to go on . . .'

'Somebody'll be beggin' but it won't be 'er.'

The voice was a hiss in the darkness as Liza was jerked from the bed and flung face down on the floor.

'I told you to leave the kid be, keep yer filthy paws off 'er!'

One hand pressed to her mouth to stop the vomit spilling out, the other holding the edges of her nightgown together, Phoebe recognised the tones of Tilly Wood; serving a life sentence, the gaunt-featured woman was the only soul in the whole prison who had shown her the faintest semblance of kindness in all of the eight months she had spent in this hell hole.

'Seems as 'ow you don't understand plain English . . .'

Suddenly there were no snores, no groans. The silence from the other beds announced that each woman was awake and listening though none moved.

'. . . well, Liza Spittle, I can mek it plainer fer you . . .'

Lifting herself on one elbow, Phoebe peered through the gloom. Tilly Wood had one knee between Liza's shoulder blades with both hands cupped beneath the woman's chin, forcing her head back.

'Play yer dirty bloody games wi' any other of the pissants you fancies but this one you leaves be, an' if you doesn't then you's goin' to be found behind one o' them bilers wi' a jam rag stuck in yer gob!

'Y'see, Liza, I ain't got nuthin' to lose – I'm already behind these bars fer life an' there ain't nuthin' Steel Arse or the likes of 'er can do to me they ain't already done in ten years. That's a long time, Liza, but you put one more finger on that wench, just one finger, and *you'll* be 'ere for eternity.

'Oh, you knows I pushed my swine of a man down the stairs, they told you that did the wardresses, but what they didn't tell you was I broke 'is neck fust. It didn't tek much . . .'

Pressing her knee further into Liza's back, she pulled the chin upward, bringing a strangled cry from the woman on the floor. 'Just a quick jerk and the spine was broke at the base of the neck. You don't 'ave to be no big bloke to do that, Liza, you just need to spend yer life fightin' off ten brothers an' a bloke you wus never married to in fust place.' The cupped hands jerked again. 'It would be easy, Liza, an' pleasurable, an' you would never know when it was comin', so if you wants to live long enough to get out of 'ere, you'll think on what I says . . . leave this 'un be!'

Rising, Tilly waited while Liza picked herself up and slunk back to bed, hearing the disappointed grunts coming from the shadows; there were many in the room who would have welcomed the snapping of Liza Spittle's neck.

''Er won't mess wi' you any more,' Tilly said, covering Phoebe with the blanket, then louder, ''cos Tilly Wood don't tell the Good Lord 'isself more'n twice.'

I order you be taken to a place of imprisonment where you will serve a term of fifteen years.

Lying in the darkness, Phoebe knew her life would not stretch that far.

How had this happened to her? Phoebe closed her eyes, letting the darkness press against her lids, and in that darkness saw again the summer ball and herself in a pink rose-trimmed gown dancing with Montrose. Montrose Wheeler, son of Gaskell Wheeler, owner of the Monway Iron Foundry, had asked for her hand in marriage and her father had agreed. The ceremony had been planned to take place at Christmas, Montrose vowing he could hardly bear to wait until then. He was so handsome and tall, his sandy hair and light blue eyes so different from the coarse overfed features of his father or his thin, sharp-faced mother. Who would have dreamed that an evening so warm with music and moonlight, so soft with the promise of love, would be the last time she would see her fiancé, for in the space of weeks her own father lay dead and with his death all her own hopes were extinguished.

'It's bad news I'm afraid, my dear.' Alfred Dingley, her father's doctor and friend, had come to Brunswick House to tell her himself of the accident in which her father's chaise fell to the bottom of a vertical pit. Old mine workings, the coroner had said. Wednesbury was riddled with them and dangerous shafts regularly opened without warning.

The funeral had been a week later, a family affair with just her father's brother Samuel and sister Annie, no one being left of her dead mother's family.

Against the darkness of her lids, Phoebe saw again the finely drawn face of Uncle Samuel, a carbon copy of her own father, and the sad blue eyes that seemed to know more than they revealed. Phoebe realised it was the only time she had ever seen her uncle outside the house he shared with his sister, and even on her rare visits to them she was never left alone with him: 'Because of his stone

deafness, dear,' was what she was always told when she
had asked the reason he never went out, an answer that
even as a child she'd found unconvincing. Her Aunt Annie
in her customary black, shrouded in the perennial air of
bitterness Phoebe had recognised from an early age, sat
straight-backed in the carriage that followed the hearse, black-
plumed horses walking slowly to St Bartholomew's Church
and her father's final resting place.

His death had been a blow but there had been worse in
store for her, much worse. The reading of Abel Pardoe's will
took place in the drawing room of his home, Brunswick
House, the following afternoon. James Siveter, her father's
lawyer, in a long old-fashioned tail coat that gave him the
appearance of a crow, rose from his seat at her father's
heavy oak desk, ushering Phoebe to a chair beside her
aunt. His impassive face as he resumed his seat betrayed
nothing of what was to come.

"'I, Abel Pardoe, being of sound mind . . .'"

Siveter's expressionless voice droned on through the
bequests to servants, only changing when he came to her
father's provision for Phoebe herself.

"'Next I come to my beloved daughter, Phoebe Mary Pardoe.
By the time of my death you will have been Mrs Montrose
Wheeler for many years and as such mistress of your own
home and in need of nothing. Therefore I leave you what
you have always had and enjoyed: my love.

"'Lastly, to my brother Samuel, and my sister Annie who
has imprisoned him for the last forty years – to you, Annie
Maria Pardoe, I bequeath the sum of one thousand pounds
annually and the house you live in for your lifetime. To my
brother Samuel Isaac Pardoe I bequeath this house and all its
contents together with Hobs Hill Coalmine, Dangerfield Lane,
the Crown coalmine, Moxley, and all lands, property, goods
and monies pertaining to me. May God give you the courage
to use them to buy the freedom I never had the courage to
give you.'"

The numbness she had felt since her father's death shielded Phoebe from the full impact of what the lawyer had said and she sat there while her aunt ushered him out. Mrs Banks, their cook-housekeeper, offered to help her upstairs.

Now, opening her eyes, Phoebe stared at the moon-filled squares of the windows, their regimented line like the yellow eyes of demons about to strike, while in the shadowed belly of the room figures from her nightmare continued to move.

'You understand, Phoebe, Uncle Samuel needs continual quiet. To have a young girl about the place, especially one with the comings and goings of a fiancé, would be much too upsetting for him,' her aunt had said not two weeks later. 'Therefore I am asking you to make other arrangements.'

'But Uncle Samuel is already in continual quietness, is he not, Aunt?' Phoebe remembered her own answer and the fulminating look that crossed the older woman's face as she added, 'Is he not chronically deaf?'

'And are you not chronically rude?' her aunt had retorted waspishly, then drawing black gloves over thin stick-like fingers, drove home her winning blow. 'I want you out of this house by one week from today, and be sure you take nothing that was paid for by your father.'

'But Father paid for everything,' Phoebe had protested. 'My clothes . . . everything.'

Her aunt moved to the door, waiting while the maid opened it. 'Then you will have less to carry. But your uncle would not want you to suffer any hardship. Therefore you may take two dresses and two changes of underwear, and to be certain you take no more, I will send my own housekeeper to pack them.'

'Surely I may take my jewellery?'

'All paid for by my brother, therefore part of his estate and now part of Samuel's.'

'Not all.' Phoebe followed the spare grey-haired woman, whom for all their family connection she hardly knew, out into the late-autumn sunshine. 'I have several pieces left me by my mother.'

Annie Pardoe did not hesitate in climbing into her pony trap. 'Paid for, no doubt, by my brother.' Picking up the reins, she clucked the horse forward. 'Unless you have a deed of gift you will be wise to leave any such pieces where they are.'

Phoebe concentrated hard on the tiny moon-filled spaces, willing the nightmare memories to go away, but on they went, passing before her eyes like some awful dance. She had been writing to Montrose when the Wheelers' carriage had arrived from Oakeswell Hall, and she had felt so relieved. Montrose had obviously been informed of what had happened and was arranging for her to be moved to his parents' home until after their marriage. Grabbing her bonnet and smiling at her maid, Lucy Baines, Phoebe rushed out of the house.

'Miss Pardoe . . .'

The formality of the greeting from Montrose's mother did not surprise Phoebe who had always found the woman cold if not positively unfriendly; neither did the absence of her husband who would be at his place of business at this hour of the day.

'Miss Pardoe,' Violet Wheeler sat stiff-backed facing Phoebe, 'have you written to my son informing him of your situation?'

'No.' Phoebe shook her head, wondering how such a sharp-featured, cold-natured woman could ever have been given the name of so lovely a flower.

'I thought perhaps you may not have, therefore I myself informed Montrose of your position. Under the circumstances I must inform you there can be no question of a marriage between you. As an officer in the Guards Montrose must be seen to make a good marriage – he cannot afford to tie himself to a wife unable to bring with her a good social standing.'

Phoebe remembered the physical sickness that had come over her at these words; how she had stuffed a gloved hand into her mouth.

'I know this must come as a disappointment to you,' Violet Wheeler went on with no more compassion than if she had been wishing her young visitor a pleasant walk about the gardens, 'but both Montrose's father and myself agree that it is for the best.'

Of course it was for the best – the best for Montrose.

'And your son, Mrs Wheeler,' Phoebe had managed, swallowing the sickness filling her throat, 'does he also think that breaking off our marriage is for the best?'

'Montrose will take the advice of his father,' Violet Wheeler's sharp features tightened, her nostrils flaring with controlled anger, 'whilst you would be wise to take mine and say no more than that you feel unable to go through with the marriage so soon after your father's death.'

Phoebe turned her head sideways, staring into the darkness of a room she shared with nine other women. In the space of three weeks she was orphaned, homeless and jilted. Violet Wheeler had said her son must have a wife who could bring with her a good social standing. What she really meant was Montrose must have a wife with a good financial standing.

Three days after Aunt Annie's visit her housekeeper Maudie Tranter arrived to supervise the packing of two dresses and two sets of underwear in a large carpet bag.

'Miss Annie says I am to see that all wardrobes and cupboards are locked in my presence and that I am to take the keys back with me.' The woman looked apologetically at Phoebe. 'She also said I was to take your jewellery box . . . I am sorry, Miss Pardoe, but that was what she said and I have to do it or lose my position.'

'Please don't worry, Mrs Tranter,' Phoebe had tried to reassure the woman, 'no one is blaming you, of course you must do as my aunt says.'

'I've made an inventory of everything in that box,' said Abel Pardoe's own housekeeper who had watched the packing. 'That sees us all safeguarded, Mrs Tranter. Your mistress can't go saying as how anything has gone astray. Tell her this sealing tape was set around the box in your presence and this here is the inventory I spoke of with a copy already sent to Lawyer Siveter's chambers in the High Street for her to check by.'

Fanny Banks's quick fingers passed brown sealing tape three times around the box before handing it to Annie's housekeeper. 'Now, as you've seen to all you came for, you best be off back to that crow you call your employer. As for me, I'll be leavin' when Miss Phoebe do.'

With Fanny Banks treading on her brown skirts, Maudie Tranter dropped Phoebe a quick bob and disappeared from the room, her footsteps almost at a run on the polished wood of the corridor and stairs.

Phoebe herself had left the next day, bidding goodbye to a tearful Mrs Banks who was joining her sister in Chester and a defiant Lucy who vowed to 'go into the workhouse rather than work for that sour-faced prune, Annie Pardoe'.

Try as she might Phoebe had never been able to remember more than walking down the long tree-lined drive away from the large house that had been her home since birth. She knew only that somehow or other she had walked the three miles across open grassland to Hobs Hill coalmine. There Joseph Leach had half carried her into the tiny brick building he called 'the office'. Injured in an explosion underground years before, her father had kept him on ostensibly as tally keeper, though the times her father had taken Phoebe with him on his regular visits to the pithead it seemed Joseph oversaw just about everything. Prising the carpet bag from her fingers, he sat her on the one chair, listening as tears and words poured from her.

'Joe . . . Joe . . .'

Even now, in the quiet of a prison cell punctured only by the breathing of its occupants, the shout seemed to throb against her ears.

'Joe . . . there's bin a cave in!'

'Christ Almighty!' Joseph Leach turned for the door as it burst open.

'Joe.' A figure black from head to foot with coal dust,

the white circles around his eyes the only patch of colour, announced, 'There's bin a fall – roof gone.'

'Where?' Joe asked tersely, all thoughts of Phoebe gone from his mind.

'North tunnel.'

'Bugger it!' he rasped. 'I knew that bastard would go, I said it would. Who's down there?'

'Manny Evans's gang.' The begrimed figure made no acknowledgement of Phoebe's presence.

'Eight men,' Joseph said instantly, with no reference to anything other than his own sharp brain. 'Right, you send young Billy for the doctor then meet me at the mouth.'

After that the girl was forgotten as Joseph organised the rescue.

Though no sound from the pit head told the women of the town what had occurred, the sight of the doctor's trap following the path across the heath told its own story and soon they stood just beyond the green-painted wooden gates with her father's name painted tall and white across them – Phoebe could see them clearly from the small office, women with chequered shawls about their heads, each face chalky with fear.

'How many, Joseph?' Alfred Dingley jumped from the trap, a black Gladstone bag in his hand.

'Eight, sir. Emanuel Evans, Evan Gittins, Charlie Norton and 'is lad Tommy, Sam Deeley, David Walker, Ben Corns and Meshac Speke.' Joseph reeled off the names as he swept papers and ledgers from the table that almost filled the office, clearing a space for the doctor to work on any injured men.

'Where?'

'North tunnel about thirty yards in. We can get to about ten yards of 'em at a guess. I've got a gang in now clearin' rest, but the shorin's be weak. We got to watch rest of roof don't come in atop of 'em.'

'You are sure there are no more than eight?'

Joseph had pointed to a line of nails hammered into the

12

brick wall of the office, each bearing a round metal plate the size of a penny. 'Tokens be all in an' Davy's be all gone for North tunnel an' there be nobody else in that part o' the mine. I'll 'ave the tokens checked again though, if you wants, for the other seams?'

'No need.' Alfred Dingley glanced at the wall where the Davy lamps were hung as each man checked in when coming from underground.

Phoebe ran out into the yard after the two men as a shout of 'They'm through' rang out, watching them make for the mouth of the mine. Her offer of help went unanswered.

Slowly, the iron cage was winched again and again to the surface, the cries of the women reaching across the yard as they recognised their men, but each in his turn waited for the raising of the cage until the last survivor, Charlie Norton, stepped out, his fifteen-year-old son carried in his arms.

In the darkness, Phoebe threw an arm across her face, desperate to obliterate the screams of the lad's mother. They had been lucky, Joseph had said later, but what use was that to Sally Norton?

'You did very well.' Dr Dingley had smiled at Phoebe as the last of the men's cuts were washed and bandaged. 'Now you'd better let me take you home, my girl.'

But Phoebe had refused, saying she preferred to walk, not wanting to admit the truth of having no home and Joseph said nothing of what she had told him.

'You'd better cum along o' me,' he said, watching the doctor drive horse and trap through the gates, 'my Sarah'll know what to do.'

And she had, leastways until Annie Pardoe landed on her doorstep.

It hadn't taken long. A fresh ripple of anger swept over Phoebe and she flung her arm from her face as if fending off an enemy. News had a way of travelling fast and it was news in the town that Sarah Leach had taken in Abel Pardoe's daughter. Days from the cave-in at Hobs Hill mine her aunt had driven down to the Leachs' cottage and marched in. The whole thing was over before it began: the house was part of Samuel's legacy, as were most others in this area, her aunt said, and either Phoebe went or they did – and with them Joseph's job at the mine.

'Yer father was good to me, I can't turn me back on 'is wench.'

Joseph's protest at her leaving echoed in Phoebe's mind. He and his family were reluctant to see her go but as Sarah admitted, jobs were hard come by, especially for 'a bloke wi' a bad leg'.

Phoebe stared upward. The light against the windows was changing as her life had changed, but where the sky was brightening her life grew ever darker. Turning on to her side she closed her eyes, squeezing the lids tight, fighting away a memory she could not escape . . . . *fifteen years' hard labour*.

Chapter Two

Phoebe breathed deeply, savouring the warm July air, not wanting to return to the stifling steam-filled prison laundry. Last night had been only one more in a long line of sleepless nights but Liza Spittle's visit to her bed had left her terrified, too afraid to sleep even after Tilly Wood had half throttled the woman. Phoebe pegged the last cloth to the line, her hand shaking. Liza wasn't the sort to give in easily, sooner or later she would try again.

'Thinkin' of doin' a runner, Pardoe?'

Sally Moreton stood in the doorway of the laundry, the long cane swishing alongside her skirts.

Phoebe picked up the empty basket.

'Wait!'

The order cracked across the yard. Phoebe stood still, watching the other woman march the length of the washing line, her cane lifting each of the cloths in turn.

'Wot 'appened last night?'

'Last night?' Phoebe hedged, knowing Sally Moreton would already have been told everything.

'Don't play the innocent with me, you bloody thief! I want to 'ear wot 'appened.' The cane whistled past, close to Phoebe's ear.

'I didn't know anything had happened.' She waited for the blow she knew the lie would bring. 'We all sat as usual, mending linen after clearing the dining hall, then at eight-thirty we dispersed to the dormitories and prepared for bed. Then at nine the light was put out and everyone went to sleep – at least that is what happened in our dormitory.'

'"At least that is what happened in our dormitory,"' Sally

Moreton mimicked, bringing the cane down again. 'Listen to me, you little snot! If nothin' 'appened 'ow come Liza Spittle can 'ardly shift 'er 'ead on 'er neck this mornin'? An' 'ow come when 'er talks 'er sounds like a glede under a door? Got a touch of this new influenza as 'er or is it somethin' else grabbed 'er by the throat? Somethin' like another woman?'

The cane tapped warningly against the drab grey skirts of the laundry superintendent. Phoebe knew that it would take very little to bring it lashing across her face.

'Lost yer tongue, 'ave yer?' Sally Moreton grinned, showing large uneven teeth, bases blackening with decay. 'You nearly lost a lot more last night. 'Ad a visit from Liza so I 'ear. Enjoy it, did you?'

Phoebe gripped the empty basket, holding it close against her as Sally Moreton stepped nearer.

'Play wi' these, did 'er?' Sally's free hand closed over Phoebe's breast and squeezed. ''Er likes tits does Liza, especially young tits.' She smiled again, bringing her face close to Phoebe's. 'The sort that is still firm. But it ain't just tits satisfies Liza, 'er likes more, 'er likes a bit of what's down 'ere . . .' The hand holding the cane knocked the basket aside, allowing the other to press between Phoebe's legs. 'I know what Liza likes. We 'as the same tastes if you see what I mean!'

Dropping the basket, Phoebe pushed the woman, causing her to take several steps backward. 'You disgust me!' she spat.

'So I disgust you, do I?' Sally Moreton brought the cane to rest against the palm of her left hand, eyeing the girl whose mouth was still swollen from yesterday's blow. It was going to be more than her mouth would be swollen this time! 'Did Liza disgust you an' all . . . could it be we ain't good enough for Miss 'Igh and Mighty Pardoe? Or is it Tilly Wood 'as staked a claim?'

'Tilly Wood isn't like that!' Phoebe flared. 'She hasn't got your filthy ways . . .' She stopped as the cane found its mark, the force of it splitting her lower lip as it threw her backward.

'So Sally Moreton 'as filthy ways, 'as 'er?' The cane whistled through the air, slicing across Phoebe's shoulder. ''Er ain't to yer liking.' The cane struck again. ''Er disgusts you, do 'er?' The cane flashed downward, cutting across Phoebe's cheek, then lifted high into the air again.

'Stop that!' Agnes Marsh caught the superintendent's arm, halting the blows raining on to Phoebe. 'You bloody fool, Sally. Ain't you got more sense than to beat the kid senseless this time o' the day?'

'I don't let nobody mouth off at me!'

'Nor you should,' Agnes allowed, 'but daytime ain't the time to teach her a lesson, you should know that.'

'No, it ain't, Agnes.' Sally Moreton lowered the cane, her eyes on the girl still shielding her head with her arms. 'But it won't always be daytime, will it? Then this one will really find out what it means to mouth off at Sally Moreton.'

'That's it, Sally.' Agnes Marsh, deputy superintendent of the prison laundry, released the woman's arm. 'Do what you like in the dark – that way there's nobody can point the finger. As fer 'er,' she jerked her head towards Phoebe, 'Governess 'as sent fer 'er, wants 'er upstairs.'

'What for?' Sally looked quickly at the woman beside her.

'Didn't say, just sent Mary Pegleg to say as 'er wanted to see Prisoner Pardoe in 'er office, now.'

'You 'eard 'er.' Sally reached out with the cane, poking Phoebe in the ribs. 'Get yerself up there . . . an' mind, I'll 'ear of every word what's said so you better be careful what you tells our new lady Governess about yer little . . . accident.' She touched the cane to Phoebe's bleeding mouth then stood aside. 'Get yerself to the bathroom and wash afore you go upstairs.'

Her eyes clouded with pain Phoebe picked up the fallen basket, carrying it into the steam-filled laundry and depositing it beside her washtub. All eyes followed her as she walked from the laundry; all eyes registered the bloody mouth and weals like scarlet ribbons criss-crossing her cheek, among them the eyes of Tilly Wood.

'Wot did 'er say?'

The evening meal of bread and potatoes finished and the dining hall cleared, the women prisoners sat at the long wooden tables, each with a piece of mending.

'She said I wasn't to be assigned to the laundry from now on,' Phoebe answered in a whisper.

'A sined? Wot does that mean?'

'It means 'er don't 'ave to scrub no more bloody jam rags, that's what it means.' Mary Pegleg, her duties as general dogsbody for the prison Governess finished for the day, sat with the others, the wooden stump attached to her left knee thrust out beneath the table. Tilly Wood looked up from her place opposite Phoebe but said nothing.

''Ave you bin sprung, Pardoe?' a thin whippet-like woman asked.

'No,' Phoebe shook her head, 'I am not being released.'

''Er's goin' into the sewin' room.' Mary Pegleg supplied the information with an air of importance. 'I 'eard through the door. I 'as to sit outside Governess's room case I'm wanted, an' I 'eard 'er say as 'ow Pardoe was to work in the sewin' room from now on.'

'By all the Saints in Heaven, I wish it were me!'

'Governess ain't that daft,' the whippet-faced woman grinned. 'Tek you in there an' Christ knows 'ow many would get clobbered.'

'It's not bloody fair! A bloke lathers the 'ide off of a woman an' 'e gets away wi' it. A woman 'its a man an' 'er finishes up doin' twelve months in 'ell, washin' other folks' dirty linen.'

'That's true an' all, Bridie Trow,' came another whisper, 'but you hit the man with a wooden stool, nearly knocking his brains out!'

18

'Holy Mother o'God, an' that's a dirty lie.' Bridie looked up from the sheet she was mending. 'Oi could never 'ave knocked out the man's brain for 'e 'ad none in 'is 'ead to start with.'

'Hey up, Steel Arse is comin'.'

The sudden whisper stilled the women's giggles and all heads bent to the sewing.

''Alf-past eight . . . pack up.' The ever-present cane swished as the superintendent of the laundry surveyed two hundred silent women. 'Put the sewin' in its proper basket then prepare for bed. Each dormitory will be inspected before lights out at nine.' She stood watching the women file silently from the hall, her eyes following the thin figure of Phoebe Pardoe.

'So 'ow come the sewin' room . . . an' why you?'

Hands and face washed, a rough calico nightgown swamping her stringy body, Tilly Wood sat on the end of Phoebe's bed, the other occupants of the room covertly listening.

Phoebe glanced at her hands, encased in the white cotton gloves which Hannah Price, the prison Governess, had given her to protect them while they healed. 'It seems Mrs Price was invited to a friend's house at the weekend. While she was there they visited the Goose Fair at Wednesbury and Mrs Price purchased a petticoat from one of the stalls. She asked who had made it because she would like to buy more but was told that would not be possible for the girl who was responsible for the petticoat had been sent to prison in Birmingham. Being told the name "Phoebe Mary Pardoe", the governess guessed it might be me. When I told her my home was in Wednesbury she asked to see some of the sewing I had done here in Handsworth, then she said I was to be assigned to the sewing room but my duties would not begin until my hands were healed.'

'An' yer face?' Tilly asked, looking at the weals still red

against the swollen flesh. 'What 'ad the Governess to say about that?'

'She asked what had happened. I told her it was an accident, the drying racks had slipped and caught me on the face.'

'Best way,' Tilly nodded. 'This is a new government prison, it ain't like the old 'uns with everybody packed in a single stinkin' underground cell, an' Hannah Price is first woman to run a prison as I know of. It will be a 'ard job keepin' it if I know anythin' about men – one breath about 'er bein' unable to control we women an' 'er'll be out. Besides . . .' she threw a meaningful look at Liza Spittle '. . . we can sort out our own problems.'

'Find yer own bed, Tilly Wood.' Sally Moreton strode into the long room, her cane slapping the foot of each bed as she passed. Reaching Phoebe's, she paused. 'Seems you 'ave more than one visitin' yer bed at night, Pardoe.' She touched the cane to Phoebe's breast. 'Already gettin' more than tits to play with, are they? P'raps we better move you from more than the laundry.' She smiled, showing her blackened teeth. 'Mebbe that little room next to mine? Be nice an' private there you would, nobody to come pawin' you in the dark.'

In her bed, Tilly's strong fingers tightened on the rough blanket.

'Now the lot of you, listen!' The cane cracked against the iron frame of each bed like a series of pistol shots as Sally Moreton proceeded to the door. 'There'll be no lovers' meetin's tonight, no moonlight walks from bed to bed . . . you 'ear that, Liza Spittle? Each of you stays put where you am now. Ignore Sally's warnin' an' you'll wish yerselves dead!'

Turning off the one gaslamp, she left.

'Goodnight to you an all, Mrs Moreton,' Bridie Trow called softly after the departing wardress.

'An' arsehole to yer warnin',' another voice added, just loud enough to be heard.

'Ar, an' you can stick yer cane up that!' Mary Pegleg laughed in the darkness.

'Sure, Mary, an' that's not the place old Steel Arse will be pushin' 'er cane in 'er lonely room,' Bridie Trow said crudely. 'It's not that 'ole she'll be a pokin' stick into, may the Divil an' all 'is demons escort her into Hell!'

Tilly Wood pulled the blanket up to her chin, remembering the weals on Phoebe's face, the broken mouth swollen to four times its size. The Devil could have Sally Moreton but it would be Tilly Wood gave her to him.

Phoebe stared at the windows high above her bed. Why had her aunt turned her out of her own home? Why after that had she ordered Joseph Leach to turn her out of his? Why did her aunt hate her so much? Why had Montrose not come to see her or even sent a note? The questions kept sleep from her.

'. . . *I find you guilty of wilful theft* . . .'

The words seemed to echo through the quiet room.

'*I want you for my wife, Phoebe.*' The figure of Montrose Wheeler rose in her mind, so tall and handsome, so dashing and attentive. '*I want to take you to London . . . to Paris . . . I want to show you off to the world . . . I love you, Phoebe, and I want you to be my wife.*'

But he hadn't loved her enough to write, he hadn't wanted her badly enough to come for her when the home she thought hers forever had gone instead to her aunt and uncle.

And her aunt had made sure she went from it quickly, just as she had made sure she had also gone from Joseph's home.

But Joseph had not left her entirely without help. He had taken her to see Elias Webb, a stumpy irascible man who owned property on the edge of the town.

'I wants no truck wi' the Pardoes,' he had shouted, his face red and angry when Joseph told the reason for their visit. 'It was Abel Pardoe ruined my business when he sold Monway Field to an iron merchant – pulled my mill down, 'e did, a mill I'd ground flour in all me life, ar, an' me father afore that, an' then she . . . Annie Pardoe . . . I wasn't good enough fer 'er . . . wanted no mill owner fer a 'usband did that one . . . bloody stuck up bitch! No matter who got 'urt so long as it wasn't Annie Pardoe.'

'Then why let 'er 'urt another, Elias,' Joseph had asked, 'why when you can stop it?'

''Ow can my lettin' Abel Pardoe's wench 'ave my 'ouse 'urt that bitch of a sister of his'n?' Elias had demanded.

''Cos your 'ouses are about the only ones left in Wednesbury as don' belong to Pardoe or Foster or Platt, or else to folk who am beholden to 'em. Annie Pardoe not only turned 'er own brother's wench out of 'er father's 'ome, 'er turned 'er out o' mine. Said if 'er didn't go, I 'ad to – an' lose me job at the pit an' all. An' if Annie Pardoe 'as seen wench off two places, what meks you think 'er will let Abel's daughter rest in any if 'er can do anythin' about it?'

Elias had looked at her then, Phoebe remembered, his eyes bright and calculating in his red face.

'Why let the sins of the parents fall upon the children, Elias? Especially the sins of Annie Pardoe.' Joseph drove home the last nail.

'That 'un!' Elias had almost spat the words. 'Annie Pardoe is still the same heartless . . . done!' He struck the table palm down. 'You can 'ave the 'ouse but it will cost you two 'undred an' fifty guineas . . . tek it or tek yerself off.'

Joseph had tried to get Elias to lower his price but Phoebe had agreed. To own her own house, however small, a house her aunt could not turn her out of, would be worth two hundred and fifty of the three hundred guineas her maternal grandmother had left her.

Wiggins Mill stood some way out of the town, close to its own pool. Set in a hollow, it was sheltered from the winds blowing off the open heath, the Birmingham Navigation Canal at its rear. With a scullery, kitchen, large living room and smaller parlour, three fair-sized bedrooms, together with the usual outhouses and a stable, it had become hers the following day.

And a week later Annie Pardoe had arrived.

'And this is where you intend to live?' she had asked, looking down her nose at the furniture which the remainder of Phoebe's guineas had bought from John Kilvert's pawn-broker's shop in Union Street. 'And what do you intend to live on?'

Refusing the offer of tea, her aunt wiped a gloved finger across the chair Phoebe indicated then refused that too.

'. . . or is there someone prepared to keep you – for a price?'

Staring at the squares of moonlight high on the shadowed walls Phoebe felt again the heat that had risen to her face and the cold steady rise of anger in her stomach. She had despised Annie Pardoe then: before that moment she had held no real feelings for the woman who was her father's sister, but at that moment the seed of hate was sown.

'Aunt,' her voice had been steady though she was taut with fury, 'this house is my home and how I choose to make my living is my business and no one else's. My father's will did not name either you or Uncle Samuel my guardian, therefore you have no jurisdiction over me. That being so, you will not interfere in my affairs.'

Her aunt's face had twisted with what Phoebe had hoped was derision but knew to be hate.

'What do you expect people will say . . . a young woman living alone outside the town?'

'That I'm what you already think me,' Phoebe had answered, 'a whore.'

Sally Moreton strode through the prison laundry, thin cane swishing beside the skirts of her grey uniform, her hair scraped back to form a knot at her neck, adding to the severity of her features.

'Call them clean?' She stopped at a basket of cloths, their sides ragged where they had been torn into strips.

Martha Ames looked at the cloths she had scrubbed at for over an hour. 'They look clean to me, Mrs Moreton.'

'Well, they don't look clean to me. Look at 'em!' Sally Moreton's black-booted foot caught the wicker basket, tipping it over to one side. Poking the contents with the cane, she strewed them across the flagged floor. 'Look at this . . .' She ground a boot into a wet cloth. 'An' this . . .' Her boot came down on another, leaving a dirty mark on each. 'An' wot about these?' Hitching her skirts, she trampled the freshly scrubbed cloths, spreading a pool of water across the floor.

Martha Ames stared silently at the cloths that had had her knuckles bleeding. She knew better than to argue.

'They'm bloody filthy!' Sally Moreton shouted, her tall man-like frame towering over Martha. 'Filthy, like all o' you scum!' She glared at the other women, watching silently. Only Tilly Wood's eyes refused to fall before her glare. 'We'll 'ave 'em done again,' she shouted, kicking the cloths across the floor, 'we'll 'ave the 'ole bloody lot done again. You!' She pointed to Bridie Trow. 'Get them boilers emptied. An' you,' she bawled at the ferret-faced Nellie Bladen, 'get fresh water in them tubs. An' you lot . . .' she glared around the steam-filled laundry, '. . . you all do the same. You are going to start all over again.'

'But, Mrs Moreton . . .' The pale consumptive face of Nellie Bladen blanched further as the superintendent swung back to her. 'That'll tek the rest of the mornin'. It'll be afternoon afore we can start washin' agen.'

'Are you arguin' wi' me?' The cane lifted, coming down hard across Nellie's thin shoulders.

'Steel Arse ain't took kindly to Phoebe Pardoe bein' teken out of 'ere,' a voice whispered behind Tilly Wood, 'looks like we am all goin' to be made to pay.'

'When I tell you what to do, you do it . . .' The cane rose again, coming down across Nellie's bent back. 'You don't talk about it, you *do* it!'

Tilly's hand tightened about the thick wooden stick she used to lift clothes from the boiling water in the huge copper.

'You 'ear me, scum? You do it.'

Nellie was already on the floor when Sally Moreton fell across her, unconscious from the blow Tilly Wood struck to the back of her head.

'That bastard has dealt 'er last blow.' Tilly looked at the figure of the wardress almost covering the thin woman half-conscious beneath her. 'Quick, you lot, 'elp me get Nellie out from under this swine.'

Bridie Trow grabbed the shoulder of the woman who seconds before had seemed set to beat Nellie Bladen to death, and heaved her aside, rolling her on to her back.

'Christ Almighty!' Martha Ames breathed. 'What've you done, Tilly? We'll all be done for when Sally Moreton comes to.'

'Holy Mother an' all the Saints.' Bridie Trow crossed herself. 'We'll all be swingin' on the end of a rope, so we will, when 'er tells Justice about this.'

''Er won't be tellin' Magistrates nor nobody else,' Tilly said, grabbing a cloth from a basket standing ready to be taken to the washing lines in the yard. 'Steel Arse 'as caned the last woman 'er'll ever cane an' spoke the last words 'er'll ever say.'

The cloth stretched between her hands, Tilly sank to her knees at Sally Moreton's head. 'Sit on 'er,' she said, looking up at the women grouped around. 'Bridie, Martha, sit on 'er – an' one of you watch the door.'

Then as the two women sat on the unconscious wardress, Tilly placed the folded cloth over the woman's face and held it tightly until any sign of breathing had stopped.

'That's you got yer comeuppance,' Tilly breathed, getting to her feet.

'An' may the Divil 'ave the dealin' of it,' Bridie added, crossing herself again.

'We'll all be meetin' 'im when Governess sees that.' Martha

touched a foot to the dead woman. 'We'll all be as dead as this one.'

'No, we won't.' Tilly looked at the woman on the floor. 'Find Mary Pegleg an' tell 'er to report to the Governess there has been an accident in the laundry . . . an' tek your time.'

''Ow do we mek this look like an accident?' Martha asked. 'The woman's dead.'

'Sure an' 'as no one ever died of an accident before?' Bridie answered as the woman watching the door set off on her message. 'Try holdin' yer gob for a second, Martha Ames, an' listen to Tilly.'

'Leave 'er be.' Tilly held out a hand to the women who stepped forward, about to lift the whimpering Nellie. 'Let 'er lie. Now listen to me. Sally Moreton was tellin' Nellie to tek the cloths outside for peggin' out when 'er started to gasp. 'Er clutched 'er chest, staggerin' about knockin' that basket over, then 'er cried out, a funny stranglin' cry in 'er throat, an' then tumbled 'ead first over Nellie there, nearly knockin' 'er unconscious. You two,' she pointed to Bridie and Martha, 'an' meself rolled Sally over an' called out 'er name, but gettin' no answer thought we best send for the Governess.'

'What d'you reckon will 'appen then?'

Tilly looked at Liza Spittle who until that moment had remained a silent observer. 'Do you reckon as the Governess will believe you?'

'I do.' Tilly looked at the woman who revolted her. 'An' I reckon summat else, Liza, I reckon you'd better keep yer mouth shut, 'cos what Tilly Wood does once 'er can do again – only next time it will be *you* lyin' there.'

'Won't the Governess be after sendin' for the doctor though, Tilly?' Bridie's look was as anxious as her question.

'I'm bankin' on 'er doin' just that,' Tilly answered. 'That Poor Relief doctor as looks after this place is more interested in the bottle than in patients. 'E's drunk no matter when 'e's sent for, be it day or night. It's my guess 'e'll tek one look at Sally Moreton, listen to what we tells 'im 'appened, an' say 'er died of an 'eart attack.'

'Amen to that,' Martha murmured.

'Holy Mother o'God, smile on the man an' grant he be as drunk as a fiddler's bitch!' And Bridie Trow crossed herself again.

Chapter Three

'Are you all right?' Bridie Trow had watched Phoebe from the start of the evening meal. 'You've not touched your taties other than chase 'em round the plate like a bobby after a babby.'

'Yes . . . I'm all right.'

'Like my arse you're all right!' Martha Ames popped the last of her own potatoes into her mouth, speaking as she chewed. 'I seen you comin' from the sewin' room an' you was cryin'.'

'Cryin'!' Tilly Wood stopped eating. 'What about . . . 'as anybody 'ad a go at you?'

'No.' Phoebe didn't look up, unable to keep more tears from filling her eyes.

'Then what am you cryin' for, Phoebe?' Mary Pegleg eased her wooden leg to a more comfortable position under the long scrubbed table top.

''Er's cryin' for to go 'ome,' Liza Spittle laughed, the beetroot mark on her face seeming to darken. 'Well, you'll cry a long time, Pardoe – about fifteen year I'd say.'

'Shut yer gob, Liza Spittle!' Bridie's eyes flashed.

'"As anybody said summat you didn't like, Phoebe? 'As anybody upset you, Phoebe?"' Liza Spittle minced, then laughed coarsely. 'You lot mek me sick the way you dance round 'er. 'Er ain't no different from the rest on we. 'Er was thievin' an' 'er was catched, now 'er's got to do time like we all 'ave so let 'er be . . . the more 'er cries the less 'er'll piddle.'

29

Tilly looked across the table, her thin face pinched with distaste. 'If you wants to chew yer next meal, Liza, then tek my advice and keep yer mouth closed.'

'Liza's right in a way, Tilly,' Mary Pegleg put in. 'Phoebe ain't no different. We all feel like 'avin' a cry at times, an' there be times when a good cry meks you feel better.'

'Give me half hour after lights out,' Liza smirked, 'then I'll mek 'er feel better. What Liza does is better for 'er than fartin' around wi' words. Ah bet you can remember 'ow it felt when that fiancy o' your'n touched you up, eh, Pardoe?'

Picking up her plate, Tilly tipped the remainder of her bread and potatoes on to Mary Pegleg's then swung the empty plate fast and hard, smashing it full into Liza Spittle's face.

'You was told to keep yer dirty mouth shut, Liza!' Tilly put the dented metal plate on the table as Sally Moreton's replacement began to move towards them. 'You should 'ave done just that, but then, they say there's no fool like an old fool.'

'What's going on here?'

Emily Pagett had been superintendent of the laundry for the month since Sally Moreton's death. She carried no cane but every prisoner in Handsworth gaol knew she was not to be played with.

'Phoebe . . . 'er's . . . 'er's a bit upset.' Nellie Bladen's consumptive face turned an even more sickly yellow.

'Why is that, Phoebe?'

Brushing at her cheeks with her fingers, Phoebe glanced up at the wardress. She had no occasion to see this woman other than at mealtimes, her place of labour being changed to the sewing room, but Tilly and the others had said she was not without sympathy.

'I . . . I was just remembering . . .'

''Er was saying that 'er father's bin dead twelve months today,' Tilly chipped in as Phoebe faltered. ''Er was very close to 'er father.'

'It happens to everybody, Pardoe.' Emily Pagett turned her

glance to Liza Spittle, trying to staunch the blood spurting crimson between her fingers. 'And what's happened to you, Spittle?'

'Sure an' 'tis the nose on 'er face, 'tis bleedin'.' Bridie Trow was angelic in her innocence. 'Sure an' it does that sometimes.'

'So her nose is bleeding. And what has happened to her tongue, why can't she use that? It's usually to be heard if she thinks none but inmates are around.'

'It'z juzt a doze bleed,' Liza snuffled through her fingers, 'it 'appenz zumtimes.'

'I see, just a nose bleed . . . not caused by anything specific like a snide remark or the promise of a midnight visit?' The wardress raised her voice so it carried over the clatter of forks. 'In the four weeks since my arrival in Handsworth I have come to know almost all of you women, and you have all come to know me and to know I will have no stepping out of line. Keep yourselves orderly, do your work well and there will be no trouble. That is *exactly* what I want and expect . . . no trouble.'

The clatter of forks resumed, no prisoner raising her head, each afraid that to catch the eye of the laundry superintendent might in some way constitute a challenge.

Her voice once more at a normal level Emily Pagett looked at Liza, blood smeared across her face, merging the beetroot mark into one red mask. 'Looks nasty, Spittle,' she said. 'Better get along to the washroom and get it cleaned up. You wouldn't want to get it knocked, now would you? That *would* be painful . . .' Then, her eyes still on the woman shuffling from the table, she added. 'And you, Tilly Wood, best try getting that plate back into shape. And next time, use your hand – there's less evidence that way.'

'How did you know?'

Phoebe slipped the rough calico nightgown over her head, fastening the flat cloth-covered buttons up to her throat.

31

'Took no guessin'.' Tilly fastened her hair in a plait, leaving it to lie across one shoulder. 'You've said one or two bits o' what 'appened afore you come 'ere, one o' em bein' as 'ow your father died sudden like.'

'God rest the puir man!' Bridie crossed herself.

'I never expected it.' Phoebe stared down at her hands, now lying in her lap. 'Father sometimes stayed away if his business took him to London or Southampton but he always told me first. I had no idea he had not come home that night until Mrs Banks announced his bed had not been slept in. Then when I heard about the accident . . .'

'Don't go over that.' Tilly fastened the buttons of her own nightgown. 'No use in rakin' spent coals.'

'Let 'er get it out if 'er wants to.' Martha Ames came to sit beside Phoebe on the low iron bed. 'Spit it out, wench, it'll feel better when you do.'

'It all happened so quickly,' Phoebe said quietly. 'Father dead, his will leaving me penniless, Montrose no longer wanting to marry me, and Aunt Annie turning me out of my own home . . .'

'By Patrick an' the Saints, ye puir girl! An' it's little wonder the Divil got his hooks into yous. So how did you manage, you never 'avin' to strike a blow yerself afore?' Bridie asked.

'I never would have managed without Joseph Leach and his family,' Phoebe answered. 'It was Joseph and his son Mathew who hired a horse and cart to transport the furniture from the shop to Wiggins Mill, and Sarah Leach and their daughter Miriam did most of the organising of the rooms. But it was providing food that gave me my worst moments. It was over an hour's walk from the house to the town and I would bring back only enough for one day. It was Sarah taught me to plan ahead, to buy in stones rather than in ounces, and it was she who got the carter to bring what I needed from the town and drop it at the crossroads on his way to and from Dudley. From the crossroads I had to carry it the half mile to the house. There were times I just wanted to give up . . .'

'I know that feelin'.' Nellie Bladen's sickly face looked death-like in the anaemic yellow light of the single gaslamp. 'But we keeps on goin' somehow.'

Phoebe smiled, recognising knowledge gained the hard way. 'Yes, Nellie, we keep going on. It didn't seem so bad once Miriam and Sarah finally taught me to cook . . . not so bad, that is, until I realised my very last pennies were gone.'

'Eeh, ma wench, 'ow did you manage?' Martha pressed a hand over Phoebe's, her eyes on the girl's face.

'I didn't know what to do,' Phoebe replied quietly, interrupted only by Liza Spittle's moans as the rough calico of her nightgown scraped her swollen nose. 'I only knew I wasn't going to take my trouble to Joseph and Sarah, they had done enough already and with my aunt only too ready to take their home . . . that was when Lucy Baines arrived. The carter had brought her to the crossroads then directed her to Wiggins Mill. I had not seen her since that last day at Brunswick House. She had found work at Sandwell Priory across the valley at West Bromwich. It was her first real day off, she said, and Sarah had told her how to find me.

'We talked a lot and laughed over some of the mistakes I had made while learning to fend for myself, then it came out about my last pennies being spent. She asked me about my jewellery, why didn't I sell it? I would get enough money to tide me over comfortably until I got work or was married.'

'But you said that fi-nancy o' your'n 'ad given you the push!' Mary Pegleg began, then stopped as Tilly's hand smacked against her backbone.

'Lucy seemed to think that was the least of my troubles.' Phoebe smiled again. 'I was better off without a "bloke with not enough oil in his lamp to light his way home", were her words, though what she meant exactly I don't know.'

'I do,' Tilly broke in for the first time since Phoebe had begun to speak. ''Er meant as 'ow your Montrose Wheeler 'adn't enough sense to hold on to a good thing when 'e'd got it, an' I fer one agrees wi' 'er. You be better off wi'out a bloke who only wants a woman for 'er money.'

'Tilly's right, Phoebe,' Mary Pegleg nodded. 'You be fortunate to 'ave found out what 'e was afore you married 'im. There be them among us as don't an' it's too late to do anythin' about it once you're wed. I know, that's 'ow I come to 'ave this.' She tapped her knuckles against the wooden stump below her left knee.

'So what did you do, Phoebe?' Martha asked, stealing Mary's moment of glory.

'I reminded Lucy of what my aunt had said. My mother's jewellery and mine must have been paid for by my father, and unless I had deeds of gift confirming they had been given to me, then they were part of the estate and as such belonged to Uncle Samuel.'

''Er sounds a proper old cow,' Nellie Bladen muttered. 'I wouldn't mind meetin' 'er one dark night. ''Er wouldn't bloody know 'er arse from 'er elbow when I'd finished wi' 'er.'

'An' the Lord give strength to ye,' Bridie Trow said fervently, 'an' the demons o' Hell be there to pick up the pieces.'

'And did you 'ave these deeds of gift?' It was Tilly who asked the question.

'No.' Phoebe shook her head. 'So when my aunt's housekeeper arrived to collect the keys to the house she was given both jewellery boxes, my mother's and my own.'

'So if your maid saw as 'ow the jewellery was took by your aunt's 'ousekeeper, 'ow come 'er asks you why you don't sell it?'

'I asked the same question,' Phoebe answered, 'then Lucy asked something else I found puzzling. What had I done with the dresses I had taken with me? I said I had not worn them since coming to Wiggins Mill, I had used only the underwear, the dresses were in a box in my bedroom. At that Lucy grabbed my hand and dragged me after her up the stairs. In the bedroom she flung open the box and threw the dresses across the bed. "Your bloody dried up fart of an auntie took your mother's jewellery but the old bag didn't get your'n," she said.' Phoebe halted. Less than a year ago she had never heard such words; now she could speak them without so much as a blush.

'But that 'ousekeeper of Annie's, 'er took both boxes, least tha's what you said.' Mary Pegleg sounded confused.

'So she did, Mary,' Phoebe answered, 'and I said the same to Lucy who laughed. She agreed Mrs Tranter had been given two boxes each containing pieces of jewellery – none of which, she said, was that given to me by my maternal grandmother. *That* she had removed from my box, replacing it with some of my mother's. She said Aunt Annie didn't know what jewellery my mother and I had so she would never know what or if any were missing.'

'Sure an' if that girl's brain is not the gift of the little people oi'll be after askin' what is?' Bridie Trow grinned. 'So tell me, what had she done wi' the trinkets an' all?'

'Sewn them in the hem of my dresses.' Phoebe looked at the women grouped around her. 'Mrs Banks and Lucy had taken my grandmother's jewellery out of my room as soon as Aunt Annie had left Brunswick House and together they had sewn it into the hem of two dresses, the two Lucy packed into a bag while Mrs Tranter watched.'

'Oi said it was the gift of the little people the girl had.' Bridie grinned again. 'Sure none but they have the guile to think of doin' the loike, sewin' baubles into a frock. Jesus, but Paddy O'Flaherty 'imself couldn't come up wi' better, an' him the smartest man in all Oirland.'

'So why 'adn't you sold the jewellery?' Tilly watched Phoebe's face, waiting for an answer.

'Because neither of them had told me what they had done. They both thought if I knew I would insist the jewellery go to my aunt, then Mrs Banks left for Chester, and with the worry of getting a new post and then not being allowed time off up until she came to see me that day, Lucy could do nothing but hope I'd found them.'

Seated on her own bed, Liza Spittle touched a finger to her broken mouth. 'If you found you 'ad jewellery to sell,' she said, trying hard to speak without moving lips swollen beyond recognition, ''ow come you was 'ad up fer thievin'? 'Ow come you am in 'ere doin' fifteen years?'

'You sew very nicely, Pardoe.' The prison Governess examined the stitches Phoebe had put into a church Psalter. 'Father Heywood will be pleased with these, I'm sure. Tell me . . . who taught you to sew like this?'

Hannah Price's office was at the front of the plain purpose-built prison and from where she was standing Phoebe could see out across the heath, out where people were living ordinary lives, where they could walk with soft meadow earth beneath their feet, where they could stand with the sun and wind on their faces, out where her own life had once been worth living.

'Mrs Banks, Ma'am.'

'Mrs Banks was your tutor?'

'No, Ma'am.' Reluctantly Phoebe turned from her view of the outside world. 'She was my father's housekeeper. I did have a tutor,' she explained, seeing the Governess's enquiring look. 'Mr Caleb Priest was my tutor until I reached the age of thirteen then my father thought my education needed a woman's hand. He engaged Miss Stephenson who did not think I would need the skill of needlework, but I enjoyed it. When she left I used to sit with Mrs Banks and Lucy. That was when I learned to sew.'

'I see.' Hannah Price returned the Psalter. 'Tell me, Pardoe, do you prefer to work out your sentence in the sewing room, or would you rather be in the laundry or the kitchens?'

Phoebe's hand tightened on the beautifully embroidered Psalter. To have to return to the laundry, even without the presence of Sally Moreton . . . a cold sickness rose in her stomach; fifteen years' hard labour, the Magistrate had said, and the woman watching her across the room had the power to return her to a labour that paralysed the soul.

'I . . . I prefer the sewing room, Ma'am.' Phoebe swallowed the sickness of despair. 'I . . . I hope my work is satisfactory?'

'It is.' Hannah Price nodded, the slant of sun through the window catching the chestnut brown hair she had coiled into a knot on the back of her head. 'And so is your behaviour. Your superintendent tells me you have given no trouble while you have been here and I have received no report of any disturbance in your dormitory.' Crossing to the table that served as a desk, she sat down, her hands clasped on its surface. 'In view of that, Pardoe, and of the excellence of your work, I am placing you in charge of the work of the prisoners in the sewing room. I hope you realise the trust I am placing in you?'

'I do, Ma'am.' It took Phoebe long seconds to find her voice, the sickness of fear subsiding into relief. 'And I will do my best to honour it.'

She had not been returned to the steamy hell hole of the prison laundry and to the hated task of washing menstrual cloths, a task Sally Moreton had taken particular joy in making totally hers. Phoebe looked at the Psalter she was embroidering. Fifteen years . . . how many Psalters would she sew in that time?

'Eeh, Joseph, I can't believe it!' Sarah Leach looked across at her husband. 'I can't believe Abel Pardoe 'as bin dead over a year.'

'You can believe it all right.' Joseph peeled off his moleskin trousers, dropping them beside shirt and waistcoat on the floor of the tiny scullery of the one up, one down that housed them, their twenty-year-old son and fifteen-year-old daughter. There was little enough room to move in the place but there would have been less had the rest of his seven children lived beyond babyhood.

'I 'elped to gerrim out an' our Mathew 'elped to carry 'im 'ome.' He slipped into the tin bath Sarah had prepared for him, the warm water easing his crippled left leg, that being the only thing that had prevented him helping to carry Abel Pardoe's body.

''Ow did it 'appen?'

Reaching for the Sunlight soap Sarah kept on a cracked saucer, Joseph lathered his face, blowing like a seal breaking the surface. 'Crownin' in,' he spluttered, 'along of Bilston Road, I told you.'

'I know you did, but I still can't believe it.'

Picking up her husband's clothes, she carried them into the small yard they shared with five other families and threw them across the rope Joseph had fastened for her between two slim tree trunks he had trimmed and hammered into the earth. Proceeding to beat them with a cane carpet beater, she coughed, catching some of the billowing coal dust in her throat. There were those in Wednesbury did this once a week, same as their men took a weekly bath, but in her house it was a nightly affair. Sarah gave the finishing whacks then gathered the clothes, carrying them back to the scullery. Wealthy they were not, but clean they would be.

'Did anybody see it 'appen?' She took up the conversation from where she had left it.

'Don't think so, not many comings and goings up that end during the week.' Joseph scooped handfuls of water, throwing it over his hair, revealing brown beneath the black. 'Folks is all at work 'ceptin' fer Sunday, an' most o' that is spent in Chapel.'

'What did Miss Phoebe 'ave to say?' Sarah had heard it all before but felt the need to go over it again.

'Not a lot, too shocked I reckon, though 'er did say as 'ow 'er father didn't go 'ome at all that night.'

'Oh!' Sarah placed trousers, jacket and waistcoat across a wooden stool. Then, 'Joseph . . . do you reckon 'e wuz theer all night . . . in that 'ole?'

'I doubt it, Joby Hackwood would 'ave found 'im. Them dogs o' his'n could find anythin' – sharp as a razor be them dogs an' Joby 'isself not far off. No, if Abel Pardoe 'ad met wi' that 'ole that night, Joby would 'ave found 'im.' His bath finished Joseph dressed. ''Sides, 'e were facing wrong way.'

Carrying the tin bath out the back, Sarah emptied it into the communal drain that ran through the street of miners' houses then brought it back into the scullery against the arrival of her son.

'What do you mean, 'e were facin' the wrong way?' In the tiny living room she passed Joseph his clay pipe from the mantle then the precious tin with the last few strands of shag tobacco.

Joseph packed the tiny white bowl of the home-made pipe, pressing the tobacco firmly down with his thumb, testing the draw of it with loud sucking breaths before holding a taper to the fire. 'It were soft Johnnie as found 'em . . .'

'Wot! Minnie Pritchard's lad? I thought 'er kept 'im close, not let 'im roam about?'

'Lad 'as fits, Sarah,' Joseph held the lighted taper to the bowl, answering through short puffs, 'that . . . that don' . . . that don' mean as 'e's daft. Lad 'as a brain . . . it's folk around 'im as is daft . . . too daft to let lad be.' Knocking the taper against the bars of the grate blackleaded to a shine like silver, he extinguished the flame, dropping the taper back into a clay pot in the hearth. 'If that mother o' his'n let lad out to work . . .'

''Ow can 'er?' Sarah was quick to defend the woman. 'Lad 'as fits . . . 'e ain't responsible. 'E can't be trusted to act proper.'

'It's folk who believe that am the daft 'uns, Sarah.' Joseph leaned back into the chair set close to the fire, pulling heavily on the small pipe. 'Lad were responsible enough to come straight to pit an' tell me what 'e'd found. If that ain't actin' proper then I don' know wot is. Seems right responsible way of carryin' on to me, an' don' 'e always put isself down somewhere when 'e feels a turn comin' on?'

'I feel sorry for 'em both,' Sarah added coals to the fire, 'the lad an' 'is mother. What the good Lord was thinkin' on the day 'e was got . . .'

'Nobody knows the ways o' the Lord, Sarah, an' it's a wise 'ead that don' puzzle over 'em.'

'That be true enough.' Picking up her mending, Sarah carried it to the hard-backed settle beneath the small window. 'Any road up, it were lad found 'im, you say?'

Joseph tapped the white bowl against the palm of his hand, loosening the tobacco. 'Ar, leastways nobody else 'ad, not to my knowledge anyway.' He replaced the slender stem in his mouth, holding it between his teeth. 'Along about three o'clock he come runnin' into yard like a bat out of 'ell, babbling on about Bilston Road cavin' in and oss an' cart at bottom of 'ole.'

Sarah waited while Joseph tapped his pipe.

'I could see lad was upset,' a wisp of grey smoke curled from Joseph's lips, 'so I left office to Manny Whitehouse an' went wi' 'im.'

'What if gaffer 'ad come an' you not at the pit? You could 'ave lost yer job.'

'No fear o' that 'appening seein' it was 'im at bottom of that 'ole!'

You didn't know that at the time, tekin' off after soft Johnnie, Sarah thought, though was wise enough not to say it.

'Any road,' Joseph puffed, 'soon as I seen trap I knowed who it was 'ad gone in. I sent Johnnie 'ome an' went back to pit for men to raise Abel.'

'So, what about 'is facin' wrong way?' Sarah asked again as Joseph settled into silence.

'Well,' he removed the pipe from his mouth, his gaze on the glowing coals, 'if gaffer 'ad bin on his way from pit to the 'ouse, as Miss Phoebe thought, then oss would 'ave bin facin' t'other way, but it were facin' *toward* Bilston with its back end toward Brummagem.'

Sarah held the needle in mid-air, a puzzled frown drawing her brows together. 'What's wrong wi' that?'

'Think on it,' he answered. 'Abel Pardoe left 'ome that mornin' fer pit only 'e didn't come to pit that day. Miss Phoebe said 'e 'adn't come 'ome from pit in the afternoon nor 'ad 'e bin 'ome all night. Joby Hackwood is certain sure there was no 'ole in Bilston Road that night nor up to eleven o'clock next mornin' when he says 'e was runnin' 'is dogs along the edge o' cornfield . . .'

'Seein' 'ow many rabbits was runnin' likely,' Sarah said drily.

'Whatever 'e was doin', there was no 'ole in Bilston Road at that time or 'e would 'ave seen it, so Abel must 'ave run into it between eleven an' two. It would tek the hour between then an' three for young Johnnie Pritchard to sort out what to do then get isself over to the pit to get me.'

'I still don't see what you reckon is wrong?' Sarah stabbed the needle into her mending.

Joseph blew another stream of blue-grey smoke, the smell of shag tobacco mingling with the smell of coal. 'What's wrong is this. Oss 'ad its back end toward Brummagem,' he said, using the local term for Birmingham, 'that means Abel Pardoe was on 'is way back from there.'

'But 'ow can you be sure?' Sarah asked.

'I'm sure enough,' Joseph replied, his glance still deep in the heart of the fire. 'I 'appens to know Abel spent a deal of time there.'

'Doin' what . . . business?'

'Of a sort.' Joseph sucked on his pipe.

'What sort?' Sarah removed the thread from the needle, using the eye end to unpick an untidy stitch.

'Use yer 'ead, woman.' Joseph bit on the stem of the clay pipe. 'What sort of business does a man do at night? Not the sort 'e does in any office! It's my belief Abel Pardoe 'ad a kept woman – either that or he med regular visits to some knockin' shop.'

Sarah almost dropped the needle. 'Eeeh, Joseph! You mean Abel Pardoe . . .'

'That's just what I mean,' Joseph continued where Sarah's shocked voice left off. 'I mean Abel Pardoe had spent that night in Brummagem with a prostitute.'

'Thank the good Lord that never came out.' Sarah held the needle poised in mid-air. 'Phoebe Pardoe went through enough with that aunt of hers wi'out 'earin' such things about 'er father.'

'Seems nobody else figured it,' Joseph sucked once more on the slim white stem of his clay pipe, 'or, if they did then they'm keepin' quiet about it same as we 'ave.'

'That poor girl in prison these twelve months,' Sarah sighed, resuming her mending. 'I can't believe that neither, 'er would never steal anythin'.'

'Magistrate said 'er did.'

'Magistrate don't know everythin',' Sarah snapped, a catch in her voice. ''E don't know what a nice carin' wench young Phoebe was.'

'Magistrate don't need to know.' Joseph stared into the glowing heart of the grate. ''E knowed only what somebody wanted 'im to know an' in my opinion that somebody be Annie Pardoe. My guess is it be 'er as supplied that evidence, if what was said in that court could be called evidence, an' that were just enough to put Abel's daughter down the line for fifteen years.'

Chapter Four

''Er's sewin' what!' Martha Ames's face creased with a mixture of amusement and disbelief. 'Hey, Phoebe, you 'ear that? Mary Pegleg reckons you be sewin' salt cellars.'

'Psalters.' Phoebe joined the laughter of the women. Apart from a half-hour break for the midday meal she didn't see them until evening. 'I'm sewing Psalters . . .'

'That another of 'er new ideas?' Liza interrupted scathingly. 'Gets a good many of them does new Governess.'

'An' all of 'em to the good so far.' Martha looked at her fellow prisoner, the beetroot stain livid on her cheek. 'Though I reckon I could suggest one we'd all find to our liking.'

'Oh, ar, an' what's that, Martha Smart Arse?'

'That 'er 'as you put down.'

'What them Psalterers for then, Phoebe?' Nellie Bladen asked as the second flush of laughter died away.

'Jesus, Joseph and Mary!' Bridie exclaimed, making the regular sign on her chest. 'Sure an oi can't be after believin' what my own ears be tellin' me, Nellie Bladen.'

'So what am they tellin' you?' Nellie's ferret features tightened. 'One thing they ain't tellin' you for all the sign o' the cross you keep mekin' . . . they ain't tellin' you Bridie Trow is an angel nor ever likely to be!'

'That's where you be wrong altogether, so you be.' Bridie's native brogue thickened. 'If oi'm not after bein' an angel when oi'm dead it would be meanin' oi was to spend the rest of me after loif with the loikes of you – an' the good Lord will never be permittin' the loike of that.'

'And what is it the good Lord will not permit?'

The women's smiles faded as Agnes Marsh halted her patrol at their end of the long table.

Bridie, eyes still malignant, half turned on the bench seat. 'Nellie Bladen was after sayin' that oi'll be livin' wi' the loike of herself after oi be dead.'

'Well, you both have one consolation.' The wardress smiled spitefully. 'After you've finished in Handsworth you'll be used to each other . . . and to the place you'll both finish up in when you're dead. Now get this lot cleared and get ready for lights out or you might be wishing yourselves there now.'

'Sour-faced cow!' Nellie muttered, watching the wardress move down the room toward its one door. 'I know what 'er could do with.'

'An' p'raps you would like to tell 'er,' Liza Spittle dropped the apron she had been mending into the large basket set beside the table, 'to 'er face.'

'Why don't you when you am doin' it wi 'er in the store room, you dirty bugger. Don't think we don't know what goes on in there.'

'It don't bother me what you think, none of you, I'll do what it teks to get by in this place.'

'An' that means mauling the tits off any woman who'll let you an' a few that's bin too frightened to refuse.' Martha Ames dropped her own mending into the basket then turned a disdainful glance on Liza. 'Yer nothing but a filthy swine, Liza Spittle, no wonder the Devil marked you one of his'n.'

'You still didn't tell me what a Psalterer was?' Nellie Bladen whispered to Phoebe as they left the dining hall.

'It is a book of Psalms.'

'A book! But you can't sew a book, Phoebe.'

'No, of course I can't.' She smiled, following Nellie out of the dining hall. 'What Mary should have said was that I am embroidering covers for Psalters.'

'Trust Mary Pegleg to get it wrong.' Nellie turned toward

the washroom. 'That woman couldn't get anythin' right, not if 'Ell fetched 'er.'

Soaping her hands and face with carbolic, Phoebe thought of the events of the morning. Hannah Price had sent for her, asking that she make two Psalter covers. She wanted them as a gift for the Vicar of St James's church in Wednesbury. Now Phoebe felt the same tug at her stomach she had felt when the Governess told her of her visit to a friend she had in the town. How long before *she* could visit friends? Phoebe buried her face in the rough cotton that served the prisoners as towels. She knew how long . . . fifteen years.

Phoebe stared at the familiar rectangles of moonlight, her brain refusing her the sanctuary of sleep. She had thought her troubles were ending when Lucy gave her the jewellery. If only she had known . . . her troubles were just beginning.

She had pawned a ruby ring first, choosing to take it to John Kilvert, the pawnbroker who had sold her the furniture, hoping to redeem it in a few weeks.

What a hope! Phoebe turned her face to the wall, finding no solace in the well of shadows.

The ring had been followed by a marcasite brooch and that by a cornelian bracelet. One by one the pieces had gone, John Kilvert giving her a fraction of their worth and that fraction swallowed by the purchase of food and the small amount of cotton she bought to make garments to sell, garments that brought her even less than her jewellery. Finally it was her grandmother's sapphire necklace. John Kilvert's eyes had glowed when she unwrapped it from her handkerchief and laid it on his counter. He had scrutinised it carefully then said, 'Two pounds ten, tek it or leave it.'

She had had to take it as the pawnbroker well knew. Two pounds ten shillings . . . careful as she had desperately tried to be, it had lasted less than six weeks.

Too proud to tell Sarah and Joseph of her circumstances, she had agreed to go with them to the Advent Fayre one

Saturday evening. 'The gentry will be there,' Sarah had said, 'mebbe they might buy some of your petticoats. Heaven knows they'm pretty enough.'

Only she had no material to sew petticoats and no money to buy more. But she would be expected to take something that could be sold to benefit the church. She hadn't thought about her two dresses until she went to bed. The next morning she had chosen the white one sprigged with tiny red flowers and carefully taken it to pieces, using the cloth to make two dresses for a child, trimming one with red ribbons and the other with pink.

Standing behind the stall allotted to her and Sarah Leach, Phoebe had seen Montrose's mother sweep into the market place and saw the doffed caps and bobbed curtsies of the townsfolk as the woman and her companions halted a few moments at each stall. Maybe they would pass her and Sarah by, maybe Violet Wheeler would not recognise her in the flickering light of candles set in jars, but even as she pressed into the shadows Phoebe knew it would not happen.

'Mama, look, how delightful.'

The two women and a girl Phoebe guessed to be around her own age paused at her stall, the cold November breeze fluttering the feathers of their bonnets.

'Look, Mama.' The girl touched a gloved hand to the dresses Phoebe had made. 'Don't you think they are pretty?'

'I do, my dear.' Lady Dartmouth smiled at her daughter then asked,'Who made these?'

'I did, Your Ladyship,' Phoebe answered, aware of the warning in Violet Wheeler's eyes.

'They are very pretty and well stitched.' Lady Dartmouth held one of the dresses closer to the lighted candles. 'Don't you agree, Mrs Wheeler?'

Montrose's mother made a pretence of examining the stitches. 'Yes,' she answered, already turning in the direction of the next stall, 'quite.'

'Mama,' the girl picked up the second dress, 'do you not think these would make the most admirable Christmas gifts for the children of the servants? You know how much you enjoy the giving of something useful.'

'They would indeed be admirable, my dear, always provided the children are not boys, eh, Mrs Wheeler?'

Forced to turn back Violet Wheeler managed an acid smile. 'As you say, Your Ladyship, useful only if they are not boys.'

'Tell me,' Lady Dartmouth returned her hand to the warmth of her fur muff, 'have you more of these?'

Phoebe shook her head. 'No, Your Ladyship.'

'Pity.' Lady Dartmouth made to move on but her daughter stayed.

'But you could make more.' The girl's cheeks glowed red in the cold of the November night. 'How many could you make before Christmas?'

'Two would be all I had cloth for.' Phoebe avoided the glare of Violet Wheeler. 'You see, Your Ladyship, I made those from a gown of my own and I have only one more.'

'You mean you made something as pretty as this out of an old gown?'

Not so old, Phoebe thought, that particular dress had been a gift from her father on her last birthday.

'Then there is no problem.' The girl turned to her mother. 'I have lots of dresses I do not wear any more. I may give them to be used may I not, Mama?'

'Of course, Sophie,' Lady Dartmouth nodded, 'that is a very good suggestion.' Then turning her glance on Phoebe added, 'My daughter and I will be returning to the Manor on Thursday of this week. You may call whenever my daughter wishes.'

'Oh, come the next afternoon.' The girl turned to Montrose's mother. 'I'm sure you too will find a few dresses for such a worthy cause, Mrs Wheeler. After all, the proceeds will go to the church, so when may she call upon you?'

Even in the darkness of the November evening Phoebe saw the colour drain from the woman's face. 'I . . . she . . . she may call Thursday afternoon of this week at three o'clock.'

'So,' Lady Dartmouth was clearly to be delayed no longer, 'bring the dresses to the Manor one day before Christmas Eve. I will send a list of how many and what sizes to the Vicar.' She turned to her daughter. 'And now, Sophie, I insist on returning to Oakeswell Hall, this night air is much too cold for either of us.'

'Looks like Violet Wheeler 'as designs, invitin' 'er Ladyship to Oakeswell.' Sarah Leach watched the departing trio.

'Designs,' Phoebe breathed, relieved when the carriage drove away, 'how do you mean?'

'Mean!' Sarah handed over a pot of her preserve, taking a threepenny piece and handing back a penny and a halfpenny to a woman with five children hanging on her skirts. 'A man wi' half an eye can see what I mean. Violet Wheeler 'as set 'er sights on that young un for 'er lad.'

'You can't mean . . .'

'I can an' I do,' Sarah said. 'That woman intends for 'er son to wed Lady Sophie, daughter of Sir William and Lady Amelia Dartmouth of Sandwell Priory.'

Phoebe remembered the feeling that coursed through her then; it wasn't pain, no, she couldn't call it pain, it was more like pity . . . pity for a young girl being prepared like a lamb for the slaughter.

She had gone to Oakeswell Hall at the appointed time to find a servant waiting for her at the gate, the dresses, two of them, draped across her arms. Phoebe Pardoe was not to be admitted even to the grounds of her former fiancé's home.

The visit to Sandwell Priory had been so different. Phoebe turned her eyes back to the greyish-yellow rectangles high up on the wall. She had looked down from the ridge of high ground on to the house nestling in the valley, its tall windows reflecting the pale watery November sunlight, windows that seemed to go on and on along the expanse of the huge building. Brunswick House was by no means small but it would fit a hundred times over into that house. She had stared until a flurry of snow blew across her face then set off down the path to the valley. A mile or so further on she had stepped aside, hearing the rumble of an approaching carriage.

'It is you, isn't it?' Lady Sophie leaned from the window, calling for the carriage to stop. 'You are the girl I spoke to at the Fayre, are you not? The girl who is to call today?'

'I am, Your Ladyship.' Phoebe bobbed a curtsy.

'Edward,' she went on to someone in the carriage, 'this is the girl I told you about, the one who makes such delightfully pretty dresses.'

The carriage door had opened then and a tall blond man of about twenty or so had jumped out.

'Forgive my sister,' he said, 'it is a failing of hers to keep people standing in the cold.' He smiled, a smile that lit deep blue eyes. 'Allow me to assist you into the carriage?'

'No.' Phoebe took a step backward. 'No, thank you, I . . . I'll walk.'

'Nonsense.' The man smiled again. 'I will not hear of such a thing, the day is far too cold. And besides,' he held out a hand, 'it is coming on to snow.'

'Of course you must ride with us.' Lady Sophie added her smile and voice to her brother's. 'There is plenty of room.'

Phoebe had made no more demur, accepting the man's hand as she climbed into the carriage.

'My sister told me of meeting you but she failed to tell me your name?'

Across the carriage the blue eyes had smiled deep into hers.

'My name is Phoebe . . . Phoebe Pardoe.'

'How do you do, Phoebe?' He said her name slowly as if wanting to hold it in his mouth, to keep it inside of him, a part of himself.

'My sister you have met already, allow me to present myself – Edward Dartmouth.'

He had introduced himself simply. Phoebe knew he was Edward Albert Richard Dartmouth whose family had owned the Priory for nearly five hundred years, but he had given himself no airs and graces.

At the Priory Sophie had heaped dresses into her arms, their colours mixing like some exotic rainbow, then laughed as Phoebe gradually disappeared beneath them.

She had not seen Lady Dartmouth, Sophie apologising for her absence, explaining that her mother's evening visit to the market had given her a chill. 'Poor Mama,' Sophie had laughed. 'She says the things she does for the church should guarantee her a healthy eternity, though she does wish it would do the same for her earthly existence.'

Four maids had eventually carried the dresses down the great staircase. Phoebe watched for a glimpse of Lucy as they passed but she was not among the servants who crossed the vast marble hall and down a wide fan of steps to the carriage Sophie insisted Phoebe should travel home in. Edward stood beside it.

'I could not forgive myself should I let you go home alone.' He had helped her into the carriage then, his eyes never leaving her face. Phoebe had not wanted him to accompany her, ashamed for him to see her dilapidated home and the tumbling outhouses, but once there he had kept her hand in his while the coachman carried the dresses indoors. 'You must allow me to call you Phoebe,' he had said softly. 'Please tell me I may?'

Phoebe closed her eyes but the face of Edward Dartmouth was printed on the lids. A handsome face, a face with more than admiration revealed in those deep blue eyes.

Lucy had been at Wiggins Mill one day when Edward paid a visit, one of many since Phoebe's going to Sandwell Priory.

'You wants to be careful, Miss.' Phoebe remembered Lucy's warning. 'Could be 'e's here after more than you should give 'im.'

'He's a friend, Lucy.'

'There's friends and friends.' Lucy's reply had been tempered with the same warning. 'The sons of gentry is no friend to the likes of us, Miss. Not unless they want a special sort of friendship. You take a tip from me an' tell 'im not to call 'ere no more.'

But Edward had not tried to take advantage of her. He had been so courteous and yet so full of life, insisting on her going out for walks along the canal bank, teaching her to skim stones across the water, piling logs on to the fire then sitting at her feet as she sewed. She had known he loved her, known even before he told her. In the darkness of the quiet dormitory, Phoebe remembered.

Samuel Pardoe put down his brush, turning from his latest landscape painting. 'It has been a year now since Abel died.' He spelled out the words on his fingers as he had been taught in childhood. 'It seems so very long, Annie.'

Annie Pardoe watched the brother she had lived with all of his fifty-two years. He had always been slight of build even as a child but of late had become markedly more frail, seeming to dwindle into himself, fading a little more each day.

'Twelve months is a long time,' she signed in return, 'but there it is. Abel is gone and we must learn to live with the fact.'

'But Phoebe is not gone,' Samuel's fingers moved quickly, 'yet we have not seen her since her father died. Why is that, Annie? Why does Phoebe not come to see us?'

'I told you, Samuel . . .' Annie walked to the window of the room that had been turned into a studio for her brother, avoiding the need to look into the face that was so like that of Abel, then after a moment turned to sign: 'Phoebe said she never wanted to see either of us again.'

'But I think perhaps if we went to see her . . .'

'No, Samuel!' Annie Pardoe signed rapidly then dropped one hand to her side as if the movement gave her pain. 'We will not go to see her. She made the decision to leave this house, hers was the choice and we must abide by it. If it be that she changes her mind then she will be welcome to return. Until that time we will have to wait and pray.'

Samuel applied another touch of paint to the canvas, his thin hand almost transparent, then signed again. 'I wonder why Abel left everything to us? It seems so very strange.'

'I see nothing strange in a man entrusting his business and property to someone old enough and wise enough to look after it.' Annie breathed deeply, holding her hand tight against the spot beneath her rib cage, then released it to sign, 'Phoebe was very young. Abel thought we would be the better guardian of what was his until she married.'

'The better guardian of what was his . . .' Samuel left off painting. 'Phoebe was his but he did not name either of us her guardian, did he, Annie?' His eyes reflected a sadness he could not voice.

'Our brother did not appoint anyone as guardian to his daughter,' Annie crossed to the door, 'simply because he thought to see her married long before he died. I have called to see our niece several times, Samuel, hoping to persuade her to come and live with us, but each time I have been met with hostility. It hurts us both to know that she has cut herself off from her family, those who have loved her from her birth, but we cannot force her to come home, my dear.'

'Annie,' Samuel signed as she opened the door, 'what happened to the idea of her marrying Gaskell Wheeler's son?'

She hesitated, the hand on her ribs pressing a little harder, then, 'I'm afraid she took the same headstrong, foolish action she took toward us,' she answered. 'She said she had been pressured into accepting Montrose Wheeler against her will, and now her father was no longer here to enforce the marriage, she would not do so. The Wheelers were understandably upset but agreed to say that following the unforeseen death of her father, Phoebe felt she could not marry so soon, therefore a postponement had taken place.'

'Is she alone?' Samuel's fingers fluttered like wounded butterflies.

Annie looked into the thin face and sad grey eyes of her brother and the pain beneath her hand worsened. It had not been his fault, he was not to blame for what fate had ordained for him or the life Abel Pardoe had ordained for her – he was not to blame yet she could not forgive him.

'No, she is not alone.' Her answer was sharpened by the pain. 'Abel's housekeeper went with her and so did her maid. They are all well cared for, I instructed Lawyer Siveter to pay an annual allowance. Phoebe might have turned her back on us, Samuel, but we will never turn ours upon her.'

Leaving the room before he could ask any more questions, Annie paused outside the door, her eyes closed, her hand pressed to the pain that refused to be ignored. Samuel had asked the same questions before and she had told the same lies.

Opening her eyes she walked to her bedroom, taking a small cardboard box from a drawer in the table that stood beside the heavy fourposter bed. Abel had slept in that bed, Abel and his pretty wife; so many nights, so much happiness. Taking the lid from the box, she put two of the white tablets it held into her mouth, swallowing them with water from the carafe on the table. Yes, Abel had shared this bed, this room with a wife while she . . . what had she had . . . what love had Annie Pardoe known, whose bed had she shared?

Putting the lid back on the box, she replaced it in the drawer, covering it with a layer of lace-edged handkerchiefs.

She had shared neither love nor bed with any man thanks to her brother. Abel could never be made to pay while he was living and death had carried him beyond her reach. No, Abel would not pay for a life he'd snatched away, a life he had destroyed so he could live his own. But Abel's daughter would . . .

Is she alone?

Samuel's question echoed in her mind, and in her mind she answered but this time with all the truth of vengeance. No, Phoebe was not alone. Some two hundred women shared her home, a home she would inhabit for the next fifteen years.

'Well, if it ain't the Governess's little pet.'

Liza Spittle's narrow eyes watched Phoebe coming along the corridor that led to the kitchens, a tray balanced in her hands. 'Ain't you goin' to stop an' 'ave a chat wi' Liza?'

'Move out the way, Liza,' Phoebe said as the other woman moved her large frame, blocking the narrow passage. 'You know prisoners must not hang around the corridors.'

'There's a lot of things not allowed in this bloody place,' Liza grinned, showing discoloured teeth, 'but the bastards 'ave to catch you at it first.'

'I have no wish to be caught,' Phoebe edged to one side in an attempt to pass, 'especially talking to you.'

'We don't 'ave to talk.' Liza stepped closer, the beetroot mark pulsing like some living thing on her cheek. 'You don't need to talk for what I want.'

'Liza, please move.' Phoebe was becoming alarmed. Why wasn't Liza in the laundry?

'Lucky me, bein' given the job of clearin' dinner plates,' she grinned as if answering Phoebe's unspoken question, 'otherwise we wouldn't 'ave this chance.'

'Chance?' Phoebe tried to control her trembling. She knew Liza Spittle had not given up in her twisted desire and for that reason took care never to be in her company without Bridie or Tilly.

Liza stepped forward again, wedging Phoebe against the wall. 'The chance for me to show you what you missed 'cos of that interferin' bitch Tilly Wood.' She leaned forward, pressing the tray into Phoebe's middle, her hand lifting the skirts of Phoebe's prison uniform, sliding high up over her thigh.

'Leave me alone!' Phoebe tried to use the tray in an effort to push the woman away from her, turning her face from the sour fumes of her breath. 'Please, for God's sake, don't!'

Liza laughed, a husky sound deep in her throat. 'They all says that first time.' Her voice was deep as a man's, her mouth touching the side of Phoebe's neck. 'But then it changes – it changes to, for God's sake, please do.'

'Stop!' Phoebe's cry cracked on a sob. 'Please, I . . . I'm not like that . . .'

'You will be.' Liza's tongue licked upward against Phoebe's ear, her hand moving toward the vee between her legs. 'You will be when Liza gets through.'

'No, please.' Phoebe's control had gone, the tears spilling down her cheeks. 'Please leave me alone. Please, for God's sake!'

'If you won't do it for God, then do it for me!'

Tilly Wood's voice rang out behind Liza as she was swung away, one arm twisted high up her back.

'I warned you,' Tilly snarled, her gaunt face twisted with contempt. 'I warned you afore, Tilly Wood tells not even the Lord 'imself twice . . .'

Grabbing the collar of Liza's grey calico frock, she spun her backward against the opposite wall.

'. . . but you don't tek a tellin', do you, Liza Spittle?'

Tilly struck out, the back of her hand slamming hard across Liza's face.

'. . . so yer goin' to 'ave to be shown that 'ands off means what it says.'

Across the narrow corridor Liza's small eyes glittered with a feral light as they flicked from Tilly to Phoebe then back to Tilly. 'I'm goin' to do fer you, Tilly Wood,' she breathed, wiping the blood from her mouth with the back of a hand. 'This time I'm goin' to kill you.'

She lunged forward, her large masculine frame threatening to obliterate Tilly who turned aside, thrusting a foot in her way. Liza stumbled but the force of her attack carried her forward, the sickening crunch of bone against brick covering Phoebe's sobs as she hit the wall beside her. Then Liza was falling, slipping sideways as she went down, her cracked skull sliding slowly over Phoebe's shoulder and breast, down along her skirt, trailing a long slow smear of red across grey.

'What did the Governess 'ave to say about it?' Martha Ames asked as the women prepared for the nine o'clock light out.

'I couldn't 'ear all that well,' Mary Pegleg answered. 'But 'er sent me to get Agnes Marsh an' that one looked none too 'appy when 'er went into the Governess's office, an' 'er looked a damn' sight less when 'er come out again.'

'But sure an' you must have heard somethin'?' Bridie said, slipping her nightgown over her head then folding the drab grey prison dress before placing it regulation fashion across the foot of her low iron bed.

Mary Pegleg unfastened the straps that held the wooden stump below her left knee, balancing it against the wall beside her bed. 'Well, I 'eard 'er tell Agnes as 'ow this was the first prison to 'ave a woman in charge an' that it would only tek summat like a brawl between the inmates to convince the Board that a woman wasn't fit for the job an' that 'er would be replaced wi' a man.'

'Sure an' that would be a black day for all,' Bridie said, buttoning her nightgown. 'Hannah Price has been fair in her dealin's with us women an' all. Could be we might have had a Governess the loike of Steel Arsed Sally Moreton, God rest her puir soul.'

'Did 'er say anythin' about Tilly?' Nellie Bladen looked across to Phoebe, sitting silent on her bed, her face pale and empty, then whispered, 'Is 'er still locked away on 'er own?'

Mary Pegleg rubbed a hand over the rounded nub of bone where her leg had been amputated. 'I 'eard summat about police, but I don't know if Governess said 'er was sendin' fer 'em or keepin' thing quiet from 'em.'

'Get the bobbies in 'ere an' it'll be more than Hannah Price will be teken out.' Martha Ames looked from one to the other of the women, their faces mirroring the tension that had held them all afternoon and evening. 'We'll all go, an' there's some of us in 'ere knows where to. 'Ell itself would be a better place.'

'Do you think Liza will die?' Nellie's normally yellow skin took on a deathly gleam under the sullen glow of the one gaslamp.

''Er looked near enough to it when we carried 'er to the infirmary,' Martha answered. 'Reckon 'er'll be lucky to last the night.'

'Holy Mother of God!' Bridie's hand lifted, making the sign of the cross several times in rapid succession.

'Did Agnes Marsh send fer the doctor, does anybody know?'

''Er couldn't.' Mary Pegleg eased her thin body into her bed, covering it with the one rough blanket before answering the question. ''Er 'ad to wait till Hannah Price got back from meeting with the Board an' that wasn't till after seven o'clock gone. 'Er said it was too late to get the doctor out then, that it would 'ave to wait till mornin'.'

'Too late my arse!' Martha spat. 'What 'er meant was the bloody doctor was too blind drunk by that time of the night even to stand up, let alone treat anybody.'

'Well, whatever 'er meant, 'er didn't send fer 'im,' Mary Pegleg stated flatly.

'Oi wonder what he will be makin' of it when he does come?' Bridie said.

'I don't know,' Martha shook her head, 'but this much I can say – drunk or sober there be no way 'e can call this a 'eart attack.'

'What will 'e call it . . . will it be murder?'

'Liza Spittle ain't dead,' Martha shot a glance at Phoebe but Nellie's words seemed to have passed over her head, 'so 'ow can 'e call what 'appened murder?'

Crossing to Phoebe's bed she pressed her back on the pillow, pulling the coarse blanket up to her chin before going back to her own place.

'But what if Liza do die?' Nellie persisted.

'If 'er does then any tears I shed won't be for 'er,' Martha said acridly. ''Er was nothin' but a filthy bitch sniffin' round women, 'er 'ad it comin' to 'er an' I fer one ain't sorry as 'er's copped it. The one I'm sorry fer is Tilly Wood.'

'What's goin' to 'appen to Tilly would you say, Martha?'

'Lord knows!' She looked at the other woman, death marked plain across her thin consumptive features. 'Depends on what the doctor and the Governess 'as ter say ter the Prison Board.'

Bridie crossed herself fervently. 'Then may the sweet Mother o'Jesus be puttin' the words into their mouths.'

Chapter Five

Phoebe lay awake in the hard narrow bed. She had not spoken since the affair in the corridor, she had not joined the discussions of the women, her mind empty, somehow detached, hearing nothing yet registering everything.

Tilly had offered no resistance when Agnes Marsh ordered two wardresses to take her away, only the eyes that had long forgotten laughter staying on Phoebe's face as they took her. What would they do to Tilly? She was already serving a life sentence for manslaughter . . . if Liza Spittle died Tilly would be accused of murder and it was certain she would hang. But she was no murderer; she had told Sally Moreton a lie about snapping her husband's neck to frighten her, it was the push down the stairs had broken it. No, Tilly Wood was not quite guilty of murder . . . yet.

Oh Lord! In the darkness, listening to the breathing of the sleeping women and the consumptive coughing of Nellie Biaden, Phoebe prayed, 'Oh Lord, don't let Liza die.'

High on the wall the windows showed a paler shade of darkness. Why was I sent to return that tray to the kitchen? Why was Liza Spittle clearing the dinner plates? Why was she in the corridor at that precise moment? Why was there no one else clearing the dining hall?

Questions vied for prominence in her brain. Lord, if only her father had not met with that terrible accident, if only her Aunt Annie had not acted as she had, if only she had never made those children's dresses, Lord if only . . . but how often had the Lord heard those words?

Above her the small rectangular windows lightened with infinite slowness, like lids lifting to reveal strange hypnotic eyes, and she turned her head away. But out of the shadows Lucy danced towards her, Lucy with eyes glowing and lips smiling.

'I'm getting wed.'

Phoebe heard the laughing happy voice rise from the depths of buried thoughts. 'Mathew an' me, we are goin' to be wed.'

Phoebe had joined in the girl's delight, returning the hug Lucy enfolded her in. They had talked a long time in the kitchen of the mill house, Lucy baking scones and mixing an amount of bread dough Phoebe thought must last a year at least, then she had asked about a wedding dress.

'I hadn't thought about it,' Lucy answered, setting the cloth-covered dough to rise besides the hearth. 'Well, not really thought about it, though I would like somethin' nice, somethin' new, I suppose, if the truth be told. But that's out of the question on what I get paid at the Priory.'

'And Mathew?' Phoebe had asked.

'Can't really ask him to sport me a dress from the money he makes, Miss Phoebe.' Lucy collected wooden mixing spoons, dropping them into the large brown earthenware bowl. 'Mathew had his wages docked same as the rest of 'em at the pit.'

'Docked?' Phoebe remembered the surprise she felt, but had it been surprise or disgust? 'Do you mean my aunt has reduced the wages of the men working at the mine?'

'Yes, Miss Phoebe, I do,' Lucy answered. 'Both of 'em, the Hobs Hill pit and the Crown mine at Moxley, and the folks who depend on it am feelin' the pinch real bad.'

'But why?' Phoebe asked. 'For what reason?'

'Annie Pardoe said as how price of coal had fallen an' men could take lower wages or take their hook.'

'She said that!'

'Well, not in them exact words.' Lucy carried the utensils

she had used in her baking to the long shallow sink in the scullery, returning for the kettle singing softly over the fire. 'But that was what 'er meant: the men could either accept a lower wage for a day's work or they could leave the pit altogether. And as you know, Miss Phoebe, that would leave them without a home as well as a job 'cos most houses in Wednesbury belong to Annie Pardoe, least at that end of the town they do.'

Phoebe might have asked what part her uncle had played in all of this but deep down she knew Samuel would know nothing of it.

'Mind you,' Lucy carried the kettle into the scullery, pouring hot water over a bowl and spoons then putting the kettle aside to be filled later at the pump in the yard, 'some of 'em couldn't be much worse off if they did leave. They 'ave little enough in their tins to feed a family *and* pay rent, and Annie Pardoe ain't one to let rent man call twice and get nothin', so some of the women an' kids am goin' more than hungry.'

'What of Joseph and Sarah?' Phoebe reached for a cloth to dry the dishes but it hung forgotten in her hands.

Lucy placed the freshly washed baking bowl on the wooden board Mathew had made to stand beside the sink. 'They are fairin' up to now though Joseph had his wage docked same as others, but they only manage 'cos Sarah can do most things herself.'

Sarah was a marvel, Phoebe thought, cook, housekeeper and gardener rolled into one, growing vegetables Joseph could no longer tend after the accident that had left him lame. But how long could she manage now money was short?

'So how will you and Mathew be fixed with him not earning as much?'

'It's going to be harder.' Lucy took the cloth from Phoebe and set about drying the bowls and spoons. 'There be no use in my denyin' that, but I'll have my position at the Priory and Mathew will 'ave his job at Hobs Hill. We can afford to rent a little house . . . just.'

'But you said yourself the wage at the pits had been reduced and what if you start a family? They won't keep you on at the Priory if you have children to care for. And if the situation at the pit gets any worse . . .'

'We've thought of that, Miss Phoebe, and we both know that if we wait for things to be perfect we will never be wed so we decided to go ahead. There will be hard times and worry for us whether we wed or not so we have little to lose except each other.'

Why had her aunt reduced the wages of the miners? Had the market price for coal really dropped or was there some other reason for her action? Phoebe picked up the bowls and spoons, carrying them back into the kitchen, replacing them on the rough wooden dresser set along one wall. Could it in some way have anything to do with her aunt's obvious dislike of Phoebe herself?

'So when will you and Mathew be married?' she asked as Lucy bustled into the kitchen, setting the freshly filled kettle over the glowing coals.

'Next month, the fifteenth,' Lucy's face radiated her joy, 'that's my birthday. Mathew said to have the wedding on that day then we would have two things to be happy for. Ooh, I am looking forward to it.'

Just as I was looking forward to my own wedding, Phoebe thought, watching the happiness light the other girl's eyes, only mine never took place.

'We want the ceremony to be at St Bart's.' Lucy lifted the bread dough on to the table, scoring it with a knife before placing it in the oven to bake. 'Just family and a few friends. We both hoped you would come, Miss? It won't be grand or anything.'

'I'm hardly grand myself, Lucy,' Phoebe smiled at the half apology, 'and I would like to come very much.'

'Would you?' Lucy placed the cooled scones on to a prettily flowered plate, embarrassment touching her cheeks with pink. 'I mean, could . . . ?'

'Would I . . . could I what?' Phoebe laughed.

'Well, Miss, me and Mathew thought . . . we hoped you might be my attendant.'

'Bridesmaid!' Phoebe grabbed the young girl, hugging her. 'Lucy, I would be absolutely delighted, and I think I have something upstairs you might be delighted with too.'

Holding on to Lucy's hand, Phoebe raced through the sitting room and up the stairs to a bedroom draped with the dresses Sophie had given her and which as yet she had not taken to pieces to make up into garments for children.

'What about one of these for a wedding dress?' she asked.

Lucy stood quite still, her eyes wide. 'You mean . . . you mean I could have one of these . . . to keep?'

'Of course to keep,' Phoebe laughed. 'Try them, I'm sure they will fit. You and Sophie are much the same size, and if need be we can soon make a few adjustments.'

'Which one?' Lucy stepped forward, touching first one and then another of the dresses. 'Which one can I try?'

'Try them all.' Phoebe snatched up a blue muslin gown trimmed with silk forget-me-nots, pressing it into Lucy's hands. 'And take whichever you wish.'

'Ooh, Miss Phoebe,' Lucy held the gown almost reverently, her eyes playing over the others, 'do you think I should?'

'No, I do not think you should!' Phoebe answered emphatically. 'I *know* you should. Now get out of that skirt and blouse and try every one of those dresses.'

Trying the blue gown, Lucy preened before a long cheval mirror that had come from Kilvert's pawn shop, then discarded it for one of pale creamy yellow, the skirt caught around the hem in half hoops of yellow tea roses.

'That looks lovely, Lucy,' Phoebe said, scooping up the girl's dark hair into a yellow silk ribbon, 'and we could make some silk rose-buds to dress your hair. The whole effect would be marvellous.'

'Oh, I do like it, Miss Phoebe,' Lucy breathed, touching a hand to the high waist, 'it's so pretty.'

'Then it's yours,' Phoebe smiled.

'But what if Miss Sophie should see me?' Lucy turned, her eyes filled with concern. 'Wouldn't 'er get mad seein' as how 'er give you these to make kids' frocks?'

Phoebe knelt, smoothing the creamy folds about Lucy's feet. 'I really don't expect the Dartmouths to turn up at Wednesbury Parish Church to witness the marriage of Mr Mathew Leach to Miss Lucy Baines, even though she'll be the prettiest bride in the country. And even if they should, I'm sure Miss Sophie would be delighted you chose to wear her gift on the most special day of your life.'

'Then if you be sure, Miss, I think I would like it to be this one. Only . . .'

'Only what?' Phoebe stood up.

'Only it do seem a shame not to try them others on, I'll not be gettin' another chance to wear such frocks!' Lucy grinned.

'And I will not be getting another chance to rescue the bread from burning.' Phoebe sniffed then dashed out of the bedroom. 'You carry on,' she called, hurrying downstairs to the kitchen, 'I'll be back in a minute.'

'Am the loaves all right, Miss?' Lucy asked when Phoebe returned a few minutes later.

'They look delicious. You are so good at cooking, Lucy.'

'Like you with sewing, Miss.' Lucy paraded a pale green sprigged dress. 'Those little frocks you've made for the kids look real pretty, I reckon Lady Dartmouth will be right pleased wi' them.'

'I hope I can get them all done in time for Christmas.' Phoebe helped to extricate Lucy from the swathes of pale green. 'There are more than I had expected.'

'Then you mustn't use your time making rose-buds or nothin' for my wedding frock,' Lucy mumbled from beneath layers of muslin.

'I shall make just as many rose-buds as it takes, Lucy Baines.' Phoebe took the dress, draping it across a chair.

'And anything else we think is necessary to make your day perfect.'

'P'raps I can 'elp, on my day off? I ain't much wi' a needle but I'm willing to try.'

'You already help enough, Lucy, I don't know how I would manage without your coming here. Sarah and Miriam tried hard to teach me to cook but I am still not very good, I'm afraid, so your help in that department is invaluable.'

'Mathew says my scones are as good as his mother's.' Lucy beamed.

'And Mathew is right.' Phoebe draped the green dress higher on the chair, leaving its folds free of the floor. 'Their only drawback being you want to go on eating them and that is not so good for a girl's shape.'

'Eeh, Miss, you need 'ave no worries in that direction.' Standing in white frilled bloomers and chemise, Lucy looked at her former employer. 'It might not be my place to say it but I reckon as you could be doin' wi' a bit more meat on your bones. You be gettin' to look right scrawny, beggin' your pardon.'

'Well, all that delicious bread of yours will soon remedy that.' Phoebe picked up the last of the dresses Sophie had given her and one which Lucy had so far refrained from touching. 'Now, Miss Lucy, I think you should try this on.'

Lucy looked at the gown, its folds streaming to the floor like a jade waterfall. 'Ooh, no, I couldn't, not that one . . . it's much too grand.'

'Nonsense.' Phoebe held it out. 'I agree it might not be as suitable to your colouring as the yellow but try it anyway. You will never know unless you try.'

'I . . . I don't think I should . . .' Lucy hesitated, a longing to feel the rich taffeta against her skin pulling her one way; a reluctance to dare try anything so grand and costly pulling her in the opposite direction.

'Oh, come on, Lucy.' Phoebe held out the dress, its fabric gleaming in the wintry sunlight, entering the tiny window sheltered by the eaves. 'Where is your sense of adventure?'

'Well, if you say so.' Lucy held up her arms for Phoebe to slip the gown over her head. 'Though I don't think it's goin' to suit me.'

'We will see.' Phoebe pulled the heavy fabric down over Lucy's shoulders then stopped as the girl cried out.

'It's somethin' in the frock,' she said, pushing the gown right down to the floor and stepping out of it. 'Somethin' cold and . . . and . . .'

'And what?' Phoebe put an arm around the frightened girl, leading her away from the dress folded in upon itself like a green island on the bare wooden floor.

'I don't know,' Lucy answered shakily, 'it . . . it felt cold and . . . and hard . . . across my chest.'

Phoebe stared at the mound of taffeta. She couldn't just leave it, she had to find out what it was lying coiled inside that dress.

'Stay here.' She pushed Lucy into the open doorway of the bedroom then, her own heart thumping, walked back to where the gown lay heaped.

'Eeh, don't touch it, Miss,' Lucy said, fear making her voice sound hollow, 'don't touch it!'

'Don't be silly, Lucy, it's probably nothing more than a dressmaker's pin that has been overlooked.' Sounding far more confident than she felt, Phoebe reached for the gown. Teeth gripped together she shook the material, then as nothing happened, lifted the dress, holding it at arm's length.

'Eeh, I could 'ave sworn there was somethin' in that frock,' Lucy said, courage returning sufficiently for her to step back inside the bedroom. 'I could swear I felt somethin'.'

'Well, let us look.' Phoebe laid the taffeta gown atop the pale green muslin draped over the room's one chair.

'I'll look.' Lucy came to stand beside her. 'I know whereabouts it was.'

Opening the bodice wide, she examined the inside of it. 'Oh my Good God!' she exclaimed, drawing back as though from the hand of death. 'Oh my Good God, will you look at that!'

'I want you to tell me exactly what happened.' The Governess of Handsworth Prison for Women looked at the thin figure of the girl standing in front of her desk. 'You were in the corridor at the time Liza Spittle was injured, were you not?'

'Yes, Ma'am,' Phoebe answered, her voice little more than a whisper.

'What were you doing there?'

Phoebe looked across the desk at the woman she knew held Tilly's life in her hands. 'I was returning a lunch tray to the kitchen, Liza blocked my way, she would not move when I asked her to let me pass . . . then . . . then she tried to force herself upon me.'

'She tried to do what?' The Governess's face blanched, her mouth pinched with disgust. 'Are you telling me Liza Spittle tried to behave like . . . like a man?'

'Yes, Ma'am,' Phoebe whispered, looking down at her feet. 'It happened once before and Tilly Wood helped me then.'

'As she did yesterday?' The Governess spoke as though she held a bad taste in her mouth. 'Tell me, Pardoe, where were the wardresses whilst all of this was going on?'

'Mrs Marsh accompanied me almost to the kitchens,' Phoebe lied, aware of Agnes Marsh standing just behind her, aware also that the woman had been asleep in her room instead of being on duty and knowing that to say so would bring vengeance not only upon herself but also on Tilly and the others. 'Then we heard the noise of a bucket being dropped on the stairs and she went to see what had happened.'

The Governess raised an enquiring glance to the wardress.

'It was one of the new intake, Ma'am,' Agnes Marsh took up the lie. 'She was scrubbing the top landing and knocked over the bucket, sending it down the stairs. I stayed to see to her mopping up before anybody could slip on the wet stairs, then I saw to her getting fresh water and soda to start again, and when I got to go to the kitchen Liza Spittle was lying unconscious in the corridor.'

'I see.' The Governess returned to Phoebe. 'You say Tilly Wood helped you? How come she was in that part of the building and not in the laundry?'

'I checked on that, Ma'am,' Agnes Marsh put in swiftly. 'She'd been sent to fetch the cooking cloths and towels from the kitchens ready for the afternoon wash.'

'Allow Pardoe to answer my next question,' Hannah Price answered coldly. 'Tell me, what assistance did Wood give?'

Phoebe swallowed hard, her eyes still on her shoes. Please God, help me to answer without making things worse for Tilly, she thought. Don't let me put her in greater danger than she is in now.

'She pulled Liza away, then when Liza tried to attack her, stepped aside. Liza crashed her head into the wall. It all happened so quickly, Ma'am, then Mrs Marsh came and had Liza taken to the infirmary and Tilly was locked away. That is all I know.'

Hannah Price glanced at the blank sheet of paper lying on her desk. Was that all the girl knew, or was it all she was prepared to say she knew?

'Have you seen Spittle this morning, Mrs Marsh?' she asked without looking up.

'Yes, Ma'am,' Agnes answered. 'There is no change from last night. She is still unconscious.'

'In that case there is no sense in sending for the doctor.' The Governess picked up a pen, dipping the nib into a glass ink-well and beginning to write on the paper before her. 'I will send an interim report informing the Prison Board that one of the inmates is unwell, and this evening I will ask the doctor to call. Spittle should have recovered sufficiently well by that time to relate to him what occurred.'

Spittle should have recovered by that time, Agnes Marsh thought, beginning to usher Phoebe from the Governess's office, or was Hannah Price giving the doctor time to drink away his senses? Either way it suited them both. The last thing the Governess or Agnes Marsh wanted was a murder inside the prison, and if Liza didn't make it then that would be another bonus.

'Excuse me, Ma'am.' Phoebe ignored Agnes Marsh pushing her towards the door. 'May I please ask a question?'

Hannah Price paused in the writing of her report and looked up at the young girl whose eyes no longer studied her own shoes but were on her, steady and unblinking. Was she truly a thief? Had she really robbed the home of Sir William Dartmouth? In all honesty Hannah could not bring herself to believe so; this girl was very different from all the other prisoners in Handsworth, so well mannered and polite, so obviously well bred it would be hard for anyone to believe her a criminal, but the law had pronounced her such and the law must always be upheld.

'Yes, Pardoe, what is it?' She signed to the wardress to wait.

'It is Tilly Wood, Ma'am,' Phoebe said, showing no trace of her true feelings. 'What is to happen to her?'

The Governess balanced the pen back and forth between thumb and forefinger as though testing its weight, her lips pursed tightly together. Phoebe waited, each tick of the tiny carriage clock sounding like the boom of a cannon in the still room.

'Ah, yes, Wood.' The balancing of the pen stopped as if some decision had finally been reached. 'I do not think it necessary to mention the involvement of any other prisoner at this stage, so for the time being Prisoner Wood will return to the laundry.'

'Thank you, Ma'am.'

Hannah Price looked up at the quiet answer and knew it was more than a simple thank you. Much, much more.

Chapter Six

Phoebe pushed the needle tiredly into the cloth, her eyes aching from a sleepless night, a night that had followed the pattern of so many since her confinement to Handsworth Prison, for though her body rested her brain refused to sleep. But last night it had not been for herself she had worried but for Tilly: locked up in solitary isolation, a place Phoebe herself had only heard of, a place the mention of which reduced the rest of the women to hushed tones.

But Tilly was free of that for the moment at least. Phoebe pulled the gold wire thread through the cloth, seating it with the tip of a finger. And what of Liza . . . would the Governess send for the doctor this evening, and if so . . . ?

'May I see?'

Phoebe looked up as a voice broke into her thoughts. She placed her needlework in the prison Governess's outstretched hand.

'This is very fine.' Hannah Price examined the Psalter cover. 'You sew very well, and such an elegant choice of colour, I know Phi— Father Heywood will be pleased when he receives them. You should be able to place yourself in some dressmaking or millinery establishment upon your release.'

Phoebe took the piece back as the Governess moved on along the line of sewing women. She should be able to secure a position. It was so easily said but who would employ a convicted thief?

'I find you guilty of wilful theft . . . you will serve a term of fifteen years . . .'

She pushed the needle through the cloth. Fifteen years for a crime of which she was innocent.

'Oh my Good God, will you look at that!' Lucy's shocked words rose to the surface of her mind and Phoebe saw again the bodice of the jade taffeta gown spread wide, revealing the necklace caught up inside it.

''Ow do you reckon that got there?'

Lucy's words replaced the quiet hum of the sewing women's conversations.

'I don't know,' Phoebe had replied, 'but we must return it to the Priory.'

'How come it hasn't been missed?' Lucy looked up from the floor of the bedroom. 'And it can't 'ave been or I would 'ave heard about it. Word gets round fast in that house.'

'It must have become caught when Sophie removed the dress,' Phoebe said, seeing how the mounting had become hooked into the dress lining. 'She probably wouldn't feel it through her petticoats, but surely when her maid came to put the gown away she would inspect it first for any mark or stain?'

'Not that one, Miss.' Lucy watched her free the necklace. 'I know 'er and lazy isn't the word I'd be using to describe 'er. She would 'ave had 'er marching orders long since but Miss Sophie is too soft. Everybody downstairs says they don't know how 'er gets away with half of the things she gets up to, but get away with it she does.'

'Maybe, Lucy, but to overlook something as valuable as this must be more than careless.'

Lucy looked at the necklace, emeralds dripping like huge green tears through Phoebe's fingers.

'Aye, Miss,' she said thoughtfully. 'Like you says, more than careless.'

They had taken the necklace to the kitchen where they both sat looking at it spread on the table, its stones gleaming in the pale sunlight, the gold of its setting turned red by the glow of the fire.

'Eeh, it's so beautiful,' Lucy sighed. 'A girl would feel like a queen with that round 'er neck.'

Phoebe glanced up, her mouth curved in a smile. 'Much as I want you to look and feel like a queen on your wedding day, Lucy, I couldn't offer to let you wear this.'

'Would make no difference if you could,' Lucy drew back as if the necklace were a living thing, 'I wouldn't dare to. Why, I'd be scared to death!'

'And rob Mathew of his pretty bride? Then it is as well this does not belong to me.'

'What *will* you do with it, Miss Phoebe?'

'Return it to Sophie as I said.'

'I 'ave to return to the Priory, do you want me to take it for you?'

'No, Lucy,' Phoebe answered as the girl reached for the cloak she had hung on a nail set into the kitchen door, 'I would not want to put such a responsibility upon you. The dresses were given to me and I must be the one to return the necklace. Not to do so personally would be most impolite.'

'If you say so, Miss Phoebe.' Lucy tied the ribbon of her bonnet beneath her chin. 'But you be careful you say nothin' to anybody as to why you be visiting the Priory. There's folk about these parts as can't be trusted.'

Lucy had left Wiggins Mill then, and for the first time since making it her home Phoebe had felt truly afraid of being alone. The next day she had wrapped the necklace in a piece of white linen, pushing it deep into the pocket of her skirt, then wrapping her cloak tight about her had set off across the heath toward the Sandwell Valley.

She had reached the rise above the Lyng Fields, so called for their covering of tiny purple wild flowers, when Edward had caught up with her.

'Couldn't you have sent someone with word?' he said, dismounting from the huge bay horse and listening to her reason for visiting the Priory. 'I would have sent the carriage for you.'

'I have no one to send.' For some reason Phoebe did not mention Lucy and her connection with his home. 'Besides I have no wish to impose, your family has already been very kind to me.'

'Yes, but out here all alone,' Edward took her hand, concern loud in his voice, 'there's nothing out here for miles around . . . anything might happen.'

'And nothing.' Phoebe smiled. 'Really, I am quite safe.'

'I suppose I know that,' he touched her hand to his lips, 'but I would prefer you didn't walk the heath alone, Phoebe. I only wish I could accompany you but I have an appointment with my father at two and it is almost that now.'

'I would not want to be the reason for your being late for Sir William.' Phoebe withdrew her hand. 'Please go, I will be all right.'

'Well, at least let me take the blamed trinket for you. It's near enough an hour's walk from here to the Priory and I can send a carriage to take you home.'

'No, Edward,' Phoebe returned firmly. 'No carriage. I want to walk back to Wiggins Mill. The fresh air will do me good.'

'If it doesn't kill you from cold first, and it will be dark before you get there.' He glanced at the grey snow clouds gathering over the valley.

'Then hadn't you better take this so I can be on my way home?' Phoebe drew the linen bundle from her pocket, unwrapping the necklace and handing it to Edward. 'Please would you give my apology to your sister and explain I did not know this was caught inside one of the gowns she gave me until yesterday evening?'

'My sister would lose her head were someone not there to fasten it to her neck.'

Edward tossed the necklace up into the air and Phoebe watched the tiny flashes of green flame dance circles in the light as it descended into his palm.

'I still wish you would let me send a carriage out to you.'

He dropped the necklace into his pocket before swinging easily into the saddle.

'I shall be perfectly safe, Edward.' Phoebe stepped back from the horse, a sudden breeze catching the animal's nostrils and causing it to prance restlessly.

Edward reined the bay, speaking softly and touching the animal's neck. 'Sophie will certainly wish to thank you herself.' He looked down at Phoebe, the breeze fanning her sherry-gold hair about her cheeks. 'May I bring her to Wiggins Mill tomorrow?'

The horse neighed loudly, its hooves stamping restlessly at being held in check, and Phoebe raised a hand to wave, relieved at not having to answer.

One week later she had been arrested.

'Governess wants to see Phoebe.'

Mary Pegleg limped into the sewing room, delivering her message to Agnes Marsh.

'What for?' The wardress's voice was sharper than usual and as she looked at Phoebe her eyes held a touch of concern and a heavier touch of warning. Whatever the Governess wanted, Agnes Marsh had better come out of it white as snow if she were to keep the promotion of Superintendent to the sewing room and not be sent back to that hell hole of a laundry.

''Er didn't say.' Mary Pegleg leaned against the door jamb easing her weight from the wooden stump attached to her left knee. ''Er just said to tell you 'er wanted to see Phoebe right away.'

'You better get yerself to the office then, Pardoe.' Phoebe put her sewing on the end of the long trestle table, feeling the eyes of the other prisoners on her as she went towards the door.

'Pardoe!' Agnes Marsh came close, her mouth merely a slit as she breathed, 'Mind what you tell 'er. Things could be made pretty bad for you . . . there are worse places inside this prison than the laundry.'

Mary Pegleg limping alongside her and Agnes Marsh marching behind, Phoebe walked along the gloomy corridors that led to the Governess's office. How many more years would she spend locked away? Her fingers curled tightly as the memory of flashes of green fire darted across her brain. She had not stolen Sophie's necklace, they had found it caught up inside a dress, she and Lucy, but neither she nor the maid had been believed.

Edward and his sister had not called the next day or any day. She had seen no one until the day the constable arrived. She had to go with him to the Magistrates' Court, he said, and no, he could not tell her why, the Magistrate would tell her that.

They had walked the several miles to Wednesbury where she had been taken to the Green Dragon Inn at the entrance to the Shambles. It was in an upstairs room there that the Magistrate had heard evidence against her.

It was alleged that she had visited Sandwell Priory and taken away several dresses, the gift of Miss Sophie Dartmouth; in the process she had stolen an emerald necklace, the property of the said Miss Sophie.

That had been the point at which John Kilvert had been asked if she was the woman who had pawned several pieces of jewellery at his shop.

'She is, Your Honour.' The pawnbroker's shifty eyes had fastened on her and his high-pitched reedy voice carried around the room. 'Some very valible jewellery, and where could the likes of 'er get such from lessen 'er stole it?'

'We will decide that, Kilvert.'

But the Magistrate's voice had held no rebuke and the pawnbroker had smirked at Phoebe as she stood up from her seat.

'Are you now prepared to tell us what you have done with the necklace?'

She had not been asked if she had taken Sophie's necklace, she had been told she had, told she had stolen from a girl who had helped her.

'The necklace you speak of,' Phoebe tried to stay calm, to keep the mounting fear out of her voice, 'I . . . we found it hooked inside a gown given to me by Miss Sophie.'

'We?' The Magistrate had looked at her over heavy spectacles. 'Do I take it someone else was with you?'

'Yes,' Phoebe answered, the trembling in her stomach increasing as she realised Lucy was not present and neither was Edward. Did he know she was being accused of stealing the necklace she had given to him? Of course he must know, the complaint must have come from the Priory, so where was he? Why wasn't he here to tell them it was a mistake . . . to tell them she had been returning Sophie's property when he had overtaken her, that he himself took the necklace from her?

'Well, was someone else involved in this theft?' The Magistrate leaned across the table that served as a desk.

'There was no theft.' Phoebe stared at the other three people in the room: the constable sent to bring her here, John Kilvert her accuser, and a woman dressed in black, her face hidden behind a heavy veil. 'Please, you must believe me, I am telling the truth. We found the necklace caught up in the bodice of the gown and . . .'

'*We* found?' The Magistrate leaned back in his high wing chair. 'You had better say who it is besides yourself makes up this we.'

'It was Lucy, my mai— my friend. She was visiting me and we decided to try on the dresses before taking them apart. We found the necklace inside a green gown. We guessed it belonged to Miss Sophie, seeing she had given me the gowns, and Lucy asked if she could return it that day when she went back to the Priory.'

'And did she?'

'No, Sir.' Phoebe swallowed hard, seeing the look of satisfaction cross the hard features of the man facing her. 'I thought that as the gowns had been given to me, mine was the responsibility of returning the necklace.'

'Which you obviously did not or we would not be here today.'

'I did not return it to the Priory.' Phoebe felt a cold desperation take hold of her: they did not want to believe her, this man had already decided she was guilty. 'The . . . the day after finding the necklace, I went to return it. I had crossed the Lyng Fields and was about to go on when Edward Dartmouth overtook me. I told him the reason for my journey and he offered to take the necklace for me as the weather was worsening and it would take me several hours to get home.'

For several minutes the room remained silent except for the anxious fidgeting of the pawnbroker. Across the table the Magistrate fingered long white whiskers then, leaning forward, he glared at Phoebe.

'You are saying that you returned a valuable emerald necklace to Edward Dartmouth, that he did not return it to his sister, and that therefore he is in fact the thief?'

'No! No, I . . . I'm not . . . Edward wouldn't . . .'

'No more.' The Magistrate's palm came down hard on the table. 'I have heard enough. You stole a necklace and now try to place the blame upon the son of a respected family, a family who have held their seat in West Bromwich for hundreds of years. You accuse a man who is not present to answer for himself against your lies. Well, I will answer for him. Edward Dartmouth would never commit such treachery against his own. You are a liar and a thief, and it is only out of regard for the young man's father, Sir William Dartmouth, that I will exercise leniency and not inform him of what you have said here, for to do so would result in your incurring a far heavier penalty than the one I am about to pass.'

He then reached out a hand to the wooden gavel lying in front of him.

'Phoebe Pardoe, I find you guilty of wilful theft. I order you be taken to a place of imprisonment . . .'

A rustle of black skirts told of the woman's leaving the

room as the gavel struck hard against the table. Behind her black veil Annie Pardoe almost smiled. Her meeting with Sophie Dartmouth's personal maid had paid off. That girl's attempt to extract money in return for her silence regarding a missing emerald necklace had failed, but the charge of theft Annie had forced her to lay against Phoebe had not. The Magistrate's final words followed her through the door.

'. . . you will serve a term of fifteen years' hard labour.'

'Wait there, Pardoe.'

Agnes Marsh held out a hand as they reached the Governess's office. Mary Pegleg limped to the stool set against one wall where she was allowed to sit between running messages.

'Why has she asked to see me, Mary, do you know?'

'No idea.' Mary Pegleg answered the question in a whisper. 'I ain't bin 'ere the whole time though I knows there be someone in there with 'er 'cos I 'eard 'em talkin' when I come up from the kitchen. Sounded deep, the other voice, like a man's.'

'Is it the doctor?' Phoebe asked worriedly. 'Has the Governess sent for the doctor, is Liza worse?'

'I don't know,' Mary hissed. 'Was some shemozzle goin' on downstairs, summat about a visitor, but I didn't 'ave chance to find out who it was. Though like I said, it sounded like a man an' 'er in there seemed in a right tizzy, 'er voice all excited, what I could hear.'

'Maybe it is Father Heywood.' Phoebe's reply was almost a prayer. 'Perhaps he has called regarding the covers for the Psalters.'

'Let's 'ope it is.' Mary Pegleg shifted position on the stool, one hand rubbing her amputated leg where it sat in the cup of the wooden stump. 'At least let's pray to God it ain't the doctor. We don't want to see 'im 'ere while 'is brains is still in 'is skull.'

The door to the Governess's room opened and Agnes Marsh stepped out, her mouth tight with resentment.

'You're wanted inside, Pardoe,' she said, barely allowing her lips to free the words. 'And you, Pegleg, get your arse off that stool and get down to the kitchen. Tell them Her Highness is wanting a tray of tea sent up to her office – *now*.'

Waiting for an answer to her tap on the Governess's door, Phoebe remembered the Magistrate's words: 'Out of regard for the young man's father I will exercise leniency and not inform him of what you have said here, for to do so would result in your incurring a far heavier penalty.'

Chapter Seven

Inside the Governess's office, its desk lit by a larger window than elsewhere in the prison and set about with comfortable leather high wing armchairs, Phoebe bobbed a curtsy to the woman standing behind the desk.

'Pardoe, this is Sir William Dartmouth.'

'A far heavier penalty'. The words screamed in Phoebe's brain, the room whirling around her in a mad dance of chairs, desk and people. *'A far heavier penalty . . .'*

'Are you all right, Miss Pardoe?'

Phoebe felt hands to either side of her as her legs began to crumple.

'Sit here,' the distant voice commanded. Then, 'Have you sal volatile, Mrs Price?'

'Smelling salts, Sir William.' Somewhere above the void that threatened to swallow her, Phoebe heard the Governess answer, 'I have smelling salts,' then coughed as a small bottle was held beneath her nostrils.

'No, do not get up!' Sir William Dartmouth touched a hand to her shoulder then walked to the fireplace that held a fire both winter and summer. 'I have something I wish to say to you.'

He hesitated, waiting for Hannah Price to acknowledge the tap on the door. A woman in the drab grey dress that marked her as an inmate entered carrying a tray, depositing it on a small oval table set against one of the wing back chairs. She glanced at Phoebe before leaving.

He had been told. Phoebe's fingers curled, pressing her

nails hard into her palms. He had been told she had accused Edward of not returning the necklace to his sister. But she had made no such accusation. Why hadn't Edward told them he had the necklace, and why after so many months had his father decided to seek his own revenge?

'You will take some tea, Miss Pardoe?' he said as Hannah Price poured the steaming liquid into a china cup. 'My presence here has seemingly upset you.'

A china cup! She had not drunk from a china cup in over twelve months. Phoebe made no move to accept the tea the Governess held out to her. A tin mug was all she had to drink from now and would be all she would have for fifteen years – and how many more? How many more years had this man demanded be added to her sentence?

'You were accused of stealing a necklace from my daughter . . .'

Phoebe raised her gaze, her soul in her eyes. 'I did not steal it,' she said softly, 'I was returning it to the Priory.'

'So I understand.'

Hannah Price returned the cup to the tray, leaving her own untouched as she studied the girl who had already served a year in Handsworth gaol.

'I gave it to Ed— to your son. He said he would give it to Miss Sophie together with my apology. They were both to call at Wiggins Mill the next day, but they never came.'

'Miss Pardoe . . .' Sir William hesitated, looking into the fire for several moments then faced her again, squaring his shoulders as if preparing for an unpleasant task he would have preferred to leave to someone else.

Frightened of what she knew was about to come Phoebe stared at Edward's father, standing tall against the fireplace, tan knee-length coat accentuating his powerful physique, hair that had once been black crested with a dusting of grey above the temples, and eyes that in the dim light of the room might have been grey or even black.

'Miss Pardoe,' he said again, as if searching for words, 'I

was told of what passed between yourself and the Magistrate the day after you were sentenced, but yesterday I was told more . . .'

Phoebe's throat closed and her head began to pound. Yesterday he had been told more and today he would have retribution.

'Yesterday,' he went on, 'I spoke to Lucy Baines, or I should say I spoke to Mrs Mathew Leach. She told me you would not allow her to return my daughter's necklace but said that you yourself would do so.' Breaking off, he turned towards the Governess. 'We will not go on with this any longer. Mrs Price, you have the Magistrate's signed document?'

'Yes, Sir William.' She touched the folded sheet of white paper lying on her desk as he moved to take up his hat and gloves lying on a small table just inside the door of the room.

'Then I will say good day.' He inclined his head the merest fraction as Hannah Price dropped a curtsy. 'Miss Pardoe.' The same slight movement of the head and he was gone.

He had spoken to Lucy. The pounding of her head mounting to a sickening crescendo, Phoebe gripped the arms of the chair. Why had he not mentioned Edward? Why had he not spoken to his son?

'Sir William took the trouble to bring this himself.' Hannah Price picked up the sheet of paper, holding it unopened in her hand.

Phoebe stared at it, the world slowly dropping away from her. He had taken the trouble to bring it himself, to see the girl who had attempted to accuse his son of theft, attempted to blacken the character of his family, to see the girl whose life he was taking away. How many more years were written on that paper? How many more years to serve in hell?

'It seems a mistake has been made . . .'

Hannah Price's face swam before Phoebe's eyes.

'. . . the necklace you were accused of stealing has been

found. This,' she tapped the paper against her fingers, 'is an authorisation from the Magistrate. You are free to go.'

'Sir William Dartmouth himself?' Sarah Leach looked in disbelief at her son and his wife seated in her tiny living room. 'Billy-me-Lord in your 'ouse? Eeh, it's not to be believed.'

'What did 'e say?' Joseph tapped his pipe against the bars of the fire.

''E said as how his family had returned from Europe the day before and 'e had asked his son if he knew anything of Sophie's missing emerald necklace,' Lucy answered. 'It seemed at first as though he knew nothing of it then he remembered taking it from Phoebe and dropping it in the pocket of his riding habit.'

'So?' Sarah urged as her daughter-in-law paused for breath.

'So 'e says 'e sent a footman or some such to search the coat an' 'e comes back wi' the necklace in 'is hands,' Mathew took up the story.

'Oh, thank God . . . thank God!' Sarah wiped her eyes on her apron. 'Now she'll be free – Abel's daughter will be free to come 'ome.'

'Oh, aye, I reckon as Phoebe will be free to come 'ome,' Mathew went on, 'but what sort of freedom will it be? Nobody will want to know a gaolbird, innocent or not. I reckon as Phoebe Pardoe ain't gonna be a whole lot better off outside o' that prison than she were inside of it, 'specially if that aunt of 'ers can do anythin' about it.'

'What does that mean?' Joseph scraped the bowl of his clay pipe with a slender bladed knife then blew down the stem.

Mathew looked over to where his father sat beside the shiny blackleaded grate. 'I mean that in my opinion Annie Pardoe is somewheres to be found in this business. She 'olds something against Phoebe, the facts tell that themselves – turnin' her out of her father's house, tekin everythin' that was hers 'cept what Lucy saved for her – an' it's my guess it was her in that Magistrates' Court in the Green Dragon.'

"Ow can you tell that?'

'I can't really, Mother.' Mathew turned his glance to Sarah, scalding tea in a large brown earthenware teapot. 'But I got talkin' to the bobby as fetched Phoebe to the Magistrate . . . 'e gets into the Gladstone most evenings when 'e ain't on duty . . . an' 'e said the woman come in a carriage – a carriage wi' A.P. on the door.'

'A.P.' Sarah held up the teapot, the first cup half filled. 'Abel Pardoe.'

'Yes, Abel Pardoe,' Mathew said. 'The carriage was Abel Pardoe's an' the woman as rode in it were Annie Pardoe. An' 'er went to the Green Dragon to hear 'er own niece sentenced to fifteen years an' never lifted a finger to stop it!'

'God 'elp us,' Sarah murmured.

'Ar, an' 'e will 'ave to an' all if anybody 'ears you goin' on like that.' Joseph glared at his son. 'Keep yer opinions to yerself, my lad. Annie Pardoe 'as done thee badly as it is but 'er's capable of doin' a damn' sight more so be ruled by one older and wiser an' keep yer tongue between yer teeth.'

'Did 'Is Lordship say what was to be done about Phoebe?' Sarah resumed filling the cups, handing a larger mug to Joseph.

'He said he would see to everything himself,' Lucy accepted the cup from her, 'but he didn't say what it would be.'

'Billy-me-Lord be a fair man,' Joseph said, using the name by which the locals addressed Sir William. 'If 'e 'as said 'e will see to things then see to 'em 'e will. Reckon we will just 'ave to bide our time til' Abel's daughter be 'ome.'

'There's no telling when that will be,' Lucy said, swallowing her tea, 'but when she does come I want to have a fire going and something hot ready for the table. So drink up your tea, Mathew Leach, it's a long walk to Wiggins Mill.'

'Aye, the wench will be wantin' a bit o' comfort,' Joseph nodded as Lucy dropped a kiss on his head. 'If you can let we know when 'er is back, Mother an' me will walk over to the mill.'

'I'll do that, Father.' Mathew grabbed his cap from one of the several nails hammered into the door that opened on to the street, respectfully holding it until he was out of the house. 'Bye, Mother.' He folded Sarah in his arms, feeling the thinness that had come in the last few months, and in his soul cursed Annie Pardoe afresh. Her money grubbing was robbing his mother of her life as surely as Phoebe had been robbed of hers. 'We will be back to see you on Sunday.'

Reaching the corner where the road curved away out of sight of the house, he turned to wave to his mother and in his heart he made a wish: May Annie Pardoe not live to see Sunday!

The heavy door banged behind Phoebe. She was free! There would be no more days locked inside Handsworth Prison for Women, no more backbreaking hours in that laundry or sewing until she could barely see the needle, no more wardresses barking orders at her. Closing her eyes she breathed deeply, feeling the fresh air bite at her throat. She was free, free to go home, but Tilly Wood would never go home.

Phoebe had not been allowed to say goodbye to any of the women who had shared her existence for more than a year; even Mary Pegleg had not been sitting on her stool outside the Governess's office when she had come out. Given the clothes she had arrived at the prison in, she had changed, Agnes Marsh in attendance, then had been taken to the door of the prison, passing no other prisoner on the way.

'Excuse me, Miss . . .'

Phoebe opened her eyes to see the man who had come to stand at her side, wearing a high black hat and knee-length boots teamed with deep blue coat.

'Sir William asks if you would be good enough to ride home in the carriage?'

'*Sir William took the trouble to bring this himself.*' The

words echoed in her mind. But he had not come to lengthen her eternity, he had come to bring her freedom.

'Miss!'

'What . . . what did you say?'

The coachman looked at the girl in the shabby brown dress and cloak, her bonnet tied over lifeless hair snatched back from a drawn pallid face. This was not the usual kind to ride in the Dartmouth coach, but then again it was certain sure she wouldn't get far on foot. 'Sir William, Miss,' he said again, 'asks if you would kindly take the carriage home?'

Phoebe glanced about her, seeing for the first time the outside of the high prison building. She had not seen where they had brought her in that black-painted cart with its iron-grilled window, nor even known apart from hearing 'the women's gaol in Birmingham'. Now she saw a bare stretch of heath broken only by a group of scraggy trees some distance to the left and a path leading to the right, and realised she had no idea in which direction home lay.

'Yes . . . yes, thank you.'

Holding both hands to her skirt, feeling every sharp stone through the worn soles of her boots, she half stumbled to where the carriage stood waiting. Then the door closed and she was on her way home. Home! Leaning her head against the cushioned upholstery, she allowed the pent up tears of months to flood her cheeks.

'Allow me!'

Phoebe felt the soft cloth pressed into her ungloved hands and opened her eyes to see Sir William Dartmouth.

Across the narrow space that separated them he saw the sudden fear return to her eyes and felt disgusted at a system that treated a young girl in such a way as almost to destroy her; but it was a system he himself had long upheld.

'Forgive me for not giving you an explanation,' he said quietly, 'but I felt the sooner you were out of that place, the better.' He glanced at her hands, nervously twisting the white lawn handkerchief, then went on, 'I was informed of the outcome of your appearance before Gideon Speke, and of the term of imprisonment to which he had sentenced you, and I felt no regret. My family's friendship seemed to have been abused and my daughter's property stolen. But yesterday I found that nothing had been stolen and that I had been wrong. Because of my action you have been made to suffer great hardship. I can only offer my most sincere apology. I will, of course, make reparation in any way you wish.'

Reparation! Phoebe stared out of the window but the passing streets and imposing buildings of Birmingham went unseen. How could any reparation make up for what she had been through . . . for what she knew was yet to come?

'Your home is at Wednesbury, I believe,' he resumed, covering her silence. 'If you will tell me where I will have Aston take us there.'

'Brunswick House,' she answered, only half registering what he had said.

'Brunswick House!' He leaned forward slightly, a small frown creasing his brow. 'You live at Brunswick House?'

'No . . . I . . . I'm sorry.' Phoebe forced her mind to attend her words. 'I do not live at Brunswick House. My home is Wiggins Mill on the outskirts of the town.'

'Then why say Brunswick House?'

For a moment Phoebe thought she heard the note of accusation so many voices had held over the past months and her head rose defensively. 'Possibly, Sir William,' she said clearly, 'because I once did live there.'

'Brunswick House?' The frown deepened, his eyes narrowing in concentration. 'That was Abel Pardoe's house . . . his sister got it if I remember rightly. And you . . . your name is Pardoe . . .'

'Yes, Sir William.' Phoebe looked straight into his dark eyes. 'Phoebe Pardoe. I am Abel's daughter.'

'So she is to be set free?' Annie Pardoe looked at the man

seated·in her drawing room, one hand tugging nervously at long white side whiskers.

'There was nothing I could do,' he answered. 'Sir William Dartmouth himself came to withdraw the charge, said the necklace had been found and demanded the girl be set free at once.'

'And you signed the document of release?'

'I had to, Annie.' Gideon Speke had been unnerved at Sir William's appearance in his office; he was a powerful man and not only in West Bromwich, there was no telling what he would do if he found out.

'Yes, I suppose you did.' Annie stood up, black skirts rustling. 'But hear me, Gideon Speke. You took my hundred pounds to put her away and if anything comes of her being found innocent 'tis you will bear the brunt. I will swear before God I paid you one hundred pounds to try buying her freedom, and that you pocketed that money while hearing no evidence in her defence. One word, Gideon . . . just one word and you will never sit on the Magistrates' bench again!'

So Abel's girl was free! Annie Pardoe closed the door on the departing Magistrate. She had been denied little more than one year of her life while she, Annie, had had no life at all. Slowly she walked through the house and out into the garden. She would not let it rest here. She had taken her niece's home and all she possessed save the paltry sum her maternal grandmother had left her, but all that would not pay for what her own brother had taken from her. Revenge tasted sweet and Annie craved its sweetness. There was more yet to be had and she would drink it to the very last drop.

Turning, she walked back into the house and up the stairs to her room. Putting on her cloak and settling a black bonnet on her head, she went to the room Samuel used as a studio.

'I have to go out for a while,' she signed on her fingers. 'I do not expect to be very long. Is there anything I can get for you while I am in the town?'

Samuel shook his head, his mouth unsmiling as he regarded his sister. Annie had always worn a look of bitterness but of late that look had changed; to what he could not rightly say but it was a look he liked even less.

'Has Tranter brought your hot drink?'

Samuel rested his brush on the palette. 'No,' he signed back, his fingers moving rapidly, 'I told her not to.'

Annie did not question his answer, knowing that in the years Maudie Tranter had spent with them she too had learned the sign language that enabled Samuel to speak.

'Then we will have one together when I return.' Annie Pardoe looked at the brother she had cared for for so many years. His features were thinned and gaunt compared to a year ago but they were still a carbon copy of the man who had been a brother to them both, still with the same keen eyes, 'Take care not to get cold, dear.' Her gloved fingers fluttered like the black wings of a crow. 'You know how unwell you have been of late.'

Samuel picked up his brush, watching his sister leave the room. The house always felt easier when she was not in it.

Annie drove the small trap, guiding the mare along the Holyhead Road that linked Wednesbury to its neighbouring towns. Passing the Monway Steel Mill of which Samuel, thanks to their brother, was part-owner, she turned off across the heath towards Hobs Hill mine, stopping at the huddle of small houses some half-mile away.

'I will say what I came to say.' She had marched straight into Joseph Leach's cottage, ownership relieving her of the necessity of waiting to be asked. 'My niece has besmirched her father's name, she has been imprisoned for theft, therefore she will be unwelcome in any house of standing.'

'But my Mathew's wife says Miss Phoebe is to be set free.' Sarah Leach stared at the woman who seemed to fill her small room with darkness. ''Er says as 'ow they 'ave found out Miss Phoebe never done it, 'er never stole no necklace.'

'Nevertheless,' Annie drew in a long breath, the effort flaring her nostrils, 'the slur remains, my brother's good name has been stained, and I will not have it perpetuated by accepting the girl's presence in any property I and my brother Samuel own. And this house forms part of that property. I tell you, Sarah Leach, you have Phoebe inside this house for one minute and you are out, bag and baggage. What's more, I will see to it that the cripple you call a husband will get no job in Wednesbury.'

'There be only one thief in Abel's family,' Sarah muttered, watching the trap pull away, 'an' that be you, Annie Pardoe. You 'ave teken everythin' that should 'ave bin his daughter's an' may the Good Lord pay you for it!'

Chapter Eight

Sir William Dartmouth watched the face of the girl he had just seen released from prison. Its pallor and thinness did not completely hide its fine-boned quality, or the unhappiness shading her green eyes detract from their lovely almond shape. He had known Abel Pardoe for many years, they had done business together on a regular basis, he buying much of the coal Abel's mines produced together with steel from his Monway works, but they had not mixed socially. Now he was looking at the daughter he had not realised the other man had, a daughter whom he guessed bore a quiet beauty beneath the mark of Handsworth Prison.

She had not spoken since telling him she had once lived at Brunswick House and though she had stared out of the window for the rest of their journey he guessed it was not the passing scenery that held her attention.

'Is this Wiggins Mill?' he asked as the carriage rumbled over a stony path worn by the carter's wagon. 'Miss Pardoe?' He leaned across, touching a hand to hers, still twisting the handkerchief, then withdrew as Phoebe jerked backward, the shadow in her eyes deepening. 'I asked, is this your home?'

'Yes.' Phoebe looked across to where the old house began to rise out of the hollow that sheltered it, the stilled windmill standing sentinel on the adjoining high ground. 'Yes, this is Wiggins Mill.'

The coach drew to a halt and almost immediately the coachman was opening the door.

'Miss Pardoe,' Sir William waited until she stepped down, 'you are no doubt in need of rest but perhaps you will do me the courtesy of calling at the Priory as soon as you feel able? There is a lot I still have not said and we must discuss how you may be compensated.'

Phoebe looked at her home. She was free, she did not have to bite back her words any longer and never again would man or woman order her life.

'Sir William,' she turned back to him, a cool gleam of assurance clearing the shadows from her eyes, 'I will call at the Priory but only to return your handkerchief. As for compensation, there is no need of any. A mistake has been made and a mistake has been rectified, we need say no more on the subject. Will the day after tomorrow be convenient for me to return your handkerchief?'

'I will send the carriage for you at eleven.' Then, as Phoebe made to reject the offer, he smiled. 'And *you* need say no more on *that* subject.'

'Miss Phoebe . . . oh, Miss Phoebe, you're home!' Lucy raced around the corner of the house as the carriage drove away. 'Oh, it's so good to see you.'

'And you, Lucy,' she breathed as her friend's hug threatened to stifle her.

'Welcome home, Miss Phoebe.' Mathew Leach smiled at the two women, laughing and crying at the same time.

'Mathew!' Phoebe broke free to hug the man she had known from childhood. 'But . . . but shouldn't you be at the pit?'

'Come in, Miss Phoebe.' Lucy's voice lost some of its joy. 'There's a fire in the grate an' tea on the hob an' I'm dyin' to butter you one of my scones.

'You see, Miss Phoebe,' she said when at last Phoebe stopped wandering through the rooms of her home and settled in the warm kitchen, 'when I was sacked from the Priory and Mathew was given the sack from the pit we had nowhere to go like an' . . . well, I thought the mill could do wi' being kept an eye on an' you wouldn't mind us being in one of the outhouses. We never used the 'ouse, Miss, honest we didn't. I just come in every day to dust and keep the rooms aired.'

'You mean, you were both removed from your employment?' Phoebe left the scone untouched. 'But why? For what reason?'

'Mathew was sacked for questioning the reason for your aunt reducing the wages at the pit an' meself? Well miss, Sophie's maid said I must 'ave put the necklace in one of the dresses sent to Wiggins Mill, that I knowed you as a friend and would be able to retrieve it when I visited you and then sell it. So the housekeeper up and sacks me. Matters of the servants is left to 'er when 'er Ladyship is away, Sir William is never bothered with little things like sacking a maid.'

'They don't 'ave to give a reason,' Mathew said sourly. 'Pit owner or gentry, meks no difference – when either of 'em wants you out it's a case of pick up yer tin and go.'

'But how have you managed with no wage between you?'

'Well, like I said, Miss,' Lucy took up the thread, 'we had nowhere to go. We thought yer aunt might turn nasty if we lived with Mathew's parents an' we couldn't live here without being wed so we just got Father Heywood to say the words over us then we come here. Oh, Miss, I hopes you don't mind?'

'Of course I don't mind, but Lucy . . . your lovely wedding? Didn't you get it after all?'

'No, Miss.' Lucy smiled at her husband. 'But I got the man and that's all that matters.'

'We'll be gone in the mornin', Miss.' Mathew turned towards the door. 'I'll go see to our bits an' pieces an' when Lucy is finished over 'ere 'er'll pack the beddin'.'

'She will do no such thing!' Phoebe answered vehemently. 'And neither will you. You will stay here and glad I'll be of your company. I . . . . I wouldn't want to stay here alone . . .'

'We understand, Miss, and we thank you,' Lucy cut in, seeing the shadow return to Phoebe's eyes. 'Mathew and me we'll mek it up to you, really we will.'

'There is nothing to make up.' Phoebe smiled. 'We are friends, and wage or no wage will survive somehow. In fact, you two seem to have found a way already, judging by the food on this table.'

'That's Mathew, Miss,' Lucy beamed. 'You remember he was quite handy with hammer and saw? Well, he gets a few odd jobs from folk in the town, mending a chair or mekin' a stool, little things like but they buy flour and vegetables. And I do a bit of sewing like you used to only I don't get no dresses from the nobs.'

'Neither will I again, Lucy.' Phoebe sipped the hot tea she had poured. 'Those doors are closed forever, I'm afraid.'

'But you didn't never tek anything!' Lucy's glance was bright with anger. 'Them at the Priory knows you never and so does Magistrate.'

'I don't think that will make any difference.' Phoebe shook her head as the other girl offered more tea. 'The very fact that I have been in prison will be sufficient for the nobs, as you called them, to reject my company.'

'Then bloody nobs ain't worth associatin' wi'.'

'Mathew!' Lucy glared at her husband. 'Language.'

'Beg your pardon, Miss Phoebe,' Mathew pulled open the door that led on to the yard, 'but that's the way I feel,' he said, going outside.

'Please don't tek no notice of Mathew.' Lucy gathered the used cups on to a wooden tray. 'But the losin' of his job 'as made 'im bitter. I keep tellin' 'im it's no use his feelin' that way but I might as well bang my 'ead against a brick wall for all the good it does. ''E just won't take a tellin', says all moneyed folk am the same: all out for themselves an' sod the likes of folk who grind for 'em. There be times I think he'll never be the same as he was.'

Never be the same. The thought lingered as Phoebe followed the other girl into the scullery. She understood Mathew's feelings. Things might never be the same for any of them. She was free, but what freedom would Wednesbury allow a girl who had been in prison?

Phoebe came up the rise from Lyng Fields, feeling the softness of the earth beneath her feet, and stood on the crest of the high ground cradling Sandwell Valley, looking down on the ancient Priory. Cool air fanned her brow and she lifted her face to it, revelling in its touch. She had deliberately not waited for the carriage as Sir William had told her to, ignoring his instruction. Never again, she told herself, closing her eyes to the delicious taste of freedom, never again would any man or woman order her life.

A breeze lifting out of the valley caught her skirts, lifting them like unseen fingers, and she pressed a hand to them, delighting in the touch of the brown bombazine after so many months of wearing drab grey calico. But the women who had been her companions of those months were still wearing grey uniforms. Her mind flashed to Tilly. She would be dressed in grey calico the rest of her life. If only they had given her time to say goodbye to the woman who had befriended her . . . but she had been rushed from Handsworth Prison as though she carried the plague and now she would never be able to tell Tilly how glad she was to have known her and to have been her friend.

Opening her eyes, she looked down at the house nestling on the floor of the valley, its mullioned windows seeming to stare back at her. Sir William Dartmouth had waited outside that prison, waited until she emerged through its heavy door; he had brought her home in his carriage, but for what reason? Reparation for what his son had caused to happen to her? Maybe, but any such feeling would be momentary, passed and forgotten in a week. As Mathew had said yesterday, all moneyed folk were out for themselves, they and they alone were all that mattered to them, and the more money they had the less those without it counted for. Well, she had none but she would count for something. Lifting her skirt, she set off down into the valley. Somehow, some way, Phoebe Pardoe would count for something.

At the foot of the high ground the valley widened into a flat swathe, the grass-covered earth rolling away to green eternity. It had been green around Brunswick House, Phoebe remembered, the lawns edged with beds bright with flowers, a shaded arbour leading to her favourite rose garden, but there had been nothing like these vast acres spreading endlessly, the ancient house at their heart.

Passing at last beneath a great stone arch, she began to walk along the sweeping approach, itself lined with magnificent beeches, their arched branches almost meeting overhead as if in imitation of the stone.

'Hey!'

The shout coming from the hushed silence of the morning took her unawares and she stopped, both hands clutched to her brown cloak.

'Where do you think you be goin'?'

A man in late middle age, his shoulders hunched, stepped from behind a tree.

'Don't you know this 'ere be private property?'

He stepped towards her and Phoebe saw his earth-stained hands move toward the heavy buckle belt fastened about his breeches.

'Of course I know.' Phoebe lifted her chin, putting every ounce of her failing confidence into her voice. There was no one around; in fact there might only be herself and this man in the world, so empty was the spread of ground. 'This is Sandwell Priory and I am here by appointment.'

'Appointment, eh!'

The man's hands still hovered about the fastener of his belt and Phoebe felt her heart jerk. What did he intend to do? Whatever it was there was no one to see.

'Yes, by appointment.' Phoebe stood her ground as he came closer. 'I am here to see Sir William . . .'

'*You*, 'ere to see Billy-me-Lord?' The man sniffed derisively, eyeing her plain brown dress. 'You'll be tellin' me 'as 'ow you be a personal friend of 'is next.'

'Hardly.' Phoebe stared into the man's eyes, pale rheumy eyes that seemed to swim in a mist of water. 'Though I do wish to return this.'

Thrusting a hand into the pocket of her cloak, she pulled out the freshly laundered handkerchief, its crested initial worked in pale blue, and held it towards him.

'Oh!' He stared at the handkerchief, his manner changing as if the owner himself had suddenly appeared. 'It's . . . it's just that 'er Ladyship don't like town folk using the main drive, an' with you not bein' in a carriage like I thought as you . . .'

'That I was one of the town folk?' Phoebe returned the handkerchief to her pocket. 'You thought correctly, I am.'

'In that case . . .' the hands stopped hovering, dropping instead to the man's sides '. . . you should 'ave come by the back way, up against Ice Pool. That way there would be less chance of them up at the 'ouse seein' you. You best go back. There be a path around to the left of the arch will lead you to the stables. You can get to the servants' quarters that way.'

'Thank you.' Phoebe's mouth did not relax.

'I ain't seen you afore,' the man went on as she turned away. 'You be the new maid?'

'No.' Phoebe halted then swung around to face the lovely stone mansion. 'I am not the new maid and neither do I enter a house via the servants' quarters.'

Feeling those watery eyes on her back she marched up the arrow-straight drive, her mouth set in a straight line. Her home might be a hovel in comparison to that of Sir William Dartmouth but she was mistress of it and servant to no man, and that was the way her life would remain.

She had almost reached the steps that led from left and right, forming an arc up to the main entrance of the Priory, when a footman in dark blue livery appeared as if from nowhere.

'You shouldn't have come this way.'

His voice was hushed, almost reverential; no servant in her father's house had been expected to speak this way.

'So I have been told,' Phoebe answered loudly.

Closing the space between them, the man glanced at the house before grabbing her elbow. 'Then why did yer? You must 'ave been told 'er Ladyship don't like servants usin' the main drive. C'mon, out of it, there'll be trouble if 'er sees you 'ere.'

The hand on her elbow tightened and for a fleeting second Phoebe was back inside that corridor with Liza Spittle's hand pushing her back against the wall, the old sickness rising in her throat.

'What is going on here?'

The words were not loud but they acted upon the footman like a starting pistol. His hand fell away from Phoebe's elbow and he stepped back as Sir William Dartmouth rounded the corner of the house.

'I asked what is going on here?'

The sickness that memory had provoked faded as he approached. Glancing at the footman, Phoebe saw the pale line of anxiety now lining that man's lips. So it was the same here in West Bromwich as it was in Wednesbury! Positions once lost would be hard to replace, especially if a man were to be dismissed with no references.

'I have a stone in my shoe,' Phoebe lied, 'your footman was about to assist me.'

'I see.'

I know you do, thought Phoebe, catching the look of gratitude in the servant's eye as he was dismissed. First you think me a thief, now you see me as a liar.

'I will send for one of the maids.'

'Please don't bother.' Phoebe bent, and removing a shoe, shook it, displacing the imaginary stone. Then she slipped her foot back into it. 'A woman learns to do these things for herself in Handsworth Gaol.'

'Take him back to the stable.' Sir William turned to the groom who had followed him from the back of the house. The man began to lead away the magnificent black horse and its master turned back to Phoebe.

'That will keep them in conversation for a few days.' He smiled.

Phoebe glanced at the departing groom, remembering how the slightest deviation from the usual could set the women's prison humming for days. The slightest deviation! What Tilly had done to Liza Spittle was no slight deviation . . . what would happen now to Tilly . . . what would the Prison Board do to her?

'Shall we go inside?'

The question cut across those thoughts spinning in Phoebe's mind, bringing her attention back to the man half smiling at her.

'There is no need.' She fished in her pocket then held out the folded square of white lawn. 'I can return this to you here. It is all I came for.'

'But that is not the only reason I wished you to come.' He regarded her from deep grey eyes. 'You have not yet been given a full explanation of the facts of what happened on that day, nor have you received my family's apology.'

'I have received my freedom,' Phoebe answered, her own gaze clear and steady, 'that is enough. Nothing more is necessary or wanted, therefore I wish you good day, Sir William.'

'Maybe it is enough for you,' his voice was suddenly hard, cutting through the quietness covering the beautiful valley, 'but what of my son? All he can do is apologise, Miss Pardoe. Would you deprive him of what little solace that can give him?'

Edward! How many times had he filled her thoughts during those long nights, how many times had she seen in her mind that handsome face, those vividly blue eyes? Yet strangely she had not once thought of him since meeting his father.

'Will you not at least let the boy speak for himself?'

Only a brief nod indicating her agreement, Phoebe followed him into the Priory. Dismissing all offers of attention, Sir William led her through the spacious rooms, each exquisite in its furnishings, until he came to a door concealed in an alcove in a corridor lined with portraits.

'My wife will be in here,' he said, pushing open the door and waiting until Phoebe passed inside.

Much smaller than the rooms through which she had already walked, this held a more intimate feel, the home of laughing children and shared secrets. Phoebe glanced quickly at the photographs in silver frames dotted on tables, the deep chairs carelessly scattered with bright cushions, the spectacles beside the newspapers that marked this a family room.

'Amelia, my dear, Miss Pardoe is here.'

Lady Amelia Dartmouth laid aside the book she had been reading. 'Miss Pardoe, do forgive my not welcoming you but I was not informed . . . William, why did no one tell me of Miss Pardoe's arrival?'

'Never mind that for now,' he replied as his wife drew Phoebe to a chair, 'ring for Edward and Sophie.'

'You will take tea, my dear?'

Phoebe looked at the elegant woman, remembering her from the evening market, only then her bonnet had hidden the traces of gold that still shone among the carefully dressed fading hair and her cloak had covered the stately, tightly corseted figure.

'Thank you,' she murmured as Amelia Dartmouth issued softly spoken orders to the man who responded almost immediately to the pull of a bell cord.

'Phoebe!' Edward was first into the room, rushing to where she sat in a deep brocade chair. 'Oh, Phoebe, I'm so sorry.'

'Edward!' his father cautioned as a maid entered with a silver tray. 'We will wait for your sister.'

He had grown. Phoebe glanced over to where Edward stood beside his father. He was taller than she remembered but still lacked three or four inches beside the older man. He had the same blue eyes and golden hair of his mother but the stance of his father, the assurance that a life of wealth and position bestows.

'Phoebe . . . Phoebe, I'm so happy to see you!' Sophie burst into the room like a boisterous puppy, grabbing both of Phoebe's hands and pulling her out of the chair. 'Was it positively awful in that prison?'

'Sophie!' Lady Amelia's voice was sharp.

'Sorry, Mama,' she said, giving Phoebe's hands a squeeze before releasing them.

'Miss Pardoe,' Sir William said as Phoebe accepted the delicate porcelain cup Sophie handed her, 'my son has something to say to you.'

'Yes, Phoebe.' Edward's blue eyes clouded. 'That day I met you coming here to return a necklace you told me you had found caught up inside a dress that Sophie had given you, I said I would return it in your stead.' He looked at his mother and Phoebe thought that despite his height he seemed just like a little boy, seeking encouragement in making a confession.

'Go on, Edward.' His mother smiled, a world of understanding in her eyes.

'Well, after I left you, The Prince caught his foot in a root or something and came down heavily.'

'The Prince?' Phoebe questioned.

'The bay I was riding,' Edward replied, 'he was a son of Satan, my father's black, and sometimes he showed it. He did that day anyway . . .'

'He was restless, I remember.' Phoebe put the delicate cup and saucer aside, her tea untouched.

'He always reacted to a sudden breeze that way.' Edward glanced at his father, still standing before the Adam fireplace. 'As if he wanted to race the wind. Anyway he got the bit between his teeth and set off like a bat out of hell. We were half across the valley when he came down, and when I couldn't get him to his feet I went for help. By the time it was all sorted out I had completely forgotten about the necklace in my pocket.'

'The Prince was a particular favourite of Edward's.' Amelia Dartmouth stretched a hand toward the tall young man who was her son. 'His father gave him the foal when it was born, you could say they grew up together were it not to sound so sentimental.'

'Edward was devastated when they had to shoot The Prince,' Sophie put in. 'It was days before he could bring himself to speak to anyone.'

'By that time,' Lady Dartmouth took up the explanation, 'the chill I had caught that evening at the street market had worsened, and it was decided we should leave for Europe earlier than originally intended. So you see, Miss Pardoe, both Sophie and Edward were out of the country when you . . .' The explanation trailed off, his mother holding on to Edward's hand.

'What my wife was about to say was that she and our son and daughter were abroad when you were arrested and imprisoned, and I did not acquaint them with that information in my letters to them. Therefore the fault is mine . . .'

'William,' Amelia Dartmouth's brow creased in a small frown as she turned to her husband, 'my dear, you were not to know the necklace would be found.'

'As you say, Amelia,' he nodded, 'but that does not excuse my behaviour. When James Siveter informed me that a young woman had been found guilty of stealing the necklace, I did nothing to ascertain the truth of what had happened.'

'But what could you have done?' his wife asked. 'You must accept the law.'

'As we all must,' his already dark eyes seemed to darken further, 'but we need not accept that the law has been presented with the true facts. I should have set in motion my own investigation.' He turned to Phoebe. 'As it was I did not, and therein lies my guilt. I was too ready to believe the friendship of my family had been abused and for that I offer my profound apology, Miss Pardoe, and ask in what manner I may make reparation?'

Phoebe rose, her plain brown garments a stark contrast to the elegant testimony to wealth that lay all about her.

'Sir William,' she said quietly, 'I told you yesterday that a mistake had been made. It was a mistake for which I attribute no blame and require no reparation. I know that as soon as you were told the truth you lost no time in securing my release. I know also that neither your son nor daughter would have wished for such a thing as my imprisonment, but now the truth is out and the necklace retrieved there is no need for the subject to be raised again.'

She turned to the woman who still clutched her son's hand, as if thinking he might be marched away to some prison. 'Thank you for receiving me, Lady Dartmouth. Now I must return home.'

'May I come to see you tomorrow, Phoebe?' Sophie was on her feet. 'I do so enjoy talking to you.'

'Sophie,' Lady Dartmouth smiled for the first time, 'Miss Pardoe may wish to rest for a few days before being concerned with callers.'

'I should be happy for Sophie to call at Wiggins Mill whenever you feel she may, Lady Dartmouth.' Phoebe dropped a polite curtsy.

'Does that invitation hold for me too?' Edward released his hand from that of his mother.

'Again, only when your mother permits it.'

'Don't bother ringing for Compson.' Sir William stepped forward as his wife made to pull the bell that would ring for a servant. 'If Miss Pardoe will allow, I will see her out myself.

'I really cannot permit you to refuse to take some form of compensation for what we have done to you.'

They had passed once again through rooms Phoebe would have loved to linger in and stood now at the foot of the curving stone steps that fronted the great house.

'You can't force me to accept either.'

'As it seems I could not force you into waiting for my carriage to collect you this morning.' William Dartmouth looked down into a face too pale and too thin but one that nevertheless whispered of beauty and character, and he smiled. 'Perhaps you will permit it to take you home?'

'Thank you, Sir William, but I prefer to walk.'

'What!' He laughed then, low in his throat. 'And get another stone in your shoe?'

'I may even take them off and walk barefoot.' Suddenly Phoebe too was smiling. 'That would give your servants even more cause for conversation. Good day, Sir William.'

Sir William Dartmouth watched the slight brown-clad figure walk away and found himself admiring the courage and honesty of the girl, the resilience that had brought her through months of imprisonment yet blaming no one at the end of it. He remembered the astuteness and honesty of the man he had known in the world of business.

'Yes, Miss Phoebe Pardoe,' he murmured, watching her disappear along the drive, 'you are truly Abel's daughter.'

Chapter Nine

Phoebe put the last of the breakfast dishes back on the kitchen dresser then settled the kettle over the coals. She would make a broth later against Lucy and Mathew's return from town. They were both trying so hard to make a living, Mathew trudging the streets in search of odd jobs and Lucy baking every night then selling scones and pies in the market place by day, while she . . . Phoebe looked around the small kitchen, its red flagstones boasting a pegged rug against the door, dresser arrayed with an assortment of plates and cups, the table whose twice-daily scrub had the wood almost white . . . apart from keeping the house clean, what was she doing?

She turned back to the fire, staring into its red heart. She couldn't go on like this, she couldn't continue to live off Lucy and her husband. In prison she had dreamed of being home, of earning her own living, of being beholden to none save herself yet . . . 'Why?' she whispered to the flames. 'Why can't I do it, why can't I at least try?'

The coals settled, sending a small glowing ember sliding between the bars of the grate. Phoebe watched the trail of sparks it made as it fell against the fender, sparks that glittered and then faded into nothing, as her life had once glittered only to fade.

If only her father's death had not come so soon, if she had been married to Montrose, her life would have been so different. Different! Reaching the tongs from the companion set that stood beside the range, she picked up the fallen ember, replacing it on the fire. Yes, her life would have been different but her world would still be empty for how long would happiness have lasted once she'd found out that Montrose's real reason for marrying her was her father's money? And now it seemed Sophie had been earmarked to become Mrs Montrose Wheeler.

Replacing the tongs, she walked restlessly into the small living room with its meagre pawnshop furnishings. Mrs Montrose Wheeler! Phoebe touched a finger to the blue glass top of the oil lamp sitting in the centre of the round chenille-covered table and knew which she would rather have.

The skirts of her brown dress swishing, she ran up the stairs and into the bedroom she had once used as a workroom, the lethargy that had lain over her since leaving prison falling away like a discarded shawl. She knew how she could make a living. Opening a chest that stood against the window wall she took out the small dresses she had made for Lady Dartmouth, dresses that had never been given as the presents they were intended for. They were pretty. She lifted them one at a time, holding them against the light from the window. There were women in Wednesbury who either hadn't the skill to make their children's clothes or else were too busy working to keep them to have the time to try. Lucy said there were customers for her baking, maybe some of those customers would buy clothing. Draping the dresses across a table she used for cutting out her patterns, she counted them. There were eight ready for sale now and she still had some of the dresses Sophie had given her.

Turning to a larger chest standing on the opposite wall she raised the domed lid and stood stock still. The pale green gown stared up at her.

'. . . *I find you guilty of wilful theft* . . .' Phoebe's hand tightened on the mahogany lid as the room swam away from her.

'. . . *I sentence you to be taken to a place of imprisonment and there you will serve a term of fifteen years' hard labour . . .'*

Hard labour . . . imprisonment . . . fifteen years . . . wilful theft . . . I sentence . . . fifteen years. . . . The words twisted and turned in her mind, louder and louder until they screamed in her head; life draining out of her, Phoebe's fingers loosed the heavy lid and it fell with a bang, the noise of it chasing away the ghosts of the past. She stood for several seconds, her breathing rapid and short. She was free of the walls but not yet free of the prison. But she would be free, determinedly she lifted the lid of the chest and took out the green gown, totally free.

Laying the gown across the one chair the room still held she hesitated at a sound from downstairs. Sophie? Edward? It couldn't be Lucy or Mathew, they would not return before evening. She crossed to the window and looked out to where the Dartmouth carriage would be standing . . . only there was no carriage.

It could have driven up unheard but it could not have left the same way. Maybe she had imagined the sound? She stood listening until the crash of breaking china told her she had not imagined it.

Maybe it was Lucy, maybe she was unwell. 'Lucy!' she called, running from the room and downstairs to the kitchen. 'Lucy, are you all right?'

'It ain't Lucy . . .' a voice behind her halted her progress toward the scullery '. . . it's me!'

Phoebe turned toward the voice. A man stood inside the kitchen, blocking the doorway to the living room. He was about five feet ten and aged around thirty, and eyed her brazenly.

'Who are you? What do you want?' Phoebe asked, suddenly knowing a new fear as his eyes wandered over her.

'Who I be don't matter.' He spoke through lips that seemed too thick for his narrow face. 'What I want, though, that be a different matter.'

'I have no work to give you.'

He smiled, spreading the thick lips, showing teeth that were strong but in need of a rub with baking soda. 'It ain't work I'm after.'

'I . . . I don't live alone here.'

'Oh, I know you don't.' His eyes glittered, he knew her fear and was feeding on it. 'I know about Lucy and 'er 'usband, same as I know about you and your visit to Sandwell Priory last week. 'Ow much did 'e give you?'

'I don't understand.' Phoebe tried to move into the scullery but the man was at her side before she had taken two steps.

'Don't play me for a fool, Miss Bloody Fancy Pardoe,' he grated. 'You understands all right an' comin' on all innocent won't pull the wool. My eyes am wide open. I knows the Dartmouths won't be lettin' things go wi'out payin' you somethin' . . . now wheer is it?'

'I did go to the Priory last week.' The fear in her was stronger now and she knew he sensed it as an animal senses fear. What would he do when he found nothing here of value? 'But I went there only to return a handkerchief Sir William had lent to me, nothing more. I . . . I took nothing from them.'

'So Phoebe Pardoe got nothing?' He moved closer. 'Look, I warned you, don't play clever wi' me. I know you done twelve months an' more on account of Mr Bloody 'igh falutin' Edward Dartmouth an' that last week you went to the Priory to collect. You talked to the 'ole bloody lot of 'em . . . compensation is what you talked and compensation is money. You got money an' it's that money I've come for . . . now wheer is it?'

One hand flashed upward, grabbing her hair, snatching her head backward. 'You might as well tell me,' he brought his face close, the thick lips only inches away, ''cos I'll find out one way or another and one of them ways you're gonna find very painful.'

'I . . . told . . . you,' Phoebe fought to speak against the constriction of her neck being pulled backward, 'I was given nothing . . . the Dartmouth family . . . they gave me . . . no . . . no money.'

'Lyin' bitch!' He released her hair, the same hand smacking viciously across her face, knocking her against the dresser, sending plates hurtling to the floor. Grabbing a poker, he thrust it deep into the glowing fire. 'If you ain't told me wheer you 'ave the money 'id by the time that's 'ot, you'll 'ave a face nobody will bear the lookin' at.'

He wouldn't believe her, he was convinced she had been given money by the Dartmouths and nothing she said would alter that. Phoebe swallowed hard, her thoughts unnaturally clear. If she could get out of the house she might be able to make a run for it.

'All right,' she said, wiping a hand across her smarting eyes, 'Sir William did give me money but it's not here . . .'

'Then wheer is it?'

He grabbed at her again, cinching her arm, pulling her forward. There was no smell of coal dust, Phoebe thought, and no tiny burn holes in his trousers so he was not a miner nor did he work in an iron foundry. That meant he wasn't local for there was little for men to do otherwise around Wednesbury. So how did he know about her being in prison or about her visit to the Priory?

'I said, wheer is it?' He reached his free hand to the poker, its steel tip indistinguishable from the crimson coals. 'But you can take yer time, it's gonna be a pleasure gettin' you to say.'

'It's outside.' Phoebe prayed her words would convince him. 'I thought it better not to bring it into the house. No one would expect so much money to be left out there.'

'Wheer outside?' He drew the poker out of the fire.

'In the old mill.'

'That's better.'

He dropped the poker, letting it rattle down the bars of the grate on to the stone hearth, dragging Phoebe with him out of the house and across the yard to where the windmill stood on a little rise.

'Wheer abouts did you put it?'

Phoebe winced as he jerked her arm. 'Up in the corn loft. There's a pile of empty sacks against the wall, I hid the money under them.'

'Yer best be tellin' the truth,' he threatened, almost frog marching her towards the door of the disused mill, 'yer'll regret it if you ain't.'

If only he would release her arm! Phoebe tried to form a plan: she could run back into the house and bolt the doors. But he did not release her. Kicking open the wooden door, he pushed her before him into the mill.

'The corn loft, you said?' He glanced upward then down to where a rickety ladder lay half buried in the dust of the floor. Holding her with one hand, he struggled to raise the ladder then rest it against the floor of the loft.

'You first.' He leered, his almost canine teeth taking on a yellower hue in the light streaming from the doorway.

Phoebe struggled up the ladder, her feet catching in her skirts, threatening to throw her off the narrow uneven struts.

'Stop there an' don't go movin' . . . . if you know what's best for you.'

Pushing her as he followed from the topmost rung of the ladder, he kicked it aside, laughing as he made for the heap of sacks lying in a corner.

This would be her only chance. There would be no more tricking him when he found there was no money under those sacks. Moving slowly, holding her skirts so they wouldn't rustle, she got to her feet, inching towards the edge of the corn loft floor. He had kicked away the ladder but that wouldn't stop her.

'Go on . . . jump! Makes no odds.'

Despite her caution he had heard and was watching her, on his knees among the empty corn sacks.

'You'll break one leg at least, mebbe both, but you won't need legs for what I'm gonna do to you . . . after I've got yer money, that is. Go on, jump . . . you won't crawl far.'

He began to laugh again, a laugh that had her spine crawling. 'What I'm gonna do to you . . .' She had heard those words before; the image of Liza Spittle's birthmarked face floated before her eyes and the sour smell of her filled Phoebe's nostrils. Closing her eyes, she jumped.

Annie Pardoe slipped the key into her black bag and left her bedroom, going to her brother's studio.

'I am going into the town,' she signed, the movement of her hands setting her bag swinging from her arm. 'Doctor Dingley has prescribed a medicine for your headaches and I do not trust Isaac Jackson to send it before teatime. That man is not nearly the chemist his father was.'

Samuel put his brush on a table beside a palette smeared with paints and looked at his sister. He could hardly remember seeing her dressed in any colour other than black, as though she were in constant mourning; neither could he remember seeing her smile, he could only recall the bitterness that had eaten away at her over the years, a bitterness of her own making. Yes, Annie *was* in perpetual mourning, grieving for a life she thought duty had required her to forgo and nurturing bitterness against the brother she blamed for taking it.

'There is no need for you to go,' he signed, his long fingers moving in rapid succession, 'my headache is quite gone.'

'Yes, it is now,' Annie's fingers relayed words of care she had never truly felt, 'but what of the night-time, dear? You know how sometimes you cannot sleep for the pain in your head. I think it better I fetch your medicine myself.'

'If that is what you wish.' Samuel's fingers seemed to flow into each other, one sign blending into another with the practice of years. 'I will take a turn in the garden until you return.'

Going into the adjoining room that was her brother's bedroom, Annie took a lightweight coat from the panelled wardrobe. Returning to the studio, she held it out to Samuel.

'You must take care,' she signed as he took the coat and slipped it on, 'you know how quickly you take the influenza.'

Yes, he knew. Samuel followed her out of the studio, making his separate way into the garden. He also knew how much he wished the influenza would take him.

Annie drove her small trap along Walsall Road turning off when she reached Oakeswell End, directing the horse toward the chemist's shop that topped Dudley Street. She would collect the medicine Alfred Dingley had prescribed and then she would complete what she had intended all along.

Ignoring the sidelong glances of the women and the looks of dislike from men she had laid off from the pits on one pretext or another, and whom the iron foundries would not take on, she trotted the horse a roundabout route, avoiding where possible the more heavily frequented roads until she came to Bescot Fields. This part of Wednesbury was still mostly pasture with only a few farms holding out against the industrialisation that had engulfed the town like the black plague; here she had lived so many years before coming to Brunswick House, here at the end of a beaten track hidden by high hedges was the house Abel had given to her and Samuel. It had not been sold or let to tenants and neither would it be until her use for it was gone. Samuel took no interest in the property or businesses left to him by Abel and none in this house: his painting was his only interest, which suited her. She turned the horse off the track, driving round to the back of the house where the trap would be screened. Yes, it suited her very well.

Leaving the horse to crop at the overgrown flower border she took the key from her bag, letting herself into the house. She would not open the shutters. The years had taught her the geography of this house and she moved easily through its shadowed dimness. In her old bedroom she drew a box from the back of a narrow shelf obscured by a marble-topped washstand set in front of it.

A finger of daylight poked between the heavy velvet curtains. Annie carried the box over to it. She removed the lid and breathed deeply, a feeling of satisfaction coursing through her. It was still there. From the depths of the box she withdrew a small finely wrought glass bottle. By the finger of daylight she read the label: 'D'Amour'. Elias Webb had thought her his the day he gave her the bottle of French perfume. But the perfume and its giver had long gone from her life.

Discarding the box, she thrust the bottle into her bag and left the house, locking it securely before climbing into the trap and leaving her former prison to its silence.

Phoebe struck the packed earth with a jarring thud and lay still. Above her, his narrow face pulled into a grin, the man watched, then satisfied she was either unconscious or worse, turned back to searching the heap of sacks.

Hearing his movements above her, Phoebe knew he had not followed. Carefully, a prayer in every move, she pushed herself to her knees, then to her feet. By what miracle she had not broken her legs she didn't know and didn't stop to reason, her one thought was to make it back to the house and bolt herself in. Gathering her skirts in both hands she tiptoed toward the open door and was almost through it when she heard him shout.

Running the last few yards, she hurled herself out of the door, slamming it behind her, eyes skimming it in search of a bolt or securing bar. But there was no way of locking it; there had been no need for locks at Wiggins Mill.

'Hey! Come here, you bloody bitch . . .'

The shout was followed by a grunt. He was down from the corn loft, had jumped as she had.

'Think you could fool me, did you? You'll 'ave nuthin' to think with when I catch you!'

Phoebe heard the scuffle as he got to his feet. She was already halfway across the open ground separating the mill from the house when she heard the door slam open against the wall.

'You won't bloody get away . . .'

The shout followed her as she ran.

'You've got that money somewheers an' I'm gettin' it!'

The last came out in a gasp as he threw himself at Phoebe's back, his hands fastening in her skirts and dragging her to the ground.

'Would 'ave gone a lot better wi' you if you had just told me wheer the money is 'cos now I'm gonna knock the truth outa you . . .'

'I told you the truth.' Phoebe tried to move but his weight sprawled half across her was too much. Her face pressed against the earth, she went on, 'I was given no money at the Priory.' It would not be enough. Her brain began to work calmly; she had to be more convincing, tell him something his thieving mind would accept. 'They . . . they offered me a hundred pounds . . .'

She stopped as he rolled off her then snatched her over on to her back, a hand about her throat. ''Undred pounds!' His fingers tightened on her neck, lifting her head then banging it hard down on the ground. 'An' you told me you got nuthin', you bloody lyin' cow!'

'I . . . I didn't take it.' His fingers tightened about her throat and behind her eyes tiny fireworks began to explode. 'I . . . I told them . . . it . . . it wasn't enough.'

His fingers relaxed but stayed about her neck; above her his thick lips drew back. 'Not enough! You told 'im a 'undred pounds wasn't enough?'

'Y . . . Yes . . .' Phoebe coughed.

'You! You told the 'igh an' mighty Billy-me-Lord Dartmouth that a 'undred pounds wasn't enough?' He laughed. 'What a bloody cheek . . . I bet 'e 'ad near enough an' 'eart attack.'

'He . . . he wasn't pleased.'

'Pleased!' Her attacker laughed again, the sound rolling off the walls of the old windmill and away toward the canal. 'I bet 'e wasn't bloody pleased, 'is sort ain't used to bein' refused, not no way. So . . .' he stopped laughing '. . . if you didn't take 'is 'undred quid, what did you tek?'

Phoebe lifted her hands to the one still holding her by the neck and pushed. 'Nothing.'

The fingers tightened again, banging her head twice against the hard earth. 'You keep arsin' around wi' me an' you gets yer brains knocked out,' he hissed. 'I don't believe you didn't get summat, you was one of a sort once till that sister of yer father's took the lot from you . . . oh, I know all about that.' He grinned down at her, his yellow teeth parted. 'Same as I know you to be too smart to miss the chance of gettin' your 'ands on some of Billy's money, so don't tell me you got none.'

'I got a lot *more* than a hundred.'

The flicker of greed in his eyes told Phoebe this was what he wanted to hear, this would convince him, this he might just accept. Pushing against his wrist, she stared up at him.

Holding her stare for a full minute, he tried to gauge the truth of what she had just said then dropped his hand.

''Ow much more?'

'A lot.' She sat up, coughing as a stream of air gained free passage to her lungs. 'Only I don't get it until this afternoon.'

'Go on.' He watched her rub her throat, his eyes lowering to her breasts.

'They were all there, like you said,' Phoebe tried to ignore his look, 'Sir William and Lady Dartmouth and their son and daughter. They said they were sorry I had been inconvenienced . . .'

'Incon-bloody-venienced.' He laughed again, the noise of it rolling in waves from the mill to its outhouses before washing out over the low embankment that bordered the canal. 'That sounds just like 'im – somebody does twelve months in the shit an' 'e calls it a inconvenience!'

Taking her chance, Phoebe got to her feet, brushing spears of dried grass from her skirts. 'I told him much the same. I also told him that this particular inconvenience was going to cost him ten thousand pounds or I would go to the newspapers. I said I was sure they would relish reporting how so prominent a member of the gentry had allowed an innocent girl to take the blame for a crime his son had committed.'

'But the necklace was found!' His eyes glittered up at her.

'Was it?' Phoebe flicked a dried straw from her sleeve, trying to guess how long she could stall him. Maybe Sophie or Edward would call and maybe not, reason told her, they had called only two days before. 'Or was it a replica? After all, who would know? And who would really care? The public's interest would not be in the recovery of the necklace but in the suffering of a young girl, and that suffering would only increase in the telling.'

'An' 'e went for it?'

He stood up, his tongue skimming his thick lips, and Phoebe stepped backwards, making a breathing space between them.

'Not at first. He argued that I would never be believed, but I argued that the damage to his family's reputation would be already done and that he might never be quite believed again in anything he tried to do. I said the aristocracy is a cautious breed. It cares to take no chances with the unreliable in case its own unreliability is brought to light.'

'Clever.' He smiled his approval. 'I said you was one of 'is own sort, y'ave brains as well as looks.'

Deep inside Phoebe shuddered at the glance he played over her but forced herself to stay calm. 'Clever enough,' she said, avoiding his eyes, 'to turn a hundred pounds into ten thousand.'

'Christ Almighty,' he breathed, 'ten thousand quid . . . it's a bloody king's ransom!'

'But it's a king's ransom I earned,' Phoebe said, 'over twelve months in hell I earned that money, and I told them either they pay what I ask or I tell the whole story plus more . . . much more.'

'So 'e agreed?' His eyes slid again to her breasts. 'Billy-me-Lord is payin' you ten thousand quid.'

'This afternoon.' Phoebe turned towards the house. 'He had to go to the bank. He said that he never kept that much money in the house, so if you come back around four o'clock you can have half.'

'Why go?' He grabbed at her, pulling her hard against him. 'It will be more pleasurable to wait 'ere . . .'

He pressed his face to the side of her neck, pulling at her flesh with his thick lips, and this time Phoebe could not hold her shudder inside. Grasping his hands, she tried to force them away, a sob of terror escaping her as he turned her in his arms. 'I . . . I'll give it all to you if you go.'

'I intend 'avin' it all,' he grinned, thick lips shining wetly, 'an' the money besides.'

Hooking one foot behind her ankle he brought her down, her spine hitting the ground hard, driving the wind out of her.

Already unbuckling the belt holding up his trousers, he looked down at her. 'Relax,' he grinned again, 'you'll enjoy what I've got fer you.'

Their hold released, his trousers fell around his ankles, revealing the naked flesh beneath, then he was on top of her, one hand clawing at her breast while the other slid her skirts above her hips.

'You'll enjoy what Liza's got fer you.'

Once more Phoebe was against that prison wall, the stink of Liza Spittle in her nostrils, the vileness of her touch rising like gall in her throat.

'Stop!' She struggled to push him away, to rid herself of the threat of his body. 'Please stop!'

'It ain't stop you'll be sayin' in a minute,' he said thickly, his hands fumbling at her underwear, 'you'll be sayin' more . . . please, more.'

'No . . .' Phoebe screamed as his fingers touched against her bare skin. 'Liza, no . . . o . . . o!'

Chapter Ten

Maudie Tranter slipped out of the back entrance of Brunswick House, her cloak covering a wicker basket.

Annie Pardoe would be gone most of the afternoon and there was little likelihood of Samuel's needing anything, poor man. Maudie shook her head. He seemed to become more drawn into himself every day, eating hardly enough to keep a sparrow alive, and those headaches! She reached the lane that backed the house, turning left towards Hall End. Yes, Samuel Pardoe's headaches just seemed to get worse despite the medicines Alfred Dingley regularly prescribed.

'Come in, Maudie.' Sarah Leach left off scraping the potatoes she had freshly pulled from the vegetable patch, wiping her hands on a square of white huckaback. 'It's good to see you, the seein' ain't often enough.'

'An' likely to be less.' Maudie followed her through to the kitchen, letting the basket on to the table with a groan. 'It gets to be a longer walk out 'ere each time a body comes, or at least that's the way it feels.'

'Give us yer cloak.' Sarah took the heavy woollen cloak, her eye on the basket.

'Eeh, ma wench!' Maudie dropped heavily on to a hoop-backed chair, its cane seat welcoming to her thin frame. 'Why do you still go on livin' out 'ere? You would be better off nearer the town an' Joseph wouldn't 'ave near so far to trot to the pit.'

'Try tellin' 'im that.' Sarah smiled, lifting the kettle from its bracket above the fire and scalding the tea in her brown earthenware pot. "E says 'e is 'ere till they carries 'im up Church Hill an' settles 'im agen 'is mother and father.'

'P'raps 'e's got the right idea 'spite what I says.' Maudie watched the flow of dark brown liquid being poured into Sarah's china cups, kept for visitors. 'Wednesbury ain't the place it once was – all steel foundries wi' their smoke an' dirt messin' place up, an' now them newfangled toob works.'

'Toob works?' Sarah asked, adding milk to the tea before passing one of the cups to her visitor. 'What do toob works be?'

'They be factories as meks toobs – 'ollow stems of steel. All sizes they can mek – long an' fat, short an' thin, big or little.'

'What they be for then?' Sarah pointed to a small glass bowl filled with sugar. 'These toobs.'

'I'm buggered if I know!' Maudie spooned sugar into her tea. 'But I reckon 'er up at Brunswick 'Ouse does. Seems as 'er's dabblin' in a lot of things lately.'

'Is 'er buyin' these 'ere toobs then?' Sarah asked over her cup.

'Not buyin' 'em.' Maudie sipped her tea, savouring both it and the moment; she didn't see much of folk and when she did she enjoyed the glory of imparting news of the doings of Annie Pardoe. 'But I reckon 'er's puttin' money into the mekin' of 'em.'

'Well, 'er certainly ain't puttin' any into them pits o' their'n,' Sarah answered, placing home-cooked scones and a jar of her own damson jam on the table. 'Joseph says that Hobs Hill mine is near to cavin' in just about everywheer and that the Crown mine up at Moxley ain't much safer. What wi' all that an' their pay bein' docked, the men would pack in tomorrer if they could get set on anywheers else. Eeh, wench, what changes we've seen since Abel went!'

'There's been changes all right,' Maudie lifted a scone to the plate Sarah passed her, 'an' not all in them pits neither.' She sliced the scone, ladling it with thick dark jam. 'You knows 'ow long I've been wi' Annie Pardoe an' 'er brother, an' in all them years I ain't known 'er 'ave doin's wi' nobody other than tradesmen, but now . . . well, all I knows is summat is goin' on.'

''Ow do you mean?' Sarah helped herself to a scone.

'There's bin a caller to Brunswick 'Ouse several times over the last few weeks an' always when Samuel be sleepin' . . . 'e sleeps quite a bit, 'e does, these days.'

She paused but Sarah did not speak, not wanting to put her visitor off her stride. Maudie was easily diverted and any news of Annie Pardoe's doings was too good to miss.

Maudie drank the last of her tea and waited while the cup was refilled. Spooning sugar into it, she went on, 'It's always the same man: Clinton Harforth-Darby 'e says 'is name is, an' you should see Annie when 'e comes. All sweetness an' light 'er is, apologisin' for Samuel's absence sayin' as 'e regrets bein' unable to come down . . .' she stirred her tea vigorously as though the action would ease some of the contempt her words roused '. . . as if 'er would ever suffer the poor bugger to come downstairs. Keeps 'im up theer like a rooster in a pen, 'cept Samuel will never get to perform like no rooster.'

'Does 'e know what's going on?' Sarah chanced Maudie changing tack. 'I mean, the say-so in all business matters be wi' 'im surely? 'E must sign papers an' things, Annie can't do that.'

'That's what you think.' Maudie accepted a second scone. 'It's what a lot of folk think seein' as 'ow the lot was left to Samuel, but Maudie Tranter knows better . . .' Sinking her teeth into the light scone, her eyes fastened on Sarah's, relishing the interest she saw in them. 'I heard 'er tell this Harforth-Darby that 'er could sign in 'er brother's stead, that 'e 'ad given 'er power of a tur . . . I can't remember the exact word but it must be legal like 'cos Harforth-Darby passed her some papers an' I seen 'er sign meself.'

'You seen Annie Pardoe write 'er name on papers that man give 'er? Eeh, I wonder what they was for?'

Maudie touched a finger to each side of her lips checking for stray crumbs before sipping her tea. 'That I don't know,' she shook her head, 'but it was summat that set a smile on that man's face that stretched from ear to ear. An' there's another thing.' Maudie finished her tea, refusing a third cup with a shake of her head. 'Last time 'er went out, 'er bought a new frock . . .'

'Who, Annie Pardoe!' Sarah asked, disbelief plain in her voice.

Maudie nodded. 'Ar, an' not just a new frock but a new lavender-coloured frock.'

'God luv me, I don't believe it.' Sarah stared at the other woman. 'After all these years, Annie Pardoe in a frock that ain't black? I can't remember last time I seen 'er outa black.'

'Oh, 'er ain't wore it, it's hangin' in 'er wardrobe. 'Er don't know I've seen it – but then, there's one or two things as Annie Pardoe ain't knowin'.'

'P'raps they be goin' somewheer special?' Sarah swung the kettle on its bracket away from the fire as the hiss of steam became louder. ''Er an' Samuel, I mean.'

'Oh, ar,' Maudie smiled acidly, 'an' pigs might fly. That one never goes out nowheer, and garden is as far as 'e goes, an' I can't see as Annie 'as bought 'erself a new frock to saunter round the roses.'

'I never could understand that, Maudie,' Sarah said, sitting down again. 'From a babby 'e never went anywheer on 'is own, 'e was always wi' his mother, an' after 'er went 'e was only seen wi' Annie – an' that weren't often, poor sod. 'E was always kept close to their skirts an' yet from what I remembers of 'im 'e was a good-lookin' lad, same as Abel. Would 'ave been the mekin' of 'im to 'ave wed.'

'Ar, well,' Maudie sighed heavily, 'it be too late fer that now even if 'e 'ad the mind. That sister of his'n wouldn't 'arbour no other woman in the 'ouse an' I can't see Samuel goin' against 'er, not now.'

'Poor soul,' Sarah shook her head in unspoken sympathy,

'but whatever the reason 'e's been kept close all 'is life it couldn't a' been 'is brain or Abel would never 'ave left 'im everythin'.'

'It ain't 'is brain,' Maudie agreed, 'there be nuthin' wrong up top. 'E might not go out of that 'ouse but it ain't 'cos 'e's short of 'is marbles.' She tapped a finger to her forehead. ''E's just got no interest in nuthin' 'cept for 'is paintin'.'

'Seems to me 'e ain't never been allowed no interests. Eeh, that family am goin' to 'ave a lot to answer for, an' not only on account of Samuel neither. There's young Phoebe an' what they've done to 'er.'

'That were all Annie's doin', an' all,' Maudie replied. 'I tell you, Sarah, Abel Pardoe would turn in 'is grave if 'e knowed what 'ad 'appened to that girl of 'is'n.'

'There was no call to go turnin' the wench out of 'er own 'ome,' Sarah said, 'that were nuthin' short of vicious. Surely Samuel 'ad summat to say about that?'

''E might 'ave done,' Maudie rose reaching her cloak from the nail in the door, 'supposin' 'e knowed the truth of it but I 'ave me doubts about that. More likely 'is sister 'as filled 'im up wi' all sorts of lies.' She fastened the cloak about her throat. 'But like I said, Annie Pardoe don't know all. Might be as one day 'er will 'ave one or two surprises comin'.'

''Ow do you mean, Maudie?' Sarah waited for Annie's housekeeper to finish fastening her cloak.

'I ain't sayin'.' Maudie dropped a hand to the wicker basket still on a corner of the table; she wasn't one to give all her news in one sitting. If it were worth the telling it were worth the holding, for a while longer anyway. 'But mark my words, Annie Pardoe be in for a shock.'

'No . . . Liza, don't . . . no . . . o . . . o!'

Phoebe's screams ricocheted off the walls of the mill and its outhouses as she struggled to push the man away.

'You won't be sayin' no fer long,' he grunted, snatching at her drawers, the cotton of them tearing in his hand. 'You won't be sayin' anythin', you'll just be moanin' wi' pleasure when you gets this up you . . .'

'Somebody is goin' to get summat up 'em but I don't think it's goin' to be no woman!'

'What the bloody 'ell . . . ?'

'Is this yer 'usband, Missis?'

Her movements jerky, like a badly controlled puppet, Phoebe sat up, pushing her skirts down over her legs, grasping the torn bodice of her dress and holding it across her breasts, fear still bubbling in her throat. The man who had attacked her was jerked to his feet by the scruff of his neck.

'Am you married to 'im?'

'No!' Phoebe looked up at the figure dangling like a rag doll in the grip of a tall, broad-shouldered man.

'So you ain't 'er 'usband!' The tall man shook her attacker effortlessly. 'Then how come you be sprawled across 'er wi' your bare arse to the sun?'

'Let go, you interferin' bastard . . .'

Phoebe made to get to her feet as her attacker struggled to free himself, wanting only to get inside the mill house and lock herself away, but fell back as her legs refused to hold her.

'Oh, I'll let you go.' Placing two fingers in his mouth, the tall man gave a series of sharp whistles. 'When I've done wi' you.'

'You'll be sorry, you bloody canal rat.' The man who had come to rob Phoebe tried to kick backward but the trousers draped around his ankles prevented him. 'I've got mates . . .'

'An' do they all go around doin' what you intended doin' 'ere?' The tall man twisted the other around. 'You call attackin' a woman fun, I suppose? Well, I call punchin' the daylights out of scum like you fun – an' I'm goin' to 'ave me some fun right now!' One hand holding Phoebe's attacker by the throat, the other smacked into his yellow teeth with the force of a sledge hammer.

Her face turned away, Phoebe heard the cries as fists found their mark again and again.

'Bert . . . Bert, no more . . . you'm like to 'ave killed 'im!'

'I could bloody kill 'im lief as look at 'im.' Anger darkening his face, the tall man answered a woman in black skirts, a white cotton poke bonnet fastened over her brown hair, as she ran up to him. 'Makin' too free wi' what God give 'im.'

'Well, 'e won't make too free wi' it no more for a while.' The woman looked at the semi-conscious figure lying on his back, legs sprawled apart. 'Mind, the Lord weren't too lavish in first place wi' what he give this one.'

''E can still do more than enough harm wi' it all the same.' He dropped a hand to the handle of a knife tucked in his wide leather belt. 'I've a mind to cut the bugger off. That way 'e won't force it up no other woman as don't want it.'

'No, Bert!' The woman put a restraining hand over the one fondling the knife. 'I reckon 'e'll 'ave learned 'is lesson by the time 'e gets round to usin' that again. Best you do what you always do when you've knocked a man senseless an' I'll see to the wench.'

Turning away as the tall man caught the other by the collar, dragging him away, trousers about his ankles, the bare flesh of his buttocks scraping the rough ground, she moved to where Phoebe still sat, arms huddled across her chest.

'It's all right, ma wench,' she said softly, going down beside Phoebe and drawing her into her arms. 'It's all right, it's all over now.'

'Tilly . . .' Phoebe sobbed against the woman's shoulder. 'Oh, Tilly.'

'That's it,' the woman murmured soothingly, 'cry it up, wench, cry it up. You'll be better for gettin' it out.'

'We best get 'er inside.'

The man called Bert returned and stood looking at the two women huddled together on the ground.

'You be right.' The woman got to her feet, gently urging Phoebe to follow suit. 'A cup of sweet tea is what 'er's wantin'.' Then, seeing Phoebe flinch as the man made to help her up,

'It's all right, me luv, my Bert won't 'arm you, you'll be safe wi' us.'

''Er don't look as though 'er can make it on 'er own.' Bert stood still a moment then, reaching out, swept Phoebe up in his arms.

'Not in there, Bert,' the woman cautioned as he turned toward the house, its rear door still wide, 'we don't know what that bloke might 'ave taken out of there an' we don't want stickin' wi' the blame. We'll take 'er wi' us till 'er feels better. Might be somebody will be lookin' for 'er by then.'

'Try to drink some of that, ma wench, it'll do you good. You be in my 'ome.' Phoebe felt the cup held against her mouth.

'Tilly,' she cried, turning her face away, 'Tilly . . . it was Liza, oh God, it was Liza!'

'I ain't Tilly.' The woman placed the cup on top of a low cupboard built against a wall. 'An' it weren't no Liza as was 'avin' a go at you, it was a man.'

'Tilly . . . ?' Phoebe opened her eyes, looking for the first time at the woman who had helped her.

'No, ma wench, like I told you, I ain't Tilly an' it was no Liza sprawled across you, it were a man.' The woman smiled, her face kind beneath its bonnet. 'But you be all right, 'e's gone, an' after what my Bert give 'im I don't think 'e'll be back – not unless 'e be glutton for punishment.' Taking the heavy cup from the cupboard top she held it out to Phoebe. 'Try drinkin' this. It's only tea, but then our means don't stretch to alcohol.'

'Thank you.' Phoebe took the thick cup, swallowing the hot sweet liquid.

'Theer you go, Mam.'

Phoebe looked up as a lad of around nine years old squeezed into the narrow room, placing a prettily painted tin jug on the cupboard top.

'The water you wanted.'

'Eh!' The woman glanced at Phoebe. 'I 'ope as you don't

mind but I sent the lad for water from your yard. That was what brought Bert to your place earlier. 'E was supposed to be comin' to ask if we could 'ave a jug of water, this in canal be none too clean for drinkin'.'

Phoebe handed the cup back, her tea finished. 'What happened?'

'Me dad kicked the shit outa some bloke as was attackin' you,' the boy answered, eyes gleaming.

'An' you will get it belted out of you when I tells 'im what you've just said!' The woman aimed a swift blow to the side of the lad's head. 'What've I told you about that sort of language? You might live on a barge but you ain't no canal rat an' I ain't 'avin' you talk like one.'

'Sorry, Mam, sorry Miss.' The lad smiled, his face proud beneath a shock of brown hair. 'But me dad still kicked the s . . . stuffin' outa that bloke. Says 'e won't be maulin' no women for many a day.'

'Out!' The woman aimed a hand at the boy who ducked expertly. 'Get out and help yer father. Eeh!' She turned to Phoebe, 'Kids today. Their mouth be grown up afore their backsides be free of the napkin.'

'Was it your husband who . . . who pulled him off me?'

'Ar.' The woman nodded. ''E could tell from your screamin' that what that one was about 'ad none of your consentin' so 'e dragged 'im off you and give 'im a punchin' 'e won't forget in a 'urry.'

'Where is he now?'

'Who? The one as 'ad you pinned beneath 'is tackle?' The woman made a noise of contempt in her throat. 'Bert will 'ave chucked 'im where it'll go rusty if 'e don't get 'isself out, an' sharpish. 'E'll be in the cut, an' if 'e drowns I 'ope there's none to mourn 'im.' She poured more tea from a tall pot, pink roses and green leaves bright against its black enamelled body. 'I thought we should bring you 'ere to the barge, I didn't want nobody thinkin' we was in any place we shouldn't be, 'sides . . .' she placed the heavy platter cup on the cupboard top near to Phoebe '. . . if anythin' be missin' from your place, could be folk might think we took it.'

'He . . . he didn't take anything.' Phoebe picked up the cup, glad of something to do with her hands. 'He came for money, had the idea I had some hidden at the mill, and it was his intention to rob me of it.'

'An' did 'e?'

'No.' Phoebe shook her head. 'I didn't have any money at all, much less the amount he expected me to have.'

'You don't 'ave to say any more if you don't feel you want to,' the woman sipped her own tea, 'though usually it feels better to get it out like.'

'I was upstairs.' Phoebe stared into the tea. 'I heard him downstairs and thought it was Edward or Sophie. When I went to see he grabbed me and threatened to burn my face with a poker if I didn't give him the money.'

'But you 'adn't got any?'

'No.' Phoebe went on staring into her cup as if the events of the past few hours were being played out in its depths. 'But he wouldn't believe me. I thought if I could get him across to the mill I might be able to run away while he was searching it so I told him I had hidden the money in the old corn loft, but he forced me up there with him.'

'But you was outside when Bert come across you.'

'He kicked the ladder away,' Phoebe ignored the interruption, 'so I jumped. He didn't come straight down. I slipped out and made a run for the house.'

'An' that's when 'e catched you?'

'Yes.' It was little more than a whisper. 'I told him then that the money he thought I already had was to be brought to the mill that afternoon. I said if he would leave right away I would hand it all over to him when he returned.'

'An' 'e said 'e would 'ave the money an' a bit more besides,' the woman finished for her. 'The dirty swine! 'E deserves all my Bert give 'im an' more. The rope is too good for the likes of that one, but it ain't always the ones that am guilty as pays the price.'

'I find you guilty of wilful theft . . . you will serve a term of fifteen years . . .'

The Magistrate's words rang in Phoebe's ears. The woman was right: it was not always the guilty who paid the price.

Maudie Tranter let herself in at the rear entrance of Brunswick House and stood for a while in the kitchen, her ear registering the silence. The mistress wasn't back yet. Removing her cloak, she hung it in a cupboard in the scullery, sitting her bonnet on a shelf above.

She had timed her visit well as always, arriving back before Annie returned. Running her hands over her tight-drawn hair, she returned to the kitchen, a bitter smile touching the corners of her mouth as she replaced the wicker basket in its place beside the large pine dresser. Annie Pardoe had cut the wages of the miners to the bone; it was only fitting that some of the contents of her larder had gone to one of them.

Going out of the kitchen she crossed the hall, the slow tick of a longcase clock measuring her steps as she climbed the stairs. Halting outside Samuel's bedroom she listened for movement but, hearing nothing, moved along the corridor to the room used as a studio. Tapping the door out of respect for the man whose ears had been sealed in the womb, she went in. Samuel was not there. Maudie breathed more easily. He was still sleeping, so neither of them would know she had been out of the house.

She was halfway down the staircase when Annie let herself in at the front door. 'Mister Samuel must still be sleeping. I have just been to see if he wanted anything but he is not in his studio.'

'Has he woken at all while I have been out?'

'No, Ma'am,' Maudie answered. 'There 'asn't been a sound out of 'im the whole afternoon.'

'Bring his tray in about five minutes,' Annie turned towards the staircase, 'we will be in the sitting room.'

In her room she removed her cloak and bonnet, hanging them in a large wardrobe, letting her fingers caress the lavender silk of the gown the cloak would conceal. Soon she would wear no more black, soon she would wear the colours her lost youth had never known, soon now . . . very soon she would share a bed as Abel had shared his. Her body would know the touches his had known. Soon now . . . soon.

Opening her bag she took out the pretty glass bottle, holding it to where the light from the window caught the faintly golden contents, then crossing to a chest of drawers she placed the bottle in the bottom one, covering it with a layer of silk petticoats carefully wrapped in blue tissue paper.

Pushing to her feet, she gasped, clutching at a point below her left breast as a pain ripped through her. Her breathing rapid, she stumbled to the bed and sat for several minutes before taking the bottle of tablets from the drawer of the side table. Pouring a little water from the carafe that always stood beside her bed, she swallowed a couple of small white tablets. Two minutes later she made her way to her brother's bedroom, the medicine she had collected from the chemist in her hand.

In the kitchen Maudie laid a tray with tea and thinly cut sandwiches of salmon and cucumber. Samuel had taken salmon and cucumber for tea almost daily for the fifteen years she had served as housekeeper; in fact, everything remained the same in Annie Pardoe's household – or at least it had until Harforth-Darby had arrived on the scene. She scalded the tea, setting the white china pot on the tray. She didn't trust Harforth-Darby with his smarmy ways, he was buttering Annie Pardoe up sure as shooting, and just as sure she was in for a disappointment. Maudie set milk and sugar on the tray. If Annie thought she was going to get that one to the altar then she was shouting into an empty gulley, lavender frock or no lavender frock!

Carrying the tray to the sitting room, she set it beside Annie, her eyes taking in the tired sunken features and thin frame of the man who sat opposite.

'You be on your last legs, Samuel Pardoe,' she murmured, closing the door on brother and sister, 'an' it's my idea there be them as is ready to kick 'em out from under you.'

Waiting until the door closed, Annie poured tea, handing one of the cups to Samuel.

'It is just as well I went to collect your medicine,' she signed. 'I swear that Isaac Jackson took near enough an hour to prepare it. Seems tradesmen don't care how long they keep you waiting these days. I tell you, dear, things are no longer the same.'

Samuel smiled wearily. 'Things have not been the same since Abel died.'

Annie watched the rapid flickering of his fingers. 'What do you mean, not been the same?' Her own fingers formed the question.

'Let us not try to delude each other. You have always seen to my welfare, Annie, and I thank you for that though it has not been in the best of ways. It was our parents' thinking that turned my home into a prison. You have merely carried on where they left off. Oh, I know I could physically have forced my way out of this or our former home but what good would that have done? So in that way things have not changed.

'No, Annie, things changed when we heard Abel's will, when we came to Brunswick House. Feelings between you and me have never been what our brother thought them to be. You have always been bitter, blamed Abel for putting you in the position of nursemaid to me, blamed him for your never having married and saw his leaving me his fortune as a means of repayment for what he did. I can't blame you for those feelings, Annie, but since Abel died the bitterness in you has grown. I can never give you back the years you have spent with me but there are some things I can do . . .'

Annie sat stock still, her eyes on Samuel's dancing fingers, a feeling of alarm, fear almost, beginning to rise in her throat.

'. . . you see, I too feel that Abel acted wrongly, that your life was yours to do with as you wished and not as his money dictated. I know I should have told you this twenty years ago but I never found the way. That was my mistake and I'm sorry for it. I also think it was wrong of him to leave everything to us, literally denying his own daughter what was rightfully hers. That was Abel's mistake but it is one I can do something about . . .'

Samuel saw the apprehension on his sister's face deepen into something more at his mention of Abel's daughter and he felt a sudden deep pity. Annie had fed on her bitterness for years. What would she do when she heard all he had to say?

'It is my intention to return Brunswick House to Phoebe,' the movement of his fingers continued, 'together with the mines and partnerships in the Monway steel works and everything else her father willed to me, except a sum of money large enough to keep you comfortably for your lifetime and maybe recompense you somewhat for the years you have spent with me. You do, of course, have the house at Bescot. Whether or not you choose to live in it will be your decision.'

Annie stared at her brother, her brain numbed by what he had told her.

'As for myself,' he went on, 'I don't think Abel or Phoebe would object to my buying a small house somewhere. And not to worry,' the same weary smile touched his lips but the old sadness remained in his eyes, 'you and my parents can rest easily – I am not about to break my bonds. The shame I brought to the family will die a secret.'

The sharp sting of pain below her breast broke the numbness encircling her and Annie stood up, her glance sweeping the now empty room. Samuel was going to give everything back to their niece. She pressed a hand to the pain, will-power forcing the nausea out of her throat. But it was not only Samuel's to give, it was *hers*; she had spent half a lifetime earning that money, earning the power it brought, and Samuel would not take it from her.

''Ave you finished with the tray, Ma'am?' Maudie entered the room, one look at her employer telling her that the suspicion she had held for some time had proved correct, Annie Pardoe had been given a nasty shock. She smiled over the tray as Annie swept out.

'Ar, you've 'ad a shock, Annie Pardoe,' she whispered, carrying the tray to the kitchen, 'a big 'un. But there be more to come yet . . . much more.'

'Excuse me, Sir, but might you be Lucy's 'usband?'

'Who are you?' Edward Dartmouth looked at the tall well-built man coming toward him across the mill yard.

'My name is Bertram . . . Bertram Ingles.'

The reply was polite but there was none of the deference men usually adopted when addressing Edward.

'Might I ask what you are doing here?'

Edward looked at the man standing inches above himself, shirt sleeves rolled halfway between wrist and elbow, trousers held up by a broad leather belt blackened with wear, brass-studded clogs on his feet.

'I've come for water.' He lifted the black enamelled bucket painted around with a band of brightly coloured flowers. 'An' I asks you agen, Sir, be you Lucy's 'usband?'

'I am not Lucy's husband.' Edward's gaze circled the outbuildings. 'How do you know of her?' The gaze came back to the man now almost barring his way. 'And where is Miss Pardoe?'

'If Miss Pardoe be the young woman as lives 'ere then 'er is on my barge.'

'Your barge?' Edward said sharply. 'And how does she come to be there?'

'You've no need to come out fightin'.' Bert saw the flame kindle in the younger man's eyes. ''Er be wi' my Lizzie. I come for to ask permission to draw drinkin' water from the pump there earlier on today an' I found a young woman wi' a bloke sprawled across 'er, 'is trousers round 'is ankles . . .'

'Phoebe!' Edward interrupted. 'Did he . . . ?'

'Rape 'er?' Bert shook his head. 'Though it weren't for the want of tryin', an' 'e would 'ave an' all 'ad I not come across 'im when I did.'

'This man,' Edward brought his riding crop across the palm of his left hand, anger drawing his mouth in to a tight line, 'where is he now?'

'Coolin' what's left of 'is ardour in the cut,' Bert said, a nod of his head indicating the canal, 'though I doubt there was much of that left after I'd finished lettin' daylight into 'is guts.'

'You didn't give him enough!' Edward's eyes glistened with rage. 'You should have killed the swine, and even *that* would have been too good for him.'

'I think I near enough did do for 'im.' Bert smiled grimly. 'Leastways 'e won't be botherin' no woman for a long time yet.'

'More likely never again if I can find him, and I will!' Edward slapped his palm with the crop. 'I'll find the man and finish what you started . . . in the meantime, take this for your trouble.'

Bert Ingles looked at the sovereigns Edward drew from his waistcoat pocket and his face hardened.

'Any trouble I took on young wench's behalf was a trouble I would tek for any woman,' he said angrily, 'an' if it were a trouble then it be one I don't need payment for. You put your money back in your pocket, lad, an' put this bit of advice wi' it: next time you offer payment to a barge man for preventin' a wench bein' raped, mek sure you steps away pretty sharpish or you be likely to find yourself in the cut wi' the light shinin' on *your* innards.'

Edward stared. What was it with these people? First Phoebe and now this man. Both had refused money though it was obvious neither had any: both had almost nothing to support them but both burned with the same fierce pride.

'My apologies, Mr Ingles.' He slipped the coins back into his pocket. 'I had no wish to offend.'

'None teken, lad.' Bert smiled. 'Now if you'll wait till this bucket be filled, I'll tek you to . . . what did you say wench was called?'

'Miss Pardoe,' Edward answered, a liking for the tall rough-mannered man already formed. 'Miss Phoebe Pardoe.'

Edward followed, stepping gingerly from the narrow towpath on to the moored barge, picking his way through an assortment of buckets and ropes clustered into the small space between the prow and the cabin, almost three-quarters of the barge housing a cargo of coal on top of which sat a young boy and an even younger girl, both watching his progress through solemn eyes.

'You pair stop on top,' Bert said to them as he led the way down four steep steps that gave on to the family's living quarters.

'Phoebe,' said Edward blinking against the gloom, 'are you all right?'

''Er's all right.' Lizzie glanced at her husband standing on the steps, the confined space not enough to hold them all. 'Though 'er's 'ad a bad fright.'

Head and shoulders stooped against the low roof, Edward squeezed down the cabin that seemed barely a yard wide. 'Let me take you home, Phoebe.'

'I don't think much of you doin' that,' Lizzie said firmly. 'That wench 'as 'ad a shakin' up an' the last thing 'er needs is to be left on 'er own, so lessen there be somebody wi' 'er in that place of 'er'n then I says 'er's best left 'ere.'

'I think perhaps that would be best.' Edward looked at the bargee's wife, a white poke bonnet still covering her head even though she was in what was her sitting room. 'It would not be proper if I stay alone with her and neither can she be left on her own whilst I fetch Lucy from the town.' He touched a hand to Phoebe's, resting in her lap.

'Don't fetch Lucy, Edward.' She looked up at him. 'I have

suffered no harm and don't want her worried. If it is all right with Mr and Mrs Ingles I would prefer to stay with them until Lucy and Mathew return. They are always home about seven.'

'That ain't no bother to me nor Bert.' Lizzie caught the nod from her husband.

'Thank you.' Edward squeezed Phoebe's fingers gently before turning towards the hatchway. 'You may have refused my money, Mr Ingles,' he said when they both stood once more on the towpath, 'but surely you will not refuse my thanks for your solicitousness.'

'I won't refuse.' Bert took the hand the younger man extended, shaking it warmly. 'An' though it don't be necessary, it be appreciated.'

'Surprised me, that 'as,' he said, half to himself, watching Edward stride away towards the mill, its redundant windmill standing sentinel on the low rise that hid the house from the canalside.

'What 'as, Dad?'

'That one,' Bert answered his son, eyes following the figure moving rapidly away. ''E don't come from no miner nor no foundryman neither, that one 'as a different breedin', yet I thought all moneyed folk was above thankin' the likes of we. But 'e ain't.'

'Dad,' the boy asked as his father stepped aboard the barge, 'what's titty us ness?'

'Eh?' Bert glanced sharply across the expanse of coal.

'Titty us ness,' the boy's eyes gleamed roguishly, 'that's what that bloke thanked you for ain't it?'

'They ears been flappin' agen?' Bert picked up a nut of coal, 'they need a set o' doors fastened to 'em.' He threw the coal laughing as his son rolled clear, 'Cheeky young bugger,' he muttered fondly.

Chapter Eleven

Phoebe looked up from the small dress she was sewing, waves of fear flooding through her at the sound from outside the house. Putting her work aside she tiptoed to the window that looked out towards the track leading to the town, breathing her relief when she saw the trap she knew to be Sophie's.

Running swiftly downstairs she opened the door, her smile of welcome fading when she saw her caller.

'Good afternoon, Miss Pardoe.' Sir William Dartmouth inclined his head with a slight, barely perceptible movement. 'I hope I am not inconveniencing you by calling?'

'No . . . not at all.' Phoebe could not entirely hide her surprise.

'Edward told me of the unfortunate incident that took place yesterday,' he said when she did not ask him into the house. 'I trust you were not injured . . . in any way?'

'No.' The tiny pause so significant in its meaning was not lost on Phoebe; he had been told not only of the assault upon herself but also the nature of that assault. 'I was not injured . . . in any way.'

'I am relieved to hear it,' he said, watching the colour rise to her cheeks. 'My wife and I were concerned to hear of what happened to you, as was Sophie. Both of them were anxious to call upon you but my wife is ill with influenza and Sophie is not happy to leave her mother at the moment. But given your permission they will call once Amelia is well again.'

'I shall be happy to see them.' Phoebe stepped aside,

clearing the doorway. 'Forgive me, Sir William, won't you come in?'

Stepping inside, he allowed her to take his gloves, and when she set them on a small mahogany stand, followed her to the tiny parlour.

'Will you take some tea?' Phoebe asked when he was seated. 'I am afraid I have nothing in the way of wine.'

Tea. William Dartmouth smiled inwardly. It was every Englishwoman's placebo. 'No, thank you,' he said. 'I will not detain you. I came only to assure myself and my womenfolk that you had taken no harm.'

'None, I assure you.'

'That is as well, for the fellow who attacked you will pay hard enough when he is caught, and he will be, you have my word on that.'

'I think he has probably paid enough already,' Phoebe said, 'judging by what I hear Bert Ingles did to him.'

'Ah, yes, Edward told me of him. A bit of a rough diamond if I'm not mistaken.'

'You're not!' Phoebe's eyes flashed green fire. 'But then, diamonds are valuable rough or cut, are they not? And the Ingleses will always be highly valued friends to me.'

He glanced around the small room with its tired, well-worn furniture. This child of Abel Pardoe's might have little in the way of worldly goods but courage and integrity she had in plenty.

'You are not here alone, Miss Pardoe?'

'Of course I am, this is my home, where else would I be?'

'But I understood a woman and her husband were here with you.'

'Lucy and Mathew,' Phoebe nodded, 'but they go into Wednesbury every day.'

'Leaving you in this place by yourself?'

'Sir William, I am not a child.'

'That much is obvious,' he replied tersely, 'and therefore

the greater the danger. This Lucy . . . she must stay home, you must not be alone here again.'

'Sir William,' Phoebe said coolly, 'Lucy is the mainstay of this house at the moment. Her earnings provide most of their living and all of mine. Mathew works hard but odd jobs pay little in Wednesbury, so you see it is impossible for Lucy to stay here all day. My explanation is more for Lucy's sake than for yours. I would not have you think she left me on my own from choice.

'There is one more thing I have to say and it is this: do not ever use the word "must" to me. I have earned the right to be my own mistress and no man or woman will ever dictate to me again.'

William Dartmouth glanced at the down-at-heel furniture. 'Accept the money I still offer and neither of you would need to work again.'

'Don't seek to still your conscience with money.' Anger made Phoebe's voice sharp. 'I asked for none and I shall take none.'

'That is your prerogative.' He smiled. 'As will be your answer to my next question, always supposing you choose to give one for of course I should not dream of saying you must.'

'You can ask.' Phoebe caught the hint of amusement behind his grey eyes and her own mouth relaxed into a smile.

'This Ingles fellow – he told Edward that when he came upon that man attacking you, you were screaming about someone called Liza, and a little later you thought you were talking to a Tilly. Neither is a suitable name for a man. Tell me, was anyone else involved? Did the one who assaulted you have an accomplice?'

Phoebe's smile faded. 'No,' she said, looking to her lap where her fingers had automatically twined together at the memory of Handsworth Women's Prison. 'At least, there was no one with him when he . . . when he came here.'

'So who are the women whose names you called?'

She didn't have to tell him, Phoebe thought, he had no claim upon her, no right to ask questions. She could tell him that and then ask him to leave.

'Liza Spittle was a prisoner in Handsworth,' she said, surprised by the decision she could not recall making. 'She . . . she had certain tendencies . . . she . . . she tried . . .'

'You mean, she tried to force herself on you much the same as a man?'

'Yes,' Phoebe said, not knowing why she wanted him to know what Liza had done and grateful when he spared her the strain of the telling. 'And Tilly helped me . . . twice. She warned Liza not to touch me in . . . in that way again, and when she did try a second time Tilly tripped her up and Liza hit her head against the wall. I think she was hurt quite badly . . . she . . . she may even have died, and if so the Governors might say it was murder and Tilly would hang. But it wasn't! Tilly couldn't . . .'

'Is Tilly an inmate of the prison also?'

Phoebe nodded. 'She always will be. She is serving a lifetime sentence for manslaughter. They . . . they said she killed her husband but . . .' She looked up, her eyes defiant behind their cloud of unhappiness. 'I don't think she did. Tilly is no murderess no matter what any judge may have said.'

He rose, collecting his gloves from the small stand where Phoebe had placed them and opening the door himself.

'You are a very stubborn young woman,' he said, smiling. 'You refuse my offer of compensation, then you tell me never to use the word "must" to you again, and now you say you do not believe the verdict of a court.'

'It would not be the first time a court had been wrong, would it, Sir William?'

Pulling on his gloves, William Dartmouth looked at the girl whom he knew would openly defy him on any matter she felt to be right. 'Yes,' he inclined his head in a gesture of farewell, 'a very stubborn young woman, but one I admire. Good afternoon, Miss Phoebe Pardoe.'

*   *   *

'Me mam says to ask can I fill this from your pump?'

Phoebe smiled at the lad, his grin cheeky, his toffeedrop eyes bright beneath tumbling brown hair.

'Of course,' she answered. 'And when you're done come into the kitchen. I've got a big fat scone that is just asking to be eaten.'

''As it got sultanas in it?'

'Yes, big ones . . . this size.' She made a circle with thumb and forefinger.

'Oooh, bostin'.' His eyes gleamed with anticipation. 'I like sultanas. Our Ruth don't, 'er picks 'em out when we 'ave cake. Me mam says 'er shouldn't, it's bad manners to pick, but I don't mind 'cos our Ruth, 'er gives 'em to me.'

'I might be able to find one without sultanas for Ruth.' Phoebe recognised the barge man's word for something good or pleasant.

'Eh, don't do that, Miss!' He grinned, putting down the large flower-painted jug then wiping his palms against the sides of his trousers. ''Er enjoys picking 'em out as much as 'er does the eatin' of the rest.'

'In that case, we will find her one with extra sultanas.'

'We am leavin' tomorrer,' he said, perched on a stool in the kitchen, pulling sultanas from a scone and squashing them between his teeth, savouring each one before swallowing it. 'We as to tek them coals to London.'

'London?' Phoebe watched him work his way around the edge of the scone, the plate she had offered it on forgotten on the table. 'That's a good way off.'

'Ar, it is,' he nodded, recovering a crumb from his knee and stuffing it in his mouth beside a sultana. 'You ever been there, Miss?'

'No, I haven't.'

'I don't know as you'd like it.' He surveyed her over the scone. 'It's quite a big place, an' dirty the parts I've seen of it, an' folks pushin' an' shovin' as if they don't 'ave a minute to live.'

'It can't be much dirtier than Wednesbury.'

'It is, Miss, you can tek it from me. Wednesbury is a picture compared to London. Oh, the buildin's 'ere am black wi' smoke an' soot but the streets, well, they ain't filled wi' everybody's rubbish like, am they? I mean, they don't drop their paper on the roads or throw the peelin's out the windows here, do they?'

'They don't do that in London, do they?'

One foot tapping a half-laced boot against the leg of the stool, he considered a partly concealed sultana. 'I don't know about the places the nobs live in,' he twisted the scone, considering the sultana from all angles, 'but the ones we dock in, the basins like, well, you finds all sorts o' stuff throwed down there. Me mam, 'er don't like London an' I don't think you would either.'

'In that case I shan't go.' Phoebe placed several scones in a dark blue paper bag that had once held sugar. 'But I do quite fancy the seaside.'

'Me an' all.' He gave way to temptation, pulling the sultana free. 'An' our Ruth. Me dad says we might pick up a load that 'as to go to a port one day . . . a port is like the seaside, ain't it, Miss?'

'Mmmm.' Phoebe twisted the top of the bag to make a fastening. 'I imagine so. A port has ships and ships sail on the sea, so a port must be the seaside.'

''Ave you been to the seaside?'

Settling the bag of scones on the table, Phoebe went into the scullery, fetching a jug of milk from a bowl half filled with water to keep it cool.

'Not since I was a very small girl.' She filled a glass with the frothy white milk, setting the linen cover back over the jug before returning it to the scullery.

'Didn't your parents 'ave the money to tek you more than once?'

'It wasn't the money,' Phoebe placed the glass of milk before him, 'my mother died while I was still quite young and my father was too busy with his business to take me to the seaside.'

'Never mind, Miss.' He looked across at her, his eyes round and brown as a well-used penny, a seriousness in them that outstripped his years. 'Like me mam says, we all 'ave our cross to bear, but when we get that load for a port you can come with we. Mam an' Dad won't mind.'

'Speaking of your mother, Mark Ingles, she is not going to be at all pleased if you keep her waiting much longer for that jug of water.'

'Bugger me! I'd forgot all about the water.' He jumped from the stool, shoving the desecrated scone into his mouth.

Phoebe followed him into the yard, handing him the bag of scones as he finished filling the jug.

'An' you'll forget me language, won't you, Miss?' He grinned up at her, crumbs edging his lips. 'Go on, Miss, be a pal, say you ain't 'eard me say what I said?'

'All right,' Phoebe laughed, 'I didn't hear you say what you said.'

'Ta, Miss.' He sauntered off across the yard, raising the bag of scones above his head. 'Tara for now.'

'Miss Phoebe,' Lucy said thoughtfully, 'whoever it was come 'ere to rob you, 'e knowed about you bein' up at the Priory, 'e even knowed as you seen all of the family together, so it seems to me 'e is either a footman or else somebody who works in the 'ouse told 'im about you bein' there.'

'I . . . I hadn't thought about it.' It was true she had not thought of how the man had known of her visit, or of the fact she had been in prison, but she had lived through the nightmare of his attack again and again through the long night, jangles of fear setting her nerves dancing at every sound, only the knowledge that Lucy and Mathew were staying in the house preventing her from screaming.

'Well, I 'ave.' Lucy went on talking as she tipped flour into a bowl. 'An' if I 'ave then Sir William is sure to 'ave an' all. 'E ain't no fool that one, 'e can put two an' two together an' come up with 'alf a dozen.'

'Do you think that was the real reason for his coming here today?'

'Don't know.' Lucy spooned a small amount of salt into the flour. ''E didn't ask any questions about 'ow anybody might know, did 'e? But that don't mean anythin'. 'E might not 'ave said as much but you can take it from me 'e 'ad thought of it.'

He might have thought about it but Phoebe wanted only to put the whole episode behind her. She wouldn't forget, she would never forget, but right now she wanted only to leave it, to talk of anything except that.

Phoebe reached for the tongs settling fresh coals on the fire, then rinsed her hands and set about greasing pie tins with a dab of lard on a scrap of cloth.

'He asked whether I had suffered any harm from being attacked.'

'What the 'ell did 'e think? It certainly ain't done you no good. Bloody soft question to ask!' Lucy exploded.

'He said Sophie and Lady Amelia were concerned and that they would call later.'

'Huh!' Reaching a small shallow basin from the dresser, Lucy pressed it into the pastry, making a series of circles. 'Why didn't they come with him?'

'Lady Amelia has the influenza.'

Taking the circles she had cut from the pastry, Lucy pressed them into the tins. 'It was their son's fault you was gaoled but even so their sort don't usually call on the likes o' we.'

'The likes of us are as good as any Dartmouths, Lucy,' Phoebe answered, pounding a pot of boiled potatoes with a wooden spoon. 'The only difference is they have money and we do not.'

'*You* could have.' Lucy scooped the remnants of the circles together, rolling them with quick deft movements, making a further mat of soft pastry. 'You was offered it an' I think you should take it. It's nothin' you don't deserve.'

Phoebe lifted the large pot of mutton from the fireplace where it had stewed gently from early morning. Draining the stock into a bowl, she added the meat to the mashed potato. 'Accepting money will not alter what happened. I prefer to earn my living.'

'Well, I think you'm daft.' Tasting the mixture of meat and potato, Lucy nodded and Phoebe began filling the pastry-lined tins.

Finishing the filling of a dozen pie tins, she draped a cloth over the unused mixture, setting the pan in the hearth. 'Lucy,' she asked, passing a smaller basin the other girl had pointed to, 'do you think my dresses would sell in the town?'

Lucy pressed the basin into the pastry, cutting out smaller circles. 'The bits an' pieces I've managed to make 'ave gone well enough an' they ain't near so good as your'n. Mind, I couldn't make much, what wi' the baking.'

Phoebe watched smaller circles of pastry being placed over each pie tin, Lucy fluting the edges between finger and thumb. 'But what you did make sold each time?'

'Ar.' Lucy nodded. 'Could 'ave sold more but like I says, it's 'avin' the time to sew.'

Dipping two fingers into an egg she had beaten, Phoebe traced the lid of each pie. 'What about your pies and my dresses?'

'What you mean, Miss?' Lucy was already busy with the next batch of pastry.

'Put them together.'

'Eh?' Lucy paused.

'Well, not together as such.' Phoebe began to load the oven with pies. 'What I meant was, if you bake and I sew we could pool the money we make.'

'No, Miss Phoebe,' Lucy began, cutting out larger circles, 'your little frocks is worth much more than mutton pies.'

Closing the oven, Phoebe straightened. 'Your mutton pies have fed me since I came home, Lucy.'

'Oh, ar!' Looking up she ran her eyes over the girl she had once worked for. 'Well, they ain't made you much fatter. Anyway you give Mathew an' me a place to stay . . . well, you did in a manner o' speakin' 'cept you wasn't 'ere to speak to, an' then when you come out you didn't make we go. Way I sees things, a mutton pie an' the odd scone don't count for much against that.'

'It counts for a great deal with me,' Phoebe said, oiling more pie tins with a knob of lard, 'so we are equal, neither of us owes the other anything.' Lifting the pan from the hearth, she spooned the remainder of the filling into the pastry-lined tins then carried the empty pot into the scullery to be washed later.

'Do you really think my clothes would sell?' She asked again, uncertainty edging her question. 'Money is not all that plentiful in Wednesbury, is it?'

'Not in all quarters it ain't.' Lucy finished fluting the edge of the last pie. 'But then everybody don't work for Annie Pardoe. Some o' the men 'er finished at the pits as got taken on at Hampstead mine. Seem to be doin' all right an' all judgin' by the number of pies them women o' their'n buy.'

'But everyone has to have food,' Phoebe said, moistening pastry lids with beaten egg.

'Ar, an' they 'ave to wear clothes an' all or they gets a slow walk to Wednesbury police station wi' a bobby on each arm.' Lucy stretched her aching back. 'Tell you what . . . why don't I take them little frocks you made for Lady Dartmouth an' see if they sell?'

'I had thought of trying, I was getting them out of the trunk when . . .' Despite the heat of the kitchen Phoebe's face paled. The fear of what had happened was still vivid. It haunted her nights and filled her days but she knew if she admitted as much her friend would stay home and that would mean very little money coming in, and Mathew and Lucy had things hard enough. Going to the oven, she took out the cooked pies, hoping the action would cover her hesitation, masking what she could not say.

Lucy rattled the cooking utensils, gathering them for washing. If that bastard hasn't drowned in the cut then I hope he's dropped down a mine shaft! she thought. Either way may he rot in hell for attacking a woman. 'I will just get this lot shifted an' we'll 'ave us a cup of tea,' she said, rubbing her hands in the bowl of warm water on the hob. 'Put the kettle back over the fire, Miss.'

Phoebe swung the iron bracket, bringing the kettle to rest over the hot coals, then picking up the basin of water, followed to where Lucy had carried bowls and dishes to the scullery.

'I'll empty this in the yard,' she said, going to the scullery door. 'Will I give Mathew a shout?'

'If you will, Miss.' Lucy set the dishes against the large brownstone sink. ''E'll be just about gaspin' for a cup of tea.'

'Lucy . . .' The three of them were sitting in the kitchen of the mill house, cosy with the glow of the fire and the smell of fresh-baked pies and scones. 'What did you mean when you said not everyone in Wednesbury works for Annie Pardoe?'

'What do you mean, what do I mean?' Lucy asked in the tongue-twisting Black Country style.

'It seemed strange your using my aunt's name. She can't have anything to do with the business, that is solely Uncle Samuel's responsibility.'

'P'raps yer father thought it would be,' Mathew looked up from the fire, 'but Annie soon put the mockers on that. It's 'er as 'as all the say in what is or what isn't to be done, an' who is to be finished an' who ain't.'

'Aunt Annie might say things,' Phoebe nursed her cup between her hands, 'but she can't do more than that, she cannot sign her name to anything. Only Uncle Samuel can do that.'

'Seems like 'er can,' Mathew replied. 'I called in me mam's afore I come 'ome an' 'er said Maudie Tranter 'ad visited earlier. Maudie told 'er that Annie be gettin' a gentleman visitor . . . quite reglar it seems . . . an' Maudie 'eard 'er tellin' 'im Samuel 'ad given 'er some sort of power . . . power of a turn summat or other, me mam couldn't rightly say, but whatever it be it means Annie Pardoe can sign any business paper in place o' her brother.'

'Power of Attorney,' Phoebe said, suddenly understanding the sacking of men and the reduction in wages. 'My aunt has Uncle Samuel's Power of Attorney.'

'What does that mean, Miss?' Lucy asked.

Phoebe let her head sink tiredly against the back of her chair. 'It means my aunt has control of everything my father left to Samuel.'

'An' that means 'alf of Wednesbury,' Mathew said. ''E might just as well 'ave left it to the Devil.'

A loud knock on the scullery door jangled Phoebe's frayed nerves and the jerk of her hands set the tea dancing madly in her cup.

'You be all right, Miss,' Mathew said calmly. 'Just stop you theer, I'll see who that be.'

'I would like a word wi' Miss Pardoe, would you ask 'er if 'er will see me?'

Phoebe breathed out long and slow, feeling the tension loosen from her stomach as she recognised the voice of Bert Ingles.

'Come in, Mr Ingles,' she said, going to the scullery. 'I hope you don't mind the kitchen? It's a bit cramped but it's warmer than the sitting room.'

'I'm used wi' being cramped, there's not much living space on a barge.' Bert Ingles nodded to Lucy and Mathew as Phoebe introduced them.

'What can I do for you?' Phoebe smiled.

'I come to bring you these.' He fished in the pocket of a jacket that should have had a decent burial long ago, pulling out two brass locks. 'Me an' Lizzie got to talkin' after we brought you back 'ere yesterday evenin' . . . well, like we said, you can bolt these doors from the inside but we couldn't see 'ow you would fasten 'em on the outside, not so as nobody could get in like, an' Lizzie said there was bound to come times when you 'ad to leave the place, so we thought if you put these on the doors you would at least be certain nobody had got in while you was away. You would 'ave no more nasty surprises waitin' for you, if you follow what I mean.'

'That is very kind of you, Mr Ingles, I am most grateful to you and to your wife. It will be a great relief to me knowing the doors of the house are securely fastened.'

'They will be with these.' He looked proudly at the locks he held, one in each hand. 'Nobody will get them open wi'out the keys. These am no ordinary locks, I made these meself.'

'You made 'em?' Mathew took one of the locks, turning it over in his hands. ''Ow could you do that on a barge?'

'I didn't make them on the barge.'

'Oh,' Mathew looked up, 'then where?'

Shaking his head at Phoebe's offer of a chair, Bert Ingles went on, a strong hint of pride lacing his explanation: 'Them locks be my own design. You can't buy them in no ironmonger's. I made them just before me father died. You see, Miss. . .' he looked at Phoebe '. . . me father was a lockmaker out at Willenhall, an' 'e taught me the locksmithing.'

'But the barge,' Phoebe said, 'I thought you worked the barge?'

'So I do, Miss,' he answered, 'but I ain't always done that. I worked wi' me father up to three years ago. It wasn't until 'e died though that I found 'e had run at such a loss I couldn't pay the brass founders an' everybody else that claimed 'e owed them wi'out selling up.' He shrugged. 'So that is what I did. There were nothing for it after that but to get a job, any job that would feed the wife and kids. That's how I come to be working the canal.'

'What be so different about this?' Mathew turned the lock he was holding, sending darts of gold flickering from the polished brass.

'I'll show you.' Fishing a key from his jacket, Bert took the lock, inserted the key in it. 'See?' He turned the key, the action shooting out a metal bar.

'Ar, it's locked,' Mathew said, a quizzical frown pulling his brows together. 'I don't see nothin' different in that.'

'But it's not locked, not altogether.' Bert Ingles smiled. 'You see, this is a doubler.'

'A whater?' Lucy asked.

'A doubler, Missis.' Bert passed her the lock. 'Least that's what I call it. You see, it's a double barrel lock.' He took the lock back, turning the key a second time, and another bar shot out. 'Now,' he handed the lock to Mathew, 'try openin' it.'

Mathew tried turning the key but it wouldn't budge. He tried again then looked at the man watching him. 'It's stuck,' he said. 'The key must be jammed or summat.'

'It's not the key nor the lock that be jammed.' Bert retrieved the lock. 'That's what you are meant to think. You see, anybody not knowing how it works would think the same, and thinking they had got the key stuck would leave off trying to get in.'

'Well, if a burglar couldn't get in, all supposin' 'e managed to get 'old of the key, 'ow do you expect we to do it?'

'Like this.' Bert laid the lock on the table so they could each follow what he did. 'You turned the key anti-clockwise to operate the bolt,' he said, glancing at Mathew, 'that would be the normal way to operate a lock, but I reversed the mechanism. On this the key has to be turned clockwise to lock it.'

'Clever.' Mathew pursed his lips admiringly. 'But what about the doubler bit?'

'This is where the key does get stuck,' Bert answered, 'least you would think it had 'cos you won't pull it out at this stage. You 'ave to turn the key once more, that releases a second bolt an' also the key; it's a double safeguard. Even if a burglar cottoned on to the fact the key had to be turned back way round from usual, its getting stuck would cause him a bit of a headache.'

'An' pickin' the lock an' then findin' it still didn't open, 'e would likely pack in tryin' altogether?' Mathew grinned. 'That's what I calls useful.'

'It is a very good way of locking doors,' Phoebe said. 'They will save me a deal of concern whenever I have to go anywhere. How much do I owe you, Mr Ingles?'

'You don't owe me anything.' He laid three more keys beside the locks on the table. 'Me and Lizzie be just glad we could be of help.'

'But I couldn't . . .'

'Ar you could,' Bert Ingles looked suddenly embarrassed, 'just show me where you keep your screwdrivers and such and I'll have them locks on the doors in no time.'

'I'll give you a hand.' Mathew picked up the locks. 'Tools am in the barn.'

'Eh! What do you reckon to that?' Lucy asked as the two men left the kitchen.

'I reckon you are going to have to pay for those locks, Mrs Leach.'

'Me!' Lucy gasped. 'I ain't got but ninepence in me purse.'

'Bert Ingles won't take money,' Phoebe handed her a clean cloth from the airer strung across the fireplace, 'but I don't think he would refuse four of your mutton pies.'

Chapter Twelve

'I said to sell them . . . both of them.'

Annie Pardoe sat in James Siveter's office in his chambers in Lower High Street, her voluminous black skirts entirely hiding the small chair beneath her.

'You will have no trouble, I have been asked to sell them on several occasions.'

'Miss Pardoe,' the solicitor cleared his throat, 'does your brother know of this intended sale?'

Annie's eyes narrowed and her mouth tightened. 'If you want to continue to be our solicitor, James Siveter, I advise you to do as I instruct. My brother gave me his full Power of Attorney and that means I can act as I see fit, and I see fit to sell the Hobs Hill coal mine and the Crown. It also means I can replace you in your capacity as Samuel's solicitor. Your sort are two a penny.'

James Siveter rolled his long-handled pen between his fingers, experiencing a strong desire to tell the woman sitting opposite his heavy desk to take her business with her to the nearest canal and jump in with it! But it was a desire he curbed; she was right when she said she could replace him, and while not exactly two a penny solicitors were not hard to come by. He could not afford to lose business, however wrong he felt it to be.

'I will bring the necessary papers to Brunswick House first thing tomorrow.'

'No!' Annie's tight mouth showed no sign of slackening. 'You will not come to Brunswick House. I will sign an agreement of sale while I am here. You can get the purchaser's signature today – we have already agreed the price. I shall call here again tomorrow at three and I expect the business to be concluded.'

Why the rush? James Siveter thought, filling out the necessary documents. And why was Annie Pardoe here instead of sending for him to come to Brunswick House as he had always done? Power of Attorney or not, she obviously didn't intend Samuel knowing of today's doings.

'I will get this to the purchaser as soon as . . .'

'You will take it to him now!' Annie snapped. 'I want this finished and done. Three o'clock tomorrow.'

Holding the door for her to pass, the solicitor watched as she swept into the street. So she was selling both coal mines, and quickly . . . too quickly even for Annie Pardoe. Yes, it was a safe bet Samuel knew nothing of it, just as he likely knew nothing of what she had sold already: the shares in the Monway steel foundry, the Moxley iron works, together with a string of smaller businesses and houses. And what was she doing with the money she'd had for them? He had drawn up no new contracts. Whatever she had done, he, James Siveter, had not been consulted. Closing the door, he returned to his desk. 'I wonder?' he mused, taking up the papers Annie had signed and putting them into a small valise. 'I wonder, Samuel, do you have any idea just how close you are to having nothing?'

Leaving the solicitor's office Annie had turned her trap left along the bottom end of Lower High Street, guiding the horse left again into Finchpath Lane. This way she could avoid the wheels of the trap becoming caught in the tramlines. There was also less likelihood of her being seen by going back to the house via the heath. She flicked the reins, urging the horse into a trot. What the folk of Wednesbury didn't see they couldn't talk about, and she wanted no talk of what she had been about today.

Samuel had spoken of reverting his legacy to Phoebe, of

giving back what his sister's sacrifices had earned. How easily, she thought bitterly, how *easily* her brothers disposed of her life, ordering hers to the comfort of their own. Abel had enjoyed that comfort, enjoyed the pleasures of his pretty wife, and now Samuel wanted the comfort of a conscience cleared of taking Phoebe's inheritance and his sister was to have no part in that decision. But she would not let it happen again; she had been given a second chance at living, a chance to have all Abel had had in every sense of the word, and this time she would not let it go. Tomorrow she would have the money from the sale of the mines and the next day she would give it to Clinton.

She clicked her tongue, encouraging the horse, seeing the figure of Clinton Harforth-Darby in her mind. In his mid-forties, he was a handsome man, tall, always well dressed, his dark hair just hinting at grey, with clear intense eyes and a manner only real breeding bestowed. Calling to see Violet Wheeler at Oakeswell Hall she had first been introduced to Gaskell's cousin, and the next afternoon he had come to Brunswick House.

The reins forgotten in her hands, she let her mind play over the events of the past weeks, events that had led her to the threshold of a new life. With the death of his wife a year ago Clinton had sold his sugar plantation in the West Indies to return to England. Interested in the manufacture of the new metal tubes, he had come to Wednesbury to discuss with Gaskell the possibility of starting up a business. That was when he and Annie had met. From that moment she had, for the first time in twenty years, been treated like a woman and not a servile catspaw. Clinton was not like her father had been, nor Abel, treating women as though they didn't have the capacity to understand anything beyond the kitchen. He had talked to her about going into the manufacture of tubes, how he saw the business expanding over the years; he had told her how Gaskell had wanted to be a partner in the venture but Clinton had refused him. He had more than enough money to finance any business, he said. He did not want a partner, what he wanted was *her*.

Annie's heart gave the same crazy bounce it had when Clinton had said those words two weeks ago. He wanted to marry her, to make her his wife. She, Annie Pardoe, would become Mrs Clinton Harforth-Darby, *she* would marry into the Wheeler family not Phoebe, and she would take the Pardoe money with her. Clinton had brushed it aside when she had told him that Samuel owned everything. It was of no consequence, he had said, he wanted her for his wife not the paltry amount her brother might have bequeathed. However, if it interested her, she could go on being the legal representative for Samuel. It was then he had given her the ring, placing it on the third finger of her left hand, a square-cut amethyst the size of her thumbnail.

It was kept in a drawer in her bedroom. Annie thought now of the lovely ring hidden beneath layers of petticoats, the same petticoats that covered the perfume bottle that had been Elias Webb's gift to her. Clinton would announce their engagement at the Wheelers' house during the party they were giving before their son's regiment left for India. Until then she would not wear it, and by then everything that had once been Abel's would be hers.

They had often talked of the new premises he would build for the making of metal tubes during Clinton's visits, her interest seeming to fire his own as she suggested sites in or near the town, pointing out their nearness to the canal that would be needed to transport the tubes. That was when Clinton had said she would have made an ideal partner for his business except she was to be his wife, refusing to entertain the idea she could be both; it had taken her some time to get him to agree, Clinton eventually suggesting she become a steel tube manufacturer in her own right; the premises, the machinery, the raw steel, everything in her name. Only that way would he be happy.

And now the coal mines, the mainstay of all that had

once constituted Abel's wealth and then Samuel's were gone. Tomorrow she would have the money that would start her in her own business and the beginning of a new life.

'I was pleased to hear Sophie's news.' Phoebe glanced at Edward walking beside her. 'She was so excited when she called on Thursday.'

'Her coming engagement to Montrose Wheeler, you mean?' He stopped, picking up a stone and skimming it into the canal. 'I wish I could feel as happy for her.'

'But you don't?' Phoebe knew she was stating the obvious.

'No.' He sent a second stone winging after the first. 'The Wheelers are simply intent on making a good match, just as they were with . . .' He stopped awkwardly. 'I . . . I beg your pardon, Phoebe.'

'Just as they were with Abel Pardoe's daughter?' She smiled. 'You don't need to apologise for telling the truth, Edward.'

'You knew!' He turned to her, surprise lifting his fair eyebrows. 'You knew they wanted you for your father's money rather than for . . . for . . .'

'For myself?' She gazed at the circles spreading on the surface where the stones had struck the water. 'No, not at the time. I only realised that when his mother told me she had written to tell him of my Uncle Samuel's inheriting everything that was my father's, and he did nothing . . . he never even wrote to me to tell me he no longer wished to marry me.'

'He left that to his mother also?'

She nodded. 'It was a shock then but at least I have been saved from a marriage that could have brought me no real love, and I am grateful for that.'

'But what will save Sophie?' He kicked a boot savagely into the spongy earth. 'Her dowry will not be signed away to an uncle, she will be handed over like so much coal or wheat, she and all she has will become the property of Montrose Wheeler – and it will be God help her after that.'

'Does your mother know how you feel about Sophie's marrying Montrose?'

'My mother thinks that it is a good match. I truly believe she is of the opinion that love grows only after marriage.'

'And Sophie . . .' Phoebe watched the circles spread into nothing. 'Have you said anything of your feelings to her?'

'No, how could I when she is so happy? I can't tell her, Phoebe, I can't be the one to hurt her.'

Far better the bubble be burst now, Phoebe thought, than let it carry her to the moon only to break there.

'What of your father?' she asked. 'Have you confided in him?'

Edward plucked a blade of grass, twisting it between his fingers. 'I have said nothing to him but I think he knows I feel such a marriage would be wrong, and that like myself he would rather Sophie widened her social circle, met other young men before making her choice. But like myself Father could never bring himself to hurt her.'

'So Sophie will marry regardless of how you and Sir William feel?'

'Maybe not.' He rolled the blade of grass between his fingers then flicked it out over the water. 'My father has no wish to see Sophie hurt and that is why he has set the date for her betrothal to Wheeler to take place when we return from Europe, which puts it several months into next year. At least that way he is giving her a little time to find out if her emotion is love or not. And who knows? She may meet someone she would rather marry than Gaskell Wheeler's son . . . anyway that is what I hope, and I think it is my father's hope too.'

And mine, thought Phoebe, no trace of jealousy colouring it. No girl should marry a man only to discover his passion was for her money. She had been saved from that. Pray God Sophie would be too.

Returning the wave of a small girl on a passing barge, Phoebe turned from the peaceful lure of the water. Sophie's visits once a fortnight were not so disruptive to her work but Edward had begun to call at Wiggins Mill weekly and sometimes more than that. She had to find a way of telling him she could not spend a couple of afternoons a week out walking with him. 'I really must return, Edward,' she began. 'I ought not to be here, it's not fair on Lucy and Mathew.'

'How do you mean, not fair?'

'Surely you must see it is not right for me to be out walking when both of them are at work? I should be working too. I have a living to make as they do.'

'There's no need for any of this,' he waved a hand in the direction of the mill, 'you should not have to work for your living.'

'Then how would I manage?' Phoebe's laugh held more irony than humour. 'People need money to live, Edward, and it does not grow on trees.'

'You would not need money,' he caught her hand, his blue eyes intense, 'not if you became my wife. I love you, Phoebe. I have since that moment I helped you into the carriage the day you came to the Priory to collect those dresses. Marry me . . . say you will be my wife?'

What would that hold for both of them? Phoebe looked into his face, so like his mother's, and knew the answer. Sir William Dartmouth's son and heir married to a woman who had been in prison . . . what gossip that would provide! What houses would receive them merely to see his gaolbird wife, only to ignore them politely from then on. She knew Edward would argue his love was strong enough to withstand the attitudes of others, but would it be? Yes, he loved her now, she had seen it in his eyes each time they met, but was it real or just the misguided infatuation of a young man attempting to right a wrong he had caused, and would a year from now see him regretting such a marriage?

Gently she released her hands. She could not take that risk. She had too much respect for his parents, Edward carried too old a family line, too ancient a name, to have anything threaten it. And marriage to her, a woman accused and convicted of theft, however wrongly, would do him no good in the eyes of society.

'I won't marry you, Edward,' she said softly. 'I will not marry anyone yet.' She smiled up at him. 'Perhaps in a year or so, providing you feel as you do now, you will ask me again.' She turned away, the cloud of disappointment on his face hurting her too. Trying hard to sound matter-of-fact, hoping that way to lighten any embarrassment her refusal of his offer might have caused him, she went on, 'In the meantime, whether we like it or not, I have work to do.'

'Phoebe,' he said as she would have walked on, 'is there anyone else?'

'No, Edward,' she replied, the truth of it shining from her eyes, 'there is no one else.'

'Eeh, what a to do in the town today!' Lucy dropped into a chair as Phoebe dished up the evening meal she had prepared. 'You know Charles West, the jeweller in the High Street . . . well, 'e was robbed the night afore.'

'Robbed!' Phoebe stopped filling Mathew's bowl with the soup she had simmered all day. 'Who did it?'

'Nobody knows,' Mathew answered. 'It 'appened durin' the night by what I 'eard.'

'Heavens!' Phoebe finished filling his bowl then ladled soup into her own. 'Was anyone hurt?'

Mathew took a chunk of crusty bread, dipping it into his soup. 'No,' he said between bites, 'nobody 'eard anythin', not a sound. Charlie West never knowed it 'ad 'appened till he went for 'is cash this mornin'.'

'But the money from the shop,' Phoebe looked up from her meal, 'surely he doesn't leave the takings in the shop overnight?'

'No, 'e don't,' Mathew helped himself to more bread, 'an' 'e don't put it in no bank neither. Seems whoever broke into 'is 'ouse last night knowed that, 'cos money was all was took.'

'Were the police called?' Phoebe asked.

Lucy nodded but it was Mathew answered. 'Ar, they was called but them bobbies don't seem to know whether they be comin' or whether they've been. It seems Charlie West wasn't the only one to get 'is pocket lightened last night. Hollingsworth the pork butcher, 'e was 'ad, an' so was Samuel Platt the iron founder up on King's Hill.'

'All on the same night? No wonder the police were at their wit's end. I don't remember anything like this ever happening in Wednesbury before.'

'I don't either.' Lucy spooned her soup. 'Me mam says nothin' like it 'as ever 'appened, least not as long as 'er's been alive.'

'Which is from the time of Adam, ain't it?'

'Watch it, Mathew Leach!' Lucy waved her spoon at her husband. 'You ain't so big 'er can't tan your arse.'

'Now *that* we would have to watch.' Phoebe joined in their laughter.

'Do you think it could be somebody local? The burglar, I means,' Lucy said finishing her soup.

'Won't know that till 'e be found.' Mathew cut a wedge of cheese from the block Phoebe placed on the table. 'An' Lord only knows if that'll ever 'appen. 'E could be miles away by now.'

Her sweet tooth preferring a sultana scone instead of cheese, Lucy spread it with the dark red damson jam Mathew's mother had sent from last summer's bottling. ''E could be,' she agreed, sinking her teeth into the scone, 'or 'e be down a disused mine shaft like that murderer we 'ad some years back. You know, 'e killed that woman Mary . . . Mary summat or other.'

'Mary Carter?' Mathew placed his cheese between two slices of bread, pressing the whole together with the heel of his hand. 'Bad business was that by what I've 'eard me mam an' dad say.'

'Any murder is a bad business.' Lucy popped the last of her scone into her mouth.

'Ar, that's right an' it ain't wrong, but that particular murder ended more'n one life, so it seemed, an' there was folks in Wednesbury was party to it 'appenin'. Me dad reckons there was no nicer bloke you would wish to meet than Joseph Bradly.'

'My father never spoke of a murder taking place in Wednesbury,' Phoebe said. 'At least, I never heard him speak of one. What happened?'

'Sit you down, Miss.' Lucy bustled up from the table. 'I'll get the teapot.'

Taking his cue, Mathew stayed silent but as the tea was poured Phoebe asked again.

'You don't want to be 'earin' about no murder, Miss Phoebe.' Lucy set the teapot firmly on the table. 'Anyway it all 'appened long ago.'

'Then my knowing can't hurt anyone,' Phoebe replied gently, realising Lucy wanted to protect her from anything she might find painful. 'Really, Mathew, I would like to know. There seems to be such a lot to this town I never knew of before.'

'If yer sure . . .' Mathew glanced at Lucy who lifted her shoulders resignedly. 'Joseph Bradly lived up along Church Hill, right against the old church. 'Is wife 'ad died while their daughter Anna was no more'n a babby an' Mary Carter used to go up to the 'ouse every day to do for 'em like. Well, 'er went missin' an' when 'er was found drownded in Millfields Pool folk said as 'ow Jos Bradly was one who done it; seems they kept on sayin' it till the poor bugger 'ad more'n 'e could stand.'

'What did he do?'

Mathew looked across the table at Phoebe then away to his mug of tea, his tongue stilled by sudden embarrassment.

'What did Joseph Bradly do, Mathew?'

''E . . . 'e got pie-eyed,' Mathew stared resolutely into the mug, 'too drunk to know what the 'ell 'e was about, then 'e . . . 'e went 'ome an' raped 'is own daughter.' The last came out in a rush. If he didn't say it quickly, he wouldn't say it at all.

'What a dreadful thing to happen!' Phoebe breathed.

'Ar,' Mathew nodded, ''er couldn't 'ave been more'n sixteen or seventeen accordin' to what was said. Left Wednesbury 'er did, left a babby . . . a lad, Aaron 'e was called . . . don't know what 'appened to 'er after that.'

'And her father, did he stay in Wednesbury?' Phoebe stirred milk into her own tea.

'Me mam said 'e couldn't do no other, not wi' a babby.'

''E could've put it into the workhouse,' Lucy joined the conversation.

'Me mam said that an' all.' Mathew leaned back, his meal finished. 'But me dad said 'e was too fine a bloke to leave a babby in the workhouse, no matter 'ow it was got.'

'Was anything ever proved?'

'Seems years after a bloke was brought up from a shaft 'e 'ad dropped into, and 'e said it was 'im killed Mary Carter.'

'So Joseph Bradly was cleared of suspicion of murder?'

'Cleared of suspicion by law but not by folk of Wednesbury,' Lucy said, collecting dishes into a pile. 'They 'ad got their claws into 'im an' wouldn't let go. Me mam said the same old tales kept flyin' around.'

'Did his daughter return?' Phoebe helped with clearing the table.

Lucy glanced at Mathew. 'Ar, 'er returned,' he said. 'At least Mam says 'er did, but only after 'er father 'ung 'isself.'

'Oh, how awful!' Phoebe looked from one to the other. 'What an awful thing to happen to a family.'

'Ar.' Mathew rose from the table, preparing to go to the workshop he had fashioned from one of the smaller outbuildings. 'First murder an' now these burglaries, there be some right crackpotical things goes on in Wednesbury.'

Burglaries! Phoebe helped carry the dishes to the scullery for washing. She had almost forgotten them. Thank God for the locks Bert Ingles had given her!

*   *   *

165

Samuel was sleeping. Annie had given him the draught Alfred Dingley had prescribed against wakeful nights, doubling the dose he had recommended. She wanted no interruptions. Everything had gone smoothly; her prices for both mines had been accepted, as she'd known they would be, and the cash for them paid without question. Siveter had wanted to ask questions, she knew, but had thought better of it; there wasn't much of Samuel's inheritance left for him to have the legal handling of, but words from her could still harm the lawyer's reputation and he would not risk that.

Reaching a box from beneath the fourposter bed Annie opened it, setting the contents in neat white piles on the counterpane. The last of everything of value apart from this house and the one at Bescot was gone, everything that had once been Abel's was sold and the money for it lay staring up at her. 'Everything!' Annie scooped the money together, the wads of notes thick in her hands. 'Everything you had, Abel.' She laughed low in her throat. 'Everything you ever owned is here in my hands, and tomorrow it will buy back my life.'

Leaving the money scattering the bed like a sudden snowstorm, she crossed the bedroom to the chest of drawers. Opening the bottom one, she took out the amethyst ring. Soon it would be on her finger for all to see, soon the whole town would know she was to be Clinton's wife. Carefully she replaced it, her fingers touching the perfume bottle, almost stroking it, before drawing one of the silk petticoats from its blue tissue paper.

Closing the drawer, she dropped the petticoat on the bed, watching several banknotes rise in the draught of air as it landed then settled back on the silk. That would be her life from now on, surrounded in money, covered in money . . . Abel's money.

Unbuttoning her black grosgrain town dress she stepped out of it. Throwing it across a chair, she slipped off her heavy cotton petticoat. She would not wear black for Clinton's coming . . . she would never wear black again.

Sliding the silk over her head, Annie let it down over her hips, her hands caressing the soft luxury of it. No, she wouldn't wear black again nor cotton either. Clinton would see her in nothing but silks and satins. Going to the wardrobe, she took out the lavender dress. She would wear it for his coming this afternoon.

The last of the tiny self-covered buttons fastened, she took a lavender fichu from her bag. She had bought it from Fosbrook's in Union Street before going to the solicitor's. Setting it on her head, she secured it with hairpins then stood looking at her reflection in the full-length cheval mirror. Stylish the dress might be but it did not give her back her youth, it could not remove the lines that bordered her mouth nor return the bloom to her skin.

Why was Clinton marrying her? She asked herself the question she knew others would ask. It wasn't for her looks. Annie touched a hand to her face. She had never been blessed with them; what there had been in the way of looks had been given to Abel and Samuel, not that they had done Samuel a lot of good. She turned away from the mirror. He had not fared much better with his life than she had with her own.

Annie gathered the banknotes, putting them neatly into the box and closing it. Looks and life, fate had denied her both, and Samuel had ideas of taking the latter away again, of returning everything to Phoebe. 'But you are too late,' she breathed, picking up the box. 'Just as it's too late for Abel's daughter.'

Chapter Thirteen

Phoebe put down her sewing, stretching her aching back, listening to the quietness of the old mill house. Handsworth Prison had been quiet, every voice hushed to whispers save those of the wardresses, but it had been a harsh jarring quiet that left the brain reeling from its unsung staccato melody. Here it was gentle, its touch lenient to the mind, settling courteously over mill and heath. Here the quiet soothed and healed.

It wanted over an hour before Mathew and Lucy returned from their day's work, the meal was simmering in the oven, she had time for a walk. Running downstairs, cheating herself of time to change her mind, she slipped out of the back door, securing the lock Bert had fitted before slipping the brass key into the pocket of her brown dress.

Refusing to let her eyes linger on the brooding pile of the corn barn she turned in the direction of the canal. It would be pleasant there with the barges passing on the way to the ports Mark Ingles dreamed of.

Coming up out of the hollow that sheltered the mill house she looked toward the ribbon of water. There was no passing barge, only a finger of smoke spiralling toward the sky, the air too lazy to spread it. Shading her eyes from the remains of the sun, she stared. It had been an extra warm day but by no means hot enough to set the heath ablaze, so how come the smoke?

"Ow do, Miss?" The shout accompanied by a wave brought a smile to Phoebe's face and she walked on to where the

169

Ingleses sat grouped about a small fire above the towpath.

'I didn't know you were back.'

'Got back yesterday.' Bert took the shawl his wife handed to him, spreading it on the grass and gesturing Phoebe to sit down. 'Fetched a load of timber up from London way an' dropped it off at Moxley, shoring for the coalmine there.'

'But the barge,' Phoebe glanced to the empty waterway then back to Bert, 'where is it? You don't usually leave it while it's being reloaded.'

'Ain't no barge, Miss,' Lizzie said, staring at the fire trying its best to boil the kettle of water balanced over it, 'an' there ain't no load – least not for we there ain't.'

'No barge? I don't understand . . . what has happened to it?'

'Nothing 'as 'appened to the barge,' Bert poked the fire with a stick, 'barge is loaded an' off.'

'Mr Ingles,' Phoebe looked from one to the other, 'Lizzie, will you tell me what has happened, if not to the barge then to you . . . why are the four of you sitting here?'

'We come up yesterday . . . early on . . . wi' a load of timber for Moxley like Bert said,' Lizzie answered. 'We was expectin' to load coals for London like we usually does only the gaffer at the mine, 'e said there was no load for we an' that we was to get our things off the barge right away. There was already another bargee wantin' to take 'er off up to London.'

'But I thought the barge was yours . . . your home?'

'Our 'ome, yes,' Bert turned away, his face to the canal, 'but not our property. Now the owner 'as done a deal wi' new mine gaffer to put only 'is men on the barges.'

'New?' Phoebe looked at the man, his back still toward her. 'Do you mean Moxley mine has a new manager?'

'Not only a new manager.' Bert kicked out, sending a shower of grit from the path, spraying into the water. 'A new owner, an' that new owner 'as no place for Bert Ingles.'

The mine was sold! Phoebe sat back on her heels. Uncle Samuel had sold Moxley mine, and what of Hobs Hill? Was that also sold, was Joseph Leach too out of a job and a home?

'We would 'ave been further along but totin' our stuff as well as Bert's tools 'as slowed we more than we thought,' Lizzie said. ''Sides the walkin' is a bit tough on the little 'un. The lad 'e can manage it but the babby . . . 'er just ain't used to it.'

'Further on to where?' Phoebe asked, watching the boy go to stand beside his father. 'Where will you go? Where will you live?'

Lizzie glanced at her husband, his shoulders slumped forward. 'It ain't too bad, sleepin' out is quite pleasant, an' anyway Bert will find work soon.'

She smiled but behind the expression Phoebe read a different story. Sleeping out? They had slept out last night, and would again for how many nights? And what about food? No job meant no money and that in turn no food. She looked at the tiny girl huddled against her mother's skirts. How in God's name could people behave in such a way as to throw a man and his family out of their home? What sort of man was it who had bought her father's mine?

'Mr Ingles,' she got to her feet, 'why not stay here for a few days, give yourself a chance to try for work in Wednesbury? There must be something there.'

'An' if there ain't?'

'Then you have gained a few nights' rest and lost nothing.' She picked up the shawl, shaking it free of dried grass and handing it to Lizzie.

'I could go wi' you, Dad, mebbe we could both find work.'

Bert dropped a hand to his son's shoulder but remained gazing into the green depths of the canal.

'Best we stop alongside o' the cut, Miss,' he said. 'That way I can keep in touch, ask if barges 'ave 'eard of work to be 'ad in other parts. News travels fast along the cut.'

'A couple o' days wouldn't make no odds, Bert,' Lizzie

said gently. 'You need not traipse into the town, you could come down 'ere 'an wait o' the barges passin', but the little un . . . 'er could do wi' a few nights restin' in one place.'

'The barn is dry and there are plenty of corn sacks in the loft,' Phoebe said. 'It isn't much, I know, but you would be more comfortable than sleeping beside the canal.'

'Thank you, Miss.' Bert's gratitude was plain to see. 'We be grateful for your kindness. A few days an' then we'll be off . . . the Ingleses will be a nuisance to none.'

'I'm all for 'elpin' folk but four more mouths to feed . . . eeh, Miss Phoebe, 'ow we goin' to manage that?'

'It will be difficult, I know, but the clothes I have made sold well . . . I have the money from those.'

'True,' Lucy heaped flour into a bowl, 'but it won't last long spread over four of 'em.'

'I couldn't let them go any further, Lucy, that little girl of theirs looks far from well.'

'I noticed.' She rubbed fat into the flour. 'It can't be 'ealthy on them barges, all cooped up like rabbits in a hutch, an' the damp . . . it's a wonder they ain't all sprouted fins.'

'So can we manage?'

'Reckon so,' Lucy answered, 'but not for long.'

Phoebe began the ritual of greasing pie tins. 'We won't have to for long.'

Lucy looked up from rolling pastry. 'It won't be no easier, Miss Phoebe, watchin' 'em go, I mean, whether they be 'ere a short span or a longer.'

Phoebe took each circle of pastry as Lucy pressed it out, positioning it in its tin. 'Maybe they won't need to go.'

'Look,' Lucy stopped cutting circles, her eyes on Phoebe filling pastry cases with meat and potato, 'I wouldn't bank on Bert Ingles findin' work in Wednesbury. Joseph told Mathew that there might be quite a few men lookin' for jobs, wi' Moxley mine changin' 'ands.'

'Who has bought it?' Phoebe put the heavy pan of meat and potato in the hearth, covering it with a cloth.

Lucy reached for the smaller dish with which to cut pastry lids. 'Joseph couldn't say. Told Mathew nobody 'ad wind of the buyer, not yet. Let's just 'ope that whoever it is keeps 'em workin' . . . like Joseph says, there might be a few others lookin' for work in Wednesbury so don't go ratin' Bert Ingles's chances too 'igh.'

Waiting while Lucy placed the lids on the pies, Phoebe dipped her fingers in milk, spreading each with a thin film of moisture. 'Maybe he won't need to go to the town for work.'

Lucy refilled the bowl with flour, a fine white cloud mushrooming up to settle along her brows and lashes. 'What do you mean?' she asked. 'What you thinkin'?'

Phoebe turned from stocking the oven, her cheeks red from the fire. 'Locks,' she said simply, 'I'm thinking of locks.'

'I ain't with you, Miss.'

'I have been thinking a lot about those burglaries in the town.' Phoebe came to stand beside the table.

'Me an' all. They worry me they do. Who knows where 'e might strike next? Makes you scared to go to bed nights.'

'Well, if they worry us here . . .' Phoebe glanced around the kitchen with its worn chairs and mongrel assortment of second hand pots and dishes '. . . imagine how worried some folk in the town must be.'

Lucy began to make her second batch of pastry. 'Ar, there be plenty like we. An' if *they* be frightened, 'ow must all the nobs be feelin'?'

'Exactly! How must they be feeling . . . mine owners, iron and steel founders, brewers, grocers, tavern keepers? Think of it, Lucy, the list is endless and Wednesbury has plenty of them as well as plenty like us. All these people have something to lose, and all of them, rich or not so rich, would pay to make their home secure, don't you agree?'

''Course I do, but I still ain't wi' you.'

'People will pay for security.' Phoebe covered the batch of pies waiting their turn in the oven. 'We can give them that security.'

'We!' Lucy exclaimed. ''Ow?'

'Wait.' Phoebe wiped her hands on the white huckaback cloth kept 'specially for the baking then went out through the scullery, running across the yard to the barn where Mathew was helping the Ingleses settle in.

'Mr Ingles.'

Lizzie Ingles looked up from covering a heap of straw with her shawl, her face clouding with disappointment as she saw Phoebe standing in the doorway, cheeks red and arms crossed over her breasts.

'It's all right, Miss.' She picked up the shawl and began to fold it, the children watching from a corner. 'We understand, you can't let we stop 'ere after all. Just give we a minute to get we things an' we'll be gone.'

'I did not come to ask you to leave, Lizzie, I said you could stay here and you can. I . . . I only wish it were more like a home.'

'It could be.' Lizzie looked around the barn, at the rusting implements and unused flour sacks. 'If only . . .'

'If you ain't askin' we to go then what was you wantin' to ask, Miss?'

Phoebe smiled at the children, each sitting on a broken quern, then looked to where Bert stood watching her. 'Mr Ingles . . . Lizzie, would you come to the house, please? And you too, Mathew, I have something I wish to discuss with the three of you.'

'You two mind what you be about,' Lizzie pushed to her feet as she spoke to her children, 'no messin' wi' anything an' no larkin' around. You can finish makin' up this bed for the pair o' you.'

In the kitchen Lucy had finished her evening baking, the bowls and basins already stacked against the scullery sink and the brown earthenware teapot filled and waiting.

'What be all this about, Miss?' Bert asked as Phoebe reached cups from the dresser.

'It's about your locks, Mr Ingles.'

'Locks?'

'Locks, the ones you made for me.'

'They ain't broke, am they?'

'No, they are not broken,' Phoebe said, 'they work very well. I was wondering if you could make more?'

'I could,' he looked puzzled, 'but for what reason? Beggin' your pardon, you 'ave the doors to the 'ouse secured an' them barns don't 'old nought save a few old tools. An' if it's Mathew's place you was thinkin' of I already 'as a lock made for 'im, made it on me last trip to London. We intended leavin' it on your doorstep afore we moved on from the cut.'

'Thanks, Bert, that's good o' you,' Mathew said. 'I knows missis was worried about 'er bits an' pieces, we bein' out all day.'

'I wasn't wanting locks for myself . . . well, not for my own use.' Phoebe passed round the tea. 'The point is, do you think you could make . . . say a dozen . . . of the same sort as you fixed to my doors?'

'A dozen!' Bert set his mug on the table. 'That's a few locks, Miss.'

'Could you make them?' She asked, emphasising her words.

'Reckon I could,' he mused, 'I 'ave me patterns an' me files. I brought them wi' me.'

'What else would you need?' Phoebe caught the look of enquiry that flashed from Mathew to Lucy and the shrug of the shoulders she returned.

Bert pursed his lips. 'Brass or steel . . . place to work . . . a fire . . . a anvil . . . then you could manage.'

'How long would it take to make them?'

'Depends.' Bert thought for several moments. 'A week, p'raps, depends on 'ow much time you 'ave to give to the work.'

'If you had nothing else to do,' Phoebe asked, 'could you make a dozen locks in one week?'

'Ar,' he nodded, 'supposin' I 'ad a week.'

'Mathew,' Phoebe turned her attention to Lucy's husband, 'where could we get the metal Mr Ingles would need?'

'Bagnall's,' Mathew answered, his tone revealing the puzzlement this conversation was causing him. 'Bagnall's in Dudley Street will 'ave what 'e needs. I could tek 'im in wi' me an' Lucy tomorrow . . .'

'That be easy to say,' Bert interrupted, 'but money be needed to buy metals an' I've got precious little o' that.'

'Don't worry about money, Mr Ingles . . .'

'That's all right for you to say, Miss,' Lizzie put in, the same cloud of anxiety that Phoebe had seen in the barn settling over her eyes, 'but we 'ave the kids to feed an' no prospect of work to fetch more money in. I don't want to sound ungrateful, God forbid, but what bit o' money we got can't go bein' spent on makin' locks.'

'I think you have every prospect of work, Lizzie,' Phoebe smiled, 'or at least your husband has.'

Standing behind his wife's chair, Bert dropped a hand to her shoulder. 'What do you mean, Miss, I 'ave the prospect o' work?'

Phoebe looked at each of the people grouped in her small kitchen. 'I have a proposition to make, a proposition that will involve all of us. I will provide the necessary materials for the making of a dozen double barrel locks and a place for Mr Ingles to work. Food and keep for himself and his family will be his wage for the time it takes. For your part, Mathew, if you are willing, I would like you to show the lock to as many shopkeepers and tradesmen as you can. Given the recent robberies I don't think they will take much persuading to buy one, and the fitting of them could provide you with extra work.' She paused then. 'So both of you, what do you say, will you give it a try?'

'I'm game.' Mathew grinned.

'And what about you, Mr Ingles?' Phoebe smiled at the man who looked as though he had been kissed with a pole axe. 'Are you game?'

'A week off the road . . . food for the kids?' Bert grinned. 'Game? I'll say I'm bloody game . . . thanks, Miss, thanks for everythin'. I . . . I'll make you the best bloody locks ever to come out of Willenhall!'

Phoebe held out a hand. 'Then we are in business, Mr Ingles, and if things go as I hope, we will discuss a more usual wage for your labour.' She smiled at Lizzie. 'All, of course, provided your wife agrees to your settling here?'

'Oh, I agree, Miss.' Lizzie laid a hand over the one resting on her shoulder. 'An' my Bert will make you the best locks you ever seen.'

'You said your proposition included all o' we?' Lucy spoke for the first time since the Ingleses had entered the kitchen. 'So where be my part in all o' this?'

'You have the most important part.' Phoebe threw an arm around her one-time maid. 'Even the strongest of men can't work without food. We need your cooking to pay Mr Ingles's wages. What I have to ask you, Mrs Leach, is this . . . are you up to it?'

Picking up a pie warm from the oven, Lucy passed it to Bert. 'Here,' she laughed, 'you tell me, Bert . . . am I up to it?'

'Didn't you hear anything . . . anything at all?'

Maudie Tranter looked at the woman she had worked twelve years for, twelve years and not one good word in all of them. Annie Pardoe was a woman twisted with jealousy and spite, a woman who deserved all she got and more. And more she would get, Maudie could feel it in her bones.

'No, Miss Pardoe,' she said, her feelings well hidden. 'I slept all through the night, never 'eard nothing.'

Annie glanced around the dishevelled room, the mantel-piece relieved of its silver candlesticks and silver framed miniatures of her mother and father, and the desk littered with papers snatched from their drawers, strewn like white confetti over the carpet.

'You am a light sleeper, Miss, didn't you 'ear nothin' neither?'

Annie looked sharply at her thin angular housekeeper, standing with hands clasped together over a white apron that reached to the hem of her black skirts, unsure whether the woman's voice held a note of sarcasm.

'No, I did not!' she snapped. 'Mr Samuel has slept badly for several nights and I have stayed up with him. Last night I took a draught in order to get some sleep myself.'

''Course, Mr Samuel wouldn't 'ear anything, not the way 'e is.'

'Precisely.' Annie glanced once more at the room, just this one, the one with the desk and little else of interest or value apart from the few bits of silver. No other room had been disturbed, so what was the thief looking for? Whatever it was he'd expected to find it in the desk and had almost torn it apart in the search. 'Whoever it was must have come in through there.' She pointed to a door still open on to the garden. 'The Leathern Bottle gives right on to this property. He was probably drinking in there all night. I knew we should have had that dividing wall heightened.' She crossed the room, slamming the door shut. 'Go at once and bring the constables.'

Much good they'll do, Maudie thought, returning to the scullery and reaching her cloak from the cupboard. Whoever had been rummaging in that desk I doubt the bobbies will find him. That lot ain't sharp enough to catch a cold!

In the room Abel had used as a study Annie gathered up the strewn papers. Bills of sale for property that had once been Abel's but none that pointed to what had become of the proceeds of those sales. There had not been time yet for her to receive the title deeds for her tube works but, thank God, she had already given the money to Clinton.

'Sergeant down the station says as constables be out,'

Maudie said an hour later. She would have liked to take the time to call on Sarah but commonsense had warned against it. Annie Pardoe could time a walk to the police station and back almost to the minute; she would know for certain if there had been any gossiping on the way.

'Out!' Annie glared at the impudence of the man. 'What did he mean, the constables were out?'

''E meant they wasn't in,' Maudie enjoyed replying.

This time Annie was sure of the sarcasm. 'As you will be out of a position if you try your lip on me, Maudie Tranter,' she said, anger barely held in check. 'Now, if you don't want to go from this house a sight quicker than you came into it, you will tell me exactly what that fool at the station told you.'

I know what I'd like to tell you, you bad-tempered old cow, and one day, with God's help or the Devil's, I will! Maudie's thoughts gave her little consolation and she answered sullenly. ''E said as constables were out 'vestigatin' a break in up at Julia Hanson's place an' across at William Purchase, top end o' Chapel Street; said 'e would send 'em along 'ere when they reported back to the station, but 'e couldn't say 'ow long that was like to be.'

Julia Hanson and William Purchase, Annie mused as her housekeeper left the room, one a brewer, the other a grocer and general dealer, both likely to have money and like as not that money kept in the house. But what was the motive for breaking into Brunswick House? Unless . . . she touched a hand to the papers she had sorted ready to replace in relevant drawers of the desk. Unless someone knew of the cash she had got from James Siveter. She made her way to Samuel's room. And if they did, who but James Siveter could have told them?

'No, there has been no damage,' she signed in answer to her brother's question. 'Some papers scattered about the desk and the silver taken from the study. I have informed the constables. They will be here later.'

'Later?' Samuel's question flicked from his fingers.

'Two more houses were robbed last night,' Annie answered, 'Julia Hanson's and William Purchase's.'

'A brewer and a general dealer.' Samuel's fingers moved with the transient fluidity of a mayfly. 'Our burglar chooses his victims well, though why us?'

Annie shrugged. 'Who knows?' she replied her own fingers having none of the grace of movement her brother's held. 'Perhaps he thought to find money here. Thank heaven we keep little but petty cash, enough for small unforeseen events, no more.'

'This event was certainly unforeseen but nothing was taken that cannot be replaced – except, of course, for the miniatures of our parents and there is the possibility they will be returned.'

'We can always hope, but I do have my doubts.'

'No one was harmed, that is truly all that matters.'

All that mattered! Annie turned away, unable to disguise the contempt she knew must show in her face. How like Samuel to adopt that attitude . . . how typical of the weakness and ineffectuality he had shown all his life, the incapacity born of relying first upon their mother to attend to all then transferring that reliance to herself. And what of that reliance once she was married? And what of the condition that had kept Samuel confined to one house or the other for the greater part of his life? How would Clinton accept that? Would he accept it or would he . . . ?

'I must prepare for the constables' arrival,' she signed, quickly leaving the room before Samuel could answer. Clinton would not have to accept, Clinton would never know; no more would she be her brother's keeper.

Chapter Fourteen

'Ar, sold 'em both.' Sarah Leach looked at the young woman seated at her table. The years since her father's death had left their mark but it was the mark of confidence, of a sureness in herself; that prison had taught her a valuable lesson and not one any Magistrate would have expected: it had taught her that even in 1900 a woman had to fight and fight hard for any sort of life of her own. Many would have gone under given what this one had been dealt, but Abel Pardoe's daughter had learned how to fight.

'For what reason?' Phoebe's question caused the older woman to shake her head in a slow rhythm. 'Were the coal seams running out?'

'Joseph says they be gettin' thinner, but they 'ave a few years left in 'em yet.'

'Then why?'

'God knows, ma wench, an' 'e ain't tellin'.' Sarah stirred the tea she had poured. 'Who can tell what they at Brunswick 'Ouse might do next?'

'I can't understand Uncle Samuel's actions . . . to sell the coal mines!'

Sarah went on stirring, the spoon rattling against the cup. 'Who's to say it be yer uncle doin' the sellin'? Maudie Tranter said that aunt o' your'n 'ad the legal power to sign in 'er brother's stead, an' the Lord knows 'er would do it, tek 'er spite out on any 'er can. There's a few poor buggers lost their livin' 'cos of Annie Pardoe.'

Such as Bert Ingles, Phoebe thought, though he was one

of the lucky ones. The locks he made were selling as fast as he could produce them, there need be no more tramping the country in search of work for him and Lizzie had the comfort of a permanent place to make a home . . . but there were others not so fortunate.

'Sarah!' She pulled back from her thoughts, sudden agitation in her voice. 'Joseph . . . he hasn't . . .'

'Been given 'is tin?' Sarah intervened. 'No, ma wench, 'e still 'as 'is job at Hobs Hill. Seems to be just cut people as 'as been laid off . . . eh, what will them wimmin an' their babbies 'ave to live on? Meks my 'eart bleed to think on 'em.'

'Then you think my aunt is the one who has sold the mines?'

Twisting in her chair, Sarah swung the kettle from the fire, stilling its shrill hiss of steam. 'Think o' it,' she said, turning back to face Phoebe. 'Like you said you can't imagine yer uncle actin' in such a way as to put men an' their families on the streets, an' neither can I. It's true nobody 'as seen much o' him but 'e were a caring soul, never a bad word for nobody an' wouldn't 'arm a fly. But the other 'un, that Annie, 'er was a bad bugger from the start. No . . . if it was me 'ad to say who was the back of all this then it would be 'er as I'd name.'

Phoebe fingered her cup, looking at the tea she had not touched. 'Do you think Uncle Samuel knows what is happening?'

'If 'e don't then you ain't the one to tell 'im,' Sarah said sharply. 'That woman 'as 'armed you enough wi'out you givin' 'er the opportunity to do more. 'Er turned you out o' yer father's 'ouse, not carin' twopence where you went, an' naught but two frocks an' two pairs o' bloomers to go in.' She could have added that she had suspicions it was her aunt who had got her sent down for fifteen years, but bit this back. 'Mark my words an' keep well away from 'er, that woman is poison.'

What Sarah had said was true, her aunt had turned her out with virtually nothing, so perhaps it was true she was the one who'd sold off the mines. Phoebe stared at her tea, now cold in the cup. If only she could speak to Uncle Samuel, but she knew there was little chance of getting past his sister.

'So 'ow is it wi' you?' Sarah took the cup from Phoebe, going into the scullery and tipping the contents into the slop pail standing beneath the shallow ironstone sink.

'I am well, Sarah.' Phoebe watched a second cup of tea being poured.

'No after effects?'

Phoebe took the cup, adding sugar and milk. She knew what lay behind the question, knew it referred to the attack that had been made upon her, and knew also it was asked out of genuine feeling for her welfare and not morbid curiosity. 'No,' she answered, 'no after effects, though I am glad Mathew and Lucy are at Wiggins Mill with me.'

'And not only them, I 'ear.'

'You mean the Ingleses.' Phoebe sipped her tea, more from politeness than thirst. 'They were one of the families laid off. It seems the new owners had their own bargees. Mr Ingles and his wife and children were on the road when I came across them, I'm only thankful I could help them.'

'Turned out well for both of you so our Mathew tells me, but tek care, ma wench, don't get in so deep as you can't get out. 'Elpin' others is all well an' good so long as you don't get drownded in your own pity.'

'I'll try not to.' Phoebe smiled. 'And you and Joseph are always there to give me advice.'

'As long as you don't get too uppity to ask for it.'

'Joseph won't allow that.' Phoebe's smile widened. 'He never would allow Abel Pardoe's little girl to get above herself, and to him I am still a little girl.'

'Ar, Joseph always 'ad a soft spot for you.' Her tea finished, Sarah set her cup to one side. 'An' to 'im you always will be naught but a babby, but I knows an' you knows babbies 'ave a way o' growin', an' you be growin' to a beauty.'

'Has Joseph said yet who bought the mines?' Phoebe reached into the bag she had brought with her, her cheeks pink from the older woman's compliment.

'Nobody really knows, though Billy-me-Lord's agents 'ave been nosin' around for the last few days.'

'Sir William Dartmouth bought them!' Phoebe straightened up, her embarrassment forgotten.

'Like I says, nobody 'as spoke of 'im but I think as the facts says it theirselves. I reckon Billy-me-Lord be the new owner of the Crown and the Hobs Hill mines.'

Phoebe held the paper she had taken from her bag, her hand resting on the table, worry in her eyes as she looked at Sarah. 'I hope he doesn't make any more changes,' she said, 'people in the town need their jobs.'

'That be right an' don't be wrong,' Sarah agreed, taking two pots of damson jam from a cupboard. 'Pity that aunt o' your'n didn't 'ave the same feelin'.'

'What will happen . . . to men who might be finished, I mean?'

Sarah hesitated, a pot in each hand. 'Be my guess as young 'uns . . . they wi' no family to keep . . . will move on, the others'll like to stand the line.'

'Stand the line?'

'Ar,' Sarah nodded again, the movement slow and deliberate, 'men wantin' work gathers in the market place every mornin' an' stands in line 'opin' that any with work to be done will choose them. Some gets lucky and some goes wi'out . . .'

'The ones who are not chosen,' Phoebe's words dropped into the pause, 'what happens to them?'

Sarah sighed heavily. 'Work'ouse like as not, poor buggers.'

'Oh, no!' Phoebe's eyes widened. 'There must be something else.'

'Ain't nothin' else.' Sarah put the pots on the table. 'If you don't work you don't eat, not in this town. It's the work'ouse or starve, there be no such thing as charity in Wednesbury . . . things be too 'ard for them wi' next to nothin', an' them as 'ave plenty keep it to theirselves. That's the way of it, ma wench, an' you heed what I've told you an' don't go thinkin' you can tek on every man as gets 'is tin. That business o' your'n is doin' well enough but you ain't your father, you ain't Abel Pardoe.'

'No, I'm not Abel Pardoe,' Phoebe said quietly, 'but I am Abel's daughter.'

Phoebe walked toward Upper High Street, the pots of jam alongside the papers in her bag. She didn't get to visit Sarah as often as she would have liked and Joseph would be disappointed she had not waited to see him but as she had explained she was still not up to walking home alone, crossing the heath in darkness. This way she would finish her business and walk home with Mathew and Lucy.

She thought again of Sarah's pleased expression when she had shown her the poster now rolled up in her bag and told her how every shopkeeper she'd asked had agreed to display one in their premises. 'The Invincible', it proclaimed in two-inch type, 'Pardoe's Patent Locks'. They would be seen by all who used the shops, and for those who didn't she was on her way to the office of the *Express and Star*; an advertisement in the newspaper would reach every businessman in the town.

'Good day, Miss Pardoe.'

Phoebe turned at the sound of her name. She glanced first at the figure in tall hat and dark knee-length coat, then at the building he was vacating, and couldn't quite repress a shudder. The Magistrate had sentenced her to fifteen years from that building. 'Good afternoon, Sir William,' she returned.

'It was my intention to call upon you later in the day.' He replaced the hat held raised as he spoke.

'Perhaps I can save you the bother of the journey.' Phoebe wanted to move on, move away from that building and the memories it evoked.

'It is no bother, Miss Pardoe.' Grey eyes that could so easily be black regarded her evenly.

'Nevertheless it is some distance and an uncalled for journey if I can help you here.'

'I wished to tell you the man who attacked you has been gaoled. But we can't talk here . . .' He glanced at the women, their heads draped in shawls, who'd turned to look in their direction as Phoebe caught her breath sharply, a hand touching her throat. 'My carriage is to the rear.'

Gaol! Phoebe tried to breathe past the lump filling her throat. She would not wish a gaol sentence on any man, but for what he had tried to do to her . . .

'May I drive you home? I will give you the details on the way.'

'Home? No . . .' The spectres of that man's attack and of Handsworth Women's Prison fused together in her mind. 'I . . . I am not going home.'

'Then maybe we can talk inside.'

'No!' Phoebe's cry as he indicated the Green Dragon Hotel drew fresh inquisitive stares. 'I . . . I'm sorry, Sir William,' she said, 'I have no wish ever to enter that place again.'

He glanced first at the hotel and then at her, realisation dawning. The Magistrates' Court. Of course, she must have been sentenced from here. 'My apologies,' he said, 'I had not thought.'

'It is of no consequence.' Phoebe looked up, not all traces of fear gone from her face. 'If you have finished what you had to say . . .'

'I have not finished.' William Dartmouth interrupted what he knew to be a dismissal. 'If you will not allow us to speak somewhere else then it will be said here on the street. It seems one of my wife's maids overheard Sophie and her mother discussing our meeting that morning at the Priory. She presumed I had given you money and said as much to a man she was walking out with. He in turn thought to take it from you. That man is now in custody and will be spending a very substantial part of his life behind bars.'

'And the maid?' Phoebe asked. 'Is she to be dismissed her position as Lucy was?'

'Lucy?' He drew his brows together enquiringly.

'Mrs Leach, the girl you questioned at Wiggins Mill.'

'Why did she not come to me sooner with what she knew of what had happened to the necklace? Why say nothing until I questioned her?'

'Because she was warned not to.'

'Warned not to?' He frowned. 'Just what exactly does that mean?'

Phoebe looked straight at him. 'It means,' she said, her voice calm and clear, 'that Lucy was warned that to involve Ed— your son – in the affair would prove disastrous for her. She tried telling Lawyer Siveter what she knew but he said you would see to it she came to regret bringing the Dartmouth name under suspicion, then she was dismissed your wife's services.'

'She was in service at the Priory?' he asked, then before Phoebe answered, added, 'I was unaware of that, it had not occurred to me. Perhaps you will be good enough to tell Mrs Leach she will be reinstated immediately.'

No apology, Phoebe thought, no word of regret for what had happened to Lucy, just a calm proposal of her reinstatement.

'Does it not occur to you that she may have no wish to return to your employment?' she asked coldly.

Sir William Dartmouth looked at the young woman, her eyes cool and steady, and found the admiration he had first felt at their earlier meetings re-kindling in him. Not many men would speak to him as she did: his title and his money made no impression upon her and certainly did not intimidate her.

'That must be her prerogative – if you will forgive the use of the word "must".' The faintest hint of a smile appeared at the corners of his mouth. 'I wish you good day Miss Pardoe.'

'You said that?' Lucy asked later when Phoebe told her of her encounter. 'You said that to Billy-me-Lord?'

'I did,' Phoebe smiled broadly. 'Naughty of me, wasn't it?'

'Naughty or no, I bet it took the wind out o' 'is sails.'

'He did look somewhat surprised,' Phoebe said, still smiling.

'What did 'e 'ave to say to that?'

Waiting while Lucy served a customer to the last of her scones, giving her change from a sixpenny piece, Phoebe answered, 'He said that must be your prerogative.'

'My what?' Lucy shook her head as a woman, shawl drawn tight about her shoulders, enquired after a meat pie. 'What on earth does that mean?'

'It means that yours must be the choice. You can return to work at the Priory tomorrow if you wish, his wife will return you to the position you held there before.'

'Oh, ar.' Lucy sniffed scornfully. 'I'll be there bright an' early in me best cardi an' me boots blacked . . . like bloody 'ell I will! Go back to skivvyin' for the Dartmouths? I'd sooner go on the roads.'

'Were they unkind to you?' Phoebe watched the hurrying women pass from stall to stall, their purchases shoved into deep-bottomed baskets draped over one arm.

'The Dartmouths?' Lucy handed a broken scone she had placed to the side of her own stall to a small girl, her face pinched and thin, a ragged dress hanging from her bony shoulders, receiving a smile in payment. 'Not Miss Sophie or 'er mother, an' I never 'ardly seen Edward or the master. No, it was that lot below stairs. Talk about mean! They'd take the sugar out o' your tea an' then come back for the milk . . . no, I ain't goin' back there no more.'

''Ow much for this?'

A woman in skirts that had parted from their colour long ago and now hung like panels of rust from below her chequered shawl touched a finger to a child's white dress, its full skirts edged with a ribbon of cornflower blue, another of the same caught around the waist.

'Six an' eleven to you, luv.' Lucy smiled encouragingly. 'It's a lovely little frock an' all muslin.'

'It be pretty enough,' the woman ran a wistful eye over

the dress, 'an' my Ginny would look a picture in that come Sunday.' She looked at Lucy. ''Er's to be confirmed.'

Holding the dress closer to the woman, Lucy spread its skirts. 'Bein' confirmed, is 'er? Well, 'er couldn't 'ave a prettier frock for it than this.'

'That's right enough,' the woman fingered the dainty material, 'but 'er wouldn't get much wear out o' it after. It ain't the stuff to stand up to wear.'

'Muslin is stronger than it seems,' Lucy said, 'an' it's so easy to wash. You only needs to show this to the wash tub an' the dirt drops out o' it nor it needs no ironin' neither.'

'It *is* a special day.' The woman lingered. ''Er won't never get confirmed again, but near enough seven shillin' for a frock . . . that'd keep the kids for a week.'

'It might do,' Lucy withdrew the dress a fraction, 'but which would your little wench remember longest – a meal or the lovely frock 'er mother bought for 'er confirmation?'

'You'm right!' The woman drew a purse from the depths of her rusty skirts. 'I'll tek it, an' what me old man don't know 'e can't grieve over.'

Lucy wrapped the dress in a piece of brown paper, religiously saved from cloth Phoebe had bought from the draper and haberdasher in Upper High Street. ''Er'll do you proud in this,' she said, handing the woman a penny change.

'You know,' the woman wedged her package on top of those already in her basket, 'if I was the one made these frocks you wouldn't find me in Wednesbury for long.'

''Ow do you mean?' Lucy shot a sidelong glance at Phoebe.

'Well, they'm so pretty, ain't they? I tell you, if I 'ad the touch in me fingers to make such I would be in one o' they big fancy places like Brummagem or London. Folk there would pay twice as much for summat like this.' Returning the purse to her pocket, the woman turned away.

'You know, Miss Phoebe,' Lucy watched the customer, her old-fashioned black bonnet set on top of hair turned prematurely grey, disappear among the shoppers, 'I reckon there be some Wednesbury folk got more in their 'eads than coal dust.'

'But there is one at least with six shillings and elevenpence less in her purse,' Phoebe answered solemnly. 'Do you really think she should have spent so much on a dress? She said it would have kept the children for a week.'

'Don't you worry about that one,' Lucy said, after selling a woman a pink petticoat. 'If 'er couldn't 'ave afforded it 'er wouldn't 'ave bought it. 'Sides, 'er will sell it for four or five shillin' once 'er own kid be finished wi' it an' then when next one be too big for it, it will fetch a couple o' bob from somebody else, an' after they be done it'll still fetch a tanner or so from old Kilvert. There's always customers at the pawnshop either pledging bundles in or buying.'

'As I bought this.' Phoebe touched one hand to her jade green suit, the jacket trimmed with darker green frogging.

'You paid for it, didn't you?' Lucy said, a slightly indignant note in her voice. 'You didn't beg from nobody so you 'ave nothin' to feel 'shamed over. 'Sides it suits you, it really does. You look lovely, Miss.'

'Lovely enough to impress the printer?' Phoebe smiled.

'You'll knock 'is eyes out.' Lucy grinned. 'Just don't let 'im charge too much for that 'eaded notepaper an' order forms you be goin' to get 'im to print for you.'

'I won't.' Phoebe took the pots of jam from her bag. 'But could I leave these with you? I don't think Mr Simpson will be too impressed by my handing him two pots of damson jam with the designs for my bill headings.'

''E might take a bit off the price if you gives 'im a pot o' me mother-in-law's damson.' Lucy took the jam, setting it to the side of her stall. 'You never knows your luck.'

'I know I had better be off.' Phoebe closed her bag. 'I am putting off your customers.'

'Miss Phoebe,' Lucy said as she made to leave, 'mebbe you should wait for Mathew to come, let 'im go with you like? Might be best for a man to do the talkin'. After all, you ain't used to talkin' prices.'

'Then the sooner I get used to it, the better,' Phoebe said. 'I intend to be talking quite a lot of prices in the future and not all of them to a printer.'

Well, let's 'ope you stands up a bit stronger to that printer than you would to that woman just bought the frock, thought Lucy as Phoebe walked away. If I 'adn't been 'ere you would 'ave finished up givin' it to 'er. There's such a thing as bein' too soft . . .

'What did Simpson sting you for?' Mathew asked as the three of them walked home.

'A shilling a dozen.'

'A shilling a dozen!' Mathew was clearly disgusted. 'Why, that be pure bloody thievery. I'll go see 'im tomorrow an' tell 'im 'e can stick 'is bleedin' printin' wheer the monkey sticks its nuts. A shillin' a dozen! Who does 'e think 'e is coddin'?'

'He wasn't fooling me, Mathew.' Phoebe switched her bag from one arm to the other. Crammed now with butter and cheese, a pork hock wedged between the pots of jam, it weighed heavily.

'But a shillin' a dozen, Miss!' Lucy came in on Mathew's side. 'That does seem a bit steep.'

'I did not accept that price unconditionally.' Phoebe winced as her foot twisted against a stone. 'We came to an agreement.'

'An agreement?' Mathew sounded far from reassured. 'Like what?'

'Like fourpence a dozen when I order a gross or more.'

'Well, that's more like it.' Mathew hitched the hessian sack of potatoes higher on his shoulder. 'But will you ever be orderin' a gross?'

'I will be ordering many gross,' Phoebe answered, 'order forms, bill forms, receipts and notepaper, and the price will be the same for all of them.'

'Phew, steady on, Miss!' Mathew laughed. 'Lock business

191

be goin' well enough but I can't see it goin' on. After all, Wednesbury ain't all that big a town, it will only buy so many.'

'Mathew be right, Miss,' Lucy said. 'It don't pay to get carried away. Don't spend your money on fancy 'eaded paper you might never get to use.'

'Mathew *is* right,' Phoebe agreed, 'Wednesbury is not all that big a town. But then it is not the only town, and what we have sold in one town we can sell in another.'

'But 'ow?' Lucy made a detour, avoiding a puddle in the track. 'I mean, it takes folk to sell locks an' we . . . well, we all be busy doin' what we be doin'.'

'I have thought of that,' Phoebe said confidently. 'When the time comes I shall find somebody.'

'Always supposin' you find somebody to sell locks for you, Bert couldn't mek no more,' Mathew pressed home his point. ''E is workin' flat out now.'

'To say nothin' of 'avin' to buy in more metal,' Lucy supported her husband. 'An' that might be the 'orse you can't ride. Brass founders don't let stuff out on the strap, least not to likes of we they don't. You got to be big in business to get things first and pay later.'

What they were saying was perfectly reasonable. Phoebe trudged on in silence, but she had taken a gamble, made her play as her father would have said, and now she must follow it through.

Across the heath the windmill stood silent witness to one such as herself, Elias Webb, who had sold her Wiggins Mill, had made his play but for him the cards of fortune had not followed through. But hers would. Phoebe clenched her teeth, defying the laughter of the fates. One way or another she would win through, she had to if the Ingleses were not to be put back on the road.

''Ello, Miss, 'ello, Mrs Leach.' From the edge of the yard the Ingles children waved then raced to meet them, the boy leaving his sister in his wake.

'I will take that for you, Miss.' The boy took the bag from Phoebe, easing it on to his shoulder in imitation of Mathew before going to walk beside him, matching his step, in his own mind at least very much the man.

'I can carry summat as well as our Mark.' The girl looked up with serious eyes. 'I'm as strong as 'im.'

'No, you ain't.' Her brother sniffed scathingly. 'You be only a girl an' they ain't as strong as men, am they, Mr Leach?'

'They ain't that, lad.' Mathew grinned. 'But I reckon most of 'em be prettier an' our Ruthie be prettiest o' the lot.'

'But I am strong, me mother says my 'elp be in . . . in . . . invalible.'

'Well, I could certainly do wi' some 'elp,' Lucy said tactfully, 'this basket be fair breakin' my arm.' Lowering it to the ground, she took out a shank end of mutton wrapped in paper tied round with string, handing it to the child. 'If you could take that it would be a powerful 'elp.' She smiled at the small girl, the meat cradled like a doll in her arms. 'But you 'ave only to say if it gets to be too 'eavy. We 'ave two strong men 'ere can carry it.'

'I can carry it, Mrs Leach,' the child said proudly. 'I can do lots of things. I 'elped Mother make a 'ot pot today, peelin' 'tatoes an' carrots, an' 'er let me 'elp wi' jam roly poly.'

'That sounds like a real meal for a workin' man,' Mathew said. 'Jam roly poly, that's my favourite puddin', you'll 'ave to show Mrs Leach how it's done.'

'I will.' She looked up at Lucy, her little face wreathed in smiles. 'It's real easy.'

'I 'opes as you ain't fond o' too much jam in your roly poly,' the boy said, hitching the bag on his shoulder as Mathew hitched the potato sack.

'I like jam, the more the better,' Mathew answered.

'A pity that.'

'Why, don't you have any more jam?'

'Oh, ar, Miss,' the answer was jaunty, 'me mother 'as

another pot o' jam, but we don't get much on a roly poly. Least there won't be much on this'n.'

'Why not?' Phoebe asked as they crossed the yard to the house.

''Cos our Ruth keeps eatin' it!'

'So that's what meks 'er such a little sweet'eart.' Mathew lowered the sack of potatoes to the ground, sweeping the child into his arms and whirling round with her. 'Who wants jam when we 'ave our Ruthie?'

'It's time our Ruthie was in bed.' Lizzie Ingles came from the barn she had turned into a home, smiling at her daughter's delighted squeals. 'An' you too, my lad,' she said, looking at her son. 'I told the pair o' you more'n half an hour gone.' She turned to Phoebe. 'I never can get 'em to bed afore you all be back.'

'I wonder why?' Taking her bag from the boy, she drew out two fat round lollipops. 'It couldn't have something to do with these, could it?'

Shoving the joint of meat into Lucy's hands, the little girl jigged up and down, eyes shining at the promise of the sweet. 'I wants the red one.' She pulled at Phoebe's arm. 'It's my turn to 'ave the red one. Our Mark 'ad it last time.'

'Then if Mark had the red one last time it must be your turn to have it this time.' Phoebe handed her the sweet.

'I've got the red one!' The child jigged away, holding the lollipop in the air like some coveted trophy. 'I've got the red one!'

'You'll 'ave a red bottom, Ruth Ingles, if you don't say thank you,' Lizzie said sternly. 'You know better'n to take what somebody gives an' return no thanks. Whatever 'as 'appened to your manners, girl!'

The child stopped dancing. 'Beg pardon, Miss.' She came to Phoebe, her pretty mouth drooping. 'I'm mortal sorry.'

'That's all right, Ruth.' Phoebe caught the twitching of Lucy's mouth. 'I was always forgetting to say thank you when I was a little girl, and to tell you the truth I sometimes forget now.'

'Do you, Miss, do you honest?'

'Honest.' Licking a forefinger, Phoebe made the sign of the cross over her heart. 'Cross my heart and hope to die if what I have said is just a lie.'

'Ooh, you knows that an' all, you can't never say that if you 'ave told a lie.' The child's mouth lost its droop, turning upward in a smile. 'So you must be tellin' the truth, Miss, you do forget sometimes.'

We all do, Phoebe thought, bending to hug Lizzie's daughter, remembering playing the same scene so many times with her father. We all do.

'Now say goodnight.' Lizzie caught her daughter's hand as Phoebe released her.

'Goodnight.' The child lifted her face to each in turn, receiving a kiss on the cheek. 'Thank you, Mrs Leach, an' you, Mr Leach.'

'Why can't we make that Aunty Lucy and Uncle Mathew?' Lucy said, her face on a level with that of the child.

'I don't know if we could,' the answer came solemnly, 'it might not be 'lowed 'cos you ain't a real aunt, am you?'

'No,' Lucy said softly, 'but I love you as much as a real aunt, and Mr Leach loves you as much as a real uncle.'

'I'd like to,' the child said pensively, 'but I don't know if it's 'lowed.'

'Why don't we ask your mother?' Lucy looked up at the face of Lizzie Ingles.

'It's allowed.' The woman smiled, her eyes cloudy behind tears. 'It's allowed.'

Clasping her red lollipop in one hand, the other held by her mother, the girl walked away then stopped to look back at the three adults. 'I do love you all,' she said simply. 'I'm so glad we come to live 'ere.'

'I would like to call you Aunt and Uncle an' all if it's all right wi' you?'

Mathew looked at the face turned up towards his own, seeing the disappointments and knocks life had already dealt the young son of Bert Ingles, seeing apprehension of another. He held out his hand, shaking that of the boy offered to meet it. 'It's a sight more'n all right, Mark,' he answered huskily. 'That would mean more to me than a medal from the Queen.'

'I'm so glad we come to live 'ere.' The words echoed in her mind as later Phoebe prepared for bed. She was glad too. Having people about the place during the day gave her a feeling of security, and the knowledge they were close, combined with the locks on her doors, had given her confidence to sleep alone in the house, freeing Lucy and Mathew to go back to sleeping in their own home.

Yes, she was glad they had all come to live at Wiggins Mill. Picking up her nightgown from the bed, she held the soft cotton to her face, the memory of rough calico vivid in her mind. She was glad they were all here, Lucy and Mathew, the Ingleses with their children . . . if only she could have brought one more. If only she could have brought Tilly . . .

Chapter Fifteen

Annie Pardoe sat in the neat parlour of Brunswick House its graceful bay window overlooking well-kept lawns. She paid a man twice a week to see to the upkeep of the gardens and made sure he earned his money. Annie Pardoe paid no one to sit around. There had been little alteration since Abel's time though she had seen to it that no laburnum or yew grew there and had grubbed them out herself from the garden of the house at Bescot years before. She caught her breath, holding it till the twinge of pain below her left breast subsided. Yes, she had grubbed them out – but not until she had made good use of them.

'Papers, Miss.' Maudie Tranter entered the room, a newspaper neatly folded on a cloth-covered tray. Wait till you reads that, she thought as Annie took the newspaper, you'll have another shock. Making her way back to the kitchen Maudie thought of what she had seen in the *Express and Star* and how the woman in the parlour would react in the knowledge that her housekeeper always read the newspaper before taking it into her. Maudie enjoyed her thoughts.

In the parlour Annie spread the newspaper on the oval mahogany table, fixing on to her nose the reading glasses that hung on a silk string about her neck. She had made a lifetime's habit of taking the papers, reading thoroughly through them before allowing them to go to her brother.

'Hmmph!' she snorted, reading of certain elections to the town council. 'Not an ounce of brain between the lot of them.' Slowly she turned the pages, finding some reports of interest to her, others not, but reading them all until her eye caught the advertisement.

Annie's fingers dropped to the corner of the page she had been about to turn, her eyes devouring the large caption: 'The Invincible'. The heading topped a representation of a lock under the sub-heading 'Pardoe's Patent Locks'. She read the advert through once and then again. Phoebe! She pressed a hand to her side but it did not still the pain biting beneath her breast. It could only be Phoebe!

Her thoughts flew to the man who had promised to make her his wife. What if he saw the advertisement? The name was the same, Pardoe, how long would it take him to wonder if it carried with it any relationship to her? He was no fool, he would put two and two together sharp enough, then how long before he found Pardoe's Patent Locks was run by her niece?

The pain jabbed viciously, bringing her teeth together, nostrils flaring with the effort of controlling it as she read the advert through again. If he should find out . . . if he discovered her niece had not quit Brunswick House of her own choice but had been virtually thrown out . . . And what of Samuel? What would his reaction be to seeing that piece in the newspaper? He had already made clear his intention of returning everything to Abel's daughter, what would he do when he found there was almost nothing to return? But it didn't matter what Samuel thought. Annie's eyes stayed glued to the advertisement. She had taken care her brother would never carry out his threat. No, it did not matter what Samuel knew, but Clinton . . . Clinton must never know. She would kill this lock business stone dead before it got started.

Leaving the newspaper on the table she walked upstairs to her bedroom. Slipping a smart grey day coat over her matching dress, she pinned a feathered bonnet over her hair. Clutching her bag, she went downstairs without calling in on her brother.

'I am going out,' she said as Maudie appeared from the kitchen, 'I don't know what time I shall be back.'

Maudie watched her mistress wriggle her fingers into grey chamois gloves. I was right, she thought, closing the door after the departing Annie, you've had a shock right enough and it won't be the last. And you taking to dressing up in fine colours won't ward them off. There be others waiting on you, Annie Pardoe, ones you won't walk away from.

Annie walked briskly along Spring Head, following it into the market place cutting across toward Great Western Street. She had not taken the horse and trap, they would be too conspicuous left standing outside the Great Western Railway Station, for today she meant to take the train to Birmingham.

'You can sit in the ladies' waitin' room, Mum, it's the next door along the platform. There be a nice fire burnin' in there.'

The man in the tiny ticket office touched a finger to the peak of his dark green cap as he handed Annie a ticket.

Putting it carefully into her bag, she nodded. It might be best to sit in the room set aside for women, there would not be many of them using the train, not when the steam tram was a cheaper way to travel. But today the train suited Annie. The fewer folk to see where she headed, the better pleased she felt.

Choosing a seat that gave a clear view of the door and of any who might choose to enter, Annie sat in the empty room. It was a bind having to go to Birmingham but it was safest. She would not be known there and there would be few in Wednesbury who knew that town in any detail. The advertisement she had read only an hour before lodged in her mind, till she felt her mouth tightening like a trap. The hundred pounds she had paid the Magistrate had been a total waste of money. What had it bought . . . a fifteen-year sentence that had been set aside after little more than one! What had that fool been about? He should have made the sentence one that couldn't so easily be revoked. It was a pity they had ceased transportation, that way Phoebe would have been out of the country, but now her niece was free and broadcasting her presence by way of advertisements, one at least published in the *Express and Star* and God only knew how many in other publications and places. Annie pressed her hands together in her lap. If you want a thing doing right, do it yourself. This time she would do it herself, and this time it would be done right.

The conductor's call of 'Snow Hill' told of having reached Birmingham and Annie alighted. Who was stupid enough to give a name like Snow Hill to this place? she wondered, taking in the soot-grimed archways of the railway station. Black Hill would have been more appropriate. Leaving the station, she followed the line of shops beside it; tailor, draper, grocer, milliner, each jostled the other, elbowing for room in the narrow streets, but she passed them by without a second look at the overcrowded windows. Pie shop, beer hall. Annie walked on, her eye scanning signs painted over shop fronts proclaiming the name of the proprietor and the wares he sold until she read: James Greaves, Hardware and Ironmongery.

Annie caught the train back to Wednesbury, six pot menders and six mousetraps in her bag. The purchase of these would raise no eyebrows in Brunswick House: pot menders were often used in her kitchen to close small holes worn in iron pots and pans and mousetraps were always set in the cellar. Mousetrap! She gazed through the window at the dingy houses set regimentally close alongside the railway line. The trap she was setting would catch more than a mouse . . .

'Has Mr Samuel been downstairs?' she asked when she reached the house.

'No, Ma'am,' Maudie answered. ''E took 'is lunch in 'is room though 'e didn't touch it none, an' when I popped in the studio about three o'clock 'e was asleep in 'is chair. 'E seems to 'ave slept more than ever these past few days.'

'That will be his medicine.' Annie took the pot menders and mousetraps from her bag, handing them to her housekeeper.

'The doctor increased the strength a little . . . you have been careful only to give him the prescribed dose?'

'Two teaspoonfuls, measured 'em out meself, Ma'am, an' 'e swallowed 'em right off, then 'e sat in 'is chair an' 'as been there all day far as I know.'

'And he ate nothing?'

'Nothin' at all,' Maudie shook her head, 'not even a bite. I carried 'is tray down same as I carried it up . . . nothin' 'ad been touched at all.'

'Perhaps a cucumber sandwich will tempt him?' Annie turned to the stairs. 'I will go in to him when I have removed my coat. Prepare a tray now.'

'Perhaps a cucumber sandwich will tempt him,' Maudie mimicked under her breath as Annie went up the stairs. 'As if she cares whether he eats anything or not. It's all bloody top show wi' that one an' underneath it all 'er couldn't care twopence whether the poor bugger lives or dies!'

In the kitchen Maudie put the hardware on the dresser and stood looking at it. Pot menders and mousetraps, nothing unusual in that – 'cept Annie Pardoe never bought anything without it had been asked for a dozen times and she, Maudie, hadn't asked for either. And why walk into the town, why hadn't she taken the horse and trap as always? And why jaunt off down into Wednesbury to get them herself when she could have had them sent up with provisions? Taking out a tray she spread it with a freshly laundered cloth and set it with china. Annie Pardoe was up to summat as sure as God made little apples, Maudie told herself, and like as not Samuel wouldn't come out of it too well.

In her room Annie spread the newspaper she had brought up from the parlour. She had spent a couple of hours with her brother before leaving him for the night. She turned a page. He had not eaten a cucumber sandwich earlier and neither had he taken any dinner, but she had expected that. She turned a second page. She had told Maudie Tranter she would go herself tomorrow and ask the doctor to call. But that would do nothing for Samuel. Her eyes scanned the columns of print, coming to rest on the advertisement for Pardoe's Patent Locks. No, nothing would help Samuel.

Going to the marble-topped washstand she slid open the narrow drawer that ran almost the full width of it, taking a sheet of paper from beneath the pile of towels. Returning to the table, she placed it beside the newspaper then took from her bag the bottle of ink and the cheap pen she had bought before taking the train back to Wednesbury. Reading the advert through one last time, Annie dipped the pen into the ink and began to write.

Phoebe heard the crunch of carriage wheels along the track and put aside the dress she had almost finished making. Going to the window, she watched it drive to the front of the house, her feelings mixed. She liked Edward, liked him very much, and was happy for him to call . . . but if only he would call less often. She had tried to tell him of her need to work, to explain the strong necessity for it, but he only said to marry him and be done with tiresome necessities.

She watched him climb from the carriage, the light glinting on his fair hair. She knew he loved her and that he would do his best to make marriage to him happy . . . so why couldn't she say yes? Why wouldn't she marry Edward Dartmouth? Turning from the window, Phoebe left the room. She didn't know why.

'Phoebe, I am so glad you are home. I told Edward we ought to send a card before we visited.'

'Sophie, how nice.' Phoebe's smile was a mixture of pleasure and relief. She had turned from the window before seeing Sophie and now the pleasure of her visit brought the added relief of not having to walk with Edward.

'Don't bother with tea,' Sophie said when Phoebe offered refreshments, 'just sit down and listen. You are invited to a farewell ball.'

'A ball?' Phoebe was surprised. 'Where?'

'At the Priory.' Sophie's face glowed with delight. 'Where else did you think!'

'That's just it,' Phoebe said, 'you gave me no time to think.'

'What is there to think of?' Sophie rushed on. 'Father is giving a ball and you are invited. There is nothing to be thought about.'

Phoebe looked from Sophie to Edward. 'You said a farewell ball?'

'My mother is to leave for Europe sooner than had been intended.' He smiled, misreading the reason for the question in her eyes. 'The influenza she suffered recently has not cleared as we would have hoped and her physician has recommended a warmer climate.'

'I am sorry to hear your mother is not yet fully recovered,' Phoebe returned her gaze to Sophie, 'please give her my regards.'

'Oh, Mother is not too ill,' Sophie burst out with the thoughtless disloyalty of youth, 'she simply has an over-fondness for Italy, and of course we have to go too which means I will not see Montrose for several more months. The whole thing would be totally unbearable were it not for the shopping en route. You really can buy the most exquisite lace in Paris. I intend to buy my whole trousseau there. Montrose . . .'

'My mother and sister cannot travel alone,' Edward put in as his sister paused for breath, 'I am to travel with them to our villa in Tuscany then I shall return.'

'Will that not be doubling a journey?' Phoebe asked, knowing he had interrupted Sophie because he hated to think of her with Montrose Wheeler and wanting to spare him as much as possible. 'To have to return to Italy again to escort your mother home will be very tiring.'

He smiled, the thought of her concern for him deepening the vivid blue of his eyes. 'I will not be returning there a second time,' he explained. 'My father will be joining Sophie and Mother after Christmas. He will bring them home.'

'With us leaving in two weeks there will be no Advent Ball at the Priory this year,' Sophie burbled on, 'hence the idea of a farewell ball. Mother has sent invitations to absolutely everybody and here is yours.' She took a cream vellum envelope from her bag, handing it to Phoebe. 'It will be absolutely wonderful and I hope to persuade Father to let Montrose announce . . .'

'It is kind of your parents to invite me,' Phoebe cut in but this time it was not to spare Edward, 'though I cannot accept.' She could not attend a ball at the Priory, she hadn't a suitable gown for one thing, and to ask her to one which Montrose would be attending . . . hadn't anyone told Sophie the man she wanted to marry had already been engaged to the daughter of Abel Pardoe, and had broken that engagement when he found out she had no money?

'But why?' Sophie demanded. 'Is it because of Montrose? You have no cause for worry there, Phoebe. He told me what happened himself. Told me you asked to be freed from your engagement to him – that after the shock of your father's death you felt you could not marry for some time, and later you found you no longer loved him and begged him not to hold you to your promise so of course he did not. But now he loves me and we are to be married. And you,' she squeezed Phoebe's hand, 'are not to worry over my feelings. You are to accept Mother's invitation and that is that!'

So Montrose had told Sophie! Phoebe glanced at Edward, reading the distaste in his face. It was not her recollection of events she had just heard but what effect would it have on Sophie should she ever find out the true story? And what effect would it have should she discover Montrose was marrying her purely and simply for her money; that for him love played no part in marriage.

'I'm so excited,' Sophie trilled on, 'I am to have a new gown, pink, Montrose says I look ravishing in pink . . .'

I wore a pink gown on our last evening together. Phoebe's thoughts suppressed Sophie's voice, drowning it in waves of memory. Montrose said I too looked ravishing in the colour. He held me in his arms while he vowed his love for me, while he told me he could not wait for our marriage, while he told me the same lies.

'. . . he is to get leave from his regiment . . .'

Wrenching her thoughts back to the present, Phoebe glanced across to where Edward sat.

'Sophie dear,' he rose, 'we really must not take any more of Phoebe's time.'

The girl jumped to her feet, colour rising to her cheeks. 'I'm sorry, Phoebe, I do prattle on. Mother is always telling me about it.'

'And so am I,' Edward laughed, 'to say nothing of Father's efforts in that direction, all of which are wasted.

'You will come, Phoebe?' He hung back as Sophie reached the carriage.

'It's not possible, Edward.'

'Why not?' The intensity of his question was echoed in the pressure of the hands he placed on her arms. 'Is it because of my forgetting that damned necklace?'

Releasing herself from his grip, Phoebe glanced at his sister but her back was still turned to them.

'You know it isn't, Edward.'

He looked at her, frustration and the need to know lending his eyes a desperation she had not seen before. 'Then why, Phoebe?' he asked hoarsely. 'Why?'

'Edward,' she smiled patiently as though dealing with a demanding child, 'for a single girl to attend a ball she requires a female chaperone or a male escort. It might have escaped your notice that I have neither of these, on top of which I own no gown suitable for a ball.'

'The escort part might have eluded me,' Edward admitted, his eyes clearing, 'but it had not escaped my father. He has expressed the wish that you give your permission for me to be your escort for the evening, and I sincerely hope you will agree. As for a gown, I . . .'

'No.' Phoebe cut short the offer she knew would follow. She would take none of the Dartmouths' money, not even enough to buy a gown to attend their ball; she wanted no reparation and she certainly did not want their charity. 'Thank you, Edward, but I prefer to provide my own gown.'

'Then you will come!'

'I think you had better be going.' Phoebe avoided answering what was more statement than question. 'Your sister is waiting.'

'A ball, and with Edward Dartmouth your escort!' Lucy held the cream card with its gold edging as though it were a priceless object. 'Eeh, Miss Phoebe, how lovely. What will you wear?'

'Nothing.' Phoebe took the card, putting it behind a jug that held pride of place on the dresser.

'Well, that'll give the women the vapours and the men a rare treat, though I 'adn't thought it of you, to go 'ob nobbin' in naught but that you were born in, Miss Phoebe.' Mathew stood in the doorway of the scullery.

'Trust a man to be there with 'is ears flappin'.' Lucy turned a reproving look as her husband grinned. 'What you be in 'ere after anyway, Mathew Leach?'

Phoebe smiled, joining in with his infectious grin. 'Yes, what do you be in 'ere after?' she asked, using the same lazy dialect, 'listenin' to wenches gossipin'.'

'Well, you be wi' one can do that all right.'

'Don't push your luck, me lad.' Lucy stretched a hand ominously towards an iron pot set on the hob.

'All right, all right.' Mathew raised both hands in a gesture of surrender. 'Bert says to tell you, Miss, as brass for locks be runnin' pretty low.'

'He knows he can get more whenever he needs it.'

'Ar, 'e do know,' Mathew answered, 'but 'e still reckons to tell you beforehand like, says that's the way it should be.'

'Tell him to get what he thinks necessary,' Phoebe said.

'I will come see him myself as soon as I finish helping Lucy with tomorrow's baking.'

'What did you mean when you said you would wear nothing to the Priory ball?' Lucy whisked about the kitchen gathering utensils.

'What I said.' Phoebe lifted the pot from the hob, placing it on a cloth she had set on a corner of the well-scrubbed table, then set about pounding the boiled potatoes with a wooden spoon. 'I will be wearing nothing to the Dartmouths' ball for the simple reason that I will not be going.'

'Eeh, Miss Phoebe, whyever not?' Lucy was already wrist-deep in flour.

'I can't Lucy.' Phoebe attacked the potatoes with a new savagery. 'I . . . I wouldn't feel right. Everyone there will know what my aunt did.'

Lucy banged lard indignantly into the flour, sending it surging upward in a cloud. 'Ar, they will, an' they'll know what an old bitch 'er is an' all.'

Phoebe ladled cubes of mutton into the mashed potato, folding them in with the spoon. 'They will also know about the business of the necklace.'

'That an' all.' Lucy rolled the pastry. 'An' they'll see that the Dartmouths 'old nothin' against you . . . not that there be anythin' for 'em to 'old . . . but you see what I mean. Billy-me-Lord can't be apologisin' any more clear, an' that's what 'e be doin'. In front of the 'ole bloomin' county 'e's apologisin', an' your refusin' to go to that ball be like chuckin' 'is apology right back in 'is face. It do an' all, Miss Phoebe.'

She had not thought of it in those terms. Phoebe watched Lucy working dexterously at her pie-making. This could well be Sir William and Lady Dartmouth's way of proclaiming the fact she had been wrongly accused of stealing their daughter's necklace and that despite her lack of fortune she was accepted in their home. For her to refuse would be seen as churlish, and worse, in her own eyes, would rank as rudeness. But to attend . . .

'I realise how my refusal may be received, Lucy, but it can't be helped. I haven't a dress anywhere near grand enough for such an occasion.'

'Is that all? Lord, it would take a bloody sight more than that to keep me from goin' to a grand do like that. Surely you ain't gonna let a frock keep you from it?'

'Not a frock, more the lack of one.'

'That be nothin' as can't be remedied,' Lucy said, watching Phoebe carry pies to the oven and load them in. 'You can buy a frock easy as winkin'.'

'You can if you have money, which I have not . . . well, not to spend on ball gowns anyway. They cost a small fortune.'

'Spendin' some on yourself won't 'urt for once.'

'Spending that much would. I need that money to buy metal if we are to go on producing locks. I will not throw it away on a gown I will never wear again.'

'I seen a lovely bolt o' satin in Underwood's window,' Lucy sounded almost matter-of-fact, 'the loveliest shade of pale yellow you ever did see – just like butter cream. Make a bostin' frock it would.'

'Make!' Phoebe stopped filling pies to stare at Lucy. 'I couldn't make a ball gown.'

'O' course you could.' Lucy loaded her bowl with a fresh helping of flour, adding salt and lard. 'You already makes frocks, don't you?'

'Little ones, yes.'

Lucy looked up from rubbing fat into flour. 'Well, then! this will be the same 'cept bigger.'

Phoebe half smiled. Lucy made it all sound so easy, make herself a gown . . . as if nothing were simpler. Supposing she did manage to make a gown, that would only be a part of what she would need. There were other things.

'A dress is not the whole of it, Lucy,' she said. 'Given that I had one, I would also require gloves and shoes . . . a bag . . . a fan. And jewellery, what of jewellery? I have absolutely nothing in that line at all. The last of Grandmother's pieces went before . . . before . . .'

'Before you were sent to prison,' Lucy finished for her. 'Jewellery be a bit o' a sticky 'un. Wonder if Bert could make anything?'

Phoebe set the second batch of pies aside, spreading the white huckaback cloth over them until there was room in the oven. 'Mr Ingles is not a jeweller.'

'I know 'e ain't.' Lucy paused from mixing dough. 'But 'e makes things out o' brass, don't 'e?'

'Brass is not gold. If it were we would be quite wealthy for there is several pounds of it in the workshop.'

'Pity it isn't,' Lucy floured the wooden pin and board then scooped the dough from the bowl a few quick light movements rolling it into a creamy mat, 'I wouldn't mind bein' wealthy . . . not too much, mind you,' she grinned cheekily, 'just enough to make the 'ole of Wednesbury sit up and take notice.'

'Oh, I understand,' Phoebe laughed, 'nothing too blatant . . . just the odd million would do.'

'I just thought as seein' Bert was so 'andy with the brass like 'e might be able to make summat as would pass for jewellery,' Lucy said when they both stopped laughing.

'And how would I explain my neck turning a delicate shade of green halfway through the evening?'

'Oh, ar!' Lucy grimaced wryly but her eyes were laughing still. 'I 'adn't thought o' that. Mind, that would put you one up over the nobs . . . you'd 'ave summat they 'adn't got.'

'How very true. But I think I prefer to do without a green neck. It doesn't seem me somehow.'

'No! Well, p'raps you be right.' Taking the last remnants of dough Lucy shaped it into the figure of a man, giving it sultana eyes and four sultana buttons.

'Ruth doesn't like sultanas,' Phoebe said as Lucy blobbed jam where a nose would be.

'I know, but Mark does!' Lucy sprinkled the figure with

a coating of sugar before placing it in the tin alongside the scones, then looked across the table to where Phoebe was watching. 'Seriously though, Miss, apart from the jewellery there ain't nuthin' you couldn't get if you wanted to go to that ball.'

'I will not spend a great deal of money on . . .'

'You wouldn't 'ave to,' Lucy said quickly. 'Gloves you can get from Underwood's, ones that reach up over the elbow for no more than ninepence. An' they 'as feathers an' buttons. Eh, Miss, wi' your sewin' I reckon as you could make a lovely frock for little or nuthin'.'

'Hardly nothing.' Phoebe covered the scones then began to take cooked pies from the oven. 'How much is the material going to cost? Think how many yards it will take . . . Lucy, the whole thing is out of the question.'

'I don't know how many yards it'll take nor 'ow much the cost would be!' Lucy banged bowls and dishes together impatiently. 'An' neither do you 'cos you ain't asked so 'ow can you say it be out of the question? An' afore you says anythin' about shoes an' the costin' o' them you could always try John Kilvert's place.'

Phoebe straightened up, her cheeks reddened by the heat of the oven. 'A pawn shop!' she exclaimed. 'A pawn shop is not going to have dance slippers.'

'There you goes again!' Lucy rattled spoons and knives into the large mixing bowl. 'You'm a right one for reachin' a answer afore askin' the question, Miss Phoebe. Who's to say what old Kilvert 'as got stored away in that pawn shop . . . it ain't always the ones looks down an' out is down an' out, there be others 'ad to visit 'im, others popped pledges as they couldn't redeem.'

'But dance slippers?' Phoebe shook her head. 'Really, Lucy, I can't see there being such as that in a pawn shop.'

'You said that when that old brown cloak o' your'n got to be too bad off lookin' to go into town in any more, but you found that good green suit in one. What I says is if you don't try you won't know. Time to say a thing can't be done after you 'ave tried an' not t'other way round.'

She could always ask, she didn't have to buy anything. Ninepence for gloves . . . say threepence for second hand slippers . . . twopence for a dozen buttons . . . trimmings . . .

Gathering the rest of the used dishes from the table, she followed Lucy into the scullery.

Maybe it could be done, but jewellery, what of that? Phoebe smiled inwardly. Perhaps the Queen may have pawned the Crown Jewels.

'Lucy,' she asked, 'you did say the satin you saw in Underwood's shop window was a *pale* yellow?'

'Yes, Miss.' Lucy looked up from scouring pots. 'A lovely colour it be, like butter fresh from the dairy. Set your colourin' off to a tee it would.'

Pale yellow. Phoebe picked up the drying cloth and began to wipe the dishes Lucy had stacked on the board beside the sink. At least it wasn't pink.

Annie Pardoe wrote quickly, her well-formed copperplate hand rapidly covering the sheet of paper. She had bought the ink and the pen in Birmingham, that way she did not have to use that which was on the desk in the study, and the paper together with its envelope was the last of a birthday gift she had received from Abel many moons ago. She had kept one sheet of paper and one envelope, hiding them away for so many years, hiding them away but never forgetting them, knowing only that one day they would serve to hit back at him. Abel had died before she had found a way to strike, but that would not rob her of the revenge she had longed for all these years. Abel might be beyond her reach but his flesh and blood were not.

Folding the sheet of anonymously white notepaper she slipped it into the same self-effacing envelope, sealing it before writing an address across it in the same sure style. Abel was in his grave but his daughter was not. Slipping the envelope into her bag, she replaced the top on the bottle of ink, wiped the pen nib on a scrap torn from a corner of the newspaper, then slipped both into her bag alongside the letter.

Tearing the advert from the newspaper she slipped it into the drawer of the washstand, burying it beneath the towels. Abel was beyond her vengeance but she would destroy his daughter.

Thrusting a long hat pin through her hat, fastening it securely to her head, Annie checked her bedroom with a long seeking stare. The newspaper was folded neatly against her bag, the scrap of ink-stained paper was in the pocket of her coat, there was no sign of a letter having been written. Taking up her bag and the newspaper she left the room, passing that of her brother without looking in.

'Mr Samuel is still sleeping,' she said as she entered the kitchen, the lie sliding easily from her tongue. 'I thought it best not to disturb him. Take him a breakfast tray at eleven o'clock. I am going to ask the doctor to call, I am not at all sure Mr Samuel's health is improving despite the medicines.' Going into the scullery she deposited the newspaper with others kept in a wooden soap box alongside the stove to be used for lighting the house fires, then carried on, leaving the house by the rear door.

'Don't think Mr Samuel's health is improving?' Maudie watched from the scullery window. 'O' course it ain't improvin' an' you don't care for all you pretend to. You don't fool me, Annie Pardoe, you don't fool Maudie Tranter not for one minute you don't. You tell me you be going to fetch the doctor but it be my guess you be about more than that. You be up to summat, that much I be certain sure of, up to summat as sure as God med little apples.'

Standing to the side of the window so her watching presence would not easily be seen from outside Maudie waited until Annie had left, driving her small trap around to the front of the house. And still Maudie waited. She wouldn't put it past that sly bitch to come back into the house from the front. For several minutes she stood listening then, assured her mistress had gone, crossed the scullery to the soap box. Picking up the top newspaper she checked the date printed on the front page and smiled mirthlessly. 'You 'ave to get up early o' a mornin' to catch me, Annie, ma wench,' she murmured, then scanned the date on several papers until she found the one delivered to the house the day before. Turning to the page number she had made a mental note of, she smiled again. The advertisement for Pardoe's Patent Locks was missing.

Annie drove the trap at a steady walking pace, she was in no hurry and had no desire to draw attention to herself. She spoke to no one and none spoke to her, her long practice of ignoring people producing in them an almost total disregard for her. Passing to the left of Oakeswell Hall she skirted the black and white Tudor house, following the track across open ground the locals called the Mounts and coming around towards Hill Top. At the foot of the swell of ground Annie reined in the horse and sat looking at the black-grey water. Millfield Pool had formed when several gin pits had flooded, their vertical shafts filling with water which merged at the surface to form a large pond. The flooding of those shafts had taken many men, drowning them in their sludgy surging tide before they could scramble free, and it had taken others since.

Taking pen and ink from her bag she climbed from the trap and walked to the rim of ground overlooking the pool. 'You robbed me, Abel,' she whispered to the still menace lying at her feet, 'you robbed me of my life. Now watch while I rob your daughter of hers.'

Throwing the small bottle she saw it wing outward then thump into the water. She sent the pen after it, standing watching the spreading circles mark their watery grave. Taking the scrap of paper from her pocket, she stared at it for several moments. 'Vengeance is mine, Abel,' she whispered, rolling the paper between her fingers and letting it drop into her palm. Slowly raising her arm, stretching it out towards the water in macabre benediction, she tipped her hand, letting the balled scrap roll off the tips of her fingers. 'Vengeance is mine!'

Chapter Sixteen

'I wrote me name for it, Miss, I 'opes as that be all right? I 'ad no way of knowin' 'ow long you would be like, an' the postman, well, 'e 'ad other letters 'e 'ad to be deliverin'.' Lizzie Ingles's features struggled between a worried frown and an uncertain smile. 'I thought as if I wrote me name to say as I 'ad taken it in place o' you it would be all right.'

'It is all right, Lizzie, thank you.' Phoebe smiled and the other woman's face brightened. 'I wonder who it can be from?' She turned the white envelope but apart from the address written in neat flowing copperplate it bore no identifying mark.

'Only one way to find that out, Miss,' Lizzie said. 'That be to open it an' read it, an' that be best done over a nice cup o' tea.'

'I agree with you there, Lizzie.' Phoebe picked up the brown paper-wrapped parcel she had set down at her feet as Lizzie had met her. 'It's a fair walk from the Tipton Road. I got a ride from the carter as far as there but even so I am ready for a sit down and a drink.'

'Would you like me to make it for you, Miss?'

'That's good of you, Lizzie, but you must have work enough without waiting on me.'

'Nothing as will take 'arm from waitin' a while.' Lizzie opened the door that led into the mill house through the scullery and waited for Phoebe to pass inside. 'Bert an' Mark be in the workshop an' the babby be playin' around the back there.'

'Then you have time to join me. I will enjoy a cup of tea the more for having your company.'

Phoebe placed the parcel on the table in the kitchen, the letter beside it, unbuttoning her coat and hanging it beside the old brown cloak she kept now for working about the yard. 'I will take it upstairs later,' she said, seeing Lizzie eye the coat she needed to keep looking its best.

'I'll run it up for you, Miss.' Lizzie released the coat from its nail, her boots rattling on the stairs as she whisked up to Phoebe's bedroom.

'You really shouldn't,' Phoebe said as the woman skipped back in to the kitchen. 'You will have me too idle to scratch myself.'

'You, idle!' Lizzie poured boiling water on the fresh tea leaves waiting in the pot. 'That'll be the day. I've yet to come across a wench as works 'arder'n you an' I've met a few in me time. You sews most o' the day, then you 'elps with the filin' down o' the locks in the workshop, then o' nights you 'elps Lucy wi' 'er cookin'. No, you ain't idle, Miss. Whatever thoughts you might be 'oldin' about yourself that 'un be wrong.'

'I bought the most beautiful material for a gown.' Phoebe began to untie the string securing the parcel, Lizzie's compliment painting her cheeks a ripe pink. 'It is every bit as lovely as Lucy said and not nearly as expensive as I would have thought.'

'Eh, that's real pretty!' Lizzie made to touch the delicate lemony-cream fabric then pulled her hand away. 'An' it be just the colour for you with your hair.'

'There were others.' Phoebe added milk and sugar to the tea Lizzie poured for her. 'Green, blue, a really deep scarlet and a soft sugary pink. They were all so nice I was spoiled for choice.'

Sweetening her own tea, Lizzie sat opposite Phoebe in the warm kitchen. This girl must have had silks and finery, all the comfort and luxury her father's money could buy, and yet it hadn't spoilt her. There was nothing bay-windowed about her, and nothing vicious either. Even the months spent in that rat hole of a gaol hadn't altered her nature. Lizzie drank her tea. That son of Dartmouth's came visiting too regular for it to be a way of apologising for what he had done. His sort might say it once if you were lucky but not a couple of times a week. There was more to his coming than that. He was looking to make this wench his wife and if he got to do it he could count himself fortunate. This one would be no high-faluting, sit-on-her-arse lady of the manor. This one would care for the folk who worked for her.

'I got these to go with it.' Phoebe delved into the basket she had carried, taking out an assortment of buttons and lace. 'I thought feathers might be a little too much, what do you think?'

'I think you made just the right choice.' Lizzie admired the lace and touched a finger to the pretty pearl buttons. 'You'll be pretty as a picture, Miss, an' no coddin'.'

'But a ball gown,' Phoebe said, holding the elbow-length gloves she had bought against the material, then looking worriedly at Lizzie. 'I hope I haven't taken on more than I can handle. A ball gown . . . it's so different from a child's dress.'

'A bit fancier, Miss, I'll give you that,' said Lizzie, gathering the teacups, 'an' a bit on the bigger side, but that be all an' that ain't different, not really.'

'You make it sound so easy,' Phoebe called after her into the scullery, 'I almost believe it myself.'

Lizzie returned from the scullery drying her hands on her rough apron. 'You believe it, Miss, 'cos it be the truth. Lizzie Ingles wouldn't lead you up the garden path, 'er tells you the way 'er sees things an' no lies. Now you best be gettin' that there cloth up to your workroom afore summat be findin' itself spilt on it.'

'Did the metal come?'

'Ar, Miss, brass founders delivered it about an hour after

the three of you left this mornin'.' Lizzie watched as Phoebe gathered her purchases into one parcel. 'Bert says as there be enough for a couple o' dozen doublers an' p'raps a bit left over as'll make a few close shackle padlocks, an' 'e says as it be good quality metal an' all.'

Thank heaven for that, Phoebe thought, remembering how she had declared to the brass founder that any dross delivered to her would be returned unpaid for and her business taken elsewhere. She had trembled inside, seeing the scorn in his eyes as he had listened to a woman trying to play at business, but the scorn had faded as she had declared the price she was prepared to pay for brass or steel, changing to veiled admiration as she stated she would pay not a penny more.

'Don't forget your letter, Miss.' Lizzie nodded to the envelope that had become hidden beneath layers of brown paper. 'I'll be off now.'

'Thank you, Lizzie,' Phoebe said as the other woman left through the scullery. 'I will just take these upstairs and then I will see what it is.'

'. . . *one gross of Invincible locks to be delivered by the close of business on the last day of the month* . . .'

Phoebe stared at the words written neatly across the sheet of notepaper, its heading boldly proclaiming James Greaves, Hardware and Ironmongery. An order for one gross of locks, the first in answer to her advertisement. She read the remainder of the letter: '. . . *should you find yourself unable to comply with my requirements please notify me by return post.*'

The end of the month. Phoebe made a swift mental calculation. That left twenty-one days all told, including Sundays. It could not be done. She sank heavily to a chair, the letter in her hand. Her very first order and it could not be met. The start she had prayed for and it was over before it had begun. Folding the letter, she returned it to its envelope.

'It is as I have told you before, your brother's constitution has been weak from childhood.' Alfred Dingley pulled on his chamois leather gloves. 'I can prescribe medicine to help him sleep or to relieve pain should he have any, but there is no real cure for what truly ails him. You know it, Miss Pardoe, and I know it, and sadly so does he.'

Picking up the black Gladstone bag that was his constant companion, the doctor pressed a hand to his patient's shoulder before leaving the bedroom. 'He is getting weaker,' he said as he reached the front door. 'You can try him with beef tea or with some chicken broth but nothing too heavy.'

'My brother eats so little,' Annie said with mock solicitude, 'I worry so for him.'

'Worrying heals no wounds.' The doctor raised his tall black hat the merest fraction. 'And seeing you fret will only add to his suffering. My advice is to treat him the way you have always done – give him no intimation of how things really stand with him, though it is my guess he needs none.'

'How do you mean?' Annie asked, her hands shaking just enough.

Placing his valise on the seat, the doctor climbed into the carriage. 'I mean your brother is probably already acquainted with the fact that he has just a few years left on this earth.' Taking up the reins, he raised his hat again. 'Good day, Miss Pardoe. I will call one week from today.'

A few years? Annie returned to the house. Alfred Dingley was wrong. Her brother Samuel did not have a few years left on this earth, he had less than a few days.

She had taken so much care. The seeds of yew and laburnum painstakingly collected from the garden of the Bescot house. Several seasons' worth gathered and stored before the shrubs had been rooted out and burned, leaving nothing that could be traced. Dried and ground to an ultra-fine powder and added to water, the seeds had produced a liquid that held death in its pale golden heart, death that had slept within a perfume bottle waiting the time to strike. That time had come on the day of the burglary.

Annie stood before her cheval mirror admiring the sheen

of her pearl grey dress. Samuel had said how nice it was to see her in a colour other than black. How much more becoming soft shades were to her, how particularly well the grey suited her. It had suited well that day. She touched her fingers to the pocket in her skirt, concealed by the folds of taffeta. She had taken the bottle from the drawer and put it in her pocket. Samuel had been so taken up with examining the other rooms in order to ascertain whether anything other than the few silver ornaments had been taken he did not see her add the liquid from the bottle to the glass of sherry she had poured for him. Clinton had arrived just at that moment. He had heard of the burgling of her home, he said, and had to call to satisfy himself no one had been harmed.

It had not mattered to her then. She had almost smiled as she had poured a second glass of the pale golden sherry for Clinton. It had not mattered that he had met Samuel, theirs would be only a short acquaintance. Placing the glasses on a small silver serving tray she had been interrupted by the arrival of the constables and had left the two men to their drinks while she showed the policemen to the study.

Clinton had been taking his leave when she returned and she had walked with him into the tree-shrouded drive. She would have the deeds to her industrial properties the next day, he had told her, then kissed her cheek before leaving.

Turning from the mirror she crossed the room to the chest of drawers. Sinking on to her knees she pulled open the bottom drawer, taking the box with its amethyst ring from beneath the tissue-wrapped petticoats. Slipping the ring on to the third finger of her left hand she twisted and turned her wrist, admiring the dancing spurts of purple flame shoot from the heart of the stone. Soon she would wear it beyond this room, soon it would shine where all could see.

She felt no regret for what she had done to Samuel, for bringing early the death that Alfred Dingley foretold. Any regret she might have felt was gone, eaten away by her wasted years; nor did she feel any guilt. That must be Abel's for the shackles forged by his money.

Returning the ring to its box, Annie slipped it back beneath the petticoats and stood up. She would be Clinton's wife and Samuel would be gone from her life. Soon she would be free from all she had despised for so long, free from all that had held her prisoner while her youth slipped away, a freedom that had no place in it for Samuel and none for Abel's daughter.

Abel's daughter! Annie turned away from the chest of drawers, catching her reflection in the mirror as she did so. She had once been as Abel's child, young, pretty enough, full of happiness, eager for life and the promise it held. But the promise had been broken, life had not been given to her, it had been snatched away, snatched by a brother intent on his own happiness to the detriment of her own; a brother who could not himself be made to pay for what he had done to her but whose daughter would pay.

Annie smoothed her grey dress but her eyes were on the reflection of her face, on the tired skin, on the lines about her mouth, on the creases across her brow, on the look of age. The gall of bitterness rose within her. 'The sins of the parents shall be visited upon the children,' she whispered. 'She will pay, Abel . . . to the very last penny.'

'It's just impossible.' Lucy read the letter then passed it to Mathew. 'Six or seven locks a day . . . it can't be done.'

'I know.' They were in the kitchen of Phoebe's house, the evening meal having been cleared, the table holding only the letter Mathew had placed at its centre. 'The first reply to my advertisement and I can't fulfil the order.'

''Ave you talked of this wi' Bert?'

'What is the use?' Phoebe glanced at the tall young man, shirt sleeves rolled above the elbow, a broad belt about his waist. His sleeked back hair was still wet from a wash at the outdoor pump.

'Maybe none,' Mathew answered, 'but you should talk to 'im all the same.'

'Like Miss Phoebe says,' Lucy turned to her husband, 'it ain't no use talkin'. Talkin' don't make no locks.'

'It don't cost nothin' neither.' Mathew's retort was sharp.

'You think I should have shown the Ingleses that letter?'

'I don't think as 'ow it would 'ave 'urt none even if it didn't do no good. Seems only right to me some'ow that Bert be told.'

'I don't see as tellin' Bert will make no difference no'ow,' Lucy said stubbornly. 'It might only make 'im feel bad 'cos 'e can't do what that order asks.'

'Lucy has a point, Mathew.' Phoebe picked up the letter, folding it into its envelope. 'Bert works so hard, I would not want him to feel that losing this order was due to him.'

'Nor you should.' Mathew's lower lip came forward as it always did when he felt his argument was the right one. 'But it seems the bloke 'as the right to know 'is locks not just be sellin' well but could be sellin' a damn' sight better.'

'An' that be supposed to make 'im feel good, is it?'

'It would bloody well mek *me* feel good!' Mathew frowned at his wife. 'A bloke slaves 'is guts out, it shouldn't be too much for 'im to know the job 'e be doin' is a good 'un.'

'You are right, of course, Mathew.' Phoebe stood up, the letter in her hand. 'Bert should see the order. I will take it to him now.'

'I realise it cannot be done but we thought you should see the order, it shows how well your work is being received.' Phoebe waited while Bert Ingles read through the letter.

'It can't given the way we be now,' he handed back the letter, 'but that don't mean to say as it couldn't be done at all.'

''Ow be that then?' Mathew asked, his broad shoulders almost blocking the doorway of the small workshop. 'I don't follow.'

'It be logical,' Bert answered. 'One bloke on 'is own can't be doin' everythin', but give 'im a little 'elp . . .'

''Elp?' Lucy squeezed in against Mathew. ''Ow can we 'elp? We be knowin' nothin' of lockmakin'.'

'Mathew do.' Bert smiled. ''E's picked it up real well, an' Lizzie does most of the filin' down, an' Miss Phoebe there 'elps out wi' that, an' the lad works the bellows an' fetches coals up from the cut.'

'Coals!' Phoebe asked, perplexed.

'Ah, Miss, coals.' Bert turned to her. 'You needs coal to fire the forge an' we gets it from the barges that pass along the cut.'

'You mean the bargees give you coal?'

'Not gives,' Bert grinned, 'they comes 'ere for fresh water an' leaves a few buckets o' coal the side o' the cut afore they goes. It's fair trade.'

'But . . . but don't they get into trouble? It . . . it's like stealing.'

'No, it ain't, Miss.' Lizzie smiled. 'The coal bosses, they knows as cut men can't carry everythin' they needs for trips to London or the coast an' they makes allowances like. They knows a bit o' coal 'as to be swapped for water an' such.'

And may the Lord shut His ears to your lies, Lizzie Ingles, she thought, glancing away. Any hint of a bargee exchanging coal for any reason would have the coal bosses slamming him into gaol, but then, what the eye don't see, the heart don't grieve over.

'So if we all be already doin' what we can to 'elp, 'ow come you says the fillin' o' that order could be done?' Mathew asked.

'I reckons as 'ow it could be given another bloke or two, a few more hours workin' a day, an' a bit o' proper machinery to work wi'.'

'But we don't 'ave another bloke!' Lucy stated the obvious.

'Then there be the metal, Miss,' Lizzie added. 'You 'ave to

'ave money for metal. Bert sometimes gets carried away. 'E don't always see obstacles till 'e cuts 'is nose on 'em.'

'I see this order could be the start.' Bert looked at Phoebe. 'This could lead to others. Get this done an' I reckon you will be lookin' at the beginnin' of a business that could grow into summat big.'

'Buying brass and steel is one thing,' Phoebe was touched by the note of hope in Bert's voice, knowing how his dreams had ended with his father's death, 'but buying machinery is another.'

'You wouldn't 'ave to.'

'Then how?'

'I think as Bert be thinkin' of 'is own,' Lizzie put in. 'The rest of 'is tools still be in a out'ouse back of 'is father's place. They were never sold . . . nobody 'ad use for 'em seemed.'

'Until now.' Phoebe's mouth set in a determined line. 'We are going to use them. What has happened once will happen again and next time we will not have to refuse an order.'

'What you thinkin' of?' Lucy asked, recognising the determined expression.

'I am thinking we should discuss this further but not here in the workshop. Come across to the house, all of you. And with your permission, Lizzie and Bert, I would like Mark to come too. He helps in the workshop, he should be part of any decision that is made.'

'So,' Phoebe looked at the circle of people grouped about her kitchen, 'we need metal, we need men, and we need equipment. Where do we find them and how much will it cost?'

'The equipment be no bother,' Bert said. 'There be several bench vices, an anvil, 'ammers, tongs, chisels, files, the lot in my old place. They only needs bringin' 'ere, and findin' space to work be no 'eadache.'

'Then we must find a way of bringing them here.'

'Reckon a couple of Lucy's best mutton pies would see to that.' Bert grinned as he had in the workshop, the excitement of regaining his own equipment showing in his eyes.

'I see,' Lucy laughed, 'it's bribery now, is it?'

'Summat like that.' Lizzie looked up from her chair by the fire, her daughter on her knee. 'Bert be good at that.'

'See, Miss,' he went on, 'the 'ole lot, bench an' all, could be brought 'ere by barge.'

'But you don't work the barges anymore, Bert, so how does that help us?'

'No, I don't work the barges any more,' he answered, 'but I knows many who does an' there be one alongside towpath who be goin' up to Wolverhampton tomorrow. That will take him through Willenhall and right past my old place, an' 'e will be back 'ere the same afternoon. 'E would cart the lot for nuthin' more'n a couple of pies.'

'Could the man do that? Alone, I mean. Some of the things you need must be quite heavy?'

''E would need another man. I thought as I might 'ave to go wi' 'im.'

'Would there be anythin' I wouldn't recognise?' Mathew caught the flavour of the discussion. 'If you give me a good description, could I find the things you want?'

Bert thought for a moment before nodding. 'Reckon you could, ain't nothin' special.'

'Then why don't I go?' Mathew looked at Phoebe, her hands resting on the table, still holding the letter with its order for one gross of locks. 'That way Bert could carry on with the locks 'e is workin' on.'

'But what of your own work?' Phoebe asked.

'Ain't much of it at the moment,' Mathew answered wryly. 'Don't seem to be anybody wantin' odd jobs done right now an' what locks I'd be sellin' round the town could be countin' towards the gross we be needin'.'

'We are still left with the matter of employing another man,' Phoebe said.

'I've 'ad me brain on that one an' all,' Bert said again, 'if it's all right to say?'

'You've 'ad nuthin' but good ideas so far Bert so let's be 'earing what else you 'ave to say.'

Bert smiled at Mathew's words but his eyes were on Phoebe.

'Mathew has said what we all feel.' She smiled encouragement. 'Without you there would be no lockmaking business. You have solved all the problems so far, I am sure you will be helpful again.'

'Well, Miss, way I look at it is this. Mathew there 'as a good 'and for the locks, 'e 'as picked the job up a treat, 'sides which 'e as the strength needed for usin' 'ammer an' anvil. Now 'e 'as said as 'ow odd jobs 'ave dropped off so why not give 'im the job of workin' along o' me?'

'I had never thought of that,' Phoebe said, 'but how would Mathew feel about it? And what of Lucy?'

'I wants Mathew to be 'appy in what 'e is doin',' Lucy said as her husband's eyes turned to her. 'Whatever 'e chooses I know 'e does it for the best.'

Reaching for her hand Mathew folded it in his own, his smile broad. 'I'd like to work wi' Bert, Miss. Tattin' for jobs be no way to mek a livin'. Seems this lock business is goin' to tek off an' bein' in on it would give a man a reglar job like.'

'So we have our new hand,' Phoebe tapped her fingers against the envelope, 'now what we must do is work out the finances.'

Almost an hour later Phoebe pushed across the table a sheet of paper covered with figures and leaned wearily against the back of her chair.

'If only I had not bought that material to make a gown we might just have managed. I'm so sorry, Bert.'

'Ain't your fault.' Lizzie handed her daughter across to Mark who placed a protective arm about his sister's thin shoulders. 'You wasn't to know about no order comin' in.' Taking the pot from the dresser, she set about making tea.

'Of course it ain't no fault of your'n.' Lucy turned to help Lizzie with the tea. 'It was your money, you 'ad a right to spend it any road you wanted.'

'What say we goes through it once more?' Bert intervened.

Her calculations were correct, Phoebe knew. To go over them a thousand times more would only bring the same result: she just did not have sufficient money to buy the metal and pay the extra wages and no amount of checking the figures would alter that. But she leaned over them again, not having the heart to say no as she saw the dream dying in Bert's eyes.

'Let's all have a cup of tea an' p'raps things will look better.' Lizzie handed out the steaming cups while Phoebe buttered a scone each for the children.

''Scuse me, Miss.' Mark pulled a sultana from the edge of his scone, eyeing it with the look of a connoisseur, 'but you said as since I was workin' along o' me father I should be paid a reglar wage.'

'So I did, Mark.' Phoebe saw the astonished face of the boy's mother and the tightening of Bert's hand on his broad leather belt.

'Well, Miss,' Mark kept his eyes on the sultana, avoiding the warning glare that was in his father's eyes, 'I don't want it.'

'You don't want it?' Phoebe glanced quickly at the angry face of his father then back to the boy. 'But, Mark, we all agreed that a shilling a week was a fair wage.'

'It's a bostin' wage, Miss, only you can keep it toward payin' for metals. But when you gets paid for them locks, I will tek a shillin' a week.' His toffeedrop eyes gleaming with the air of a satisfied businessman clinching a deal, he popped the sultana into his mouth.

His anger forgotten, Bert touched a proud hand to his son's shoulder. 'He be right, what you reckon to pay 'im do be a good wage. Reckon lad 'as shown the way we was lookin' for,' he said. 'You can 'old my wage over till job be done an' locks paid for an' all.'

'I could not do that.' Phoebe looked up, astonished at Bert's words. 'Thank you, both of you, but you cannot work for nothing.'

''T'wouldn't be for nuthin',' Bert answered solemnly. 'Look at it my way. As things be Lizzie an' me 'as a roof for the children an' food for their bellies. Anythin' over an' above that be a luxury, an' luxuries can be gone wi'out. I know Lizzie will agree to what I says an' it be this. We will do as we did the first week we come 'ere. We 'ave enough to live on for the next three weeks so Mark an' me will tek no wage. You can make it up once locks be paid for.'

'Lucy an' me be of the same mind,' Mathew came in quickly, preventing Phoebe's refusal. 'We can manage same as Bert an' Lizzie.'

'I don't know what to say.' Phoebe's eyes glistened.

'Ain't nuthin' to be said, 'cept get these cups outa the way an' let's go over them figures again.' Bert came to stand at her shoulder. 'This time we're goin' to make 'em work.'

'We are still short,' Phoebe announced later as Lizzie carried her sleeping daughter out of the kitchen, Mark at her heels. 'I don't see there is anything more we can do.'

'I do 'ave one more suggestion.' Bert ran a hand through his hair. 'You 'ave down there the wage for another workman along o' Mathew. That be countin' for 'alf a crown a week. Now Mark, 'e knows lockmakin' inside out. Long nights on a barge leave a lad wi' little to do. 'E 'as a good brain, an' what's better 'e listens to what 'e be told. 'E can do all I do 'cept for the anvil an' that be a bit too 'eavy for 'im as yet.'

'So what are you saying?'

'I'm sayin' this. You got to pay 'alf a crown a week for summat my lad can do, and on top o' that you will need a coupla weeks to show a new bloke the ropes an' a damn' sight more'n a coupla weeks afore 'e can be left to work on 'is own, where the lad can do that now.'

Phoebe pressed a hand to her back, more tired than she wished to show. 'I don't understand, Bert.'

'I think I do,' Mathew said. 'You will be payin' a man's wage for a job 'e won't be able to do for weeks, the same job as Mark can do now, so why not let 'im work on the locks an' get another bloke to work the bellows an' bring up the coal, right, Bert?'

'Almost.' He grinned. 'My way you will be gettin' job done quicker an' for less money.'

'But if Mark is doing what a man would do he must be paid the same wage.'

'That ain't the way of things, Miss.' Bert straightened from where he had been stooped over the figures. 'Lad won't be doin' quite all a man would 'ave to, like I say 'e ain't up to 'ammerin' on a anvil, not yet. An' anyway, young 'uns gets paid less on account of the trainin' they be given. I 'preciates your thinkin' but I would rather 'e learned the usual ways of the world.'

'Bert be right in what 'e says,' Mathew nodded. 'This be one o' the facts you 'as to learn if you be goin' to run a business.'

'I expect so.' Phoebe smiled. 'And I understand we have no time to train a man in the skills of lockmaker, but we will still have to employ one to do what Mark was doing so where is the saving in that?'

'I said Mathew was almost right.' Bert pointed to the column of figures. ''Alf a crown for a bloke against ninepence for a lad, so why set a bloke on doin' a lad's work? Pumpin' bellows be a lad's work so why not get a lad to do it? It will cut nearly two-thirds off what you will pay in wages.'

Phoebe ran a swift eye over the figures, her tiredness evaporating as the import of what Bert was saying struck home. Mentally deducting the wages of Mathew, Bert and Mark, together with the revised wage of a youth, she felt a tremor of exhilaration. She could do it!

'Supposing you can make that many locks in a day, then we can accept our first order.' Rising from her chair, she held out a hand to each of the two men. 'Thank you,' she said simply, 'thank you both very much.'

'An' I'll thank you both to leave,' Lucy bustled into the scullery in search of baking tins, 'otherwise there'll be no mutton pies for that there bargee an' that'll put the cobblebosh on the lot of it.'

Taking his flat cap from his trousers pocket, Bert held it in his hand. 'I'll go down to towpath now an' 'ave a word wi' 'im, but 'e will bring my stuff right enough, no need to lose sleep over that. Night, Miss. Night, Lucy.'

'Goodnight, Bert,' Phoebe answered as he moved toward the scullery door. 'And, Bert, you have a good son in Mark.'

'Aye, Miss,' Bert fitted the cap to his head, 'Lizzie an' me, we knows that.'

Chapter Seventeen

'I instructed my own barrister to look into the affair of your time in prison.' Sir William Dartmouth looked at the young woman standing before him, hands folded across the front of a print dress, hair that was neither gold nor brown caught back in a knot that tried in vain to add years to her face. 'The result, I regret to say, showed a lamentable lack of justice. I have here a warrant signed by a magistrate – not, I might say, the one who consigned you to prison in the first place. What I ask is, will you return to Handsworth Prison for Women with me or would you prefer the constables to escort you there?'

Instructed my own barrister, I have a warrant, will you return, would you prefer the constables . . .

The words whirled together, dancing a crazy fandango, whisking in and out of her understanding. Phoebe clenched her hands together, hoping the bite of nails into flesh would stop the screams rising to her throat. He had not forgotten though he had been told of her innocence of the theft of his daughter's necklace, he wanted vengeance, never mind if the victim be free from blame. He had pretended friendship, even to the length of asking that his son be her escort to a farewell ball, and all the time he had been searching for a way to send her back to hell.

'You . . . you say you have a warrant?'

'Here.' He tapped the folded sheet against a gloved hand. 'Do you wish to read it?'

'No . . .' Phoebe breathed long and deep, fighting the nausea that was laying claim to her stomach. 'There will be no need, Sir William.' She could read it, Phoebe thought, fetching her coat, but she could not alter it. This time the Magistrate would not be wrong. This man would have his revenge and would make certain there could be no way he would be cheated of it.

Thanking the coachman for the hand he held out to help her up, Phoebe climbed into the carriage, her gaze on her home until it fell away below the rise of the ground.

How long had he been planning this? Phoebe watched the passing landscape but saw only the devils of fear dancing in her brain. Was it in his mind when she met him outside of the Magistrate's rooms in Wednesbury . . . was he thinking of it when he sent Edward and Sophie to invite her to the ball? And Edward, was he party to his father's action? Had he known of it even when he had asked her to marry him?

She closed her eyes, leaning her head against the padded upholstery of the carriage. No one save Sir William Dartmouth would know where she had gone or what had happened. Lizzie had watched from where she had been hanging washing on a clothes line Bert had set up beside the old windmill to catch the best of the breezes, but it had been too far for her to see any distress which might have shown. How long would Lucy and Mathew wait before making enquiries as to her whereabouts? Tomorrow? The next day? No, not that long, they knew she would not stay away from Wiggins Mill that length of time unless she had told them beforehand. And what if they went to the Priory? Would he see them, or would he have them dismissed without a word?

'Miss Pardoe, Miss Pardoe, we have arrived.'

This was not happening, it was a bad dream that would vanish when she opened her eyes, but it didn't and as she stepped from the carriage to be faced by that blank wall with its solid oak door Phoebe came face to face with the nightmare she had thought was over.

The door opened in answer to a knock from Sir William's malacca cane and they were inside. Inside the jaws of Hell.

Phoebe followed the grim-faced wardress in her grey soulless uniform, their footsteps sounding sharp in the carbolic-laden air of the narrow bare brick corridors. *I sentence you to fifteen years* . . . The words seemed to echo from the brickwork. How many years would it be this time? How much of her life would be spent paying for a crime she did not commit?

'Begging your pardon . . .'

The wardress had led them to a small, sparsely furnished waiting room Phoebe had heard of but had not seen and now stood looking at her, a faint shadow of near-forgotten concern on her long, drawn features.

'. . . but are you feeling unwell, Miss?'

Sensing Sir William move toward her, Phoebe stepped away.

'We do 'ave a infirmary 'ere, Sir,' the wardress looked at Sir William, 'if the lady would like to rest? She do look pale.'

'Thank you, but I am quite all right.'

Phoebe forced the words past a throat tight with fear. Resting in the infirmary would delay her return to the dormitory and the laundry only for as long as it took the man who had brought her here to leave. It had to happen, she had to return to the torture of long days and nights locked in this Godforsaken place, so why delay the inevitable? Let her sentence begin.

'Then I will tell the Governess you are 'ere.' The wardress bobbed the tiniest of curtsies. ''scuse me.'

'Miss Pardoe,' catching her arm as the wardress left the waiting room Sir William pressed her to a chair, 'are you quite certain you are not feeling unwell? You were very quiet during our drive here and now . . . as the wardress said, you are looking very pale.'

Looking very pale? Phoebe wanted to laugh but stared at him instead, rage at his treatment of her suddenly destroying the fear that had been suffocating her.

Pushing his hand from her arm she stood up, her features calm and icy as if carved from some glacial peak. 'I am looking very pale, how unwarranted of me!' Every word clipped into the quiet room like ice cubes falling into a glass. 'Please forgive my thoughtlessness. How ungracious of me to look so when you were kind enough to escort me here personally . . . how ignorant to repay that kindness by looking pale! So tell me, Sir William, how do you expect a woman to look when she is being returned to the grave?'

'Returned to the . . . I don't understand?'

'Of course you don't understand!' Phoebe spat, anger and fear overcoming her reserve. 'How could you understand? You to whom a girl dare not come with the truth for fear of tainting the name of Dartmouth. You who have been protected from reality all your life, whom the people raise their hat to, the powerful Billy-me-Lord, how could *you* understand what it is to be imprisoned? The degradation, the total lack of privacy, the utter soul-destroying mindlessness of it, the complete waste of a life . . . how would you know the torment of being accused of something you did not do, of having your life ripped away, of being condemned to a living hell, to be released only to be returned? To have the torment begin all over again!'

'Miss Pardoe . . .' He made to touch her then his hand fell to his side. He stayed where he was, watching the shades of passion flit across her face. 'I am sorry my bringing you here has caused you distress . . .'

'Sorry!' Phoebe glared contemptuously. 'You are *sorry* to have caused me distress? What did you expect returning me to prison would cause?'

'I did not think . . .'

'You did not think!' Phoebe cut across him, her tone lacerating. 'Do not insult me with lies, Sir William. You could have thought of little else all the time you were planning your revenge.'

'Revenge? I . . .'

'Yes, revenge.' She refused to let him speak, anger still uppermost. 'You pretended friendship towards me, you and your family, when all you really wanted was to have me re-committed to this prison. Why, Sir William? Why when you know I am innocent, when you have the necklace back? Why . . . is it to show the great Sir William Dartmouth is not to be played with?'

'Miss Pardoe, listen . . .'

'To what? More lies?'

'Call what I have to say lies if you will, but you shall listen. I brought you here . . .'

'Good day, Sir William.'

He stopped in mid-sentence, turning to see Hannah Price standing in the doorway.

'Miss Pardoe, my dear, how are you?'

Habit bent Phoebe's knee to a slight curtsy as she faced the Governess of Handsworth Prison for Women, fear surging up through the anger.

'I am well, Ma'am,' she murmured.

'But you look so pale.' She glanced at the man standing tight-lipped beside the young woman who had spent over a year locked behind the walls of this prison, a young woman she had come to like, whose loyalty and courage she had grown to respect. 'Sir William, perhaps the infirmary . . .'

'No, Mrs Price, thank you but we will get our business over. I want no further delay.'

'As you wish.' The governess nodded to the wardress who had remained at the door and she stood aside, allowing a third figure to enter the room.

'You wanted to see me, Ma'am?'

Everything stilled in Phoebe: her mind, her heart, the very blood in her veins.

'Yes, come in. Would you wait outside, Mrs Marsh?'

'Yes, Ma'am.'

Phoebe refused to let the exchange register, waiting only for the voice that had stilled her world to speak again.

'I think you know one of our visitors?' Hannah Price said.

In the stillness of her soul, Phoebe waited.

'Phoebe?'

The voice was uncertain but Phoebe was not. She knew that voice, recognised it from the long months of her captivity. 'Tilly!' She whirled to face the gaunt-faced woman, her hair tied in the compulsory plaits, the regulation grey skirts hanging loose about her thin body. 'Tilly! Oh, Tilly!'

'Sir William.' Phoebe stood at the front entrance to Wiggins Mill, her cheeks pink with embarrassment of what she knew she had to say. He had remained silent during the drive back to the mill, watching her hold a sobbing Tilly in her arms, then had waited until she had been settled with tea in a china cup, the kindly Lizzie in attendance. 'Sir William . . .' Phoebe began again.

'You do not have to say anything.' He placed a hand on her elbow, leaving it there as he added, 'It was thoughtless of me to act as I did. There is no need for apology.'

'There is every need,' Phoebe said, her eyes still holding traces of the tears of relief and happiness she had shed. 'It was wrong of me to speak to you as I did.'

'I think harsh words a mild punishment given the circumstances.' His grey eyes grew warm. 'Were I in your shoes nothing short of a horsewhipping would satisfy my feelings, I do not consider you at fault in any way.'

'That is kind of you, Sir William.' The colour deepened in Phoebe's cheeks, 'but I was at fault. I should have asked your reasons for taking me back to that place before I railed at you.'

'What did you think my reasons were?'

'Revenge.' Embarrassed as she was, Phoebe forced herself to meet his gaze. 'I thought you planned to have me returned to gaol, to have me serve the sentence originally passed upon me or perhaps an even longer one.'

'You thought the warrant I had was an order returning you to prison?'

'Yes.'

'But you had not been brought before a Magistrate, there

had been no new charge laid against you, how could you have thought you were being returned to serve that sentence?'

'Fear makes you suspect many things you would not normally think. I was afraid – afraid of being locked into Hell.'

'Miss Pardoe,' his eyes darkened and the fingers holding her arm tightened, 'I would never have you afraid because of me. Believe me when I say I was thinking only of the pleasure my actions would afford you. Causing you fear or concern never entered my mind. You told me of the circumstances of your friend's trial, of how you suspected there had been a miscarriage of justice. I thought it would in some way make amends for the suffering my family caused you if I could get a review of Mrs Wood's trial. I put the whole of what I knew before my own barrister who set in motion a further investigation of the so-called murder of the husband. It appears that other occupants of the lodging house where they lived had witnessed the argument. They had seen the man strike his wife and her attempt to defend herself. They had seen him fall backward down the stairs, causing his death.'

'Why didn't they say so at Tilly's trial? Why didn't they tell the Magistrate that?'

'It appears the constables did not report there being witnesses to the fall.' He did not remove his hand nor did his eyes leave hers. 'Or at least that is what the prosecution claimed. My barrister pressed for a complete review of the trial on the grounds of suppression of evidence, with the result that Mrs Wood was given a Queen's Pardon. Had I thought to tell you of all this before we went to Handsworth Prison you would not have been subjected to so much worry. I am deeply sorry and apologise most profoundly.'

'You are sorry and I am sorry.' Phoebe broke into a smile. 'We are a sorry pair, you and I, Sir William.'

'Yes.' His fingers tightened fractionally and the grey of his eyes turned to smoke. 'A sorry pair,' he finished softly.

'Sir William,' she said as he withdrew his hand from her

arm and turned towards his waiting carriage, 'I will not forget what you have done, for Tilly and for me.'

I will not forget either, Miss Phoebe Pardoe, he thought, climbing into the carriage. I will not forget what you have done to me.

'Annie dear, tomorrow I would like to see James Siveter.' Samuel's fingers moved without hesitation. 'I told you I wish to return most of what Abel bequeathed me to Phoebe.'

Annie's mind moved like quicksilver. He could not know that Phoebe still lived here in Wednesbury. She scrutinised the newspapers closely before passing them to him, removing those advertisements that referred to Pardoe's Patent Locks, and there was no one who could communicate with him other than herself. She alone had learned to speak with her hands; even Abel had not troubled himself to do so, relying on her to relay what he wished to say to Samuel.

'I want the papers drawn up tomorrow.'

She caught the quick movements, her thoughts outstripping them. Let Samuel say all he wished it would achieve nothing. There would be no tomorrow. She had thought the poison she had concocted from the yew and laburnum seed would have acted more rapidly than this; she had tried it often in those early years, feeding it to mice then cats then a dog, and in every instance it had brought death in less than two days. But for Samuel it had not worked. He had shown no more than his usual signs of illness. Was that due to Alfred Dingley's potions? She doubted it. The medicines he prescribed were no more than coloured sugar water prescribed as a salve to his own conscience for the fees he charged.

'I will go to his office in the morning,' she signed. 'I will tell him what you want and ask him to bring the papers here to you when they are ready.' That way she could delay long enough, she thought. A day would be all she needed.

'No.' The shake of Samuel's head signalled his refusal while his fingers flashed the rest of his words. 'I do not wish Mr Siveter to call at the house. I intend to visit him in his office myself tomorrow.'

You may intend to visit him, Annie thought, but I intend you do not.

'Will you be kind enough to drive me there in the trap, Annie dear?'

'Of course.' She smiled, her hands moving nimbly. 'If you are feeling as well tomorrow as you are today then certainly we will visit Mr Siveter.'

If he was well. Annie resisted the temptation to laugh. He would not be!

Samuel looked about him, the colours of late summer glowing the borders to the lawns. He loved the garden in all its phases but perhaps this was his favourite time.

'Brunswick House is such a kind house,' he motioned, 'it is almost a shame to leave it.'

A shame for you, Annie's thoughts raced, but not for me. I shall not be sorry to see the last of this place, to see the last of Wednesbury. I shall have a home of my own at last, a home with Clinton.

'Like you say, Samuel,' her fingers answered, 'it will be a shame to leave, but if it will give you peace of mind then of course that is what we must do.'

'Thank you, dear,' he smiled his weary smile, 'you always were so understanding, I will ensure you are well provided for.'

'Nonsense,' she returned, 'whatever makes you happy is all I want. But tell me, dear, how do we go about finding Phoebe? We do not know where she went, she may not even live in Wednesbury any more.'

'I know,' Samuel answered, 'but I am sure Mr Siveter will have methods of enquiry. We may leave it to him to find her.'

'Then we will tell him to begin tomorrow.' Annie touched a hand to the pain below her breast. It troubled her more often as the days passed, forcing her to take the white tablets several times each day, waking her in the night with fresh demands.

'It's time for Mr Samuel's medicine, Ma'am.' Maudie Tranter set a tray on the wicker table set between the garden chairs. 'Will I measure it?'

'Yes,' Annie nodded, 'but carefully. Two dessert spoons, no more, we must not exceed the amount the doctor advised.'

Bloody hypocrite, Maudie thought, carefully filling the dessert spoon she had placed on the tray then pouring the liquid into a glass before repeating the process. ''Er wouldn't care if 'e swallowed the lot, bottle an' all. But the Lord missed nothing and he wouldn't be missin' Annie Pardoe's doings. There was evil in that one, an old evil that had festered from her mother's passing, an evil that wouldn't be quenched this side of the grave.

'Will I pour the tea, Ma'am?' she asked as Samuel took the glass, swallowing its contents.

'No.' Annie reached for the dainty flower-patterned milk jug. 'I will do it myself.'

Samuel would take his tea then would go to his room and rest, probably sleep for several hours. That would give her time. Annie took her own cup, sipping her tea as the seed of her plan germinated in her mind, temporarily banishing the pain from her side.

'I want you to go into town.'

'Yes Ma'am.' Maudie had answered the bell summoning her to the study.

'Mrs Gaskell Wheeler told me of a herbal tea she was sure would be of benefit to Mr Samuel,' Annie went on. 'I have written the name of it on this paper. Take it to the herbalist in Meeting Street and wait until it is made up, I want my brother to have it today.' She handed the paper to her housekeeper together with a florin. 'There will be change from that,' she said as Maudie turned to leave. 'That herbal tea will cost no more than sixpence.'

'I'll get 'im to mek a bill out,' Maudie said, and banged the door behind her.

Samuel had been sleeping half an hour, Annie looked at the fob watch she wore pinned to her dress, and Maudie had been gone five minutes. Opening the doors that led directly into the garden she walked its length, turning at the tall privet hedge that screened the brick boundary wall and making her way to the low bothy building housing garden tools.

It was not one of the days the gardener-handyman was employed at Brunswick House. What she was about to do would be observed by no one. Going into the building she searched quickly along the shelves. It was there, the cardboard carton the gardener had bought, a carton containing rat poison. He had shown it to her, labouring the importance of keeping it out of reach, stressing the potency of its contents.

Taking her handkerchief from her pocket, she tipped a little of the powder into it, wrapping it carefully in the folds of the small white square of cloth before pushing it deep inside her pocket. Then, after replacing the carton on the shelf, she left.

From his bedroom window Samuel watched his sister return along the garden and knew where she had been. The colour of the dress she wore had changed. She no longer wore black, but that was the only thing about his sister that was different. Inside the same bitterness that had plagued her youth plagued her still.

Entering the house through the scullery, Annie glanced at her fob watch, checking the time once more. Maudie Tranter would be another hour at least. She had time yet.

'What did you think when you knew there was to be a re-investigation?'

They sat together in the warm kitchen. The fire had settled low in the grate and one oil lamp spilled a pool of yellow light courted by shadows.

'I didn't know.' Tilly's eyes strayed for the hundredth time around the kitchen, not yet believing it would not disappear like some dream-built world at the chime of a clock.

'But you must have been given some hint? The Governess or the wardresses, surely they said something?'

'If they knowed they said nothin' to me.' Tilly returned her gaze to the glowing coals. 'You knows what it's like in that place. If anythin' good was goin' to 'appen then that lot would be as close-mouthed as a Jew in a presbytery. They'd keep it to theirselves on purpose, drag out the agony a bit longer.'

'I can believe that of the likes of Agnes Marsh but I had thought better of Hannah Price,' Phoebe answered. 'I always got the impression she acted fairly.'

'Ah, me wench, we all thought that, an' 'er was fair an' all. 'Er was a decent woman an' a good prison governess. You kept yer nose clean and you 'ad no worry from 'er.'

'Do you think she knew?'

'Can't say.' Tilly looked again to the rough wooden dresser, studying the motley assortment of cups and dishes. 'Maybe yes, then again maybe no. There was some comin' an' goin' about a week ago, 'er was off out somewhere two or three times, but we put it down to meetings wi' Prison Board.'

'Mary Pegleg heard nothing?'

'You can bet yer life 'er didn't.' Tilly stretched a hand to the lamp Phoebe had set in the middle of the kitchen table, running a finger over the gleaming brass body. 'Mary Pegleg gets to know summat an' 'er's like a cat wi' a maggot up its arse – 'er can't get it out quick enough.'

Phoebe bent over the spent fire, adding fresh coals, the move hiding her smile at her friend's rough language. Tilly had been in gaol a long time and the ways of others had touched her. It would take time for them to fade.

'If those meetings with the Prison Board concerned your release and Hannah Price said nothing of it to you, then she must have been told not to. I can't imagine there being any other reason for her to keep it from you,' Phoebe said, sitting down again.

'Like as not yer right,' Tilly nodded, 'an' come to think on it p'raps it were the sensible thing to do. I think if 'er 'ad told me there was a chance I'd be gettin' outta that place, then told me later that I weren't, I'd of got meself out another way.'

Phoebe looked perplexed. 'Another way? But surely there was no other way.'

'Oh, ar, there was, me wench.' Tilly looked up from the fire, her laughterless eyes haunted by the spectre of hopes long dead. 'A way I'd thought on many a time. A sharp knife across the throat gets you out of anywheer.'

'Oh, Tilly!' Leaning forward, Phoebe pressed the other woman's calloused hands. 'It's all over now.'

'For me it is.' Suddenly Tilly sounded far away. 'I'll never go back theer again, I'll put meself in me box first.'

Phoebe rose, kneeling before Tilly to put her arms about her. 'You won't ever go back, Tilly, I promise, I promise.'

Holding each other, the two women stared into the flickering flames of the rebuilt fire, each seeing their yesterdays in its heart.

'Phoebe,' Tilly asked after several minutes, ''ow come that man knowed about me an' what I'd done?'

'Sir William?' Releasing her, Phoebe stood up. 'I am afraid I told him after . . .' She broke off, the horror of the attack on her flooding back.

'After what?'

'Nothing.' Phoebe made a business of taking cups from the dresser and setting them on the table. 'Nothing.'

'Yer 'ands be shakin' an' yer face be the colour of a corpse. That don't be tellin' me it was nothin'.'

Locating a brown-coloured tin labelled 'Bournville', Phoebe spooned cocoa into the cups, spilling as much of the powder over the sides as went into them.

'A man came to the house,' she said, knowing Tilly would repeat her question until it was answered. 'I . . . I was upstairs. He thought I had been given money by Sir William and that I had it hidden somewhere.'

''Ad you?' Tilly watched the cocoa powder sprinkle like brown snow over the cups. It was her bet the girl had told nobody the full story of what had happened, and no matter what it had been it was better told and in the open; fastening it up inside herself would only see the fear grow.

'No.' Phoebe loosed the spoon into one of the cups, the clatter loud in the stillness of the kitchen.

'But 'e didn't believe you?' Tilly led her on, knowing each answer would relieve the pain.

'No, he didn't believe me. I thought if I could get him out of the house I might somehow escape him so I told him the money was in the old corn barn. He made me go there with him and while he was searching among the sacks I managed to run out into the yard, but he . . . he . . .'

Tilly rose from her chair. This was the part that was buried deepest, the core of the pain etched across that young face. Taking the tin from Phoebe's trembling hands, she stood it on the table then drew her into her arms. 'Get it up, ma wench,' she said softly, 'let it all come out, Tilly's got you.'

Slowly, between long shuddering sobs, the full story of the attack came out. Tilly listened without intervention. The dam was broken, let the water flow.

'I thought it was Liza,' Phoebe sobbed against her shoulder, 'I thought it was Liza!'

'Ssshh.' Tilly stroked her hair. 'Liza won't 'urt you no more, an' neither will anybody else so long as I be livin'.' She stood with Phoebe in her arms, holding her as she would a child until the sobbing had stopped.

'Now I think we're both ready for that cocoa,' she said, pushing Phoebe into a chair. 'An' I thinks I'll be meking it, you spills too much.'

'I never thought Sir William would do anything to help you,' Phoebe said, sipping the hot frothy liquid.

'An' why should 'e?' Tilly held her own cup cradled between both hands, savouring the heat on her fingers. ''E don't know me from Adam, so why put 'isself to all that bother?'

'He said he did it to try to make up for what his family had caused to happen to me.'

'Well, whatever 'is reason, I thank the Lord for it. 'E got me from Handsworth Prison when I never thought to see the outside of it never again.' She looked across at Phoebe, sudden concern in her eyes. 'Eh, wench, I've just thought! I never even said thank you. 'E's gonna think I'm a right 'un.'

'You didn't say anything as I remember,' Phoebe smiled at last, 'but I am sure Sir William will understand.'

'Do yer think as I might see 'im agen?' Tilly asked. 'Might 'e call 'ere agen sometime?'

Phoebe dropped her eyes to her cup, surprised at the answer rising silently within her. I hope so, Tilly, I hope so.

'P'raps it might be better to write 'im a note, just in case like,' Tilly went on. 'Would you 'elp me, Phoebe?'

'Of course.' She looked up. 'We will do it tomorrow and Lucy will post it for you in Wednesbury. The post office is just a stone's throw through the Shambles.'

'Is there work in Wednesbury?' Tilly asked. 'For a woman like me?'

'A woman like you!' Phoebe said sharply. 'What does that mean?'

'It means, will anybody employ a woman they know 'as been along the line.'

'If you are referring to a certain Tilly Wood,' Phoebe adopted her most cautionary tone, 'I advise you speak of her with respect. She happens to be one of my greatest friends and one who stands in no need of employment for she is to live, and work I might add, here with me at Wiggins Mill.'

'Oh, Phoebe, me wench!' Tilly choked. 'Phoebe!'

Carrying the cups to the scullery Phoebe washed them then returned them to the dresser, giving Tilly time to regain her composure, then she asked, 'Tilly, what happened to Liza?'

'Huh!' She snorted. 'A bad 'un that if ever I met one. It seemed for a long time as 'er wouldn't get over 'ittin' 'er face agen that wall, but 'er did. 'Appen there be no stoppin' the Devil's own, an' Liza Spittle was that all right. 'Er 'adn't been outta that infirmary no more than a fortnight when we 'ad a new inmate, pretty little thing wi' 'air the colour of corn fresh scythed an' eyes blue as a kingfisher's wing. Well, I don't need to tell it but Liza took a shine to 'er an' you won't believe this but so did Emily Pagett. You know, wardress as took Sally Moreton's place.'

'I remember.' Phoebe took a chair on the opposite side of the fire, resting her feet on the hearth.

'Well,' Tilly smiled sardonically, 'that pretty little thing looked like a angel but 'er weren't none. 'Er played them two women one agen another, lettin' both touch 'er up then tellin' each in turn the other 'ad forced 'erself on 'er. It would 'ave been summat for the rest o' we to laugh at if we 'ad any laughter left in we. Any road up, outcome was Liza 'ad the blue devils an' went for Emily Pagett wi' a knife.'

'Did she kill her?'

'No, me wench,' Tilly shook her head, 'though 'er nearly did. Knife just missed 'er lung so Mary Pegleg 'eard the doctor tell the Governess. Anyway, they took Pagett off to some 'ospital in Brummagem an' that be the last we seen of 'er.'

'And Liza?' Phoebe stared at the fire, seeing in its redness the birthmark that spread across the woman's face.

'Prison Board dished out thirty strokes of the cat.' Tilly's voice was devoid of emotion. 'No more than 'er deserved.'

'But is she all right?' Phoebe had to ask. 'She did get over it?'

Tilly was silent for a moment before answering the girl Liza Spittle had tried so many times to assault. 'Might 'ave been,' she said quietly, "cept 'er 'ung 'erself wi' laces out of 'er own stays.'

Chapter Eighteen

Letting the fob watch drop back into place over her left breast, Annie listened. The house was silent, no movement from overhead. She breathed slowly. Samuel must still be sleeping.

Going into the pantry she brought out the one small chocolate-covered cake delivered to the house fresh each day. Samuel had never liked the taste of medicine, any medicine, complaining of the bitterness after every dose and the cake was a treat that took the taste away.

Annie placed it on a plate. Shaped like a cup, its thick chocolate sides daintily fluted, it was filled with a generous depth of fresh cream and topped with a thick chocolate lid embedded in which was a walnut. Working quickly, Annie removed the lid, scooping out the cream on to a saucer. Taking the powder from her pocket, she tipped it into the cream, mixing the two together. Would Samuel detect the taste? What if he left it uneaten after the first bite? Annie thought for a moment, then going back to the pantry brought out a box of finely powdered sugar. Adding a large spoonful to the cream, she folded it in then carefully returned it to its chocolate case, replacing the lid.

It was done! Putting cake and sugar back in the pantry, Annie cleared all traces of her activity from the kitchen then carried the plate to the scullery, washing both it and her hands and rinsing them in several bowls of water before drying them. Replacing the plate on the dresser in the kitchen, she returned to her chair in the garden, dropping her handkerchief in the stove as she passed through the scullery. Tomorrow she would not be talking to James Siveter, tomorrow she would be talking to Thomas Webb, Wednesbury's undertaker.

'The 'erbal tea, Ma'am.'

Annie opened her eyes, blinking rapidly, pretending to chase sleep from them. But she had not been sleeping though she had been dreaming – dreaming of her life with Clinton.

'The 'erbal tea.' Maudie held out a bottle in which a sludgy brown mixture reached almost to the cork. 'The 'erbalist said to give a small wineglass o' this twice a day.'

'Was that all he said?' Annie hitched herself straighter in the chair.

'No.' Maudie still held the bottle at arm's length.

'Then what else did he say?'

''E said we was fortunate to be 'avin' such fine weather though like as not we'd be payin' for it come winter.'

Snatching the bottle, Annie glared at her housekeeper. The woman deliberately tried to anger her. Was she hoping to be dismissed? Hope or not she would be in very few weeks from now. Rising from the chair, Annie stalked into the house, a smirking Maudie at her heels. 'I will leave this here.' She put the bottle of herbal mixture on the table Maudie kept well scrubbed.

'Will I be tekin' a draught up to Mr Samuel?'

'No.' Annie looked at the bottle then at Maudie, busy fastening the straps of her long white apron. 'No, you can bring a glass with the afternoon tray.'

'The bill for that be there on the dresser an' the change from the florin alongside o' it. You best count it.'

'Didn't you count it when the herbalist gave it to you?'

'Oh, I counted it,' Maudie looked bland, 'but then I ain't the one was worried over it.'

Sweeping to the dresser Annie snatched up the bill, reading the words 'One eight-ounce bottle of herbal mixture, sevenpence'. Scanning the change, one shilling, a threepenny bit and two pennies, she scooped them into her hand. 'Mrs

Gaskell Wheeler was confident this mixture would help Samuel.' She moved across the kitchen toward the door linking it to the rest of the house. 'And Mrs Gaskell Wheeler is most knowledgeable in the use of herbal remedies.'

Mrs Gaskell Wheeler this, Mrs Gaskell Wheeler that! Maudie grabbed the tea tray from beside the dresser, her thoughts acid. Annie Pardoe was possessed by that woman. Would kiss her arse if asked to.

'I think Mr Samuel would quite like his afternoon tea in the garden,' Annie went on. 'It is still so pleasant out there we should take advantage of the warm spell while we can. It is not often we get the chance with a climate such as ours. I will see if my brother is awake yet.'

She had thought of everything but as she moved up the stairs Annie went over it all again in her mind. The herbal tea had been Violet Wheeler's idea and Maudie Tranter had collected it. She, Annie, had left it unopened in the kitchen and would leave it to Maudie to administer it as she would leave it to her to give Samuel the cake. Should anyone question the cause of his death there would be no finger pointed at her and there would be no trace of poison having been added to either the herbal tea or the medicine Alfred Dingley prescribed.

And the cake? Who could prove poison had been added to that? Annie paused at the head of the stairs, pressing a hand to the pain that shot upward through her breast. The cake would be eaten. Samuel was too fond of sweet things to leave any of it uneaten. What if anyone asked the reason for there being just one cake? Annie pressed harder, clenching her teeth against the fire clawing at her side. Maudie Tranter would answer that. She could tell them Annie Pardoe never ate cake or sweet desserts. And the doctor? He would not look too closely, he had been expecting Samuel's death for too long. Pulling in a deep breath, she walked along the corridor to Samuel's bedroom. Yes, she had thought of everything, just as she had with that letter.

* * *

'They all be so pretty,' Tilly fingered the dainty dresses and lace-edged petticoats Phoebe had ready for market, 'an' they sells well, you say?'

'They have up to now.' Phoebe held a strip of ribbon against a length of delphinium-sprigged cotton cloth, matching the colours. 'Lucy says we could sell more.'

'Then sell more is what you must do!'

'It is not that easy.' Phoebe changed the ribbon for one of darker blue. 'I can't sew any more than I do already. I was hoping to buy one of Mr Singer's new sewing machines – I read about them in a newspaper Lucy had wrapped around some fish.'

'Bet that made a change from the smell o' brass filin's.'

Phoebe glanced across at Tilly, noticing the smile about her mouth, a smile that came more easily as each day passed.

'Then why ain't you?'

'Why haven't I what?' Phoebe went back to her first choice of ribbon.

'Why ain't you bought one o' Mr Singer's newfangled machines?'

'Money.' Phoebe spread the flower-strewn cloth on her workroom table and began laying paper pattern cut outs over it. 'I haven't got enough money. My clothing sells well but buying metal for locks swallows it as fast as I get it. I use every penny either on that or cloth or food.'

'An' what does this be for?' Tilly touched the delicate cream-yellow satin still lying in its paper wrapping.

'It was to have been for a ball gown.' Phoebe glanced at the gleaming satin then returned to her cutting.

'Was to 'ave been?' Tilly questioned. 'Why "was to 'ave been"? Why ain't it still goin' to be?'

'Because I will not have the time to make it,' Phoebe said, her lips pursed as she cut around a tricky piece of pattern.

Tilly waited until the manoeuvre was finished then asked,

'But won't the woman it be for be put out wi' your not mekin' 'er gown after gettin' that cloth an' all?'

'I don't think so.' Phoebe gathered the paper pattern pieces together, laying them aside. 'You see the woman was me.'

'You was mekin' yourself a ball gown?'

Phoebe gathered the pieces of cloth she had cut out. 'I had intended to do so but sometimes plans have to be set aside.'

'That means you ain't no longer goin' to mek it.' Tilly covered the cloth with its paper wrapping. 'Why?'

Sitting at her work table Phoebe began to pin the pieces of cloth together, matching sides to sides. 'Because it would be wrong of me to spend time sewing something that was not intended for sale, something that was bringing no money to Wiggins Mill when everyone else was working so hard.'

'But it must 'ave been special for you to 'ave spent money buying that cloth in the first place.'

'I have been invited to the Priory,' Phoebe explained. 'Sir William is giving a farewell ball in place of the more usual Advent Ball, the reason being Lady Amelia is leaving for the continent earlier than she would normally do. Her Ladyship took the influenza some weeks gone and is not yet over the effects.'

'An' you 'ad accepted the invite?'

'Not exactly.'

'Cockeyed way o' carryin' on, ain't it?'

'What is?' Phoebe asked, her mouth half full of pins.

'Buyin' stuff to mek yourself a fancy frock an' you not accepted the party invite exactly.' Tilly retrieved a pin from the floor, dropping it into the tobacco tin Phoebe kept them in. 'Strikes me you 'ad every intention of goin' to that ball. P'raps it could still be done if I 'elped you with the sewin' of it.'

'I did not know you sewed?' The words pushed past the pins still locked between Phoebe's teeth.

'There be a lot you don't know about Tilly Wood, me wench.'

Phoebe removed the pins from her mouth, putting them in

the tobacco tin that had once belonged to Mathew. 'This much I do know, you already work hard enough. You have taken on the running of the house and preparing the meals . . .'

'Lizzie does a fair share o' all that,' Tilly said quickly.

'And you do a fair share of the filing down of the locks.' Phoebe smiled gently. 'I wanted you to rest, Tilly, I didn't want you working just as hard as . . .'

'As hard as I had to inside.' She took up the words Phoebe couldn't say. 'Phoebe, wench, what I does 'ere at Wiggins Mill be paradise compared to Handsworth Gaol. I thank God every minute I breathes for what 'e done for me, an' 'elpin out wi' a bit o' sewin' ain't too great a burden. I'd like to see you go to that there ball.'

'Very well,' sorting a needle Phoebe broke off a length of blue thread, 'we will do a little each evening.' She looked up from threading the needle, her eyes smiling. 'Unless, of course, a fairy godmother should exist somewhere and decides to bring me a gown already made.'

'Oh, they exist all right.' Tilly picked up the tin of pins, staring into it. 'An' not all o' em be old neither. You be my fairy godmother, Phoebe. What you did for me be nuthin' short o' magic.'

'It was not I who got you released from prison, Tilly,' Phoebe reminded her softly. 'It was Sir William Dartmouth. He is the one who worked the magic.'

'Ar, wench, 'e is, an' grateful I be to 'im.' She replaced the tin on the table close by Phoebe's hand. 'Only some'ow I can't see 'im wi' wings an' wavin' of a wand.'

'Bert says the new lad Mathew got to work the bellows is doing very well,' Phoebe said when they had both stopped laughing.

''E is. Lad works like a little Trojan, nuthin' ain't too much trouble for 'im.'

'Do you think carrying coals might be too heavy?'

'No, wench, I don't. The lad be strong enough, Bert wouldn't set 'im no task 'e thought too much.'

'No, he would not.' Phoebe examined her line of stitching. 'Bert is a kind man.'

'They'm a nice family an' willin' workers the lot o' 'em.'

'Including Ruth. I have seen the way she gets under your feet, you can't do anything without her being there.'

'Ar, you be right.' Tilly smiled. 'But I don't mind that, 'er be a pleasant little thing, an' Lizzie 'as seen to it 'er knows 'er manners, never forgets a please or a thank you. An' talkin' of folk gettin' under other folks' feet, I better be off an' leave you to get on wi' what you be about.'

'How are the locks coming along?' Phoebe called after her.

'Nearly 'alf done,' the answer came back. 'Bert says you will 'ave 'em all on time.'

'How can you be certain?'

The evening meal finished, Lucy and Mathew sat for a few minutes before starting their evening's work.

'I can't, but it do seem strange me not seein' 'im once since 'e started.'

Mathew lit his pipe, sucking the stem much as his father did. 'P'raps 'e's found some other way.'

'Such as what?'

'Such as followin' the cut.'

'Could be as you're right but it wouldn't make a lot o' sense,' Lucy said. 'Cut would take 'im right out o' 'is way – 'e lives other end o' Wednesbury. Least that be what 'e told you, wasn't it?'

'Ar.' Mathew tapped his pipe against the heel of his hand. 'Then why would 'e be followin' the cut 'ome?'

'Who knows why kids do 'alf the things they does?'

'They does some daft 'uns, I'll give you that,' Lucy began to clear the table, 'but to go a mile or more outta your way 'ome after a day's work don't strike me as no kid's lark.'

'So what do you reckon?' Mathew blew down the stem of

his white clay pipe. 'You've got some bee in your bloomers, wench.'

'You watch the way you be talkin', Mathew Leach, I ain't no fish wife to be listenin' to your vulgarities.' Lucy flicked out with the cloth she had taken to the dishes but she was smiling.

'You ain't seen 'im, not once?' Mathew resumed, sucking his pipe.

'Not once,' Lucy affirmed. 'An' I thinks that be more'n strange. You know what I really thinks? I thinks 'e ain't goin' 'ome at all.'

Several puffs of blue-grey smoke curled into the room, suspended like a delicate veil above Mathew's head. 'Then where do 'e be goin'?'

Carrying the enamel bowl with its washing up water into the yard, Lucy emptied it into the drain running along its width then stared at the old windmill, secretive and brooding against the fading light. ''E be goin' there,' she whispered. 'It's my guess 'e be goin' there.'

Back in the outhouse they had made into a comfortable home Mathew finished his pipe, knocking the burned ash of the tobacco out against the bars of the fire. ''Ave you said anythin' to the others?'

Lucy fitted the cups and plates on to the rack Mathew had made and set on the wall, then folded the cloth she had dried them on and hung it across the length of string set across the grate. 'I thought as I would talk to you first.'

'You am sure?' Mathew put his pipe alongside the tin of shag tobacco on a cupboard that had come with a job lot of furniture from a tat man who had delivered it all for a shilling.

'Sure as I be talkin' to you.' Lucy reached for the white apron she wore only when baking, fastening the straps around her waist.

'Then we best tell the others.'

Phoebe listened, concern deepening on her face as Mathew spoke of Lucy's suspicions.

'He could not have crossed the heath without you seeing him?'

'I swear 'e couldn't, Miss Phoebe. A body can see for miles across there, it bein' mostly flat ground, an' I ain't seen 'im nowhere on it, not when I've been goin' in to Wednesbury on a mornin' nor when I've been comin' back at night. I be tellin' all o' you, that lad ain't passed me an' I says that shows 'e ain't goin' 'ome nights.'

'But his parents would have enquired before now surely?' Phoebe said. 'They must know where he is employed.'

'Maybe not,' Bert said. 'Maybe the lad 'as got no parents.'

'Was nobody wi' 'im that day I picked 'im out o' the line,' Mathew put in. 'Leastways nobody spoke to 'im when we set off.'

'If 'e don't 'ave no parents it could follow 'e don't 'ave no 'ome.' Lizzie looked at Phoebe. 'That would explain Lucy not seein' 'im on the way to an' from the town, wouldn't it?'

'It would.' Phoebe nodded. 'But if he is not going home at night, where is he going?'

Lucy's glance strayed to the rise of high ground, to the silent windmill painted black against the sky. 'I thinks 'e be goin' nowhere,' she said, 'not for the 'ole night anyway.'

'Then where is he spending his nights?' Phoebe asked, worry plain in her voice. 'I hope he is not sleeping on the heath.'

'I don't think 'e is,' Lucy glanced again at the windmill standing tall into the glow of the setting sun, 'I think 'e be sleepin' in there.'

'The windmill?' Bert followed the line of Lucy's eyes and her reasoning. 'Could well be. I could think of worse places a lad might get 'isself 'oled up in. You women wait indoors, Mathew an' me will go look.'

'You have been sleeping in the old windmill since the first day Mathew brought you here?' Phoebe said ten minutes later when the bellows boy stood in her kitchen, Mathew and Bert to either side of him.

'Yes, Miss,' the boy answered, chin on chest.

'But why? Is the walk from Wednesbury to here and back too much for you?'

'T'ain't too much!' The boy's chin came up defiantly. 'Ain't nuthin', that tiddly walk. I could walk six time further'n that wi'out feelin' tired.'

Bert placed a hand on the boy's shoulder, feeling the bones through his ragged coat. 'Tell 'er, lad.'

'Ain't nuthin' to tell.'

'If there ain't another reason you be sleepin' in that mill then Miss Phoebe be right in thinkin' the walk be too much for you, an' that bein' the case 'er might give you your coppers, lad, an' that means you'll be out o' a job.'

The boy looked quickly to Phoebe, the subtle warning Bert had given bringing fear to his eyes.

'You wouldn't, would you, Miss? You wouldn't go givin' me the sack?'

Phoebe looked at him. The sleeves of his threadbare coat were short of his wrists by several inches, his trousers halfway up his legs with more holes in them than sultanas in one of Lucy's scones, and her heart twisted with pity. What was it drove him to sneak back to sleep in the mill?

'I would have to if I thought it too far for you to walk, Josh.'

''T'ain't, Miss. Honest 't'ain't.' He looked down to where his toes peeped through boots that lacked the laces to fasten them. 'It's . . . it's . . . I ain't got no 'ome.' The reservoir of pride breached, the words tumbled from him. 'Me dad 'e buggered off years ago, left me mother to fend for 'erself an' me. We managed not too bad while she could tek in washin', then when 'er got sick we couldn't pay the landlord an' 'e chucked we out. It was the work'ouse or the road an' me mother wouldn't tek the work'ouse, least not till 'er could 'ardly walk no more. 'Er died the day after 'er went in. So you see, Miss, I ain't got other than the 'eath to sleep an' that windmill be a shelter from the wind.' He looked up at Phoebe. 'I didn't think as you would mind, Miss, I meant no 'arm, really I didn't.'

'And you did none.' Phoebe resisted the urge to take him in her arms, knowing that his fierce pride would resent any offer of childish comfort. 'But I wish you had told me.'

'You would 'ave chucked me out if I 'ad.'

'Miss Phoebe wouldn't 'ave chucked you out,' Mathew said.

'Mebbe 'er wouldn't,' the boy remained stubborn, 'but it was a chance I wasn't tekin'. Long as nobody seen me go in I 'ad a place to sleep.' He twisted free from Bert's hand. 'Who told you I was in there anyway?'

'Nobody told we,' Bert answered. 'Well, p'raps that's not strictly true. It were Mrs Leach not seein' 'ide nor 'air of you not comin' to work in the mornin's nor goin' back of an evenin'. Seemed strange to 'er that did, set 'er to wonderin' just 'ow you did get to Wiggins Mill.'

'I couldn't 'ave missed sight o' you, Josh,' Lucy said apologetically. 'The 'eath be mostly flat 'tween 'ere an' Wednesbury. You could spot a grass'opper a mile off.'

'I knows you didn't mean to drop me in it,' the boy tried to smile as he looked from her to Phoebe, 'an' I'm sorry to 'ave been the cause o' trouble, Miss. I won't go in the mill any more, you can be 'sured o' that. Just let me keep me job an' I'll bugger off every night cleaner than me father did.'

'You won't go nowhere every night, same as you won't be usin' that foul language no more.' Lizzie pushed further into the kitchen. ''E can't be sleepin' on that 'eath, Miss Phoebe, so unless you 'ave any objections 'e could bed down the side o' our Mark. There be room a-plenty in the corn loft, an' 'im an' Mark, they gets on well together.'

'Bert?' Phoebe looked at the man standing beside the young boy.

'That be all right by me, Miss Phoebe. Lad can stay wi'

Lizzie an' me long as 'e as a job at Wiggins Mill. An' if I knows Lizzie, 'er will look after 'im.'

'What do you say, Josh?' Phoebe asked.

A smile splitting his face, the boy looked at Lizzie. 'Bostin',' he breathed. 'I say that be bostin'.'

'I thought we would have afternoon tea in the garden, it is still quite warm enough,' Annie signed, finding her brother in his studio. 'And you do so enjoy the garden.' She stopped speaking, her mouth half open with surprise as she caught sight of the canvas on the easel. It was a finished portrait of Phoebe, only the paint that formed the signature still gleaming wetly. The face looked serenely back at her, a calmness beyond its years radiating from it. It was also the image of Abel's pretty wife, she realised.

'I . . . I did not know you had painted this.' Annie caught her brother's eyes on her and struggled to regain her composure. 'It is very good, especially considering you have seen so very little of Abel's daughter.'

Samuel's long narrow fingers moved rapidly. 'I worked from this more than from memory.' Going to a drawer set in a long bench-top table on the opposite side of the room, he drew out a photograph, handing it to Annie. 'It was in among some of Abel's papers. I found it when I went through them.'

Among Abel's papers? Annie stared at the photograph. She'd thought she had weeded everything out but obviously she had missed this and Samuel had said nothing of it, as he had said nothing of the portrait he'd now finished. What else had he said nothing of? What other secrets lay hidden from her? None that mattered, surely. She had held his Power of Attorney long enough to take everything from him save this house, and now it was too late for him to make good his intention of naming Phoebe his heir. She handed back the photograph. Their niece would get none of the wealth that had once been her father's.

'It is a very good likeness,' Samuel signed. 'We must hang it opposite the one of her father, they will look very well together. Perhaps James Siveter will find her and persuade her to come home. It would be nice to have her here with us, don't you agree, Annie?'

'Of course, dear,' Annie's fingers carried the lie. 'Nothing would give me more happiness than to have Phoebe return to us. We must pray that God will make it so.' She watched Samuel clean his brushes, immersing each in a jar of turpentine then wiping the bristles on a soft cloth. He could pray as much as he liked but he would find God as deaf as himself. She looked at the lovely painted face, her fingers curling into her palms. The portrait could hang with that of Abel but his daughter would never again live here.

She would sell this house, she thought as Samuel poured water from a tall flower-twined jug into a matching basin and washed his hands. She would sell it and give the money to Clinton to invest in more tube works. After all, there would be no need to keep this place on when she became his wife.

Clinton's wife. The thought stayed with Annie as they walked downstairs to the garden. How long would it be before they could marry? Not for several months that was certain, a suitable period of mourning for her brother must elapse before they could be wed, the proprieties must be observed. But Clinton would not mind the waiting, not when he saw her grief for Samuel's passing.

'Will you be wantin' tea now?' Maudie followed them into the garden.

'You have not mashed it yet, have you?' Annie asked sharply. 'I have no taste for stewed tea.'

You've no taste for anythin', if you asks me! Maudie sucked in her cheeks, looking at Annie's lavender dress with ill-concealed disdain.

'Tea ain't been mashed, not yet,' she replied. 'I knows 'ow you likes yer tea, an' so I should after all the years I've spent mekin' it.'

That won't go on for much longer, Annie thought. Once I am married you can count yourself dismissed. Aloud she said waspishly, 'Not long enough to do it graciously but I suppose we must make do. You may bring the tray now.'

Sour-faced old cow! Maudie returned to the kitchen. But then, that one had never had a good word for the doings of anybody other than herself – not that she had ever done good in her life.

'You have forgotten the herbal tea.' Annie looked at the tray her housekeeper set down on the wicker table.

'I ain't forgot nothin',' Maudie replied. 'I set it on a sep'rate tray. Seein' as 'ow Mr Samuel don't care for medicines I thought it might suit better for it to be on another tray altogether.'

'I see.' Annie began pouring milk into the cups. 'Then bring it out. It will do Mr Samuel no good left sitting in a bottle.'

'Yes, Ma'am.' Maudie turned away. If that mixture were only poison, she would gladly pour the lot down Annie Pardoe's throat!

'It is just a herbal tea, dear,' Annie's fingers signed rapidly to her brother. 'Mrs Gaskell Wheeler recommended it, she is convinced it will help you build up your strength, and I am sure Mrs Tranter has something that will relieve the taste should it prove unpalatable.' She looked at Maudie, carefully measuring the mixture into a cup, adding a little of the hot water from the tea tray. 'Have you something sweet?' she asked.

Maudie nodded a smile to Samuel, knowing he could not hear but wanting him to understand. 'Yes, Ma'am,' she said. 'I took a chocolate cake from the baker this mornin'. It be Mr Samuel's favourite sort.'

'Bring it for him then,' Annie said, 'he will take the herbal tea much easier with a chocolate cake to follow.'

Pouring the tea, she watched Maudie set the cake at Samuel's elbow then hand him the herbal mixture. Swallowing it in two long gulps, he handed the cup back to her.

'There now, that didn't be so bad, did it?' Maudie crooned to his silent ears. 'Now eat up your cake an' you'll soon forget the swallowin' o' that stuff.'

Annie picked up her own cup as Samuel took the cake, sinking his teeth into the chocolate-covered mound. Eat his cake and Samuel would soon be forgetting everything!

Chewing the last vestige of chocolate, Samuel touched his mouth with his napkin, eyes straying to the privet hedge that shielded the end of the garden. Annie had walked the length of it and when she had walked back she had held a hand close against her skirts.

It had gone as she'd known it would. Annie stood beside the four-poster bed that had been her brother's marriage bed. Samuel had eaten the cake. The ground yew and laburnum seeds had not worked, why she could not guess, but the poison she had mixed in the cream of that cake would. This time there would be no mistake. Come the morning Samuel would be dead and she would be free to enjoy her life as Mrs Clinton Harforth-Darby.

The pain that had gnawed at her all day spiralled up from her side and into her breast, the rawness of it stealing the breath from her lungs. Sinking on to the bed, she groped for the bottle of small white tablets, taking two into her mouth even as she poured a glass of water from the carafe on her night table. Waiting for the pain to pass, she checked the fob watch pinned to the shoulder of her dress. It wanted a quarter of an hour to nine o'clock. Samuel always retired at eight-thirty, he would already be in his bed.

Annie forced herself to stand. She must say goodnight to him as she always did. Tomorrow he would be beyond remembering whether she had or not but that sharp-nosed Maudie Tranter would remember the least thing that was different, and though you may not see Maudie Tranter, you could be certain the woman missed nothing.

Tapping on Samuel's bedroom door as her mother had

insisted everyone must though no sound passed his barrier of silence, Annie pushed open the door.

'Goodnight, dear,' she signed.

Samuel's hands rose like white wounded birds. 'Goodnight, Annie,' he signed, a slowness in his fingers. 'You always did what you thought best. Thank you, dear.'

What did he mean? Annie asked herself, leaning down to kiss his brow. Then in the soft glow of the oil lamp she caught the look in his eyes. He knew! Samuel knew what she had done. He was thanking her for giving him death!

Chapter Nineteen

Dead!

Phoebe walked across the heath toward Wednesbury, her mind still trying to reject the news Lucy had brought with her the night before. Her Uncle Samuel was dead.

She had not seen him since the reading of her father's will. In all that time he had not tried to contact her, not even when she was in prison. True she had never seen a great deal of Uncle Samuel, even as a child, but for him to ignore her very existence seemed somehow unnatural.

Reaching the town, she walked along Lower High Street, taking the turning that would lead her past Oakeswell Hall. She glanced at the black and white half-timbered building as she passed its curtain wall. Would Sophie live there when she married Montrose? The thought brought a twinge of pain, but it was pain for Sophie not for herself.

At the gate of Brunswick House she paused. This had once been her home, a place of happiness and love. Now it held neither. She had always been so glad to return here yet now she wanted only to turn and run. But she had to go in. Uncle Samuel was her father's brother and she must show her respects.

At the door she tugged the bell pull, her eyes avoiding the mourning wreath set at its centre. Her aunt hated her, that much had been made plain, but she was not here for the sake of her aunt.

'Eh, Miss Phoebe!' Maudie Tranter looked at the girl standing on the doorstep. 'What be you doin' 'ere?'

'Lucy told me my Uncle Samuel has passed away.'

'Ar, Miss, 'e 'as. In the night it was . . .'

'Who is it, Mrs Tranter?'

Inside Phoebe shivered at the sound of her aunt's voice but she stepped determinedly into the hall. 'It is me, Aunt.'

Annie Pardoe's hand flew to her side. She had not expected this, had had no intention of informing Abel's daughter of his brother's death. 'What are you doing here?' she rasped. 'You are not wanted in this house.'

'You made that clear enough more than two years ago,' Phoebe replied.

'That will be all, Tranter.' Annie glared at the listening Maudie, waiting until the door leading off to the kitchen had closed behind her. 'If I made it so clear,' she said, turning back to Phoebe, 'then how come you are here now?'

'I was given the news my Uncle Samuel was dead. I have come to Brunswick House to pay my respects, and that is the only thing I am here for.'

'Respects!' Annie let her gaze travel slowly over her niece. 'What respect does it show to come dressed in green? You have not even the respect to adopt mourning.'

'I apologise for the colour of my clothing,' Phoebe's chin came up, 'but this is all I have. You did not allow me an extensive wardrobe, did you, Aunt?'

'I want you to leave.' Annie placed a hand on the door handle.

'And I want to leave, Aunt, very much, I find you a most unpleasant person to be with, but I will not leave until I have done that for which I came.' Phoebe walked to the foot of the stairs. 'Is Uncle Samuel in his room?'

'No,' Annie looked towards the door of the parlour, 'he is in there.'

Phoebe stood for a moment, unmoving. Uncle Samuel had not wished her to visit him in life. Would he wish the same in death? Was her presence in this house an intrusion he would have resented? Somewhere deep in her heart she felt that to be untrue. He had been so kind to her on the few occasions they had met. Taking a long breath, she walked into the parlour.

Nothing had changed. The chiffonier held the same Staffordshire china figurines, the same high-backed sofa stood against the wall, only the mahogany table below the central ceiling gasolier was different. It stood where it always had but its heavy Brussels lace cloth was gone and in its place was draped the black velvet that had lain beneath her father's coffin and now lay beneath Samuel's.

Phoebe stared at the features that seemed to be cut from marble, her heart full of tears that would not reach her eyes. Though his eyes were closed and no smile lingered at his mouth the strange haunted look that had constantly drawn his face was no longer there. Her uncle seemed to have found a peace in death he had never known in life.

'Aunt,' she said softly, 'why do you hate me so much?'

Stood on the opposite side of the coffin Annie felt the breath catch in her throat but the rising gall of bitterness was too much for her to swallow.

'Your father stole my life!' she screamed. 'He took it, him and his fancy wife, and gave me this in return.' She struck the side of the walnut casket with her hand. 'I have had no life of my own now for nearly twenty years, I have known a living death all that time and it was your father's gift to me. He made me responsible for Samuel – Samuel who could not be cared for by any other than his own family, who could not be taken into your father's house for fear of causing distress to his pretty wife. Oh, yes, *she* must be shielded from his affliction.'

Phoebe looked from the face of her dead uncle to that of her aunt, twisted with bitterness. 'Affliction?'

'Yes, affliction!' Annie spat. 'That which kept him from leading a normal life, which kept him from taking a wife, which used up my life in keeping his secret.'

'But surely Uncle Samuel's deafness was not a good enough cause to turn him into a recluse.'

Annie's eyes burned as she answered, 'No, it was not a good enough cause. But it was not only deafness my brother suffered from – it was this!' Reaching into the casket she lifted the long white robe that covered her brother's body, snatching it open to the waist.

Phoebe gasped then turned away, her senses stunned.

'That was what made my brother a recluse!' Annie cried viciously. 'That was the shame that must be kept hidden from the world. That was what kept him from taking a wife for what woman would marry a man who was no man, who was neither male nor female, but had the genitals of both!'

'How strange we meet in the same place, Miss Pardoe. Miss Pardoe!' Sir William Dartmouth caught the arm of the young woman whose eyes set in a chalk-white face seemed to look straight through him. 'Are you feeling unwell?'

'Uncle Samuel,' Phoebe mumbled. 'Uncle Samuel, he . . . Lucy will . . . I must . . .'

Supporting her with his arm as she sagged against him, he helped her into the George Hotel. 'A doctor, quickly,' he ordered the attentive manager. 'Then a brandy. Move, man!'

'Nothing physically wrong,' Alfred Dingley said an hour later. 'She is suffering from some sort of shock, though . . . I have given her a sedative that will help but she needs rest and will get that better at home than she will here.' He nodded towards the door of the upstairs sitting room Phoebe had been taken to. 'I will have a carriage sent round to take her. Was there anyone with her, do you know?'

'She was alone when I met her in the street,' Sir William answered, 'so I presume no one was accompanying her, and as for a carriage there will be no need. I will see Miss Pardoe gets home. Send your account to the Priory.' He stood aside for the doctor to leave. 'Good day, Doctor.'

Tapping first at the door he went into the room where Phoebe sat, the wife of the hotel manager hovering at her elbow.

'Are you feeling better, Miss Pardoe?' he asked.

She looked up, the shock still showing in her eyes. 'Yes,' she said. 'Thank you, Sir William. I am sorry to have been so much trouble.'

'You were no trouble.'

'That is kind of you to say.' Phoebe stood up, her legs still not quite her own. 'But I have delayed you. I thank you again for helping me. I can manage on my own now.'

'Were you alone?'

'Yes.' Phoebe smiled at the woman handing her her bag.

'You said something about an Uncle Samuel and Lucy, were they not with you?'

Phoebe breathed deeply, her fingers curling tightly about the bag. 'My uncle is dead, Sir William. I have just come from paying my respects and I was going to speak to Lucy.'

'Lucy?' He frowned slightly. 'Is that the Lucy you told me was once in the employ of my wife?'

Phoebe nodded.

'Mrs Leach, so where is she now?' he asked.

'She will be in the market place.'

Sir William looked at the woman still hovering close to Phoebe. 'Send to the market place. See if Mrs Leach is there.'

'I know 'er, Sir,' the woman bobbed a curtsy, 'I'll fetch 'er.'

'There is no need,' Phoebe protested, 'I can go there myself.'

'Go to Mrs Leach,' Sir William spoke to the woman, ignoring Phoebe's protest, 'ask her to be good enough to come here, and tell your husband to have my carriage brought to the door.'

'Yes, Sir.' The woman bobbed again then disappeared through the door.

'I am sorry to hear of your uncle's death,' he continued to Phoebe, 'please accept my condolences. If I can be of assistance, do not hesitate to contact me.'

Phoebe walked from the room and down the stairs to the lobby. 'My aunt will be handling everything,' she said. 'She has cared for my uncle for many years.'

'Miss Phoebe, are you all right? What happened?' Lucy rushed in from the street.

'Lucy!' Phoebe caught her hands, holding them tightly. 'Lucy, I am so glad you are here.'

'Miss Pardoe has suffered something of a shock,' Sir William answered Lucy's enquiring glance. 'The doctor says she will be all right but she is in need of rest. Will you see her home?'

'O' course.' Lucy put an arm about Phoebe. 'You take a seat, Miss, while I finds the carter. 'E'll be 'avin' a drink in the Turks 'Ead round about this time. 'E'll give us both a ride as far as the Tipton Road.'

'Do not trouble yourself with the carter, Mrs Leach,' Sir William said as Lucy made to get a chair. 'My carriage is just outside. My driver will take you home and return for me here.'

'I'll collect your things from the market, Mrs Leach. They will keep 'ere till you collect them.' The manager's wife hovered nearby, eager to be seen offering assistance.

'Ta, Mrs Jinks.' Lucy led the way out of the lobby. 'I'll pick 'em up tomorrer.'

'Sir William, there is no need for me to take your carriage,' Phoebe hesitated at the door, 'a ride with the carter will do as well.'

He smiled suddenly, a light dancing behind his grey eyes. 'Miss Pardoe, you once told me that I should never use the word "must" to you again, but I will if I have to. Now spare me the retribution that would bring by accepting my carriage.'

Phoebe smiled. 'I would not have retribution fall upon you, Sir William, so I will accept. And thank you.'

Inside the carriage Phoebe leaned back, her eyes closed against the horror of what had taken place at Brunswick House, a house that had once held so much love and laughter and now held so much unhappiness.

Poor Uncle Samuel. She flinched as the picture of his thin disfigured body flashed before her closed eyelids. To have spent a lifetime with such a deformity would be terrible enough for any man to suffer, but knowing his sister's resentment, thinking that he was responsible, albeit indirectly, for her solitary life, as he must have done, could only have added to that suffering; and Aunt Annie, so consumed with her bitterness, so twisted with hate for her own family, had she ever made any attempt to hide her true feelings or had she shown them to Samuel as she had shown them to Phoebe?

Behind her closed lids a pale finely drawn face smiled back at her, a gentle kindly face, but one whose blue eyes held the shadow of pain.

'Are you all right, Miss Phoebe?' Lucy asked, feeling the shudder that passed through her.

Phoebe saw again the figure of her aunt standing over the casket which held that malformed body, her face distorted with the hate she held for her brother's child. All right? Phoebe turned her face, pressing it into Lucy's shoulder. Would she ever be all right again?

Five days to the end of the month. Phoebe looked at the calendar. She had crossed off each day as it ended, making a note of the number of finished locks. Now less than thirty were needed to make the gross. They had all worked so hard; even Ruth had helped put the finished locks in the wooden soap box Josh had got from the carter.

Brushing her hair, Phoebe remembered the grin on the boy's face as he had related his deal with the man. She had sent Josh with twopence to pay for the box. He had offered the carter one penny.

'A penny!' Zach Coates had laughed. 'It cost me more than that to cart it out 'ere.'

'It'll cost you twice as much if you 'as to cart it back,' Josh retorted. 'You might as well let me 'ave it.'

'Not fer a bloody penny I ain't. I might as well use it fer firewood, at least it'll keep me warm.'

'Why not swap it for this?' Josh had opened the sack he had carried with him across the heath, displaying the lumps of coal. 'It'll burn a lot longer than the few sticks that old box'll mek an' give off a lot more 'eat.'

'An' where 'ave you pinched that from?' Zach had demanded.

'Never you mind,' Josh told him. 'If I tell you you'll only get a 'eadache worryin' about it an' you'll 'ave to pay tuppence for a bottle of Aspro to cure it. So you see, you'll still be outta pocket.'

'You be a right bloody smart arse, don't you!' Zach grumbled, handing the soapbox down to Josh.

'Ar, an' you'll be a right 'ot 'un if you stands too near that coal,' Josh returned, handing over the sack. ''Eat that gives off is more than the fires o' Hell you've 'eard talk about.'

Tying a ribbon to the plait in her hair Phoebe could not resist a smile. Josh had bounced into the workshop, placing the box on the floor, his grin wide as the heath as he handed back the two pennies.

He was a nice boy. Phoebe climbed into bed, the smile still warm on her lips. Things were going so well, maybe he could stay on after the locks were finished.

Climbing into bed, she turned off the oil lamp that stood beside it on a table and lay back, staring at the moonlight filling her window. It was the same moonlight as filled the windows of Handsworth Prison only the spectres it held were different. In gaol the moonlight had brought memories of her life outside. Now it often brought memories of her life locked away behind those walls. How many women were lying behind them now, their freedom snatched away, and how many were staring at the moonlight?

She would never forget. Every moment spent in that place was etched deep in her soul, every word and every blow. No, she would not forget, nor would she forget Sir William. He had brought the release she thanked God for each night, but more than that he had shown her kindness at every opportunity. But why? For what reason? If he had been indebted to her because of her imprisonment he had more than made up for it. Or could it be her friendship with his son, did he know of Edward's feelings toward her? Phoebe looked away from the light of the window but the tall figure of Sir William Dartmouth remained lit in her mind. No, that was not the reason behind his kindness to her. A man with an ancestry graced by the best families in the county for so many generations would not allow his son to break with tradition. Whatever reason lay behind his friendship she was sure her possible marriage to Edward played no part in it.

Edward . . . Phoebe closed her eyes. Was he blind to his illustrious name? Could he honestly not see his parents could never accept her as his wife, a woman who had been in prison, or was he just too stubborn to accept it? He had asked her to marry him again when he and Sophie had called, bringing their mother's regrets that Phoebe would not be attending the ball and also her condolences for Uncle Samuel's death.

Phoebe turned restlessly, her eyes returning to the moonlit window. She had refused as gently as she could, trying not to hurt Edward, and now he was gone, left for Europe with his mother and sister. Painful as she knew it would be to him, she had felt bound to tell him she did not love him, her feelings were not those of a girl desiring to be his wife. He had smiled then, masking the hurt, and Phoebe had seen the strength of his father in him. Edward Dartmouth had been hurt but that hurt would never be allowed to affect his friendship toward her. Phoebe closed her eyes again but it was not Edward who stayed with her as she drifted into sleep. It was not his mouth that smiled or his eyes that watched her. The face that bent toward her was that of Sir William Dartmouth.

'That is the last of them, Tranter.'

Annie Pardoe folded the sheet of paper, slipping it into the envelope she had just finished addressing. There had been more messages of sympathy for the death of her brother than she would have expected and she had let a suitable time elapse before answering them. Let people believe her too grief-stricken to write replies before the two weeks that had gone by. Gathering the envelopes together, she handed them to Maudie.

'People will understand why it has taken so long before I answered their messages,' she said, wiping the pen nib clean of ink before moving from the desk. 'They will realise how much pain it causes me.'

Pain my arse! Maudie thought caustically. The only pain Samuel caused you was the pain of wanting him out of the way, and that pain worsened with the arrival of that Harforth-Darby!

'Take them to the post office now.' Annie took half a crown from a small black lacquered box, handing it to her housekeeper. 'That will be more than enough to pay for stamps.'

'Yes, Ma'am.' Maudie did not bob a curtsy. 'An' there'll be change an' all, I know that wi'out yer tellin'.'

Annie bit back the anger that rose in her as Maudie walked from the study. Maudie Tranter knew a lot of things and in a very few weeks she would know one more. She would know she was out of a job.

Following her from the study, Annie walked up the stairs. Maudie had seen her leave the study, she would think the last of the letters written as she had been told, but there was one more yet to do. Watching from the window of her room she saw Maudie leave the house by the rear door, crossing the yard and taking the path that led through the grounds to a door set in the garden wall. Looking at her fob watch, Annie remained at the window. She would give Maudie five minutes before writing that last letter.

The minutes gone she took the sheet of writing paper from where she had slipped it into the packet of her skirts. It was not exactly the same as the one that had lain so long in the drawer of her washstand but it was white and that was near enough. Going to the wardrobe she took her bag from the shelf, taking out a fresh bottle of ink and a new pen. She had thrown the others into Millfield Pool not thinking of the letter she must write now but her visits to Alfred Dingley's consulting room had afforded the opportunity to purchase more. Stress, the doctor had called the pain in her side, stress due to the passing of her brother but it would cease with time. She'd known it had to come, he had told her, slipping tablets into a small brown glass bottle. They had all known, even her brother himself. Annie levered the cork from the bottle of ink. Yes, Samuel had known. The look in his eyes as she kissed him goodnight had told her so.

Reaching once more into her bag, she took out the bill she had been given when she went back to that shop near Birmingham railroad station. It had been clever of her to pretend to have forgotten to buy pot menders when she bought those mousetraps. It had given her two receipts.

Fetching the small nail scissors she kept in a drawer of her dresser, she carefully cut the heading from the receipt. Quickly pouring a small amount of water from the carafe on her night table she placed it beside the ink then, drawing her handkerchief from her pocket, tipped into the water the spoonful of plain flour she had taken from the pantry while Maudie Tranter had been on her half day off. Using the long handle of the pen she mixed the flour and water to a paste then, with the tip of one finger, smoothed a little of it on to the back of the heading she had cut from James Greaves's receipt, attaching that to the top of the sheet of white paper. That done, she carefully washed pen and glass in the bowl on the washstand, wiping them on the towel folded beside it. Opening the window, she emptied the water she had used on to the flower border below. Maudie Tranter would find no trace when she came to clean.

Annie sat at the table and began to write. Tomorrow she would post this letter herself and the ink and pen would follow the others to the bottom of Millfield Pool.

The letter finished and sealed, all trace of its having been written hidden away, Annie returned her bag to the wardrobe, caressing the silk of the pearl grey gown and the rustling lavender taffeta. She must wear black for appearance's sake but once the period of mourning was over she would never wear it again. She would wear only gowns of coloured silk, the colours Clinton liked. Soon she would be with him. But how soon would that be? Annie tried to push away the thoughts that held sway in the shadows of her mind but they would not be denied.

Three weeks and more, it had been all of that since she had given him the money which the sale of the last of Abel's bequest had brought. Three weeks and she had heard nothing from him. He had told her she would have deeds of ownership to land on which to build her tube works in a couple of days, but those days had grown into weeks and she had seen nothing of him or the papers. But he would come, he would! She closed the door of the wardrobe, gritting her teeth as a spasm of pain bit upward to her breast. Clinton would come.

'Change from the post office.' Maudie entered the sitting room where Annie now sat, a newspaper spread across the table.

'Leave it there.' A nod of her head indicated the opposite side of the table but Annie did not look up.

'Do there be any mention of the Wheelers' trouble in the paper, Ma'am?' Maudie asked.

'Trouble!' Annie looked up sharply. 'What trouble? What are you talking about?'

'I 'eard it when I was comin' from the post office.' Maudie stood with hands folded in front of her. 'Two women was sayin' as 'ow Oakeswell 'All be in mournin', said as they 'ad it from one o' the maids.'

'In mourning?'

'That be what them women said, I 'eard for meself.'

'But for whom?' Annie asked, not quite believing what her housekeeper had said. 'Is it Gaskell?'

'Don't know, Ma'am,' Maudie replied. 'They said as nobody knowed.'

'How ridiculous! There couldn't be a death in the house without its being known who had died.'

'No, Ma'am, but there could be one as 'adn't took place in the 'ouse. That way could be the maid wouldn't know who it was 'ad died.'

'Well, it is no member of the family,' Annie glanced at the newspaper, 'otherwise there would have been an entry in the Obituaries column and there is none. Most probably it is a remote aunt of Mrs Wheeler's. She did sometimes talk of one living in southern France.'

'Likely that be who it is then.' Maudie turned to leave then paused as Annie spoke again.

'Nevertheless it is only polite to call and offer my sympathy, I shall go to Oakeswell Hall now.'

Fastening her cloak, Annie thought rapidly. She would go to the post office first and post the letter she had written. Then she would make her way to Oakeswell Hall, passing Millfield Pool where she would dispose of pen and bottle of ink.

From childhood she had been used to harnessing pony to trap and needed no help with either. Twenty minutes from hearing the news Maudie had brought, Annie was driving across the open ground that skirted Millfield Pool.

'I heard it being talked of in the town,' she said when she was shown into Violet Wheeler's sitting room, 'and felt

275

I must call and offer my condolence were it true for I saw no announcement in the newspaper.'

Violet Wheeler sat down, her black skirts flowing over the edges of her chair. 'Gaskell made none.'

'Then your husband is still with us, thank the Lord.'

Ordering tea from the housemaid who answered her ring, Violet looked at her visitor. 'Gaskell? But of course he is still with us.'

Uncomfortable beneath the other woman's gaze, Annie apologised. 'Forgive me, but with there being no announcement . . .'

'Of course,' Violet cut in, 'but as you say, Gaskell is still with us, thank the Lord.' Waiting as the maid reappeared with the tea tray, then with a bobbed curtsy left again, she went on, 'My husband is recently returned from London.'

'It is not Montrose, I hope?' Annie said. 'Not your son?'

Violet poured the tea with the grace of long practice. 'If you mean you are hoping it is not my son's death we are mourning, Miss Pardoe, then your hopes are fulfilled. My husband was in London on a business trip, not concerning our son.'

So it was Violet Wheeler's aunt who had died. Annie took the cup held out to her. 'It relieves me to hear your son is well.'

'Yes, Montrose is quite well though he is disappointed that given the circumstances we will not now be holding a farewell reception for him before his regiment leaves for India.'

Replacing her cup on the tray, Annie stood up. 'I will not intrude upon you any longer, Mrs Wheeler. I came only to offer my sympathy in your loss.'

'Before you go there is something here we believe was intended for your brother.' Crossing to an elegant mahogany sideboard she took a large envelope from a drawer, handing it to Annie. 'Gaskell saw his name on this but it bore no address so he brought it back with him from London.'

'Oh!' Annie turned the envelope in her hand but it bore no mark other than the name 'Pardoe' scrawled shakily across it.

'It was among Clinton's effects.'

Effects! Annie's hand tightened convulsively on the envelope. Why was Gaskell Wheeler dealing with Clinton's effects? Why was Clinton in London when he had told her he would be in Wednesbury? The answer was staring her in the face. Clinton had gone and her money had gone with him!

'Thank your husband for me.' Annie's lips struggled with the words.

'Gaskell's cousin was so ill before he left Oakeswell Hall . . .' Violet Wheeler's words followed Annie to the door.

'Ill?'

'Yes, it all came upon him so suddenly,' Violet answered the query in Annie's voice, 'stomach cramps and symptoms so akin to fever he thought it a return of the malady that struck him when he lived in the Caribbean. He went to London to consult his doctor there and we heard no more until a mutual friend wrote to tell Gaskell that his cousin was dead. Who would have thought it?' She fluttered a handkerchief to her eyes. 'A man as vital as Clinton, dead in a couple of days.'

Clinton was dead! Annie stood in her own bedroom with no memory of the drive back to Brunswick House. He had died after so short and so unexpected an illness. Clinton was dead! Taking the scissors she had used earlier that afternoon, she opened the wardrobe door. Clinton was dead and with him her dreams. Stabbing the scissors into the cloth, she slashed the grey and the lavender gowns. Clinton was dead, she would have no need of colours. The gowns in shreds about the floor, Annie slumped to the bed. *Such a short illness, so sudden, dead in a couple of days* . . . Violet Wheeler's words reverberated in her brain, circling round and round. What was it that had caused the death of a man who had appeared the picture of health when he had last called on her?

When he had last called on her. . . . Annie stared at the remnants of the pearl grey gown. She had been wearing that when he had been shown into the sitting room, when she had handed sherry to him and to Samuel. She had given Samuel the glass she always used for him, the glass with a small air bubble in the stem, one that she could not confuse with her own. She had handed it to him as Maudie had announced the arrival of the constables. But she hadn't! Fear closed her throat as memory returned. She had not handed Samuel his sherry. The tray had been taken from her by Clinton.

So sudden. . . . The words seemed to scream in her mind. Stomach cramp followed by fever, the same symptoms the powdered seeds of yew and laburnum produced. She had not handed Samuel his sherry, Clinton had after she had left the room. That explained why her brother had not fallen ill as she had expected. He had not drunk the poison, Clinton had. She had killed Clinton!

Pain surged into her breast but Annie ignored it. She had killed Samuel for nothing, she had sold his inheritance for nothing, she would never be Mrs Clinton Harforth-Darby. And the money she had handed over to him, what had happened to that? Was it in some account that would most likely pass to Gaskell Wheeler? And the envelope Violet Wheeler had handed her, what lay in there? Reaching for it where she had dropped it on the bed, she looked at the name sprawled across it. Was it some lies as to her money or did it contain the barefaced truth? He had played her for a fool and now thank you, Annie Pardoe. Thank you and goodbye.

Breaking open the seal she drew out a letter, the writing spidery. '*Annie, my dear,*' she read, '*I wanted to bring you these myself but I am afraid I feel too ill. I will post them to you from London. You will be in my thoughts until I return. Yours, Clinton.*'

Taking the rest of the contents from the envelope, Annie looked at the stylised wording . . . *land and buildings appertaining thereto the property of Annie Mary Pardoe* . . .

Slowly she began to laugh, a low empty laugh that echoed round the room, laughing as her soul died.

Chapter Twenty

'They be a fine job, Miss, you'll 'ave no trouble wi' them.'

'Thank you, Bert, you have worked so hard.' Phoebe looked at the wooden soap box filled almost to the top with shining brass locks.

'I couldn't 'ave done it by meself, everybody 'as worked 'ard and that includes yourself.'

'Four days, Bert,' she reminded him, 'four days to delivery. Do you think we will do it?'

'We be good as done now,' he smiled. 'Mathew an' me we be on the last batch. Tomorrow will see the lot finished.'

'I must admit I had doubts when we started. It seemed impossible for you to have made so many in the time we were given.'

'Would 'ave been if Mathew 'adn't stepped in, an' them two lads 'ave worked like Trojans. I tell you, without that pair there would 'ave been no order to deliver in four days' time.'

'I wish I were the Queen."

'The Queen?' Mathew glanced up from the lock he was freeing from a vice attached to the work bench. 'Whatever do you want to be 'er for?'

Phoebe's eyes danced. 'Because then I could give you all a medal. You certainly deserve one.'

Josh looked up from pumping the bellows, his face red from his efforts. 'Medals be no good, you just 'ave to keep on cleanin' 'em. 'Sides, like me mother used to say, you can't eat medals.'

'In that case, Josh, I will make yours a fish supper.'

'That be more like it.' He looked across to where Mark was working alongside Mathew. 'What you say, Mark?'

'I say mek that two suppers, an' mek me eat both.'

'Them pair, eatin' be all they think on,' Bert joked. 'I swear neither of 'em 'as a bottom to their belly.'

'Hard work makes men hungry, which reminds me – Tilly and Lizzie said to tell you the meal was ready and waiting on the table.'

'I would rather 'ear news like that than that the Queen was to visit.' Josh laid the brass-studded bellows aside, running his palms along the sides of his trousers.

'Well, I might not be Queen, Josh White, but rubbing your hands on your trousers will not do for me nor will it do for Lizzie. You know her rule: no hands washed, no dinner given.'

Josh looked at his hands then at Phoebe, his grin cheeky. 'I might 'ave known there'd be a price to pay! Mind you, I wouldn't mind 'avin a bath for one o' Mrs Ingles's dinners, only don't tell 'er I said so.'

''Ave you thought on what you be goin' to do wi' them locks when they be finished?' Mathew asked as they ate their dinner.

'Do with them?' Phoebe asked, a certain amount of surprise in her voice. 'I am going to deliver them to Mr Greaves, of course.'

Mathew chewed on some cheese. 'I know that be your intention but 'ow?'

'I've been wonderin' the same, Miss.' Bert looked up from his plate of cheese and pickles. 'Carryin' two or three o' them locks be one thing. Carryin' a gross on 'em be summat else.'

'Carryin' 'em be summat you ain't never goin' to do. You needs transport.' Mathew cut a slice of onion, sliding it into his mouth from the blade of his knife.

Across the long trestle table that the men had set up at one end of the corn barn, and where Lizzie and Tilly had laid the midday meal, Phoebe looked at them both, her brows drawing together in a worried frown. She had been so busy, so preoccupied with her sewing and with helping in the workshop, she had totally forgotten the need to arrange transport of the locks to Birmingham.

Mathew continued to eat. 'So what be you goin' to do?'

'I don't know,' Phoebe admitted. 'That part of it never seemed to enter my head.'

'We could 'ire a 'andcart?' Mathew suggested.

Bert nodded. 'We could, but it be a long push to Brummagem. It be all o' ten mile.'

'What about Zach Coates?' Mathew took a pull from the mug of beer he had brewed himself. 'If we could carry 'em between we up to the Tipton Road, 'e could put 'em on 'is cart down into Wednesbury and then on 'a train from there.'

Phoebe's frown turned to a look of dismay. 'That would mean paying carriage charges and a return fare for one of us to go with them.' She spread her hands on the table, defeat in the gesture. 'I just do not have the money.'

'Would it tek more'n four shillin', Miss?' Josh asked through a mouthful of food.

'I would not have thought so, Josh,' Phoebe answered, 'but I do not have four shillings.'

'I 'ave,' he swallowed noisily. 'Least I 'as three an' another 'un this comin' Friday'll mek four, so if as you says four shillin' be enough to pay to get them locks to Brummagem, then they'm as good as there already.'

'Those three shillings,' Phoebe looked at the tousle-headed boy regarding her with eyes like molten bronze, 'are they the same three shillings you have been paid as wages since you came to Wiggins Mill?'

'Ar.' He took another bite.

'And the fourth shilling is the one you will be paid for the work you have done this week?'

He nodded, the food in his mouth leaving no room for his tongue to manoeuvre.

'Thank you, Josh,' Phoebe said, her eyes grateful though her mouth would not smile. 'But I cannot take it. You will need that money to keep you until you find other employment.'

The boy's grin faded at her mention of finding work elsewhere but his eyes lost none of their brightness. 'I managed afore I come 'ere,' he said, allowing the food in his mouth to slide past his throat, 'an' I can manage when I be gone so you tek them shillin's an' get them locks to Brummagem. Could be when the bloke as 'as ordered 'em sees what 'e be gettin', 'e will up an' order another gross on the spot.'

Phoebe shook her head. 'No, Josh.'

'Why!' the boy demanded. 'That money be mine. I've earned it so I can do what I likes wi' it, an' I wants you to 'ave it.'

Pushing herself up with her spread hands, Phoebe rose from the table. 'You are right, Josh, that money is yours. You earned it and you are going to keep it, I . . .'

''Ang on, 'ang on!' he cut in on her refusal. 'I've been 'ere near a month as meks no odds an' in that time I ain't paid no board nor lodgin', I've 'ad three good meals a day an' supper besides, an' on top o' it all I've 'ad a bed. Now then.' Putting aside his knife, he held up his left hand, fingers curled into his palm. 'Three meals a day would cost tuppence a go an' they wouldn't be 'alf the tucker I've 'ad from Mrs Ingles neither, so wi'out supper I would 'ave been set back a tanner a day.' Two at a time he raised the fingers of his left hand, counting slowly before raising one finger of his right. Satisfied with his numbers he went on: 'A penny to 'ang the line in Joe Baker's lodgin' 'ouse would mek it seven.' He raised another finger. 'Sevenpence a day that would be, an' nowhere near the comfort I've 'ad 'ere so I reckons I owes you that money, Miss, an' a damn' sight more aside it.'

'If you owe anyone, Josh, it is Mrs Ingles. She is the one who has given you food and found a bed for you to sleep in.'

''E don't owe me nothin'.' Lizzie smiled at the boy. ''E 'as earned more'n a meal or two, the 'elp 'e gives me around the place, an' as for a bed, 'tain't nothin' outta me way lettin' 'im lie in the loft along o' me own so 'is money be 'is own to do whatever 'e likes wi' it.'

'There you am!' Josh grinned triumphantly. 'Now will you tek it?'

Phoebe shook her head. 'No, Josh, I will not.'

'What about the cut?' Mark had remained silent until now. 'You could get them locks straight into Brummagem if you sent 'em along the cut.'

''Course,' Bert nodded, 'I never give a thought to the cut.'

'What! An' you workin' the narrow boats this three year?' Lizzie smiled across at her husband. 'Some bargee you be, Bert Ingles. Back at the locks for a few weeks an' you forget the cut exists.'

'I 'ad forgot it an' that be no lie,' Bert said sheepishly, 'but Mark be right. Get that box o' locks on a boat an' you could bring 'em right into Gas Street Basin. An 'andcart from there an' you as 'em delivered.'

'It sounds easy, Bert,' Phoebe said, the worry in her tone not diminished, 'but will there be a barge going to Birmingham in the next day or two?'

'Sure to be.' The words were Lizzie's. 'Barges be up an' down to Brummagem as often as a barman serves beer on a Friday night.'

'Might be one comin' now.' Josh jumped up. 'Shall I go an' see?'

'Ar, lad,' Bert nodded, 'an' if one passes as ain't due for Brummagem ask if 'e knows when one is. An', lad,' Bert pointed a finger at him, 'no dawdlin'. There be work still to do.'

'Can I come?' Ruth scrambled up from the table. 'Take me wi' you, Josh, I want to come.'

''Old on to 'er,' Lizzie said as Josh looked at her for permission. ''Er can be off like a ferret down a rabbit 'ole if you leave go of 'er.'

''Er'll be all right wi' me, Mrs Ingles.' Josh caught the girl's hand. 'We'll be back quicker'n a navvy sups a pint.'

'There be a boat along o' the towpath.' Josh was back at the bellows in under five minutes. 'Bloke says if it be on for 'im to fetch water from the pump, 'e'll cart your locks up to Brummagem.'

'Can you carry on if I goes for a word wi' 'im?' Bert asked from the yard.

'Ar,' Mathew nodded. 'Mark 'ere can put me right should be I needs it.

'Settled?' he asked when Bert returned to the workshop later.

Sitting in his place at the workbench Bert took up a lock, removing it from the pattern mould. ''E goes up to Brum' wi' an empty boat, 'as a load to pick up from Gas Street in the mornin'. 'E 'as agreed to lay up 'ere for the night to give we the time to finish the last o' the order.'

'That be a bit o' good news for Phoebe.' Mathew put the lock he had finished on the pile set aside for filing down. ''Er was worried, you could tell that.'

'Well, the worry be groundless now,' Bert answered, 'but somebody 'as to go wi' them locks an' I don't think as Phoebe be the one. There be no other woman on that barge an' while I ain't sayin' as it be the bloke would touch 'er, I am sayin' as 'ow it wouldn't look right.'

'So what you reckon?'

'What I reckon is one o' we men should go wi' 'em.'

'It be the sensible thing,' Mathew agreed, 'an' that one should rightly be you, Bert. You can talk locks better'n me and you knows what they be worth. A bloke won't find it so easy diddlin' you as 'e would me.'

'Mmm.' Bert reached for a screwdriver. 'I'll go tell 'er when I've finished this, but we'll 'ave to bide by 'er decision.'

'It would have been the answer to our problem,' Phoebe said when Bert told her the reason for his being in her kitchen, 'but it will no longer be necessary. The locks are not going to Birmingham.'

'Not goin' to Brummagem?' Bert looked surprised. 'Then where do they be goin', Miss?'

'They won't be going anywhere, Bert. Perhaps you had better read this.' She handed him a white envelope. 'It came just a few minutes ago.'

Drawing a folded paper from the envelope, Bert read the neat copperplate hand. 'But why?' he asked. 'There be no reason given an' the month's end be three days clear away.'

'I do not know why.' Phoebe took the letter from Bert, her eyes scanning the heading James Greaves, Hardware and Ironmongery. He had given no reason in his letter, merely stating the gross of locks ordered on the second day of the month would no longer be required.

'I don't believe it!' Bert pushed a hand through his hair. 'I just don't bloody well believe it! Three days from finishin' an' the bloke 'as the gall to say 'e no longer wants 'em, an' not even a reason.'

'I am afraid we have to believe it.' Phoebe folded the letter, returning it to its envelope. 'But we do not have to accept it without a reason.'

'What you be goin' to do?'

'I am going to Birmingham, Bert.' Phoebe's chin came up. 'I am going to see Mr James Greaves.'

Phoebe sat on the slatted wooden seat of the steam tram, her bag with the one lock in it held close in her lap. The journey would take longer by tram but the fare by train was more than she had. The tram moved along Holloway Bank, complaining at the rise in the ground.

'Nice day, ain't it?'

A large woman in an even larger flowered hat nodded at Phoebe.

'Very nice,' she replied, her thoughts not with her words.

'It'll get nicer an' all if it don't get no worse.' The

woman's head bobbed, setting the flowers on her oversized hat wobbling dangerously.

'My rheumatiz says it be a-goin' ter rain.' A second woman joined the conversation.

'Oh, ar!' The flowers wobbled again. 'My old man says as 'ow 'e's goin' to get up off 'is idle arse tomorrer an' find isself a job – only tomorrer never comes, an' when it does 'e ain't in, so don't you go believin' all you 'ears.'

'You 'ave one o' them sort an' all, does you, wench!' The second woman laughed wheezily. 'I thought as I was the only woman wi' a bloke too idle to blow the froth off 'is beer.'

The large woman's assortment of chins wobbled in rhythm with the flowers on her hat. 'You knows what thought thought.' She laughed. ''E thought 'e weren't dead till they buried 'im!'

'Boundary,' the conductor of the tram called loudly. 'Boundary, all change.'

'Change?' Phoebe had been to Birmingham several times but always in her father's carriage. Now the conductor's call confused her.

'You 'as to get off 'ere, luv.' The large woman eased herself out of her seat. 'It's the boundary, did you want to go further?'

'I want to go to Birmingham.' Phoebe got out of her seat as the conductor called again.

The woman began to move along the narrow aisle separating the wooden bench-like seats, her ample hips brushing both sides. 'Wednesbury tram only runs as far as West Bromwich,' she said as Phoebe followed. 'To go on to Brummagem you 'ave to change at the boundary.' Alighting heavily, the woman eased her basket more firmly on to her arm then pointed. 'Just go a bit further down the road an' you'll see the tram for Brummagem. It be navy blue an' cream where this one be red, you can't miss it.'

Murmuring her thanks, Phoebe followed the way that had

been pointed. It took several more enquiries before she found the shop front announcing James Greaves, Hardware and Ironmongery. Taking a deep breath, she pushed open the door.

'Mr Greaves,' Phoebe took the letter from her bag, placing it address uppermost on the smooth polished wood of the counter that ran the length of the small dark shop, 'can you please explain to me why you have cancelled your order for one gross of Invincible locks just days before that order was due to be delivered to you?'

'I beg your pardon!' The man's smile faded to be replaced by a bemused look.

'I have no doubt you do,' Phoebe replied tartly, 'but begging my pardon is not enough. I require an explanation.'

'Are you sure you have come to the right shop?' He sounded almost apologetic. 'I have ordered no locks.'

'Yes!' Phoebe glared, her mouth tight with anger. A reason with or without an apology she would accept, but not bare-faced denial. 'You are Mr James Greaves, are you not?'

'I am, Miss,' the shopkeeper answered politely.

'And this, if I am not mistaken, is a Hardware and Ironmongery store?'

'It is.' He nodded, following Phoebe's cursory glance at the various articles of hardware hanging from every available space.

'Then this must be yours. Please read it and tell me if I am wrong.'

Taking the letter from the envelope, he fitted a pair of wire-framed spectacles to his nose, looking first over them to Phoebe's angry face then through them to read the words written on the paper. 'I am afraid you are wrong,' he said, after reading it through, 'I did not send this letter and neither have I sent any order for locks.'

'But it has your name and business address.' Phoebe took the letter, tapping a finger against the heading.

'I do not deny that,' he answered levelly, 'but I deny having written that letter. If you would care to look at this ledger you will see the handwriting is not the same as is on that letter.'

He could have disguised his writing. Phoebe glanced at the ledger. But why should he go to so much trouble? What did he have to gain from ordering a gross of locks then cancelling that order days before delivery?

'Then who?' Phoebe's hand fell limply on to the counter.

'I don't know who,' the man answered gently, seeing misery slowly spread across Phoebe's face, 'but it must be somebody who holds a grudge against you.'

Drawing in a deep breath, Phoebe folded the letter returning it to her bag. 'I apologise for having accused you of such an action, Mr Greaves,' she said, 'I should not have spoken as I did.'

'I understand, Miss. You pay it no more mind. These locks you spoke of, what be they like?'

'I have one here.' She took the lock from her bag, laying it on the counter where its polished brass gleamed against the dark wood.

'That ain't no botched up job.' James Greaves took the lock in his hands, examining it closely. 'This be a good bit o' work. Man as made this knows his job.' He looked up at Phoebe. 'Bet they teks a bit o' time making and all. And you have a gross, you say?'

He examined the lock again as Phoebe nodded. 'A man can be proud of making something like this,' he said. 'He's a craftsman and no mistake. Look here, Miss . . .?'

'Pardoe,' she supplied.

'Miss Pardoe,' he handed back the lock, 'I will be willing to take some locks off your hands.'

Phoebe sat on the steam tram, finding the journey home no less a strain than the outward one had been. James Greaves would take some of the locks but to whom could she sell the remainder? She looked through the window towards a sky that was already darkening. But it is not as dark as my horizons, she thought miserably. How do I tell

Mathew and Bert and Mark, and Josh there is no money to pay what I owe them?

'So there you have it.' Phoebe looked at Bert and the others grouped in her kitchen, their faces solemn. 'It appears that James Greaves did not send us an order for one gross of locks and neither did he send the letter that cancelled that order.'

'Then who the 'ell did?' Mathew had listened silently to all Phoebe had said and now his temper broke. 'Some stupid bugger wi' a twisted mind, an' if I finds out who it be 'e'll 'ave a bloody twisted neck to go wi' it . . .'

'You said as this Greaves bloke showed you a ledger of 'is 'andwritin'?' Bert said, interrupting Mathew's explosion, his own voice still level and calm. ''Ow good a proof do you take that to be?'

Phoebe looked up with eyes shadowed with disappointment and worry. 'Well, the ledger did go back several years and all the entries were in the same hand, quite different to this.' She touched the envelope lying on the table in front of her. 'I can't believe a man would go to so much trouble as to disguise his own handwriting to play a practical joke on someone he does not know, on someone he never even met before today.'

'There be no tellin' what folk'll do if they 'ave a mind,' Mathew cut in, his anger still hot.

'True,' Bert agreed soothingly, 'but what would the bloke be gainin' by doin' such? There was nothin' in it for 'im.'

'P'raps 'e thought 'avin' been turned down once 'e could get them locks cheap,' Tilly ventured her opinion. 'Mebbe 'e thought you would be only too glad to get shut of 'em.'

'There is no telling,' Phoebe answered wearily. 'The fact is I am left with a gross of locks for which I have no sale, and whether the ordering of them was a practical joke or not will not pay wages.'

'The ironmonger did offer to buy some of 'em and at the

price you first said. 'E made no attempt to cut you down, you told me?'

'None.'

'Well, to me that seems to say 'e wasn't tryin' to buy more on the cheap,' Bert thumbed the buckle of his broad belt. 'But like Tilly says, you never know 'ow a man's thoughts be turnin'.'

'Mine be turnin' to murder,' Mathew growled. 'Whoever it be 'as done this, pray God I never comes across 'im 'cos I won't be responsible for what I does to 'im – but it'll be a long time afore 'e walks again.'

'It's done now an' what's done can't be undone.' Lizzie took her daughter's hand. 'Best for all of you to get some rest. The problem will still be wi' us in the mornin', it can be talked on again then. Might be as you will see a way out when you be feelin' calmer.'

'Lizzie be right, Miss.' Bert followed his wife through the scullery to the yard. 'P'raps summat will make itself plain come mornin'.'

'I hope so, Bert, goodnight.' Phoebe stood as the Ingleses and Josh followed by Lucy and Mathew crossed the mill yard to their respective dwellings. They had all worked so hard, and for what! She looked up at the night sky, its inky void strewn with stars heavy with light. It could not all be for nothing, there had to be a reason. Why would someone want her to throw her last penny into a venture, only to see it sink? It didn't make sense. But then sending her to prison for a crime she had not committed had not made sense. She drew in a deep breath of the night air, carrying the sweet smell of the heath to her nostrils. She had been imprisoned but not defeated, and the failure to sell her locks would not defeat her either. Bert and Mathew had put their trust in her and it was up to her to ensure that trust was not in vain.

'But what can you do, wench?' Tilly asked later as she handed Phoebe a cup of steaming cocoa. 'It's all right you sayin' it's up to you to mek things good, but what do you reckon to do? You 'ave no money to pay the men an' none to buy more metals wi'. Not that you needs 'em with so many locks unsold.'

'I don't know what I can do,' Phoebe's hands shook as she put the cup on the table, 'I only know I have to do something. Mathew and Bert need their money to support their families and somehow I have to find that money.'

'Somehow, somehow!' Tilly fussed about the grate, banking down the fire for the night, the kettle already filled with water for the morning sitting on the hob above the oven. 'You can go on sayin' somehow till the cows come 'ome but it still won't put money in yer purse.'

'There has to be a way.' Phoebe closed her eyes, a thin film of tears glistening along the edge of her dark lashes.

'You could let James Greaves 'ave the dozen locks 'e said 'e would tek. That would be little, I know, but a little be better'n none at all.'

'And if I can't sell the rest, what then?' Phoebe spoke more to herself than Tilly. 'The Ingleses can't stay where there is no job to support them. They will have to move on, and that means being on the road for God knows how long, on the road with Ruth and Mark. And then there is Josh, what will he do? Go back to the streets of Wednesbury, standing in line for a job that breaks his back for a penny, sleeping under a hedge because that penny is not enough to buy him food and a bed. I can't let that happen, Tilly, I can't.'

'Mebbe you won't 'ave to, wench.' She rested a hand on Phoebe's slumped shoulders. 'The good Lord only lets we tek as much as we can bear then 'e teks the rest. 'E as give you a burden an' it be 'eavy for you, but 'e won't let it break your back. 'E'll lift it, you'll see. P'raps 'e won't tek it away altogether but 'e'll lift it enough for you to mek your way.'

'I don't mind for myself, Tilly,' Phoebe looked up, 'you and I have known worse, but I feel I have let the others down.'

'You've let nobody down, my wench!' Tilly said fiercely. 'You found 'em food an' a place to live when nobody else

would 'ave 'em, an' they won't go blamin' you for what's
'appened. If it be as the Ingleses 'ave to move on then that
will be 'cos the Lord is wantin' it that way.'

'No, Tilly,' Phoebe pressed the hand resting on her shoulder,
'the Lord has no desire to see children suffering on the streets
or men dragging their families from town to town in search
of work. While we have food in the house we will share it,
and with God's help we will stay together.'

'Amen to that,' Tilly answered fervently. 'Amen to that!'

In the moonlit shadows of her bedroom Phoebe slipped
her nightgown over her head. They would go back to selling
Bert's work one or two a day as before, but the profit from
that would not be enough to keep his family and pay Mathew
for toting them around Wednesbury. That in turn would mean
extra work for Lucy, trying to cover the shortfall with her
baking, and the strain of the past month was already showing
in her face. She could not go on like this much longer. And
then there was Josh. The Ingleses could not go on feeding him
when they had next to nothing to keep themselves with.

Going over to the window she stared out over the silent
night: over the windmill, its folded sails thrust out like a cross
stark against the dark sky, over the corn loft into which she
had been forced by the man who had come to rob her, and
to the spot in the yard where he had almost raped her. 'Why?'
she whispered softly. 'Why is all this happening to me?' But
out of the quiet shadows there came no answer.

'Can I see you for a minute, Miss Phoebe?' Bert stood cap in
hand at the doorway to the scullery.

Leaving the breakfast dishes she was drying as Tilly washed
them, Phoebe laid the huckaback cloth aside. 'Of course, Bert.
Come in, please.'

Nodding a greeting to Tilly, he followed Phoebe to the
kitchen but as she made to go through to the parlour he
held back. 'It will do 'ere, Miss.'

Phoebe's heart skipped a beat. She had lain awake the

greater part of the night trying to find a solution to their difficulties but none had come. If her burden was to be lifted it seemed the time was not yet, and if Bert had come to tell her that he and Lizzie must move on she had nothing to offer that would hold them to Wiggins Mill.

'It's like this,' he twisted his cap between his fingers, 'Mathew an' me, we been talkin', an' we thinks as 'ow p'raps them locks would be better taken down to Liverpool.'

'Liverpool!' Phoebe exclaimed.

'Ar.' Bert looked at her, his eyes candid. 'Mathew an' me, we says we got nothin' now so if we get nothin' there then we lost nothin'. We thinks it should be given a try, but we 'ad to ask what you thought. 'Ow you felt about it.'

'Liverpool.' Phoebe sat down, her hands together on the table. The night had brought her no idea of what to do with the locks but the same could not be said of Bert.

'Ar, Liverpool, Miss.' He reinforced the theme, his voice enthusiastic. 'You see, Liverpool be the docks from where ships sail to America. Mathew an' me reckon if we can get them locks over there, they will sell.'

'How do you reckon that?'

Bert shuffled from one foot to another, his hand nervously throttling his cap. 'Well, Miss, from what I 'ear tell, you can sell spectacles to a blind man in that country.'

Trying but failing to hide the smile his words brought to her mouth, Phoebe asked from whom he had such information.

'Word gets round the docks,' he told her. 'Sailors comin' in from America an' the West Indies talks of 'ow the country be growin' that fast an' 'ow they be 'ungry for all sorts o' goods. They tells the cut men you can find a market over there for anythin', an' if they be buyin' goods fast as we can ship 'em over seems reasonable they 'ave to be stored for a time in warehouses. An' warehouses need locks – good locks as can't be broken.'

'And you and Mathew think our locks will sell over there?'

Bert smiled. 'Like Mathew says, they might not be the first locks to 'it America but they'll be the best.'

'But it will take weeks, Bert, maybe months, and you have already gone a month without wages. You can't go for several more. It is different for Mathew, he can go back to oddjobbing in the town and they have the money Lucy makes selling pies, but you and Lizzie will have nothing and I have not enough money to buy more metals for you to carry on while you are waiting – not unless we let Mr Greaves buy the one dozen locks he offered to take.'

'We've thought of that, me an' Lizzie, an' we both say the same. Leave the gross of locks intact an' send 'em off to America. We will find a way to manage till we gets word back.'

'But if they should not sell as you think, Bert,' Phoebe added a cautionary note, 'Lizzie and the children . . .'

'Lizzie an' Mark knows the score,' Bert said quickly. 'They also knows that should it fail to come off we will be back on the road, but if we never takes a chance then we'll never 'ave the answer, one way nor t'other, so the final word rests wi' you, Miss.'

'Has Mathew discussed this with Lucy?'

'They spoke of it this mornin' as he walked 'er to the crossroads.'

'And Lucy was in agreement?'

'Sees 'er was,' Bert nodded, 'but t'would be better all round to talk the matter over wi' all concerned brought together. That way everybody gets to 'ear all the fors and all the agens, and gets to say their piece fair like.'

'Agreed. But in the meantime have you thought of the cost involved in transporting the locks to America? It is going to be a great deal more than getting them to Birmingham and I did not have sufficient money to do that.'

'I 'ave thought of it.' Bert stopped mangling the cap he had taken to wearing to keep the dust of the workshop out of his hair. 'An' if you agrees then I think as we 'ave the answer. You see, while you was off to Brummagem to see James Greaves I went down to the cut side an' a mate of mine was takin' a load o' coal up to London. From there 'e 'as to pick up a load that'll take 'im to Liverpool. 'E will call 'ere day after tomorrow an' if I asks 'im 'e will take them locks wi' 'im. Won't cost no more'n a couple o' pies.'

'A couple of pies might get them to Liverpool, Bert, but it will take more than that to get them across the Atlantic. How do you propose we do that?'

'This way.' Bert stuffed the cap in his trousers pocket. 'The bargee as will be passin' 'ere in a day or two 'as a brother-in-law who is first mate on a cargo steamer that makes a regular run to America. 'E takes aboard various items to sell over there.'

'What sort of items?' Phoebe asked.

'Anythin' the bargee picks up along 'is route.' Bert grinned. 'Anythin' they think will sell, which seems to be most things. An' this brother-in-law sells them for a cut of the profit.'

'Is he allowed to take things aboard the ship to be sold for his own profit?'

'Put it this way,' Bert smiled, ''e is allowed to take aboard anythin' that nobody else knows about.'

Phoebe looked at him, uncertainty in her eyes. 'There is something that does not seem quite honest about it, Bert. He is taking things on board to sell for himself and not for whoever is paying for the ship to carry cargo, and that can't be right.'

'Crew be allowed to take their own box aboard,' Bert explained. 'Don't nobody ask if it be 'olding clothes or anythin' else. One box be all they be allowed, it be up to them what they 'ave in it, so if this first mate wants to fill it wi' things 'e wants to sell that be 'is concern so long as 'e don't overdo it. It be a recognised thing, Miss Phoebe, that be 'ow seamen makes up for the low wage they be paid, same as do cut men.'

'This brother-in-law of your friend,' Phoebe asked, 'is he

to be trusted? I do not wish to call his honesty into question but . . .'

''E won't do the dirty, Miss Phoebe.' Bert's grin faded. ''E knows the cut men, an' 'e knows to cross one o' them is to wake up one mornin' wi' a knife in your ribs. No, if 'e sells 'em you'll get your money, an' if 'e don't sell 'em you gets the locks back, 'e makes nothin' an' we makes nothin'. That way benefits nobody so you can rest your mind easy: if them locks will sell at all in America then 'e will sell 'em. You tell 'im 'ow much you wants for 'em, that way 'e won't bring you less, then you pays 'im for 'is part.'

Phoebe sat silent, thinking over what Bert had said. She had little to lose either way. 'Very well.' She met Bert's quizzical stare. 'We will discuss it together this evening and if everyone is agreed, we will send the whole lot to America.'

Chapter Twenty-One

It had been a month. Phoebe picked up the bucket of water she had filled from the pump in the yard. A month since the locks had gone off to Liverpool, a month in which the small workshop had been silent.

She carried the bucket into the scullery, emptying it into the copper to heat for washing the household linen, feeling the empty pull of her stomach. The food stocks had diminished quicker than she had expected due to her giving more than a share to the Ingleses and she would take from Lucy only the small amount her needlework paid for. How much longer could it go on? she thought, slicing thin slivers of Sunlight soap from a thick bar and dropping them into the copper. A few shillings a week to feed herself, Tilly, the Ingleses and Josh.

Josh! She stirred the soap slivers into the water with a wooden stick. She had not yet found the courage to send him back to the town yet she knew she was merely putting off the moment, that it had to come. 'But not yet,' she whispered staring into the soap clouded water, 'not yet.'

'What be not yet?' Tilly came into the scullery, her arms filled with sheets.

'I was thinking we cannot keep Josh much longer.' Phoebe felt almost relieved as she said the words she had admitted to no one but herself. 'Lizzie is finding it hard to feed her own even with our help.'

'I've known that for some time, my wench.' Tilly took the wooden stick, using it to push the soiled linen into the wooden tub that stood beside the copper, pressing the sheets beneath the soapy water. 'An' I knows you won't be able to 'elp much longer. There be almost nothin' left in the 'ouse.'

'Has Bert gone looking for work?'

'Ar 'e 'as.' Tilly took the wooden maid to the clothes in the tub, banging it up and down on the linen. ''Im an' the two lads, same as they does every day, but it be a waste o' time. There be no work, not even in the foundries seems like.'

Phoebe watched the other woman pound away at the washing, her thin body bent by the weight of the heavy wooden wash tool that pressed the dirt from the linen. 'Do you think he will wait much longer before taking to the road?'

'Who can say what a man like that'll do?' Tilly brushed a wet hand across her brow. 'All I know is you can see it's gettin' 'arder day by day for 'im, comin' 'ome wi' nothin'.'

'But Lizzie and the children, he wouldn't take them on the road again, would he?'

Using the wooden stick she had taken from Phoebe as a rod Tilly fished the pounded sheet from the wooden tub, lifting it across to the brownstone sink, sloshing clean water over it and rinsing away the soiled soapy suds before carrying the sheet across to the copper to be boiled. 'Could be Lizzie would refuse to stay behind,' she said, recovering from the effort of carrying the water-soaked fabric. 'A woman like Lizzie Ingles ain't easy separated from 'er man.'

Nor from her children, Phoebe thought, lifting another sheet into the wooden tub. Lizzie would not leave her children at Wiggins Mill while she and Bert went to look for work.

'When you goin' to tell 'em?' Tilly took the maid to the sheet in the tub, pounding it with a steady rhythm.

'Yer goin' to 'ave to,' she said as Phoebe turned away. 'You 'ave to tell 'em that sewin' night an' day you still ain't got the means to support 'em more'n another couple of weeks at the outside, an' you try to do more'n you be doin' already an' you'll work yerself into the ground an' that'll be a lot o' good to nobody.'

Tilly was right. Phoebe made her way slowly to her sewing room. She would tell them tonight. To tell Bert and Lizzie she could help them no longer would be painful but what would she say to Josh? How do you tell a young boy he must leave the home and people he loves? That would not be painful, that would be heart-breaking.

Pausing before the brown paper that held the creamy yellow satin, Phoebe ran a finger over the cloth. She was to have worn that to the Dartmouths' ball where she would have been Edward's partner. Edward who loved her and wanted to marry her. Her life would be so different had she said yes, had she loved him as he did her. But she did not love Edward, she did not love any man. Closing the brown paper back over the satin, she walked to her chair, taking up the petticoat she was making, but the stitches were blurred by the face in her mind. The face of Edward's father.

Her thoughts going again and again over the problem of keeping the Ingleses and Josh, Phoebe sewed until the light from the window was too dim to see the tiny stitches clearly. The whole day and only one petticoat to show for the hours of work. She smoothed the narrow pin tuck pleating that wound around the skirt above the flounces of cotton lace. If only she could afford one of Mr Singer's sewing machines! Laying the petticoat aside, she stood up, stretching the aching muscles of her back. If only she could buy just enough metal for Bert to make one or two locks it would help, but money would stretch just so far and buying brass or steel out of what little she earned was that much too far.

Maybe I don't need money. Phoebe stood stock still, the words singing in her brain. Maybe she did not need to pay for metal when it was ordered. Maybe she could pay at the end of the month like her father's customers always had. She could but ask. Tomorrow, she would ask tomorrow.

She had walked across the heath from Wiggins Mill and now stood in the ledger room of Thomas Bagnall's iron foundry, conscious of the dust on the skirt of her green coat.

'This way, Miss.'

Phoebe followed a small man, his shoulders permanently stooped from bending all day over ledgers.

'In 'ere, Miss.'

The man stood aside, holding a door open for Phoebe to pass into an inner office.

'Miss Pardoe.' Heavy-jowled, his hairline way back from the front of his head, Thomas Bagnall pushed himself to his feet as the door closed behind her. 'I 'aven't seen you in a long time. Sit down, my dear, sit down.'

'Thank you.' Phoebe perched nervously on the chair he indicated, aware of the glance that took her in from boots to hair.

'So, my dear, you're well, I 'ope?'

'Quite well, Mr Bagnall,' Phoebe said, unable to furnish the words with a smile. There was something in Thomas Bagnall she did not like and the sooner their business was finished and she could leave the greater would be her relief.

'Then what is it Thomas Bagnall can do for you?' He smiled, the heavy folds of flesh on his face shuttering his small eyes. 'Nothing 'olds more pleasure for me than serving a pretty woman.'

'I want to order some metal.' Phoebe tried not to wonder how his eyes would re-emerge from the enfolding flesh.

'That's easy done,' Thomas Bagnall's eyes stayed buried by his broadening smile, 'you only 'ave to say what it is you want.'

'Twenty-four pounds of brass and half that of steel.'

'That don't be much.' The folds of flesh gave a little ground, allowing his eyes to show.

'No, Mr Bagnall, it is a smaller order than my previous one but it will suffice for now.'

Dropping a thick-fingered hand on to a bell set on his desk he bawled the requirements to the same stoop-shouldered man who came in answer.

'We will 'ave that out to you tomorrow, Miss Pardoe,' he said when the clerk had left for the second time, 'if you will pay Simms on your way out?'

'I wish to speak to you about that.' Phoebe fingered her bag, her nerve threatening to run out on her. 'I – I wish to settle my accounts monthly in the future.'

'Monthly!' He smoothed the whiskers that ran the length of his flabby cheeks, at the same time coming from behind his desk to stand beside her chair. 'Now that be a different arrangement . . .'

Phoebe eased her knees away from the figure standing so close his legs touched hers. 'I am aware of that, Mr Bagnall, and though I have always paid in advance when purchasing metal from you, I believe it is not unusual to pay a month after delivery.'

'It's not unusual,' his small eyes glittered, 'not unusual at all between men. But you don't be a man.'

'I do not see that it makes any difference, I can pay as well as any man.'

'Except you ain't got any money.' Thomas Bagnall's smile registered triumph as he saw Phoebe wince. 'If you had the money you wouldn't be asking to pay at the end of a month, now would you, Miss Pardoe? And that being so we need to talk terms.'

'Terms?' She hitched herself further from him, sitting almost sideways in an effort to avoid the touch of his legs. 'Do you mean a charge for interest?'

'Some might see it that way.' The small eyes hovered about her breasts and his podgy hands pulled at his side whiskers as if tearing away her clothes. 'I see it as a way of saying thank you for a favour.'

'Do you charge a man interest for the privilege of settling his account after a month?' she demanded.

'How I conduct my business is my business.' He smiled, sending waves of flesh coursing toward his eyes. 'And if you want my metal without paying cash on the nail, you must meet my terms.'

'Which are?'

He touched a finger to her face, stroking it across her cheek and along the side of her throat. 'A little of your company, a private dinner somewhere secluded. Not much to pay for a month's credit.'

Not much to pay? Phoebe felt her stomach reach for her throat. A little of her company? Thomas Bagnall would want more than that.

'I find your terms too much!' Phoebe pushed to her feet, moving quickly to the door and snatching it open.

'P'raps you do but when you find nobody'll give credit to a woman then come back to Thomas Bagnall. You'll find his terms easier to fulfil when you've no money in your pocket and no food in your stomach.'

Phoebe walked back across the heath. She had not gone to visit Sarah or to see Lucy at her stall in the market place, knowing the contempt and disgust she was feeling would show in her face. But why had she avoided both of her friends? She sat on a half-buried stone, her feet aching from the long walk to the town and halfway back again. Why did she not want either of them to know what had gone on in Thomas Bagnall's office? Turning her face to the sky she closed her eyes. She had not gone to visit them for fear of their finding out what she only now admitted. She could not let the Ingleses take their children out on the road nor could she allow Josh to sink back into the poverty and misery of living in the streets. She had to go back to Thomas Bagnall, she had to agree to his terms.

* * *

'You have no need to take me.' Phoebe smiled at the stoop-backed clerk who looked up as she entered the ledger room. 'I know where Mr Bagnall's office is.' Knowing his eyes were following her, she went along the corridor that led to the comfortably furnished room she had been in less than an hour before. Pushing open the door without knocking, she stepped inside.

'Well, now!' Thomas Bagnall's self-satisfied smile obliterated his eyes. 'You've come to your senses, I see. I thought you would so I didn't cancel your order for steel and brass.'

He moved around the desk to stand close, his body brushing hers, bringing a fresh surge of revulsion to Phoebe's throat. If she were to help Josh and the others she had to do it now for she would never have the courage to do it later. Her voice little more than a whisper, her legs trembling with weariness from her long walk but mostly from fear of what she was about to agree to, she said, 'Dinner with you one evening, that was what you proposed as payment for extending me credit, was it not?'

He lifted a hand, stroking his knuckles across her breast. 'One evening for brass,' he said thickly, 'an' one for steel.'

'But you said one evening!' Phoebe pushed his hand away, her cheeks flaming.

'So I did,' he agreed, his tiny fat-shrouded eyes sweeping the length of her before settling on her face, 'and I'm still saying one. One evening for brass, one evening for steel. Those be my terms. You may take 'em or leave 'em.'

She had no choice. Trembling she turned to the doorway, stumbling through it in her eagerness to get away from a man who revolted her, yet a man to whom she must submit. 'Mr Bagnall,' she said, her voice low and shaky, 'I agree to your terms.'

'And what terms might those be?' Sir William Dartmouth caught Phoebe's arms as in her haste to be gone from the office she cannoned into him. Steadying her, he released her, asking again, 'What terms?'

'Miss Pardoe an' me had business together.' Thomas Bagnall's eyes receded behind their barrier of fat as he glanced warningly at Phoebe.

'How interesting!' William Dartmouth looked from one to the other, his glance pausing on Phoebe's flushed face. 'I am always interested in business and in the terms that conclude it. Perhaps, Miss Pardoe, you will tell me of yours?'

'It was nothing of consequence.' Thomas Bagnall stepped back from the doorway, leaving it clear for the other man to enter the office, but he did not move.

'What do you call "nothing of consequence" Thomas?' Sir William asked the question of the iron founder but his eyes were on Phoebe.

'Twenty-four pounds of brass and half that of steel, a piddlin' little order!' Bagnall snapped, annoyed at being questioned.

'Little indeed,' Sir William nodded, 'though it could have been more politely described in the presence of a lady, don't you think Thomas?'

What little could be seen of his eyes glittering venomously, the iron founder looked at Phoebe. 'I beg your pardon, Miss Pardoe,' he ground, 'a slip of the tongue.' Then to Sir William, 'Miss Pardoe was just leaving.'

'So I see.' William Dartmouth remained blocking Phoebe's way in the narrow brown-painted corridor that smelled strongly of the foundry. 'And hurriedly. Is that because you have other business, Miss Pardoe, or is it due to the terms you have just agreed with Thomas Bagnall?'

'I . . . I asked Mr Bagnall to allow me to settle my account at the end of the month from the date of purchase.' Phoebe straightened the quaver from her voice though her cheeks still flamed.

'That is the usual practice.'

'Not for me, Sir William.' Phoebe raised her head, a mixture of pride and despair in her green eyes. 'I have always paid the full amount at the time of placing an order but today it is not possible for me to do that therefore I asked for the month of credit I knew it was usual to extend to customers.'

'And the terms?' he asked, the temperature of his voice dangerously low.

'There were no terms. She asked for a month. I . . . I gave her a month, that's all we agreed.' Thomas Bagnall glared at Phoebe. 'There were no other terms.'

'And there will be none!' Sir William glanced past Phoebe to the other man, a world of meaning in his cold grey eyes. 'Miss Pardoe's order will be delivered in the morning and paid for one calendar month following that day and there will be no extra charge any sort whatsoever. The same terms will apply to any and all future orders she may wish to place.' He turned to Phoebe. 'Do you find those terms acceptable?'

'Most acceptable,' she nodded, 'thank you.'

Inclining his head so slightly his eyes did not leave her face, he answered quietly, 'Then your business here is settled. Good day, Miss Pardoe.'

The brass and steel would be delivered tomorrow! Bert would have the means of earning a living again! Phoebe walked home across the heath, her tiredness forgotten. She had a month in which to get the money to pay for the metals and thanks to Sir William she would not have to dine with Thomas Bagnall or suffer the attentions she knew would have followed. It was more than fortunate Sir William had arrived when he did, it was heavensent. She breathed a long deep breath of air flavoured with the scent of ling and wild flowers. It had been many months since her release from Handsworth prison but she still felt the same wonder and relief at being free to walk across the heath, just to stand and listen to the hymn of a skylark rising to the sky or the chorus of crickets in the grass. William Dartmouth had brought her that freedom just as he had brought another different kind of freedom today. 'Thank you,' she murmured using her inner eyes to look at the tall dark-haired man whose grey eyes seemed to smile back at her. 'Thank you.'

'When did he go?' Phoebe asked Tilly, her voice throbbing with concern.

'About a hour after yerself,' she answered. ''E come swannin' into the kitchen an' said 'e was off somewheres else to find work 'cos there was none to be 'ad in Wednesbury. It wasn't till later I found that in the parlour.'

Phoebe glanced at the coins lying on the table, a tiny pool of silver glistening in the last of the daylight.

'Did he say where he was going?'

'I've told you what 'e said, word for word,' Tilly answered patiently, ''ad 'e said more I would 'ave told you more.'

'I know, Tilly, and I am sorry to keep on questioning you, it's just that I am so concerned.'

'We all be that, my wench, but I don't see as worryin' yerself sick will do any good – you already be worn out wi' walkin' to that town an' back. Sit yerself down an' wait for Mathew gettin' in. Could be 'e was told more'n me.'

But Phoebe could not sit down. The meeting with Thomas Bagnall had unnerved her, and now this.

'Has Lizzie said anything?' She looked at Tilly peeling potatoes in an enamel bowl, black chip marks leaving a pattern of dots around its white edge.

'Nuthin' 'er can say.' Tilly hacked a hole in a potato, digging out the brown rottenness attacking its heart. ''E be gone an' that be all there be to it. Talkin' will mek no odds to that.'

Phoebe had talked yesterday of not being able to keep them all together at Wiggins Mill; now she had found a way, only she had found it too late. If only he had waited just one more day.

'That be Lucy and Mathew 'ome.' Tilly dropped a half-peeled potato into the bowl, rubbing her hands on her apron. 'Could be they seen 'im somewheres.' Following Phoebe into the yard she heard Lizzie already asking the question and Mathew's answer.

'I seen 'im this mornin' afore Lucy an' me went into Wednesbury an' I ain't seen 'im since.'

'Neither 'ave I.' Lucy shook her head.

'It ain't 'ardly dark yet.' Mathew glanced at the golden-red rim of the horizon. ''E'll be back soon, you be worryin' over nuthin'. It ain't as if 'e ain't never been out in the dark on 'is own afore.'

'Mathew's right,' Lucy agreed, ''e 'as most like gone into the town an' met up wi' somebody 'e knows. Give 'im an hour or so an' 'e'll be back.'

'I 'ope you be tellin' true, Lucy,' Lizzie said tearfully. 'I 'ope you all be tellin' true.'

'Tell you what,' Mathew scooped Ruth into his arms as she came squealing with delight into the yard, 'let me give my best girl a cuddle and then I'll go look for 'im.'

'Who you goin' to look for, Uncle Mathew?'

Kissing the little girl's cheek he set her down beside her mother. 'I'm goin' to look for the prince who will marry my little princess, but not till you be older.'

'Can I come? Can I, Uncle Mathew?'

Mathew smiled at the child, her tumbling red-gold hair caught with a strip of cornflower blue ribbon Lucy had bought for her. 'We can't 'ave a princess walkin' the 'eath an' gettin' 'er royal feet dusty.'

'You could carry me,' she answered, her eyes wide and serious.

'I might be able to, Ruthie,' Mathew hid his smile, 'but I be gettin' very old. Could be as I couldn't carry you back.'

Catching his hand the girl smiled up at him, craning her head back on her neck. 'Don't worry, Uncle Mathew, I will carry you back.'

'Come along, miss.' Lizzie caught her daughter by her free hand. 'You can carry yerself to the wash bowl and wash yer 'ands an' face ready for bed. Say goodnight to everybody.'

'You will let me know if you find 'im?' Lizzie asked when the goodnights had been said.

'Don't worry,' Lucy smiled sympathetically, 'I'll come right over.'

'I think I'll go wi' Lizzie,' Tilly said quietly. ''Er 'as took this 'arder than I would 'ave thought. I'll stop with 'er till Mark be 'ome then I'll be back to finish them 'taters.'

'I will finish them.' Phoebe looked towards Lizzie leading her daughter to the corn barn that had become their home. 'Stay with Lizzie as long as she needs you.'

'Who would 'ave guessed Lizzie would 'ave been 'it that 'ard?' Mathew lifted his cap, running a hand through his hair.

'When you grow to love somebody it be 'ard when they ups an' leaves wi' 'ardly a word,' Lucy answered. 'Beats me why 'e did it. 'E ain't goin' to find no better 'ome than 'e's got 'ere.'

'He did it because he thought we could not keep him at Wiggins Mill any longer,' Phoebe said. 'He was no fool, he knew how long it had been since any money other than the few shillings my sewing brings had come into the house. He knew I could not support them all for much longer so he left.'

'Poor soul!' Lucy sighed. 'An' now 'e is Lord knows where, but at least 'e as *some* money in 'is pocket an' 'e is well used to mekin' it stretch as far as it'll go so at least 'e will eat for a week or two.'

'But he does not have any money.' Phoebe turned towards the house. 'He left what he had in the parlour.'

'What, all of it?' Lucy asked as Mathew set off to search the heath.

'All of it,' Phoebe nodded. 'All four shillings.'

'Poor soul!' Lucy said again. 'Poor little Josh!'

'If only he had waited, we will have brass and steel tomorrow enough for Bert to start again.'

'Eh, Miss Phoebe! How did you manage that?'

'It's a long story, Lucy.'

Catching her arm, Lucy hustled her towards the house. 'Then let's 'ave a cup o'tea wi' the tellin'. I'm that parched I couldn't spit a tanner.'

'Eh, the dirty old bugger!' Lucy exclaimed when Phoebe finished relating the happenings of the afternoon. 'I wonder 'ow the 'oity toity Rachel Bagnall would take to knowin' 'er old man be no better than a lecher!'

'I hope she never has to know.' Phoebe poured tea for both of them, handing a cup to Lucy.

'Prob'ly wouldn't worry 'er none.' Lucy blew indelicately into her cup to cool the steaming liquid. 'From what folk tell 'er ain't no better than 'er should be.' She looked up suddenly, shock slackening her mouth. 'Eeh, Miss Phoebe, you wouldn't 'a gone, would you? Wi' old Bagnall I mean!'

'I think that at the time I was prepared to do anything, Lucy,' Phoebe admitted.

'You would 'ave been called on to do more than eat a dinner wi' that dirty sod!' Lucy's shock retreated before an onslaught of indignation. 'Thank God Billy-me-Lord turned up when 'e did. Which reminds me,' she put her cup on the table, 'there was talk in the market today about the Dartmouths.'

'Sir William?'

''Im an' all,' Lucy said quickly, 'but mostly 'is family, about them comin' 'ome to England.'

Edward was coming home. The thought was pleasant but it brought no rush of excitement. It had been the truth when she had told him she was not in love with him but he had said that would change while he was in Europe, that when he returned he would ask her again to become his wife. But her feelings for him had not changed. Edward Dartmouth was a kind attentive man who would make a wonderful husband but she could never marry him.

'When are they expected?' Phoebe asked.

Across the table Lucy's eyes were bright. 'They ain't!' she said bluntly.

Phoebe's brows drew together with a hint of puzzlement. 'But you said they were coming home?'

'They *was*,' Lucy emphasised the last word, 'but it seems there was a almighty storm at sea somewheres an' the ship they was on was sunk. 'Pears there was quite a few of the passengers didn't find a place in them lifeboats an' was drowned.'

'No!' Phoebe's face blanched. 'No, not Sophie, she was to be married . . . she . . . she can't be drowned!'

'That seems to be what 'er father said,' Lucy continued. ''Cordin' to what be told in the market the ship was sunk some time ago but 'e wouldn't 'ave it that 'is family was drowned. 'E kept on waitin' for word that would tell they was still alive.'

'But it did not come?'

'Seems not.' Lucy picked up her cup, sipping the tea. 'Seems he 'eard to the contrary. 'E must 'ave for word to be goin' around.'

'I never thought when I saw him in Thomas Bagnall's foundry today, it didn't seem to register.'

'What didn't?' Lucy looked up from her tea.

Phoebe frowned as though trying to recall some inner picture. 'He, Sir William, he wore dark grey. The collar of his coat was faced with black velvet and he had a narrow ribbon of grosgrain about the sleeve. He was in mourning and I never noticed.'

'Don't blame yerself, Miss,' Lucy said soothingly, 'after what you 'ad just been through wi' old Bagnall, 't'ain't surprisin' you never noticed.'

'But *he* noticed.' Phoebe condemned her own oversight. 'He noticed my discomfort even in his own sorrow and I . . . he must think I am so heartless!'

Rising from her chair Lucy went to stand beside the girl she had once served as a maid, the girl whom life had

moulded into a woman. ''E won't think nothin' like that,'
she said, bending to place her arms about Phoebe. ''E could
see you was upset an' 'e won't tek no insult from you not
offerin' 'im sympathy. Billy-me-Lord be too fine a man to
'old a grudge, 'specially from summat 'e knows full well to
be not meant.'

'I hope you are right, Lucy.' Phoebe turned to her friend,
hiding her tears against her waist. 'He was so kind to me, I
never wanted to hurt him.'

'You ain't 'urt 'im, Miss Phoebe.' Lucy stroked a hand across
sherry-coloured hair, her voice gentle. 'You ain't 'urt 'im, an'
when you be feelin' more like yerself you can write to tell
'im of yer sympathy wi' 'is loss, but for now go an' wash yer
face while I finishes peelin' these 'taters. You will feel better
for it.'

'Ain't no sign o'the lad,' Mathew was saying when Phoebe
returned to the kitchen. 'Bert an' Mark went over towards
Tipton way an' I went towards the Lyng but it be blacker
than the devil's tongue out there an' wi' no moon I couldn't
see no more'n a spit in front o' me an' same wi' Bert an'
Mark. Ain't no more we can do tonight.'

'But he might be sleeping out in the open,' Phoebe
protested.

''E might an' I can't say as 'e ain't,' Mathew answered,
'but it be no use our lookin' any more. 'Sides if it be as 'e
left the parish like 'e told Tilly 'e was goin' to do 'e could
be anywhere by this time. We can't tell whether 'e 'eaded
for Brummagem or took Walsall way, an' in any case, even
if we does find 'im we can't force 'im to come back to
Wiggins Mill, not if 'e don't want to.'

'But he was happy here and the work with Bert interested
him.'

'Ar, the work interested 'im,' Mathew looked from Phoebe
to Lucy, 'but who knows 'ow long a lad's interest be 'eld by
anythin'? They changes their minds quicker'n a kingfisher
flaps its wings. One minute they be fascinated by one thing

an' the next minute they wants no more to be doin' wi' it.'

'I don't think Josh was like that,' Phoebe said quietly. 'I think he left because he saw it as the only way to help the situation. He thought one less mouth to feed was one less to worry over. Why else would he have left every penny he had earned in my parlour?'

'You be right, Miss Phoebe.' Lucy added salt to the potatoes she had placed in a pan set over the coal fire. 'But so is Mathew. If the lad 'as med up 'is mind to go then there be nothin' we can do about it. We just 'ave to accept it.'

'Lizzie has taken it so hard you would almost think it was Mark had left.'

'Lizzie be a good soul,' Mathew said, ''er treated that lad like 'er treated 'er own. 'Tain't surprisin' 'er be tekin' it 'ard.'

'And Bert?'

''E were the same, treated Josh as 'e treated Mark.'

'One as worries me be Ruth,' Lucy said. 'That little 'un thought the sun shone out of 'is eyes, 'er followed 'im every chance 'er got. 'Ow do you explain to a child as young as that the one 'er took to be God 'as up an' left?'

'Lord!' Mathew breathed. 'Nobody thought about Ruthie.'

Phoebe stared at the window. The night sky had lightened into dawn and still she had not slept, her mind living and re-living the times spent with Sophie and Edward. Edward had loved Phoebe, and he had died knowing her love for him was not returned. And Sophie . . . she was so full of marriage plans, so happy at the thought of becoming Montrose's wife, and now she was lying somewhere on the sea bed. Son, daughter and wife, all taken in one swoop. Phoebe closed her eyes against the picture her mind formed yet again, a picture of people helpless against waves that engulfed then swallowed them. His whole family lost together, what must Sir William Dartmouth be feeling?

'Ruth . . . Ruth, where am you?'

Phoebe's eyes snapped open as Bert's voice rang across the yard.

'Ruth . . . Ruth, my girl, ah'll tan yer arse for yer if you don't come 'ere this minute!'

This time it was Lizzie's voice that rang on the dawn stillness. Flinging aside the covers Phoebe jumped from the bed, crossing quickly to the window that overlooked the yard. Bert and Lizzie, still in their nightclothes, were looking around the outhouses. Raising the sash, Phoebe called to ask what was wrong.

'It be Ruth.' Lizzie looked up at the window, her face a mask of concern. ''Er be gone from 'er bed.'

'Have you searched the barn thoroughly?' Phoebe realised the futility of her question only after asking it.

'We looked just about everywhere,' Lizzie said, her voice near to breaking, 'me and Bert been lookin' an hour or more.'

'I'll be down in a moment!'

'What be the matter?' Tilly came into Phoebe's room as she withdrew her head, leaving the sash open.

'Ruth.' Phoebe reached for her dress and petticoats. 'She is not in her bed and Lizzie and Bert cannot find her in any of the out buildings.

'Lord, not summat else!' Tilly threw up her hands in despair. 'If it ain't one thing it's another. When is it all goin' to end? I'll get me dress an' then I'll be down. That poor woman . . .'

Phoebe threw off her nightgown, scrambled into her day clothes. Unmindful of her unwashed face or her uncombed hair she thrust her feet into her shoes and ran downstairs to the yard.

'How long has she been gone?' she asked, reaching Lizzie's side.

'I don't know for true,' Lizzie answered, her face crumpling. 'I put 'er into 'er bed last night like always an' when I woke this mornin' 'er were not in it no longer.'

'Try not to worry.' Phoebe held the crying woman, realising the unreasonableness of her request but hoping it at least sounded confident. 'We will have her home in no time. She has probably gone over to the windmill to pick you some flowers. I noticed some very pretty ones around there the other day.'

'Or 'er might 'ave gone across by the cut.' Lizzie's body shook. ''Er might 'ave 'eard we talkin' after 'er 'ad been put to 'er bed. We said about Josh 'avin' left, an' Bert was sayin' 'ow 'e might never come back.' She stepped out of Phoebe's arms. 'You know 'ow 'er 'ad taken to the lad,' she said, her eyes darkening with fear. 'Summat tells me 'er 'as gone lookin' for 'im an' 'er'll 'ave little fear o' the cut. 'Er'll 'ave no understandin' o' the danger of it.'

'But she may not have gone to the canal.' Phoebe tried to sound reassuring. 'Why should she have?'

'I know 'er 'as.' Lizzie spoke more to herself than to Phoebe. ''Er 'eard Bert say the lad could well 'op a barge somewhere an' barges means the cut an' that be where my babby 'as gone! My Ruth be somewhere in the . . .'

'Don't talk like that!' Tilly snapped, coming into the yard in time to hear Lizzie's fear. 'That babby o' your'n be up to 'er arse in flowers over by that windmill an' 'er father will 'ave 'er back 'ere afore you 'ave time to blink, so stop yer snivellin' an' go mek 'er some breakfast to come back to!'

'Tilly is right,' Phoebe said as Mathew and Lucy joined them. 'Ruth will be back before you know it. Leave it to the men. You come with Tilly and me, a cup of tea will help.'

'Will it?' Lizzie sagged against Tilly. 'Will it 'elp that?'

Phoebe turned, following the line of Lizzie's stare. 'Oh no!' she whispered. 'Please God, no.'

'Ruthie!' Bert's agonised shout rent the quiet sky as he caught sight of his daughter, her white nightgown clinging to her small body, her red-gold hair a bright splash against a dark jacket. 'Ruthie!' he shouted again, running towards the boy who carried her in his arms . . .

* * *

'I were a few yards, along the cut,' Josh explained as Lizzie held her daughter, dry and in a fresh nightgown, tight in her arms. 'I know I'd said as I was leavin' Wednesbury altogether but when it come to it I couldn't, I just wanted to be near all of you, especially Mrs Ingles.'

'But why go in the first place, Josh?' Phoebe looked to where he sat, his fingers curled about the girl's hand.

'I knowed you was short o' money, Miss, an' 'ad been for some time. It sort of makes sense, don't it? One less body in the 'ouse meks one less mouth to feed so I went, but I come back when it was dark. I found a place to sleep the other side o' the lock. I would 'ave liked to have slept in the old windmill but I wouldn't 'cos I 'ad promised Miss Phoebe I wouldn't never sleep in that place again an' there were nowheres else so I kipped along o' the cut.'

'Thank the good God 'e put you there, lad.' Bert took the child from his wife, carrying her into the loft to her bed.

'But if you was sleepin',' Mark asked, ''ow come you knowed our Ruth was in the cut?'

'I was sleepin',' a puzzled look crept over Josh's face, 'an' I was dreamin'. I was dreamin' o' me mother only it were not me mother. Well, the face were not me mother's, it were Mrs Ingles's, but 'er were wearin' a lovely white frock an' 'er face were all shinin' like a light were on it an' 'er called me name.' He paused as if living the dream again. ''Er called me name two or three times an' then 'er told me to get up an' bring Ruth 'ome. I said as Ruth already be 'ome but 'er just smiled an' said it again. "Josh, get up and bring Ruth 'ome."'

He looked at the group of people watching him. 'I 'eard 'er say it plain as day an' then I woke up. I looked all around but I couldn't see nobody an' I was just goin' to lie down again when the water up along the canal by the lock went all bright wi' the sun an' I seen summat white floatin' in it. Well, I run like buggery to see what it might be an' . . . an' it were Ruth. I went in 'ead first an' brought 'er out but I couldn't bring 'er to wakin' so I carried 'er back 'ere to 'er 'ome like I was bid.'

'You did well, lad.' Tilly pushed a dish of thick porridge to each of the two boys.

'You did that.' Lizzie caught her husband's hand as he came down from the loft. 'An' don't you ever go leavin' we again, Josh, or I'll 'ave Bert 'ere belt the 'ide off you. This place or any other the Ingleses might find theirselves in be your 'ome an' we be your family.'

Josh looked up, a spoonful of porridge hovering at his lips, his eyes filled with something near to longing. 'Mrs Ingles,' he asked, 'could . . . could I call you Mother?'

'It was a strange dream Josh had,' Phoebe said as she walked with Tilly across the yard toward the mill house, 'strange but very fortunate.'

'It were fortunate all right an' a dream it might 'ave been.'

'Might?' Phoebe stopped walking and looked at the woman beside her. 'Now just what does that mean, Tilly Wood?'

'Mek on it what you will,' she answered, 'but to me that were no dream young Josh 'ad.'

'What else could it have been?'

'I ain't sayin',' Tilly's mouth set in a straight line, 'but the lad said as the sun shone on the water just about where that little wench was floatin', didn't 'e?'

'Yes,' Phoebe answered, puzzled by Tilly's attitude.

'Well, it 'pears to 'ave escaped everybody's notice but there ain't no sun, leastways none as can be seen through clouds that be thicker than a grorty puddin'.' She glanced skyward. 'There's been no break in them from first light. I knows 'cos I ain't been to bed. I sat watching against that lad comin' 'ome.'

Chapter Twenty-Two

'But this is more than I expected.' Phoebe looked at the banknotes on her kitchen table then to the man shuffling from one foot to another, clearly uncomfortable at being inside the house. 'It is more than I asked.'

'Ar,' he nodded, 'I knows that but my brother-in-law says they Americans were willin' to pay more for such good locks so 'e sold 'em for more. That bill 'e sent along wi' 'em be from man as bought 'em an' tells the price 'e paid. You will see when you check that it all be there.'

'I am sure of it,' Phoebe smiled, 'but why has your brother-in-law not taken his percentage?'

'You trusted 'im, Miss. Now 'e be trustin' you. If it be as you be satisfied wi' the deal 'e struck then you will be sendin' 'im what 'e earned, that be the way 'e looks at it.'

'I am more than satisfied and I think Bert and Mathew are too.'

'It be a right good deal so far as I sees it.' Mathew grinned delightedly. 'Bert was right to suggest it.'

'There be a market for many more, so I was instructed to tell you, an' they can cross over same way as before.'

'Take some time,' Bert said thoughtfully. 'We couldn't go on workin' flat out like we did to make that gross, not all the time we couldn't.'

'Well,' the man shuffled again, his clogs loud on the red scrubbed flags of the kitchen floor, 'I be away up to London termorrer and back this way along o' a week. I will call, if you allows, for water an' you can be givin' me yer answer

319

then. An' if you don't mind, Miss, would you keep me brother-in-law's cut till I be comin' back 'cos it don't be doin' to 'ave money wi' you on the barges?'

'It'll be 'ere when you wants to pick it up,' Bert said, following the man from the kitchen, 'an' there'll be some for you an' all for the 'elp you 'ave been.'

''Elp where you can,' the bargee refastened the muffler wrapped about his neck, 'that's what me mother learned all 'er kids, an' if you can't be a 'elp then don't be a 'indrance.'

''Er couldn't 'ave learned you better,' Bert said, shaking the other man's hand. 'Safe journey to London an' I'll see you a week from now.'

'That went better'n I'd guessed,' he said as he re-entered the kitchen. 'Seems you 'ave a solid market if you wants to follow it up, Miss Phoebe.'

'We *have* to follow it up, Bert.' Phoebe glanced at the bill signed 'Hiram B. Rosmeyer'. 'It would be foolish not to. The only thing we have to decide is how many locks we can make in a month. As you have said, you can't work at the pace you were before so how many would you expect to make?'

'That depends,' he mused. 'As we be now I would say between a dozen or dozen an' a 'alf a week.'

'Half a gross a month,' Phoebe calculated quickly, 'two months before we could ship another worthwhile batch.'

'The market could be gone in that time,' Mathew said, 'could be somebody else will get a notion to do the same thing an' if they be quicker at it than we . . .' He shrugged his shoulders.

'I don't see we can do anything about that, Mathew.' Phoebe looked rueful. 'You all do your best and no one can do better than that.'

'Might be a way o' speedin' up the makin' . . .' Bert touched a hand to his chin. 'Mathew an' me 'ave both spoke o' the way young Josh picks things up. 'E be a quick learner an' already knows near as much of locksmithin' as do Mark. Now if we could tek 'im off the bellows an' set 'im to work on the benches along o' we three then you could turn that dozen an' 'alf into two dozen or more a week.'

'But who would work the bellows? You need those to keep the forge burning, don't you?'

Bert nodded. 'We need the bellows, that be right enough, but they don't need to be sat over full time. What I was thinkin', if Mathew be agreeable, was for each o' the four on we to tek the bellows to the forge when we uses it an' the two lads to tek a turn when Mathew an' me be too busy. An' as for the coal, I was of a mind to suggest that Mathew an' me hauls a load up from the cut each night.'

'Easy done,' Mathew grinned, 'I could knock up a cart on a couple of wheels to mek it less of a task.'

'I think though, Miss, in all fairness Josh should 'ave the same wage as Mark, learn the way o' the world ain't paved wi' gold like fairy tales would 'ave 'em believe.'

'Whatever you say, Bert.' Phoebe smiled her thanks. 'Pardoe's Patent Locks are in the export business.'

She had smiled confidently at Bert and Mathew but counting the banknotes later that evening Phoebe felt that confidence seeping away. Deducting the wages owed to the men and to Mark, and the money she would pay Bagnall tomorrow, plus setting aside even a minimum for food and household expenses, left the sum much depleted. Then she would need to order a further supply of metal if the workshop was to be kept in full production and that she would pay for in advance – she would take no more chances with the odious Thomas Bagnall. Phoebe counted in her mind. She was playing near the edge but she had done that before. Folding one of the white five-pound notes she shoved it deep into her bag. Perhaps it might be enough for what she wanted.

Leaving the iron foundry Phoebe smiled to herself. Thomas Bagnall had been surprised to find her settling one account two days before it was due to be paid and paying for a further, larger supply in advance.

With the five pounds in her bag she walked along Dudley Street, turning left against St James's Church, following Holyhead Road toward the Lodge Holes coal mine.

Joseph had given her the idea when she had visited on Sunday. He had mentioned that the old pit ponies were to be brought out of the mine and sold. Phoebe shuddered to think of these animals, most probably condemned to the glue works after years toiling underground, but that was the way it had always been.

Joseph had somehow seemed more than usually lame, needing Mathew's arm to walk around Sarah's tiny vegetable plot, and Phoebe knew they were worried for his job. If the new mine owner sacked him then they would have to leave their home.

Holding her skirts free of the dusty ground Phoebe left the road, striking left across open ground that gave on to the mine.

But Joseph had not been sacked as yet, and if she could only keep a supply of locks going to America, then maybe in a couple of years she could help Joseph and Sarah to find a new home.

'Please let things work out this time,' she breathed to the morning. 'Please don't let this order be a hoax.'

It was going to be hard work turning out the number of locks Bert had specified every week and she really ought to be at the mill helping all she could or at least busy on her needlework, Phoebe thought, feeling guilty at being away from the house. But for a few hours things were going to have to take their chances.

Reaching the large wooden gates that closed off the pit yard from nothing but open land, Phoebe saw her father's name, not painted out as yet. Nothing moved fast in Wednesbury. Loosing the skirts of her green coat, she took a deep breath and stepped hesitantly across the yard trodden black with coal dust. Today she would not be dealing with Joseph Leach, as she would have a few years before, now she would be doing business with a new yard foreman. Joseph had been dismissed when the mine had changed hands.

'Can I 'elp you, Miss?'

Phoebe smiled at the man who answered her knock on the door of the office. Of medium height but powerful across the shoulders, his splendid moustache wiggled as he spoke.

Phoebe swallowed the smile the dancing moustache threatened to bring to her lips. 'I have reason to believe you are bringing several ponies out of the pit today?'

'Ar, Miss, so we am.'

'Then I would like to purchase one of those ponies.'

'Purchase!' The moustache jigged. 'What do you mean, Miss?'

'May I step inside?' She glanced about the yard, seeing the heads of several men turn in her direction. Maybe Joseph would be in the office.

'Well, it be all dusty in 'ere like, it ain't clean for a lady.' The man hesitated, clearly unused to his working domain being encroached on by a woman.

'We won't let that worry us.' Phoebe stepped inside, glancing about the shed she remembered so well: at the heavy ledgers on a bench to one side, the row of nails hammered into one wall, each with a numbered tag that indicated a man underground, and the table where the dead Norton boy had been laid by his father. Pushing the image away she looked at the man who stood as if trying to bar her entry into a holy sanctum.

'As I said, I wish to purchase one of the ponies that are to be brought up from the pit.'

'You can't, Miss,' he said. 'Them ponies ain't to be sold.'

'What do you mean, they are not for sale!' Phoebe demanded.

'What I says, Miss.' The moustache danced indignantly at her question. 'Them ponies ain't to be sold, not to you anyway.'

'Not to me, but they are to be sold?' Phoebe pressed.

'Mebbe,' the man conceded grudgingly.

'Then why not to me? Why can I not buy one of them?'

''Cos you can't, that's all I know.' He touched a hand to his top lip as if to prevent the moustache leaping from his face. 'The ponies ain't to be sold.'

'You mean perhaps they have been sold already?'

'Maybe they 'ave, then maybe they ain't.' He held on to the moustache that seemed to want to lead a life of its own. 'All I know is what I'm told, an' I was told them ponies was not to be sold.'

'But they have always been sold,' Phoebe defended her case.

'They might 'ave bin, but that were before. This be now an' things am different. Seems new bloke don't want them ponies sent to no glue works.'

A tiny frown formed over Phoebe's eyes. 'Then what does he intend doing with them?'

'Look, Miss,' the man began to sound exasperated, 'I already told you I only knows what I'm told an' I ain't bin told that.'

'Then if you do not know perhaps you will direct me to someone who does?'

'You best talk to the manager,' he said stiffly, 'if anybody be told diff'rent it'll be 'im.'

Phoebe was taken aback. The pit ponies had always been sold off at the end of their working life to any who saw fit to buy them. It had nearly always been the glue works but others had never been barred from buying. 'Then please show me to the manager. Perhaps, as you say, I had best speak to him.'

'Can't do that.' The man grinned, triumphant in his small victory. ''E ain't 'ere.'

'Then where is he?' Phoebe felt a strong desire to slap both moustache and its owner.

'Could be anywheres in the pit, might be one place might be t'other, ain't no tellin'.'

'It is clear you did not win a Sunday school prize for honesty nor one for helpfulness,' Phoebe snapped.

'Maybe not, Miss Pardoe, but *I* did so perhaps you would do better to talk to me?'

Phoebe turned at the sound of a voice that echoed almost nightly in her mind, a faint hint of pink staining her cheeks.

'Might I ask what you are doing here?'

'Sir William,' the blush on her cheeks deepened at the unexpected encounter. 'I – I was told some of the pit ponies would be finished today.'

He waited, eyes taking in the bloom of her face.

'Oh!' His well-defined eyebrows lifted quizzically. 'Were you also told the ponies were to be sold to the glue works?'

'No.' She looked away awkwardly. What was he doing at the mine? Why did she suddenly feel like an erring child?

'But you presumed they were?'

Phoebe lifted her head, re-engaging his eyes defiantly. Wanting to buy a pony to save it from the glue works was no crime. 'Is that not what always happens to ponies taken from the pits?'

'Not all pits, Miss Pardoe.' He glanced at the yard foreman watching them covertly and the man turned back to his ledgers. Sir William led her out. 'Certainly not those belonging to me.'

'You bought my father's mines?' Phoebe asked, surprised.

'I did,' he nodded, 'and that means no more ponies from here or the Crown at Moxley will go to the glue works. Once their working life is over they will be returned to pasture at Sandwell Priory.'

'Then if they are to be put to pasture, why can I not buy one?'

Almost at the gates that closed off the pit head from the open heathland, he halted. 'Why do you want a pit pony?' he asked bluntly. 'When these animals have served so long underground they are virtually worked out. They will not be useful for heavy work.'

'I do not want a pony for heavy work.'

'Then what do you want it for?'

She did not have to tell him, of course, chances were he would not sell her a pony if she *did* tell him, but then she had nothing to hide.

'I wanted it for Ruth.'

'Ruth?' His brows rose again.

'She is the Ingleses' daughter – they live at Wiggins Mill,' Phoebe explained. 'There was an accident and she fell into the canal and though she seemed to suffer no serious injury she has not been the same child since. She used to be so full of life, always playing about the mill, but now she seems so withdrawn. I thought a pony of her own, one she would have the caring of, would give her something of interest.'

'How old is Ruth?'

'She is just a child, no more than eight years old.'

'Would she be able to handle a pony?'

'I am sure of it,' Phoebe answered. 'Her family worked the barges along the canal so she is well used to horses – that was why I thought a pit pony used to being handled by young children would suit her.'

He smiled, his eyes taking on a new warmth. 'Then perhaps we should discuss the possibility of furnishing Ruth with a pony, but here is not the most suitable of places.' He looked at the film of black dust covering her shoes and edging the hem of her coat. 'Might I suggest we go to the Priory?'

'The Priory is at least an hour and a half's walk and I have little time to spare, as I'm sure is the case with yourself, Sir William.'

'You are sure of so many things,' he said. 'Sure my ponies are to be sold off to make glue and sure I do not have time to discuss the provision of one for Ruth.'

'I beg your pardon,' Phoebe coloured afresh at his mild rebuke, 'but I have so little time and a walk to the Priory will take a great deal of it.'

'Not so much if you will accept a ride in my carriage.' He

smiled again. 'It would also relieve me of walking there as I must if you refuse.'

'But could we not just agree a sale here?' she protested.

'I think the pit ponies deserve the peace of the pasture,' he answered, 'even though Ruth would cherish one of them.'

'Then there is no cause for me to accompany you to the Priory.'

'There is every need if you wish the child to have a pony. Please,' he said, seeing the query on her face, 'there is a pony there that will answer your needs perfectly if only you will take enough of your precious time to look at it.'

It would take more of her time than she had accounted for. Phoebe thought of the others working at the mill. She really ought not to be away so long but Ruth seemed so dejected, so apart from them. If two or three more hours would serve to restore the child's interest in life then it would not be too much to pay.

'She's beautiful,' said Phoebe later, stroking the sand-coloured pony nuzzling her hand. 'What's her name?'

'Pippin,' Sir William answered quietly. 'Sophie gave her that name when the mare foaled. She said the newcomer was the colour of the pippins in an apple she fed to the mother.'

'I was so very sorry to hear of what happened to your family.' Phoebe saw the sadness shadow his face. Then in an effort to chase away a little of the shadows, she asked, 'Was this Sophie's horse?'

'The mother was Sophie's so I suppose the foal was too.'

'Then I cannot possibly take her from you.'

'Why not?' He signalled a groom who came and led the horse back to its stable. 'Sophie would have wanted the child to have it, and I want her to have it. I also want her to have this.' Leading the way to a long stone building set with graceful arched windows, he swung open a pair of heavy doors showing a line of broughams and carriages at the end of which stood a small blue-painted governess cart. 'This was my daughter's when she was a child,' he said, going over to it. 'Now I wish it to be Ruth's.'

'But I can't!' Phoebe thought of the five-pound note at the bottom of her bag. It could not possibly be enough to purchase horse and cart.

'Would the child not like it?' he asked, turning to her.

'I'm sure she would.' Phoebe glanced again at the cart, its blue-painted side edged with a pattern of daisies. 'But . . .'

'Once more you are sure,' he said gently, 'so why the "but"?'

'Ruth would love the horse and the cart would be her delight,' Phoebe decided only the truth would conclude this discussion, 'but five pounds is all I have and I know that to be insufficient to pay for them.'

'I am not selling you the horse or the cart, they are a gift.'

'No!' Phoebe's mouth set in a straight line. 'What I cannot pay for I will not take, whatever the need. Thank you for your kindness but I must refuse.'

Touching a hand to the pretty cart he seemed to see into the past, to the child who had once ridden in it so happily. 'If you will not accept a gift from me, accept it from Sophie,' he said softly.

Seeing the droop of his shoulders and hearing the pain in his voice, Phoebe's heart twisted with pity. If only she could take him in her arms and hold him until the pain had gone but she could not. Offering a gift on Sophie's behalf then having it refused would add to the hurt he was feeling. But such a gift . . . Phoebe hesitated, torn between her wish to spare him any more hurt and her decision to accept no man's charity.

Almost as if he sensed her thoughts he turned suddenly, a half sad, half amused smile at the edges of his mouth. 'I will make a bargain with you, Miss Phoebe Pardoe. You are, I take it, familiar with the handling of a horse?'

'I both rode and drove my own governess cart until . . .' She paused. 'Until a few years ago.'

'Then you take this.' He touched the prettily painted cart. 'Tell the child's parents I wish to make a gift of it to their daughter. With your permission I will drive over to Wiggins Mill tomorrow and if they do not wish to accept it I will have it taken away and no more will be said on the subject. Agreed?'

'Agreed.' Phoebe smiled, a part of her already looking forward to tomorrow.

'I ought not to have said I would do it,' she said that same evening.

'Then why did you?'

Why had she? She pondered Lucy's question. Was it because she wished to repay a kindness? Part of her owned to that but the greater part denied it. She had agreed to William Dartmouth's request, not to humour him but out of a desire she could not acknowledge.

'Why did you agree to be 'is 'ostess at the staff Advent Ball?' Lucy asked, her hands deep in flour.

'I suppose it was because he might otherwise have cancelled it,' Phoebe answered, 'and that would have been disappointing to his workers. It is the one really big celebration in their working year.'

'Why 'ave to cancel?' Adding water to the bowl, Lucy began to knead her pastry.

'Sir William explained he has no female relatives, no one he could call upon to fill the role of hostess for the evening.'

'An' so you said as you would do it?' Tipping pastry on to a board, Lucy began to roll it out. 'Was it 'cause 'e gave that 'orse an' cart to the Ingleses?' She looked up, her eyes asking a question she did not speak.

'It seemed churlish to refuse when he had been so kind.'

Phoebe avoided Lucy's eyes, knowing her own would betray the secret she had only fully recognised in the long reach of a sleepless night, a truth that had hit her like a bolt from the blue. She did not feel only pity for William

Dartmouth – she felt love. She had felt it for a long time, she realised, hugging the truth, trying to drive it from her mind as the hours passed. She could not love Edward because she had always loved his father!

'I reckon the ball'll do you good,' Tilly joined in. 'A chance to meet folk and mix a while wi' others will bring you no 'arm.'

'Perhaps not.' Phoebe spooned filling into pastry cases. 'But have you two thought about my gown? Brown grosgrain is hardly suitable for an Advent Ball.'

'Seems like that there satin'll 'ave a use after all.' Tilly carried pies to the oven, packing them inside in neat rows. 'And before you starts on about tekin' time from yer other sewin', I will tek that on till yer frock be done.'

'I don't have much choice, do I?' She smiled at Tilly.

'Not lessen you wants an argy bargy,' her friend replied, 'an' Tilly Wood don't lose no argument – 'er be determined to win.'

'An' you can forget 'elpin' in the workshop.' Lucy lined a fresh batch of pie tins with pastry cases. 'Me an' Lizzie can see to the filin' down.'

'Did I ever tell the two of you?'

'Tell we what?' Lucy asked.

'Tell you how dear you both are to me,' Phoebe said softly.

Annie Pardoe pressed a hand to the pain eating away below her breast. It was constant now, sometimes vicious, sometimes bearable, but always with her. Taking the bottle with its white tablets from the drawer of her bedside table, she eased the cork from its neck then angrily banged the bottle down on the polished mahogany surface. The pills did no good, they did not ease the pain, nor did the laudanum that fool Dingley had prescribed.

Her steps slow and heavy, she crossed the room, drawing a large brown envelope from the chest of drawers and carrying it held to her chest as she returned to sit on the huge bed. Her breathing regulated by spasms of pain, she stared at the sprawled writing before her. Her name in Clinton's writing, his hand shaking as a result of the poison she had given him. But it was not meant for you, my love! Her heart screamed. It was not for you. But he had taken it and had died and with him had died all her hopes, all her reasons for living. But Clinton would not be forgotten. Pressing the button mounted on the panelling beside the bed, she waited until Maudie Tranter entered the room.

'I . . . I have some letters . . . to write,' she said, pain interlacing the words so they came out haltingly. 'Bring . . . bring me pen and ink from . . . from the study. I . . . I will write them here.'

'Yes, ma'am.' Maudie glanced at the pill bottle, its cork still removed. 'Will you be wantin' paper an' envelopes?'

'Yes.' Annie paused, a sudden jab of pain forcing her eyes shut. 'Yes, bring paper and envelopes.'

It's a doctor you be needin', Maudie thought as she went to get the things Annie had asked for. And if you don't be callin' on one soon it won't be a letter you'll be writin' – it'll be yer will.

Drawing the documents from the brown envelope, Annie stared at the titles to properties Samuel's legacy had paid for, properties she was to have built a new life upon, a life shared with Clinton. But now he was gone and without him her life no longer held meaning.

'Will you be wantin' a tray in the garden, ma'am?' Maudie set the writing materials on the table that had been moved near the grate in which a fire was laid but as yet unlit. 'Or will I fetch a pot o' tea up to you 'ere?'

Annie glanced at the fob watch pinned to the left shoulder of her black dress. 'I will have tea here in . . . in about . . . an hour,' she said, pain snatching at the words.

'Very good, ma'am.' Maudie left the room. There don't be many hours left to you, Annie Pardoe, she thought, making her way to the kitchen. With or without the potions of old Dingley, you be walking the last stretch and how far that be only God in Heaven be knowing, and he won't tell.

Alone once more, Annie glanced at each of the documents Clinton had intended to post to her. She had doubted him, had judged him guilty of theft. But you will have it all, my love, she thought. You will have it all, every penny, as you would have had when I became your wife. I would have given it to you then as I give it to you now.

Crossing to the table she sat down, her black skirts rustling in the quiet room. Dipping the pen into the ink, she began to write.

Slicing cucumber sandwiches, Maudie placed the wafer thin triangles on a china plate, arranging a few sprigs of watercress across them before covering them with a food net. It had been an hour since she had taken the writing materials to Annie's bedroom and though she knew her mistress would probably not touch the sandwiches or even drink the tea she would take it up to her nonetheless. Annie had eaten less and less every day since hearing of that man's death. Maudie filled the tiny flowered jug with fresh milk, setting a dainty bowl of sugar beside it on the tray.

I guessed you would not be getting him to no altar, Annie Pardoe, she thought, scalding tea from a kettle bubbling softly over the kitchen fire. But I never thought he would avoid it by turning up his toes.

Taking the tray upstairs, she tapped at Annie's door with the toe of her boot, waiting for the call that would give her permission to enter and tapping more loudly when it did not come. Balancing the tray awkwardly on one arm when her second tap went unacknowledged, she turned the door knob and pushed open the door.

Annie sat on the bed, her voluminous black skirts spread over the cover like a storm cloud.

'I brought your tray.' Maudie crossed to the table set before the fireplace but seeing that the letters Annie had written were still open upon it, she took the tray to the washstand, setting it down beside the jug and bowl.

'Will I clear the table or will you take yer tea on yer bed?' she asked, shoving bowl and jug a little further along the marble top of the washstand. 'Do you want to tek yer tea at the table?' She turned, repeating her question when Annie did not answer.

'I'll pour you out a cup.' Pouring a little milk into the fragile china cup, Maudie filled it with tea then carried it across to where Annie sat on the bed, a large sheet of paper in her hands.

'Drink this up while it be 'ot.' Maudie held the cup towards Annie. 'C'mon, tek it.' She offered the cup again. 'It be fresh brewed, the way you like it.'

Annie carried on staring at the paper in her hand and Maudie tutted with irritation. Maybe she didn't fancy the tea now she had it but it was only good manners to answer a body. But then, when had good manners ever bothered Annie Pardoe? Never, unless that Clinton be about, and then it was all please and thank you. Clinton Harforth-Darby! Maudie put the cup beside the open bottle of tablets on the bedside table. What kind of a name had that been to go to bed on?

'Don't leave yer tea standin' there,' she said, the irritation she was feeling colouring her tone. 'It'll get stewed an' you knows you don't like stewed tea.'

Pausing as she turned to leave, Maudie looked at the woman seated on the bed. She hadn't spoken but that in itself was no surprise. Annie Pardoe often ignored her. But she hadn't moved either, not even to shield the paper she was holding from the possibility of being seen by another. That boded no good. But her eyes be open, Maudie told herself, 'er be readin' that paper so 'er be all right!

'Yer tea be to the side o' you,' she said again. 'Leave what you be doin' an' drink it afore it gets cold.'

Returning the few steps to the bedside table, she took up the cup with one hand, the other touching Annie lightly on the shoulder – only to draw away again quickly. Annie Pardoe was holding a sheet of paper and her eyes were open but she was stone dead.

'Oh my Lord!' Maudie breathed. 'Oh my dear Lord!'

Her hands shaking, she set the cup back on the table beside the still full bottle of tablets. Whatever had killed Annie Pardoe, it was not an overdose of them. She looked to where the body had fallen backward at her touch, the head lying a little sideways on the pillow, the open eyes seeming to watch her.

'I thought you was on the last stretch,' she murmured into the stillness, 'but I little thought you was *that* near thy end. May the Lord rest you, Annie Pardoe.'

Bending to lift the dead woman's legs on to the bed, Maudie noticed the hand that still held the paper had dropped palm down across her breast, showing a large amethyst ring on the third finger.

'That be yer weddin' finger!' she said as if Annie could hear. 'That must be a engageyment ring but I never seen you wi' it afore.'

She bent to look closer at the ring. 'Did 'e give you that?' she asked the silence. 'Or did you buy it yerself to mek it look like 'e was goin' to marry you?' Ignoring the open eyes, she eased the paper from the already cold fingers, reading the letter Clinton had written. *In his thoughts till he returned* . . . Carefully she replaced the single sheet of paper. Then he was going to marry her, seemed like. But if he was, it was unlike Annie to have let the fact go untold.

Glancing around the room, her eyes lit on the letters Annie had written that afternoon. Picking them up she read the neat copperplate hand. *'The Last Will and Testament . . .'* Maudie continued to read to the last word.

'You bitter, twisted old bugger!' she gasped, her hands falling to her sides. 'May the Lord see fit to forgive you for I never could.' She lifted the letters, looking unbelievingly at the second one. She could understand the feeling behind the first, if a woman wanted to leave her all to a man then that was her prerogative, but to write a letter like this to a girl who had done her no harm! Still unsure of what her eyes had told her, Maudie read again the letter addressed to Phoebe.

I want you to know whose was the hand behind the one that signed you to prison. I paid the Magistrate £100 to have you put behind those bars. It was I told Lawyer Siveter to advise Lucy Baines not to take what she knew of that necklace to the Dartmouths, and it was I paid John Kilvert to testify that you had pawned jewellery once before in his shop – jewellery he knew to have been stolen from another town altogether. But you were released, released from your prison though there was no release for me from the prison that held me. Abel's child was free but Abel's sister remained in the prison he had paid for.

Then there was the order for one gross of Pardoe's Patent Locks. How did you feel when you received that? I cut the heading from James Greaves's bill and pasted it to my own letter, and I did the same to the one you received cancelling that order.

And why? I will tell you why. Your father took my life. To me fell the task of living with Samuel, of ensuring no one would ever discover the twist of fate that held him and me prisoner in the same house, that none would ever learn of the affliction the medical world held out no cure for. Your father took my life so he might live his to the full. I could not make him pay so I exacted that payment from you, and though you might still live after I do not you will not have a penny of that which was first your father's and then Samuel's, for everything of that is for my husband that was to have been.

Signed, Annie Pardoe.

''Ow could 'er do all that to 'er own flesh an' blood?' Maudie said when she had finished reading. ''Ow could 'er do such bad things to a young wench who 'ad never done 'er no 'arm?'

Glancing at the first letter that was Annie's will she scanned the words again: '. . . *all land, property and jewellery belonging to me shall be sold, the realisation such land, property and jewellery shall produce is to be used for the erection of a monument to be dedicated to Clinton Harforth-Darby and is to bear the inscription, "Dear to the heart and to the memory of his betrothed, Annie Mary Pardoe . . ."'*

Maudie dropped the letters back on to the table. How could there be a spite so strong as to strike at a wench from the grave, as Annie Pardoe was here striking at her own niece? She had turned her from her father's house and even now was denying her the last of what should rightly be hers.

Maudie looked again at the figure on the bed and the papers spread about her. Going to the bed, she picked them up, quickly scanning words she did not understand but guessed to be legal proof of ownership of the properties they named. And all this was to be sold to build a monument to a dead man and feed the pride of a dead woman!

'An' Phoebe be to get nothin',' she said aloud. 'P'raps that be what you 'oped, Annie Pardoe, an' for all I know you may be 'opin' for it still but you reckoned wi'out Maudie Tranter. An' if you wants to stop me now you 'ave got to get up from that bed to do it!'

Seating herself at the table, Maudie began to copy the wording of the will until she reached the words 'shall be sold'. Careful to spell each word correctly, she changed the text to read 'shall become the property of my niece, Phoebe Mary Pardoe', then she signed Annie's name.

Taking both of Annie's letters, she pushed them into her pocket. They would burn on the kitchen fire. 'If what I be doin' be wrong, Lord, then you must punish me for I'll not change it,' she murmured. Then, slowly and methodically, she searched the room for any other paper Annie might have written and that could be compared with the Will now on the table.

Satisfied the room held no other documents she went to the rooms Samuel had used and searched them, finding nothing. She would collect the tray then search each of the downstairs rooms. Only then would she go for the doctor. Once more in Annie's bedroom she looked again at the dead figure, feeling no pity for the woman who could plot so much wickedness against her own kin. Reaching for the cup, she changed her mind. It would look more natural for it to be there; she would tell them she had left the tray earlier and on going back for it had found Annie lying on the bed and the letter she had said she wished to write on the table.

'You 'ave 'urt that wench enough, Annie Pardoe,' she murmured, leaving the room to go downstairs. 'You'll not 'urt Abel's daughter no more.'

It had been a month since Phoebe had agreed to William Dartmouth's request for her to stand as hostess for the annual party he gave for the household staff. The creamy satin falling in soft folds about her feet, Phoebe wondered if she had done right to consent to attend this evening at Sandwell Priory. Sir William had called at Wiggins Mill several times since the day he had shown her the little cart and the horse, each time saying he wished to enquire after Ruth's well-being, and with each of those visits she'd had to try harder not to read more into his grey eyes than friendship. That she loved him she could not deny, but to imagine that love returned was foolish as well as hopeless. Sir William Dartmouth might take another wife but he would not look for one at Wiggins Mill.

'You look beautiful, Miss Phoebe,' Lucy said, adding the last tiny yellow silk rose-bud to Phoebe's hair.

'Do you think he will expect jewels?' She looked at her reflection in the cheval mirror. The gown held her body in a close sheath, the satin drawn to the back in heavy swathes and the front of the skirt relieved by a trail of yellow roses

Lucy had spent hours making. The décolleté neckline was ornamented with one yellow rose, showing the swell of her breasts.

'That man 'as more sense than to go lookin' for jools other than the ones that be shinin' in yer eyes,' Tilly said, taking the gloves Phoebe had bought so many months before from the drawer and handing them to her. ''E don't need no finery – 'e can see what a woman be wi'out artificial 'elp.'

'Tilly's right,' Lucy added, 'you don't be needin' no jewels. They couldn't mek you look any more beautiful than you do now.'

'I hope you are right.' Phoebe took up her gloves and after checking one last time in the mirror, followed the two women downstairs.

'Afore you go, Miss,' Lizzie came hesitantly to the door of Phoebe's front parlour, 'the lads an' Ruth 'ave somethin' for you. Would you mind if they come in?'

'Of course I would not mind.'

'Eh, Miss, you look bostin'!' Josh was first through the door, his eyes round with admiration as he looked at her. 'Don't 'er, Mark?'

'Good enough to eat,' he grinned. 'I might even be tempted to tek you out meself, Miss.'

'Cheeky young sod!' Lizzie cuffed her son but could not help smiling.

'I think you looks like a princess!' Shy at being in the front parlour, Ruth pressed against her mother's side.

'Go on, Ruthie,' Josh urged the child, his hand gently taking hers, 'give Miss Phoebe what we got for 'er.'

The little girl looked up at her mother and at her nod allowed Josh to pull her forward. 'We buyed this for you, Miss,' she said, shyly holding up a fan of the palest lemon lace, each of its struts tipped with a tiny yellow crystal. Then as Phoebe bent to take it she piped, 'It be a new one, it ain't from the pawn shop.'

'Oh, you sweetheart!' Phoebe felt a rush of tears as she took the child in her arms. 'That is exactly what I needed.'

'We thought you might like a fan,' Mark's cheeky lopsided grin stretched across his mouth like a wedge of melon. 'You can 'ide yer yawns be'ind it if you gets bored.'

'I don't think I will be bored, Mark,' Phoebe said, giving Ruth one last hug before turning to him. 'Though I might need it to hide my embarrassment at having no jewellery.'

'No need for you to feel embarrassed,' Josh said gallantly. 'There ain't not one thing you could do would better the way you look.'

'Josh be right, Miss.' Mark wasn't to be outdone in the field of compliments. 'Ain't nothin' would mek you look prettier'n you look now. Ya looks real beautiful an' that be no lie.'

'When experts such as them two agree you look beautiful then you can be sure it's beautiful you look,' Lucy said.

'You could marry a prince,' Ruth said solemnly, 'you be beautiful enough to be a princess.'

'If I do,' Phoebe smiled, 'it will all be because of my lovely fan.' She flicked it open, holding it below her eyes. 'Any prince would be glad to marry a princess with a golden fan.'

But she did not want to marry a prince, Phoebe thought as she rode in the carriage sent to collect her. The man she loved held a title, albeit not a royal one, but he did not want her for his wife.

'Good evening, Miss Pardoe,' William Dartmouth greeted the young woman alighting from his carriage. 'Ruth is well, I hope?' He escorted her into the great hall of his ancient house.

'As well as she was when you called three days ago.' Phoebe smiled up at him, glancing quickly away as she met the look in his eyes, a look she so wanted to be saying what she knew he never would.

'And the boys?'

'Cheeky as ever.' Phoebe held out the fan. 'They bought me this.'

'Rogues, the pair of 'em.' He smiled. 'But rogues with good taste.'

'Mark said he might be tempted to take me out himself.'

'Did he!' Sir William laughed, the sound drawing the glances of his staff lined up to be presented to Phoebe. 'The young hound! There'll be many a man takes a horsewhip to that one before he settles, though I say again I admire his taste.' He glanced at Phoebe, seeing the colour steal the paleness from her cheeks. 'You look very beautiful, Miss Pardoe.'

'I think we should look to your guests.' She turned towards the line of waiting men and women.

'Our guests,' he murmured at her elbow. 'For one night at least allow them to be that.'

Later William watched the young woman dancing a waltz with his estate manager. For something like four hours she had mixed easily with the people of the estate, men and women alike, a smile and a word for each, her simple manner making her readily acceptable to them. Watching her now, the light from the chandeliers glistening on the bronze silk of her hair piled high on her head, tiny buds of yellow satin nestling in its coils, her slim body outlined by the lines of her gown, he felt a pang of jealousy that the arms holding her and the eyes looking down on her smiling face were not his. Impatient with his own thoughts, he turned to his steward.

'It is all going very well,' he said. 'Give my thanks to everyone in the morning and tell them I was very pleased at the effort they have all made.'

'I will, sir.' The steward smiled, pleased at these words of thanks.

'And now I think we should announce supper.' William watched the man make his way to the end of the great hall, to where the musicians were seated in a large alcove, not sure whether announcing supper or wanting Phoebe out of the arms of his estate manager was the real reason behind his having the music stopped. Watching the man escort her back to him, William carefully lowered his gaze, hiding the answer that throbbed in his heart.

'A glass of wine, Miss Pardoe?' he asked as the estate manager took his leave of them.

'I would find a glass of lemonade more acceptable,' Phoebe answered, a little breathless from the constant round of dancing.

'Lemonade it shall be.' He led her to the supper table. 'May I help you to a plate of something?'

Phoebe shook her head. 'Like the princess in the story, I am too happy to eat.'

'Unlike the princess in the story,' he said softly, 'don't disappear when the clock strikes midnight.'

'How does Pippin be gettin' along, Miss?' The groom who had led the horse from its stable to show to her smiled as Phoebe came up to the supper table.

'Being spoiled terribly.' Phoebe's own smile broke out spontaneously. 'She is loved by all of us but especially so by Ruth.'

'The master told us of Pippin's new mistress and with his permission we would like to send her an Advent gift.' He looked at Sir William and when he nodded permission the groom handed Phoebe a package. 'It be from all the 'ouse, an' we 'oped you would take it for we an' give it to the little girl.'

'May I peep?'

'Ar, Miss.'

The groom nodded and Phoebe peeled away a layer of brown paper, exclaiming with delight at sight of blue leather reins. 'How lovely! Ruth will be enchanted. Thank you all so much, it is so kind of you.' She smiled at the assembled staff, all of whom had their eyes turned to her and all of whom shared her delight.

Arranging for the gift to be placed in the carriage against her return, William Dartmouth accepted the glass of lemonade handed him by one of the housemaids, dressed now in a pretty print frock. 'You are a victim of your own popularity,' he said as Phoebe was kept continually busy answering the polite addresses of his staff, 'you have made too favourable an impression and I fear you will have to pay the penalty.'

'Talking to people as friendly as these is no penalty.'

'But you would like a quiet interlude before the evening resumes?'

She nodded. 'It would be nice. I have not been called upon to be hostess to a party before and it is tiring.'

'Exhausting would be my word for it. Let's go to the drawing room, it will be quiet there.'

He led the way to a room furnished with sofas and chairs upholstered in a deep cream brocade, the curtains over high arched windows echoing the same colour and the huge square of carpet patterned in cream and soft peach.

'I admit I prefer a glass of something other than lemonade.' Crossing to a large figured cabinet he drew out decanter and glass, filling the latter. Raising it to his lips, he looked at the young woman sitting on the sofa, her hair turned to glistening amber by the soft light, her lovely face smiling at him – and turned quickly away, staring into the fireplace.

'Miss Pardoe,' he said, the thickness in his throat not quite under control, 'I believe my son asked you to become his wife?'

Phoebe's smile faded. 'Edward did me that honour.'

'But you refused?'

'Yes.'

'Not once but several times, is that not so?'

Phoebe stared into her glass, the happiness of the evening draining away. Was this why he had asked her to come to Sandwell Priory? Was this why they were now alone in this room, so he could bombard her with questions? Glancing at a side table, she looked at the silver-framed photographs of his family, at Edward's face staring solemnly back at her. 'It is so,' she answered quietly.

He remained staring into the empty fireplace. 'Might I ask the reason or would that be considered too rude?'

Putting the lemonade aside, Phoebe took a long trembling breath. He had brought her to his home in order to question her and she would answer his questions, all of them, and then she would return to Wiggins Mill. 'No, I do not consider there to be any rudeness in your question. The reason for my refusals was simple: I did not love Edward in the way a woman should love the man she agrees to marry, and I would marry no man I did not love.'

'I see.' He waited for several moments, the silence marked by the ticking of a graceful clock on the mantel, above his head. Then: 'Was there someone else?'

Phoebe watched him, her emotions crying out to comfort him, knowing the pain these questions must be causing him, understanding his wish to know as much as possible of the son he had lost. 'When your son asked me to marry him there was no one else,' she said gently.

'And now?' He swivelled to face her, his question hard and sharp.

Phoebe hesitated, taken aback by the knife edge of his tone. 'I . . . there . . . no, I am not being called upon by anyone.' In the hushed light of the room Phoebe saw the play of emotion on his face, saw his fingers about the glass whiten with tension.

'I ask your pardon,' he said. 'I had no right to ask such a question.'

'No, you did not.' Phoebe looked at his face, still handsome behind the pain. 'But had I not wished to answer then I would not have done so.'

'Miss Pardoe . . . Phoebe.' He wrestled with the words, wanting to say them yet stubbornly denying them freedom. 'I, I . . .'

Phoebe remained silent. Whatever it was William Dartmouth had to say to her, he must say it alone.

'Miss Pardoe, had my family lived I would never have said to you what I must say now. Had Edward survived I would not have spoken, whether you had married him or not. You have told me there is no gentleman calling upon you, that you have promised marriage to no one.'

His fingers closed tighter, threatening to crush the glass in his hand, and a film of perspiration glistened on his forehead.

'That being so, allow me the honour of asking you to become my wife?'

Phoebe felt the rush of blood leaving her face, the fan falling from fingers suddenly without strength. Why did he want to marry her? Did he still feel Edward was somehow obligated to her, an obligation he must make good by making her his wife? That alone could be the reason, she decided.

'Sir William.' She spoke evenly though her heart was breaking. This was the thing she had dreamed of for so long; she loved this man deeply but he saw marriage to her only as a means of reparation. 'Edward was under no obligation to me, you have no debt to repay.'

'For God's sake!' He flung the glass from his hand, shattering it against the stone of the hearth. 'I love you. God help me, I love you!' He turned back to the fireplace, one hand on the mantel, his head bent, the anger in his voice replaced by a mixture of longing and recrimination.

'I have loved you since I brought you from that prison, may Heaven forgive me. It was wrong of me but I had no power to prevent it. I loved you even as Edward loved you, the thought of you married to my son or to any man haunted my days. I know it is useless to speak of it, I am afraid I allowed my emotions to override my judgement. It is unforgivable of me to have spoken to you as I have. I realise you would not dream of marrying me . . .'

'But I have dreamed of it,' Phoebe interrupted, her own voice soft with an answering surge of love. 'I have dreamed of it for many months and I dream of it still.'

'Phoebe!' He turned from the fireplace, his face lit with hope. 'You said you would never marry a man you did not love.'

She smiled across at him, her eyes tender with love. 'Nor would I, but I love you. I think I always have.'

'Phoebe!' He crossed the room with one bound, snatching her roughly into his arms. 'My love – oh, my love.'

He loved her, *he loved her*, and he wanted her for his wife. Phoebe leaned against him as he kissed her. But how would a wife who had been in prison be accepted among his circle? Would marriage to her slowly destroy his life? And children, what if they had children? What would they think of having a mother once accused of theft?

Pulling away from his arms Phoebe put her fears into words, asking each of the questions her soul told her she must.

He smiled at her, his grey eyes a deeper shade with the love he no longer feared to show. 'I want you for my wife because I love you. I love you so much I cannot conceive of life without you. I love your honesty and integrity, your loyalty and tenderness of conscience, your dignity and your constancy. I want more for my children than the emptiness of a society that prizes none of those qualities.

'The world is changing, Phoebe, and we must change with it. It might take some time for people to forget the past but give them that time and they will see for themselves that trueness of spirit that would never allow you to commit any crime.'

He drew her into his arms again, looking down into her radiant face. 'You told me once that I should never use the word "must" to you again, but I am going to do so one more time. Your father is unable to answer my request so you *must* do that yourself. Phoebe Pardoe, I ask for your hand in marriage. Will you marry me?'

Turning her face up to him, her eyes soft with love, Phoebe smiled. 'My father cannot answer you, William,' she murmured, 'but the answer would be the same. That answer is yes, you may marry Abel's daughter.'

If you enjoyed ABEL'S DAUGHTER, here's a foretaste of Meg Hutchinson's new novel, FOR THE SAKE OF HER CHILD:

For the Sake of her Child

Anna Bradly sat on one of the two wooden chairs that, together with a scrubbed wooden table, almost filled the tiny kitchen. Her feet, bare below the cotton of her blue print dress, rested on the drab hearth.

How long had it been? Leaning her head sideways, she let it rest against the rough brick of the wall. Light from the oil lamp on the mantelpiece caught the movement of her rich auburn hair. How long since Mary Carter had been pulled drowned from Millfield Pool . . . how long since the accusations had started?

Mary Carter had come twice a week to this house since Anna's mother had died in childbirth ten years ago. Mondays were given over to washing. The fire already lit beneath the brick-lined copper before she arrived, she would hang her shawl on the nail behind the kitchen door and go straight into the poky wash-house. Anna had been allowed to watch as she ladled heavy buckets of steaming water into the round wooden washtub and sometimes Mary let her help cut thin slices of yellow scrubbing soap and drop them like dusty curls in among the wash.

Thursday Mary baked.

Anna breathed deeply, remembering the smell of freshly baked bread and sugar-topped cinnamon cake. This had been her favourite day. A half-burned coal settled further into its glowing bed, sending flakes of grey ash falling into the hearth.

Anna looked back across the years since her mother's

death. Standing on a chair beside a table white from years of scrubbing, she would pour the liquid yeast and sugar mixture into the huge earthenware bowl of fluffy white flour after Mary had said the devil had been raised.

'Does yeast and sugar really raise the devil?'

She remembered the smile on Mary's face as she answered, but even more clearly remembered the answer she had never understood.

'There's more than yeast and sugar can raise that one.'

Only now could she see just how true that was.

The coals settled again and Anna stared into the depths of the fire, hypnotised. Oh, the devil had been raised all right! Only not in a cup of yeast and sugar water.

It had been on a Friday morning. Two men crossing the fields to work had seen the floating mass of clothes caught in the reeds; they had pulled the body on to the narrow path skirting the water-filled mine shaft . . . the body of Mary Carter.

'Death from misadventure' had been the Coroner's report but people hereabouts had called it murder, a murder they accused Anna's father of committing. That had been three years ago and not one of them had set foot in this house since.

At thirteen Anna had taken on the running of it, watching the taunts and jibes turn her father from a quiet man to a morose, withdrawn shadow.

He had murdered Mary Carter, they said, because she'd refused his advances. She would have nothing to do with his filthy suggestions so he had forced himself on her, then, knocking her senseless, thrown her into Millfield Pool.

Anna closed her eyes. Her father was innocent, that much she knew. Mary Carter had always arrived at the house after he had left for work and had long gone home before he returned. How could he have murdered her?

The hollow echo of the old tin bucket rattling across the cobbled yard woke Anna. The low fire now gave little light, and for a moment she could not make out the shape looming in the doorway as the door was thrown back on its hinges.

'Where are you, you bloody bitch?'

The harsh shout rang in the silence. Her father was drunk again. This had become the pattern of his life: trying to sink his pain at the bottom of a pint tankard.

'Where are you . . . you lying, stinking bitch?'

Stumbling forward, he half-fell across the table, sending the cups she had set out for tomorrow's breakfast crashing to the floor. Anna stood up, reaching for the oil lamp, turning the wick a little higher. She would help him to bed as she had done so many times; once there he would sleep off the beer.

'There you are, Mary Carter!'

He had pushed himself upright. Eyes glazed with alcohol and hatred stared at Anna. Her hand fell away from the lamp; he had called her by that name before, always when the accusations had been flying thick and his drinking heavy.

'No . . . it's me, Father . . . Anna.' She didn't move, watching the swaying of his head as he continued to stare at her.

'Do you know what you've done to me, Mary Carter?' The question was thick and slurred. 'Do you know what I've gone through because of you? The lies and insults I've suffered. Do you, you cow, *do* you?'

'Father.' Anna spoke softly, carefully. She had never seen him this bad before. 'Father, it's me, Anna . . . Mary has gone home.'

'Do you know what they are saying down there, those bastards!' He banged a heavy fist on the table, setting the knives dancing a crazy jig. 'I'll tell you what they're saying: they are saying I screwed you, forced you when you said no, then knocked you senseless and threw you into the pool.'

Swaying, he moved around the table, dim light filtering through the open door, turning him into frightening solidity. His hands hung at his sides, his head lolled tipsily forward on his neck. 'But that's not true, Mary Carter, and you know it. Screwed you? – Pah! – Christ knows I never laid a finger on you.'

Across the short distance Anna could smell the beery fumes exhaled with each breath. Something must have happened, someone in The Collier must have baited him more than usual for him to have drunk himself into such a state. Nervously she stepped forward, bare feet soundless on the flagged floor.

'C'mon, Father, I'll help you upstairs.'

His eyes continued to stare. Locked on her face, they did not see her, but what they did see contorted his expression to a twisted mask of bitterness. He moved slowly, head thrust forward, feet shuffling on the stone floor and Anna wanted to cry out but was afraid. If she remained calm he would recognise her and that terrible look would be gone from his face.

'No, by God, I never laid a finger on you. Was that why you did it? Was that why you told your cronies that every time you came to this house I made you lie with me? Was that pretence to cover the fact that I never did?'

He came closer. The dull yellow pool of light cast by the oil lamp flickered over his face, touching the long smear of blood on his left cheek, paling before the glitter of his almost transparent blue eyes.

'And why didn't I, did you tell them that, Mary Carter? Did you tell them Jos Bradly takes no whore?'

Anna clutched her hands tightly, pressing them against her sides as her father took another swaying step towards her. She had thought to help him to bed but now instinct told her to get to her own room. He would shout and swear for a few hours, smash a few dishes, but she could clear up in the morning. Right now she was safer out of his sight, for in his drink-fuddled mind he was seeing not her but Mary Carter.

'For months I've taken the brickbats,' he began again, but this time he didn't shout. His words were little more than a whisper, almost as if he were talking to himself. 'For months they've pointed the finger at me, accusing me of that which

4

I never thought to do. Well, now I've changed my mind. I've taken the insults so I might just as well take the pleasure.'

For the first time in her life Anna was afraid of her father. He would never harm her in her normal state. But tonight he was not normal, he was in drink. And there was worse than that wrong with him; the long months of mental torment since Mary's death, months of being a social outcast, treated like a leper by those who had called themselves his friends, had at last broken him.

Heart thumping, she stepped sideways. The light from the lamp, what little there was of it, was shining into his eyes. If she moved slowly, chances were he would not notice.

But she was wrong. One hand shot out, grasping the hair tied at the back of her neck and at the same time wrenching her forward, her scream muffled by the rough material of his jacket.

'You can go, Mary.' Above her head the words came out in a quiet sing-song voice. 'You can go, but this time it will be the truth you'll tell those bastards.'

Pulling back her head, Anna's anguished cries did not register on his fevered mind. Wiping his free hand across his face, mixing blood and sweat together, Joseph Bradly swore with the soft vehemence of one who has waited long for vengeance. Then, grasping the neckline of the cotton dress, he ripped it violently downward, tearing the cheap thin material to the hem.

For a moment he stared at the creamy skin above Anna's bodice then that garment too was torn away, his hand leaving a smear of blood across her breast.

'This is what you've talked of so often to your dirty-minded women friends, you filthy, bloody bitch! That you were crucifying a man didn't matter to you, did it? Well, now you're going to pay.'

'Father . . . please, Father, it's me, Anna. Father, please . . .'

Anna's screams died as a blow to the side of her head sent her spinning to the floor and the blackness of nightmare began. A nightmare that would stay with her for the rest of her life.

His weight pinning her to the floor, he dragged away her underclothes, freeing his own body as he did so. Then, with one knee forcing her legs apart, he drove deeply into her. Each thrust was like a red hot knife but Anna was already beyond pain. Her mind closed to what was happening to her body, she did not cry out. Eyes closed too, she waited while her father vented his rage and passion.

At last it was over and with a low grunt he rolled away from her.

Anna lay still, his sweat drying cold on her bare skin. Above her the yellow flame flickered a warning of the lamp's need for oil but she did not move. How long she lay there she could never later remember but at last, limbs as numbed as her mind, she pushed herself to her feet.

Her dress lay half under the snoring man stretched on the floor and there she left it. Pulling the remnants of her underwear about her, she walked slowly upstairs.

Moonlight silvered the tiny room that had been hers from birth, but Anna saw none of its magic. In a trance-like state she filled the bowl on the wash stand from its matching jug, unaware of the icy sting as she plunged her hands into the water, lifting palmsful to her face. For long seconds she threw the water over a face almost as cold, then stripping off her torn garments, reached for the thick greyish bar of soap. Again and again she scrubbed herself, covering every inch of her body, ignoring the sting of carbolic where the violence of his entry had lacerated her. She scrubbed her breasts, washing away the smear of blood; scrubbed her stomach where the flesh felt sticky; and still she scrubbed, trying to wash away the smell of his breath from her nostrils, the touch of his sweat-soaked flesh, the memory of what he had done to her.

Silver light turned a cold grey before Anna finally slipped a clean white calico nightdress over her frozen body. Her hair, still wet from the merciless scrubbing, dripped spots of icy water on to the front. In the small mirror hanging from a nail on her bedroom wall she watched them spread and join, forming a smear, the way the blood from her father's hand had smeared her breast. It was only then, hands blue with cold covering her face, that she sank into a heap on the bare wooden boards and cried: the desperate, hopeless crying of a soul doomed to everlasting torment.

The same grey light paling to opalescent pearl fingered past the undrawn curtains of the tired kitchen. The last embers of the fire had long settled and the lamp gave no more light. Groaning from the stiffness of his cold limbs, Joseph Bradly stood up. Shaking the last clouds of alcohol from his brain and remembering. That whore Mary Carter had got what she deserved. From now on the insinuations of the townspeople would carry some truth at last. Satisfaction in the grim set of his mouth, he reached for the poker, stabbing ash from the grate with hard jerky movements. Now she would have something to talk about, the bloody bitch. It was this last thought that halted his assault on the cold cinders. Mary Carter was dead! He had seen her bloated corpse laid on the path by Millfield Pool. He couldn't have been with her last night, it could not have been her, but he had . . .

Turning from the grate, he saw in the faint blush of morning the heap of torn blue cotton where he had lain. He reached for it, the iron poker dropping loudly to the stone hearth. He knew this dress. He had seen delight spread across the face of the child he had bought it for. Lifting the cloth to his face, he could smell the faint scent, as if the pattern of cornflowers gave off a living perfume . . . and then he knew. Last night he had not wreaked vengeance on Mary Carter. Last night he had raped his own daughter.

Chapter One

The long climb up Church Hill seemed neverending. Glancing at the black, smoke-grimed walls of the ancient Parish Church that crowned it, Anna thought it still seemed as far away as when she began the trudge up Ethelfleda Terrace.

Back aching with the effort of freeing every step from mud that threatened to suck her down, swollen mound of a stomach making her lean awkwardly back, she willed herself on.

Pulling her foot from the squelching earth, she gripped the basket she was carrying, forcing the bamboo handle painfully into the flesh of her palm. But the pain went unnoticed, hidden beneath the breath-snatching agony that suddenly lanced through her.

Clutching at the nearest gate, Anna leaned heavily against it, her breath coming in short frightened gasps.

It had started, she thought through the pain. The long hopeless months of waiting were about to end. The child that had been set inside her with so much pain and bitterness was about to enter the world, about to begin a life that would be led the same way, could only continue in the malice and hatred that had been her lot since the finding of Mary Carter's body.

One hand gripping the grey splintered wood of the garden gate, Anna gasped, waiting for the pain that flared through her to diminish. Drawing in a long ragged breath, she lifted her head, glancing along the path of beaten earth that led to the door of the house. But though the curtain at the window twitched, no one emerged to help her.

She was Jos Bradly's daughter, his whore. No decent woman in Wednesbury would be seen helping her.

Sweat bathing her face, Anna pushed herself upright. She had to climb the hill. She must get home or give birth like some animal in the hedge.

Stopping every few yards, panting against the recurring stabs of pain, she dragged on to the house that once had held so much happiness for her, the house where her mother had loved and cherished her for the first seven years of her life.

Pushing open the door that gave on to the kitchen, she stumbled inside, grabbing the edge of the table that almost filled the little room, fighting the red hot spasms that threatened to cut her in two.

'Mother . . .' she moaned softly into the emptiness. 'Mother, help me . . . help me.'

But her mother could not help her. Her mother had died ten years before, died in the agony Anna was suffering now, the boy she had carried dying with her.

Letting the basket fall to the table, Anna breathed hard. She must fight the pain. She was alone and would be until past her usual bedtime. Only then did her father return to the house that had become his prison and her penitentiary.

Trying to keep her breathing calm and even, she took an enamel basin from the shabby wooden dresser. She was placing the eggs she had bought into it when fresh searing pain ripped through her, jarring every nerve with searing, brutal agony. The eggs jerked in her hands, splashing the front of her with oozing stickiness.

Anna gazed at her dress, the terror she had known once before returning with stark clarity.

Her stomach had been covered in the same slimy mess when he had finally lifted himself off her.

'No! No, mother, no!'

The cry was dragged from her as she rubbed at her dress in a vain attempt to wipe it clean.

* * *

It was too early to go back.

Jos Bradly walked out of the yard of the steel foundry in silence; no friendly wave acknowledged his going, no voice called a goodnight.

Shoving his hands deep into his pockets, he walked quickly in the direction of Church Hill. This was the wrong way, he told himself, he had never gone home before ten since . . .

He closed his eyes, momentarily trying to shut out the scene that never left him.

He never went back to the house until he knew she would be in bed, until she would not have to look at the man who had raped her. And he would not see, at least in the flesh, the hurt and fear in his daughter's eyes.

But tonight, try as he might to tell himself he must not return, his steps carried him home.

He could see from the gate that the door to the kitchen was wide open. Suddenly sick with new fear, Jos ran up the narrow path.

She was there, a crumpled heap on the kitchen floor, her red-gold hair covering her face – a face he did not need to see to know it was crumpled with pain.

'Anna! Anna, my little wench!'

Blood draining from his face, he stepped towards her then turned back to the open door.

Clear of the house he began to run, streaking away down the hill as if Gabriel's Hounds were already snapping at his heels.

'Will yer come, Polly?'

He fell into the tiny house that was one of a ribbon of tumbledown dwellings edging Trouse Lane.

'Say yer'll come? There's none other I can ask. I don't want none o' they touchin' 'er.'

Polly Shipton twisted round on her stool, her withered left leg dragging on the bare flagstones. She had wondered where he would turn when the girl's time came. Well, now she knew.

She looked up at the face she had known since childhood, a face smeared by tears mixed with the dirt of the steel foundry.

Was it true what they said of him? Had he murdered one woman and then raped a young girl, and that girl his own daughter?

Polly sighed. She didn't have the answers and was never likely to have them.

'Please, Polly . . . yer must come.' At his sides, Jos's hands balled into fists. 'Anna, my little wench, 'er was on the floor. I . . . I couldn't . . . I don't know how!'

Shoving herself from the stool with her sound right leg, Polly reached for the heavy woollen shawl hanging on a nail in the scullery door. She pulled it close as she followed Joseph Bradly past the mocking eyes of the quickly gathered women – women who took care to keep their opinions in their mouths until he had passed.

Hobbling painfully, Polly kept her own head high. From this day on she would be as much an outcast in the town as the man she was following. No matter. Whatever else he might be, he was now a man sharing his daughter's agony, and the fact that she would be ostracised and ignored for helping either of them was of no consequence compared to a young girl's pain.

'It be all right, Anna.'

Pushing past Jos into the kitchen, she bent over the girl huddled on the stone floor.

'It'll be all right, me wench. Polly Shipton 'as come to be with you, Polly will take care of you. Come on now, there's a good wench, let's 'ave you upstairs.'

Hair plastered to her cheeks with sweat, Anna lifted her head and Polly saw the look of terror in her eyes as Jos Bradly bent to take his daughter in his arms.

'No . . . o . . . o!'

The scream filled the tiny kitchen and Polly Shipton knew she need go no further to find the father of the child struggling to enter the world.

*　　*　　*

Standing beside the wooden crib, Anna stared at the son she had borne a month ago, hearing in her mind the taunts and sneers that met her whenever she ventured out of the house.

She tucked the blanket closer around the sleeping child.

It had grown into something of a sport; women gathering in twos and threes as she approached, calling after her from the safety of their married respectability.

'That father o' 'er's . . .'

Words emerged from the shadows of her mind like silent wraiths.

'. . . 'e be bloody jailbait. 'Ow come the bobbies ain't fetched 'im afore now?'

They passed their taunts from one to the other, each woman raising her voice, ensuring Anna could hear.

'Ar, why ain't they? 'E killed Mary Carter, we all knows that, an' 'e be the one who 'as fathered that babby. That by blow belongs to Jos Bradly as sure as there be a God in 'eaven.'

'You didn't hear them, did you, sweetheart?'

Anna stroked a finger across her son's downy head.

'You didn't hear what they said or realise what they think, and you never will my precious . . . you never will.'

But those women had been partly right. Anna sat on her bed, one hand resting on the crib that her father had made for her own birth.

The child now sleeping in it was Jos Bradly's, in that they had been correct, but the rest of their accusations bore no truth. There was no God in heaven. She looked at the sleeping child, her heart filling with pain at what she knew was in store for him as he grew.

No, there was no God in heaven. Had there been she would not have been raped.

Rising from the bed, she lifted the child from the crib, a wild surge of love and sorrow sweeping through her as the tiny body touched her own.

'They have judged him too,' she murmured, her mouth against the tiny head, 'my father and yours. They have all judged him and, right or wrong, he will pay their price. All the years of his life will not wash away the sin of which he is guilty, even though he would have suffered death before committing it had he been sober.'

In her arms the tiny face crumpled, one arm freeing itself from the swaddling blanket, and Anna rocked gently back and forth, her lips touching her son's face, soothing away his complaining cry.

'Shhh,' she whispered, folding one finger into his clutching palm. 'Shhh, no one will hurt you. No one in this town will ever call lies and filth after you.'

But as she lifted the tiny hand to her mouth, Anna knew they would.